THE MATE GAMES BOOK ONE

OBSESSION

K. LORAINE

USA Today BESTSELLING AUTHOR
MEG ANNE

Cover Design by CReya-tive Book Cover Design

Photographer: Michelle Lancaster

Model: Lawrence Templar

Edited by Mo Sytsma of Comma Sutra Editorial

For Suzi,
Just remember you're the one responsible for the battery
shortage.

"My first obsession is you.
My second is having sex with you."

— ANONYMOUS

OBSESSION

AUTHOR'S NOTE

Obsession contains sexually explicit scenes, as well as mature and graphic content that is not suitable for all audiences. **Reader discretion is advised.**

Welcome to The Mate Games, a detailed list of content and trigger warnings is available on our website. For those of you who prefer to go in blind, keep reading.

CHAPTER
ONE
THORNE

I t was a shame Sunday Fallon had to die tonight. And that I would be the one to kill her. But there was nothing I could do now that I'd caught her scent. Not after two solid days of her existing in my space. Black-thorne Hall was my domain, the place I ruled without question because it bore my family name. Until now, I'd spent the last three years in complete control. Until her.

She called to me. Drew me to her with that irresistible, decadent scent. Made me mad with hunger. Desperate with need. Obsessed.

My father told me stories of how mother had tempted him, how her blood had been like no other. I'd never experienced it until now. I was hunting her. Not because I wanted to. I *had* to. I had to sample this irresistible creature. To know if she could possibly taste as delicious as she smelled.

Each one of her rhythmic footfalls teased me as she jogged through the campus trails, her measured breaths and elevated heartbeat strong in my ears. It took everything in me not to rush to her and sink my fangs into her throat, just as it had each night as she went about her routine. Tonight, I was within arm's reach, ready to take her, but that would mean it was over almost before it began. The monster in me wanted to draw it out, to savor the chase, because once I had her, that would be it.

She slowed to a walk, hands on her hips as she stared up at the moon and sighed. "This is it. This is what you get for being different. You finished college but still ended up being shipped off to a glorified boarding school for the supernatural's elite to keep you out of trouble."

Her voice was smooth and silky with the barest rasp to it. Music to my ears. If I killed her, I'd never hear it again. Perhaps I'd turn her instead. Make her mine forever. The thought had merit. Except, of course, for the fact that she was the princess of the Fallon wolf pack. Something told me her family would take issue with a Blackthorne vampire draining her dry and then making her one of us. We didn't want to start a war now, did we?

Her sharp intake of breath had me slinking into the shadows as she glanced over her shoulder in the direction where I'd been standing. "Is someone there?"

I smirked. Someone was definitely there. A predator. A hunter. The creature who'd change her life irrevocably.

Not tonight, though. I'd keep myself on the edge of euphoria a little longer. It was more fun that way.

As she rounded the corner, I kept my distance, now following just to ensure my prey returned safely home. I couldn't risk someone else catching her. She was mine. Whether she knew it yet or not. Her dark hair swung back and forth in the high ponytail she wore, the ends brushing her shoulders and calling attention to her slender white neck. I wondered if her skin would change from porcelain to pink when she blushed and her blood rushed to the surface. Instinct took over, lengthening both my cock and my fangs. Arousal pulsed through me, eclipsed only by my hunger. I wanted her with every cell in my body.

"Everything all right there, Thorne?" The Irish lilt of Father Caleb Gallagher's voice stopped me mid-step.

"Priest." I acknowledged him with the barest tilt of my head.

His jaw clenched at the title, a reminder of his past life as a man of God before he'd been turned into one of my kind. "Leave her be, Mr. Blackthorne. She's not for you to toy with."

"My instinct says different."

"Do not think your family name will exempt you from consequences if you kill her. The war—"

I waved my hand. "Yes, I know. The Families are on thin ice as it is, a war will start, death, bloodshed, etcetera." We had shared a relative peace between the head Families of our supernatural kinds the last twenty-five years. Since my father took control of the Blackthorne vampire kingdom and created a sort of treaty with the remaining shifter packs and witch covens. The alliance was nothing short of fragile after our kind spent centuries trying to rule over every preternatural species in existence.

I sighed heavily into the darkness. "No blood was spilled."

He arched one dark brow. "Yet."

"I will keep my distance."

"See that you do. You may be a prince, but I'm still in charge here."

I scoffed. "You're a professor. You have no control over me."

3

"One call to your father and you'll spend a week in the well. You know as well as I that he won't hesitate to isolate you if you pose a risk to the stability of our world, Noah Blackthorne."

I shrugged, trying to play it cool, but I'd spent two days in the well back home once simply so I'd know to fear it. My father was still ruthless when he needed to be.

"Keep her away from me if you want to ensure she's safe."

"You're hunting her."

I swallowed past a burning throat. Yes, I was. "I can control myself."

"Perhaps she'd be safer living in my quarters until you've found a new distraction."

A low snarl escaped before I could stop myself. The thought of Sunday spending any time in this man's home, sharing his space and his air, made unreasonable jealousy unfurl in my gut. Vampire or not, he was still a priest. A veritable eunuch, castrated by his faith and vow of celibacy. He couldn't have her, even if he wanted her. She was mine to claim.

"She's fine here. We're separated by three floors of concrete. I won't ravish her until she asks for it."

He shoved his hands into the pockets of his dark slacks, a wary expression on his face. "Goodnight, Thorne. Best get behind closed doors before you lose hold of your monster."

I shook my head before turning away and heading off in the direction Sunday had.

Which of the dorms in this hall was hers? My gaze swept over the doors, senses on high alert as I searched for her, but all I smelled now was a mixture of creatures, from vampire to shifter to witch. Until I caught it again as I stepped into my elevator. Sweet and rich with a darkness I couldn't name. Unlike anything else. Sunday Fallon called to me, begged me to claim her. To taste her. I palmed my aching cock as the doors to the top floor opened, and I strode to my suite.

I would have the beautiful little shifter if it was the last thing I did. And it just might be.

CHAPTER
TWO
SUNDAY

One Week Earlier

My grandfather only ever summoned me for two things. To ask me if I'd shifted yet, or to berate me for being an absolute failure of a Fallon. Which, to be fair, was really the same thing. If the grand-daughter of the head of North America's largest wolf pack couldn't shift, what good was she?

So when our pack's beta found me in the library and said the Alpha—not my grandfather, the Alpha—wanted to see me, I knew I'd gone and fucked up. The problem was I couldn't for the life of me figure out what I'd done this time. Other than the obvious, of course. And the sick, oily feeling in my stomach told me I wasn't going to enjoy finding out.

I jogged up the steps to the pack house, stopping just before going inside to shake out my nerves and put on my 'Fallon' face. Because a Fallon never shows fear. A Fallon would never dare to arrive at a meeting with her Alpha with fear spiking her pulse, slightly out of breath, limbs trembling. A *real* Fallon would never embarrass her family by showing any weakness at all.

Pushing open the door, I crossed the threshold and turned right, heading straight for my grandfather's office. Before walking in, I knocked twice—anything less was rude, and anything more was annoying.

He didn't bother looking up from his work before snapping, "You're late."

I gritted my teeth, knowing better than to try to defend myself, even though the words of protest were already attempting to crawl up my throat. I'd been trained long ago that there was only one acceptable answer. Staring straight at his forehead, I forced myself to say, "Sorry for wasting your time, Grandfather. It won't happen again."

"I very much doubt that," he said cooly, finally looking up from the stack of papers in his hand before giving me a once-over tinged with disgust. Tossing the papers onto the open file folder on his desk, he leaned forward, adding, "At least you won't be my problem much longer."

"W-what?"

"I've enrolled you at Ravenscroft University. You leave tomorrow."

His answer, while a surprise, was not an unwelcome one. It had always been a foregone conclusion I'd end up at Ravenscroft. The equivalent of graduate school for the supernatural elite, Ravenscroft was where the Families' future leaders learned how to navigate the complex political waters between species.

Seated as it was in a remote part of the English countryside, there would be thousands of miles between me and this place. Not to mention between me and the series of never-ending failures I seemed to rain down upon my family. But most importantly, I'd be free of him.

Instead of the punishment he seemed to think it was, this was a gift. I knew better than to let him realize it, though.

"But Grandfather—"

My protest seemed to enrage him, his hazel eyes turning the brilliant gold of the beast hidden beneath his skin. A warning snarl slipped into his voice as he cut me off. "I don't care what you want, Sunday. You either pack your bags and be waiting outside for the car when it arrives to take you to the airport tomorrow, or I drag you through our land kicking and screaming with nothing more than the clothes on your back. The choice is yours."

"You misunderstood. I only wondered how I was granted admission without my shifter abilities."

Ravenscroft was no mortal school. It was the training ground of the world's most deadly and powerful supernatural up and comers. One of the only places on earth where shifters, vampires, and all other supernatural kinds were forced to set aside their centuries-long blood feuds and play nice. It was where diplomacy was supposed to be cultivated, potential alliances forged, and vendettas both strengthened and born.

My grandfather never wanted to risk showing any weakness to his many enemies knowing their spies closely watched the school, including the other packs itching to take him out and claim his territory for their own. It was growing harder to hide my shortcomings, though. At twenty-three, I was well past shifting age, and people were starting to sniff around, asking questions about why my wolf hadn't presented. Shipping me off must be one of the only ways for him to save face. I'm pretty sure he wouldn't risk it otherwise.

Just when I was sure he wasn't going to answer my question, he surprised me. "You may be useless, Sunday, but you're still a Fallon. That name means something, so don't go getting any ideas about dragging it through the mud while you're there. You have one job, and one job only. Find. Your. Wolf. Do you understand me?"

"Yes, Grandfather. I won't let you down. What time do I leave?"

"THIS PLACE COULDN'T GET MORE Gothic if it tried," I grumbled as my driver pulled up to the gates of Ravenscroft.

"Miss, would you like me to pull 'round front or take this to the rear for a more discreet entrance?" the driver asked, his posh British accent reminding me we were, in fact, in the middle of the English countryside.

Not that I could forget. I was on my way to freedom. There was nothing forgettable about that.

"The rear, please. I'm already showing up here two weeks after the year started. I don't need to draw more attention to myself than necessary."

"Very good, Miss."

He drove past the tall wrought iron gates and followed the ivy-covered stone wall that spanned the entire edge of the school's property. Although the walls were high, the building was higher. Spires soared toward the sky, reminiscent of the stereotypical Dracula's castle Hollywood always got wrong. *Maybe they used this place as inspiration?* It had been here for over a century. Nestled in the heart of England, where the humans were none the wiser regarding the creatures that roamed the halls. If only they knew.

I shook my head and chuckled. If they'd known, it would have been burned to the ground, salted, and consecrated until the earth wept the blood of the covenant. Which was why the Families had one common goal—play nice and stay in the shadows. So far, so good ... except for a few incidents here and there.

The car pulled to a stop outside of a huge set of carriage doors where a tall, severe-looking woman with skin so pale it glowed was waiting. Her long blonde fell to her waist and was shot through with gold highlights. Every time she moved, the gold glinted in the light. Her expression wasn't friendly. She looked like I'd seriously inconvenienced her by being here.

Excellent. Seems we're already off to a great start.

Without a word, my driver exited the car and came around to my side, holding open my door for me as I climbed out. While he took my belongings out of the boot of the car, I approached the walkway to my left, where the fair-haired woman stared at me. The pressure from her gaze nearly pinned me to the pavement. What kind of creature was she? I reached out with my senses to get a feel for exactly what she was. Not a human, not a vampire. The tinge of darkness surrounding her sent a chill through me as the word *deity* flashed in my mind. What the hell was a deity doing here?

"Mademoiselle Fallon, I'm glad you had the good sense to use the private entrance rather than make a spectacle of yourself." Her velvety voice, with its French accent, mesmerized me. "I'm Antoinette le Blanc, the Headmistress of Students."

I opened my mouth to speak, but she simply turned on

her heels and headed for the doors, which opened on their own. "My things—" I protested.

"Are already in your chamber."

Glancing over my shoulder, I saw the pile of suitcases and bags I'd brought with me were gone, along with the sleek black car. "Eat your heart out, Dumbledore."

"We are not some made-up school from children's books, Mademoiselle Fallon. Ravenscroft University is a prestigious institution where the future leaders of our world learn to work together. You'll find no trolls in our dungeon. You should count yourself among the lucky to even have a place here. Especially"—she looked me over—"considering you have yet to manifest." She leaned in and took a long moment to assess me. "Not a whiff of wolf on you. There's something . . . dark about you, but I can't place it."

I bristled. How had she known? Does this mean *everyone* knew? "I have a wolf. She's just not ready to come out to play."

Antoinette smirked. "We shall see. Now, come along. Moira will be waiting for you."

"Moira?"

"Your flatmate."

"I'm sharing a room with someone?"

She snorted. "Would you rather sleep outside? That can be arranged."

"No. It's fine. I just . . . I've never had a roommate."

"This is your first year at Ravenscroft. I assure you, having someone to show you the ropes, as it were, is going to be to your benefit."

She escorted me through winding hallways, the click of her heels on the stone floor echoing in the cavernous space. It was like being trapped in a labyrinth of never-ending halls until she stopped at a tall door and opened it, revealing another building across a courtyard. People milled around the open air space, some reading, others laughing together, and one staring straight at me.

My blood ran cold as my gaze connected with the one man I never wanted to see again in my life. Kingston Farrell. Son of the Farrell pack Alpha and future leader of their Family. And, according to my grandfather, my destined mate.

THREE

SUNDAY

I stood transfixed in the doorway, my chest a messy tangle of emotions. Embarrassment. Shame. Anger. Even the tiniest flicker of lust, which I immediately stomped out. All because Kingston's furious gaze was on mine.

I hated how after everything he'd done, after all the things he said about me over the years, I could still find him so damn attractive. I mean, some of that was genetics; the guy had been biologically predisposed to making women pant even when we'd met as teenagers. But now, he was all grown up. Towering six-foot-something frame, heavily muscled sun-bronzed skin with hints of . . . was that black ink teasing from the one open button of his flannel? Shaggy golden-blond hair practically begged you to run your fingers through it, and his chiseled jaw, covered in a slightly darker five-o'clock shadow, promised you'd feel his kisses for days after. Even narrowed in anger, his green eyes still made me want to discover their secrets.

If his looks alone weren't enough to make a woman drop her panties, all that big dick alpha energy would. His aura conveyed how utterly savage he'd be protecting those that belonged to him. Too bad my shortcomings kept me from falling under that umbrella. No, Kingston Farrell had made it perfectly clear just how beneath him he thought I was. Time and time again.

But hadn't I been the one who rejected him in the first place?

"Mademoiselle Fallon, if you make me stop and wait for you again, I'll leave you here to figure out your living arrangements on your own. I know you've been raised to believe that the world revolves around your schedule and whims, but it doesn't. Not here. Do not waste my time."

My gaze snapped to Antoinette's face and the pinched, slightly annoyed expression she'd worn ever since I pulled up. "I'm sorry, Antoinette."

"That's Madame Headmistress to you. Now, come along."

My feet hastened to obey without my conscious command. *Geez. Madame Moody here could teach grandfather a thing or two. They'd probably get along like a house on fire.* I smiled to myself. *If they didn't kill each other first.*

"Something funny, Mademoiselle Fallon?"

"Nope."

She gave me a long, withering glare and then took off up a set of stairs leading to a building that seemed to have pride of place among the others in the courtyard. I only had a second to read the plaque declaring it Blackthorne Hall before she was ushering me through its front doors.

"You're on the third floor. Room eleven." She pulled something out of her pocket and handed it to me. It was a key. Heavy, ornate, and colored with age. "I suggest you don't lose that. Replacements are hard to come by." She pointed to a set of winding stairs. "Take those and then the set on the left."

I figured it was best not to ask about the elevator since although I saw one, it was not offered as an option. Three flights of stairs weren't so bad. "You're not coming with me?"

"Your tardiness this morning has made me late for another meeting. But I trust even you can manage to count to three. Just take the stairs up and then look for the door with the eleven on it." She left before I could ask anything further.

The headmistress was a bit cold. But then, I figured most deities probably were. I didn't imagine etiquette or a pleasant disposition ranked really high on the list of things they cared about.

Thankful I didn't have to worry about lugging my belongings up to my room, I made my way up the stairs and then down a hall that reminded me of an upscale bed-and-breakfast more so than a dorm. The carpets were plush, the fixtures expensive, and I was pretty sure the wallpaper was original. Not because it was faded, it was actually in perfect condition, but I was fairly sure they didn't make it that way anymore.

Still holding the key, I slid it into the ornate lock of room number eleven, wondering if they even made keyrings large enough for this sucker as I stepped inside.

Moira, my new roommate, looked up as soon as the door opened, her expression of surprise morphing to disgust as she raked her eyes slowly down and then back. *Perfect.* I really had a way of making people fall in love with me, didn't I?

Since she made no effort to hide the fact she was sizing me up, I used the opportunity to do the same. Her blonde hair was styled in an artful tumble around her shoulders, thick black liner winging her amethyst-colored eyes, and a seriously hot shade of fuchsia expertly applied to her lips— which were currently twisted in a scowl. She wore head-to-toe black, a stark contrast to her alabaster skin which was dotted with a spray of freckles, but not in the rebellious style of someone going through their goth phase. Her high-waisted, wide-legged slacks screamed money. So did her sheer silk blouse and the lacy bralette she wore beneath it.

From the looks of things, I'd interrupted her painting her nails, a glittering drop falling from the brush and splattering onto the varnished wood of her fancy desk. Since she hadn't noticed, I decided not to tell her. No need to go and give her other things to hate me over. She seemed to have more than enough reasons already.

"You must be Sunday," she said with a resigned huff. "I'm Moira Belladonna."

My eyes widened at that. The Belladonnas were a notoriously scary coven of witches.

"Good, I see you already know better than to fuck with me. Stay out of my way, and we should get along just fine." She turned her attention back to her manicure, calling over her shoulder, "That's your bed over there. I've already filled the closet, so you'll have to make do with the dresser. You're just lucky I was willing to let you share my room. No one else wanted the pampered Fallon princess disrupting their lives."

Pampered princess? That was laughable. More like dirty little secret.

I eyed the furniture in question, which had clothes spilling out of two of its four drawers. The bed hadn't fared much better. While it was made, its linens the same decadent quality as the rest of the place so far, Moira's cast-off outfits were strewn all across it. I was pretty sure this was some kind of test, and my reaction would likely solidify or change whatever assumptions she'd made about me. But I'd been playing power games like this my whole life, and I didn't scare easily.

Without a word, I picked up the first of my suitcases and tossed it on the bed, right on top of a bunched-up Armani dress. She snorted, but I caught her eyeing me as though waiting for me to challenge her or break. I was used to people like her. Rich kids were the same from Family to Family. Show no weakness. That was the only way to establish where you belonged in the pecking order. Me? I might have been hidden away for most of my life, but I belonged on top.

I scooped all the clothes off my bed, carrying them in my arms as I strolled across the room toward her. She didn't even look up as she continued painting her toenails a deep crimson. Until I dropped the pile of designer garments straight onto her freshly painted feet.

"You really should put your clothes away. They could get ruined."

Eyes trained on me, she smirked. "Well played, Fallon. Maybe you're not a runt after all."

Ah, home sweet home.

EXHAUSTION WEIGHED HEAVILY ON ME, seeping into my bones as I came through the door and headed straight for my bed. The room was empty, thankfully. Wherever Moira was, I hoped she stayed there.

My first day of classes had been a complete fucking disaster. Any hope I'd had about Ravenscroft being my fresh start had been shot straight to hell. It seemed like my class-mates were determined to hate me. If they weren't staring, they were whispering, and the wide berth everyone gave me made me wonder if someone told them I had some kind of communicable disease.

I bet it was that alphahole, Kingston. He'd probably told them all how deep his disdain for me ran. Who knew what kind of lies he'd been spreading?

I almost longed for the solitude of the Fallon estate and what I'd dubbed my 'little ivory tower.' It was neither a tower nor ivory, but at least there I'd be surrounded by familiar things, and I could avoid seeing the people who hated me. Maybe freedom wasn't all it was cracked up to be.

Tossing my arm over my eyes, I fought the wave of tears that threatened to crest. I would not cry on my first day here. I was stronger than this, dammit. But I hadn't expected to feel such loneliness so quickly.

The bed dipped, startling me because I'd thought I was here alone. I opened my eyes and found Moira; at least, I thought it was her. Her hair was a startling violet shade now, cropped close to her head and putting her pretty face on display.

"Nice hair," I grumbled.

"You are pathetic."

"Is that always how you respond to a compliment, or am I special?" I grunted in response.

"No wonder you have no friends."

"Seriously? Who the hell shit in your Cheerios? What did I ever do to you besides befoul your fucking dorm room with my mere presence?"

Moira sighed. "Listen, you didn't do anything. You exist in our space, and that's enough. Especially since Kingston

Farrell has said nothing but terrible things about you since we heard you'd be joining us."

"I hate that jackass."

"Seems the feeling is mutual. But"—she cocked her head to the side—"you aren't giving off the she-bitch from hell vibe he describes, so I think I need to figure you out for myself."

"He's just butthurt because I rejected him. I haven't actually done anything to him. Hell, I haven't even seen or spoken to him since I was sixteen. You think the guy would grow a pair and get over it after seven years, but apparently I made an impression."

Her brows, a matching violet to her hair, lifted, and she snagged me by the hand, tugging me up until I was sitting. "Oh, you humiliated him. I knew there had to have been something like that. He went from zero to douche canoe over one summer. Girl, you created a monster. I bow down."

"What?"

"Anyone who can crush a man enough to change him like that is basically a goddess in my eyes. So, on that note" —she stood and propped her hands on her hips—"we should be friends."

I laughed. "Just like that?"

"Do you want me to make it harder? It's not like you have folks beating down the door with other offers. And truthfully, you'll never have a better offer than this one right here, sweetness."

Heaving a sigh, I stared at this little spitfire of a woman and nodded. She was right. I needed a friend, not another enemy. "Sold."

CHAPTER

FOUR

SUNDAY

L ibraries were all the same no matter where you were. Human or supernatural, they smelled of dust and paper, leather and ink. It was one thing I could always count on. The Satori library here at Ravenscroft was no different. I tossed the heavy tome I'd been studying onto the table in front of me, a loud thud calling attention my way from the scattering of students up and down the rows of workspaces. I'd been spending more and more time here during the evenings because any time I was alone on the grounds, I could swear I felt someone watching me. I wasn't ready to get caught alone in a dark corner with yet another person who despised me.

"Careful, treat the books badly, and the banshee will wake up." Moira pulled out the chair next to me and flopped onto the seat, somehow still seeming as graceful as a prima ballerina.

Today her hair was fire and spice, with dark cherry red roots gradually lightening to flame yellow at the tips. What had been a sleek blonde and blunt cut at her shoulders only yesterday now fell to the small of her back.

23

"Nice wig," I said, not paying her warning any heed.

"It's not a wig. This is all me, babycakes."

She tugged on the end of her hair.

"How? I thought magic wasn't allowed here."

Rolling her eyes, she muttered, "Newbies," before leaning in close. "In class, maybe. But they have no say in what I do when class is over. Besides, when I'm not on school grounds, I want to look good."

My eyes must've widened because she laughed loud enough to earn a stern glare from the librarian sitting at the desk.

"They just let you leave?"

Another laugh escaped her, this one quieter. "They don't *let* me do anything. But what they don't know won't hurt them. If I couldn't escape this place, I would go full cuckoo's nest within a week."

"Don't they notice you're gone?"

Shrugging, she toyed with the flaming end of her hair. "As long as the tuition is paid and I come back with all my appendages, they don't care."

"I'm coming with you next time."

She flashed me a brilliant smile. "Of course you are. You're my main bitch now."

Nodding, I reached for another book, this one about the history of the war between angels and demons. As thick as it was, it must've weighed fifteen pounds. At least.

"So, I know he hates you and all, but do you want to explain to me what the hell is between you and Kingston Farrell now?"

Alarm ricocheted through me, starting in my chest and ending as a cold pit in my belly. "What do you mean?"

"I mean, that man is looking at you like he wants to kill

you . . . right after he fucks you to within an inch of your life."

I followed her gaze up to the balcony that spanned the second floor. Sure enough, Kingston leaned against the polished wood railing, eyes blazing with heat and menace as he pinned me with his stare.

"It's nothing. I told you, just a stupid grudge."

"Nope. You don't get to brush this off. You have tea, and I'm ready for you to spill it all over."

I flicked my gaze back to where he'd been standing, but he was gone. The energy he'd radiated stayed behind, though, humming through my veins.

"Our Families have been at odds since before I was born."

"Of course they have. Every person here is the designated tribute of one of the Families. I don't think any of them really get along."

"Yes, well, Kingston and I were supposed to . . . bring the Fallon and Farrell packs together."

"Wait. *That* was the rejection you were talking about? You're his mate? No fucking way."

I winced. "Could you keep your voice down? I'm sure neither of us wants the whole world knowing what happened."

"Sorry. Go on."

"When I was presented to him on my sixteenth birthday, I . . . rejected him. He's hated me ever since."

She let out a low whistle. "Ouch. No wonder. Think he still has a thing for you?"

"No. He's probably searching for a dark corner he can pull me into so he can get rid of me."

"Sure, we'll pretend that's why." Standing, she stretched and rolled her shoulders. "I sure wish someone hated me enough to look at me like that. I'd let her hate me right out of my clothes and into bed."

"Oh, I'm sure there's someone out there for you to have hot hate sex with."

"From your lips to the goddess's ears." She blew me a kiss before strolling away with her fiery hair swaying.

Picking up the three books I'd pulled from the reference section, I returned them to the librarian's cart and headed for the mythology shelves, which were tucked deep in the back of the library. The eyes of the stained glass sphinx that made up the entirety of the west wall seemed to follow me with every step I took. The remaining glow of the last rays of the setting sun made the art appear alive.

An uneasy tremor built in my center as I scanned the books, searching for anything that stuck out as important for the class I was already behind in. The hair on the back of my neck rose, and I whirled around just in time for a large hand to grip me by the throat as I was pushed hard against the shelf.

Kingston's stare burned straight through me, settling deep in my core. "What the fuck are you doing here, Sunday? Are you stalking me?"

A warning growl built in my chest, the only response my wolf ever gave me. "Believe me, if I knew you would be here, I would've run away."

"Doesn't smell that way to me." He leaned in and dragged his nose across my collar and up my neck. Right to the spot where he would've marked me as his if I hadn't rejected him. "It smells like you still want me even though you threw away your chance."

"In your dreams."

"It was. Every fucking night, in fact. Until I realized how defective you were. I should thank you, you know? You saved me the embarrassment of being mated to a weak excuse of a wolf."

My chest fluttered, the anger boiling inside ready to escape. The urge to let my wolf out had my skin itching, too tight, desperate for the change.

"Look at you, so needy," he whispered. "I bet if I touched your little cunt right now, you'd be slick and hot for me."

"Fuck you," I spat.

One brow cocked. "That's the idea, Sunshine. You know, we may not be mates, but you'd still be good for a hard and fast fuck. What do you think?" His palm left my throat and slid down between my breasts before traveling farther, settling just over the top of my pussy. "Would you say no this time?"

Before I could answer and fight him off, Kingston was gone, flung across the aisle and into the wall, knocking books off the shelves.

"That's quite enough from you, wolf." The tall, broad man's voice boomed through the space, his Irish accent almost lyrical. "Need I remind you of our earlier lesson in restraint?"

"Not all of us are as controlled as you, Priest," Kingston bit out. "And we don't want to be either."

This guy was a priest? He was hot as fuck. Dark, wavy hair, cropped close at the sides but long enough to run your fingers through. The harsh slashes of his defined brows spoke of someone used to commanding respect. And then there was the jawline. Sharp, strong, sexy. What a waste. Curiously, even though Kingston called the Irishman a priest, his complexion bore the trademark pallor of a vampire.

"Miss Fallon," the priest said, "Come with me. You're late for our first session."

"Session?"

"Yes. I am sure if you look at your schedule for the week, you'll find my name there every evening."

"Gallagher?"

His jaw clenched, annoyance flickering in his eyes. "Americans, can't pronounce anything correctly."

I bristled. "What was that?"

"*Gallagher.*" He said it, Galla-her. If eyerolls could be verbalized, he'd just nailed it.

"Oh. I've never heard it said that way."

"Of course you haven't. You privileged little creatures live life in your ivory towers, never expanding beyond what you already know."

God, he was grumpy. "Okay, Father Gallagher. Did I say it right this time?"

"Aye. My name is Father Caleb Gallagher, and I am going to help you find your wolf."

CHAPTER
FIVE
SUNDAY

"Slow down. Not everyone here is a vampire," I called as Father Gallagher strode down the darkened hallway.

His long legs ate up the space at double the length mine did, but add to that his preternatural speed, and he was halfway down the hall while I trailed behind, forgotten.

"Walk faster, and we won't have a problem."

God, he was surly. And he smelled divine. Why did a priest need to smell so good?

We left the main hall and headed down a set of stairs that led into the bowels of the building. The air shifted to damp and heavy, the scent of earth and age filling my nose. We reached a doorway marked with his name, simple and unassuming, befitting a man of the cloth.

"Come in and kneel at the altar, Miss Fallon."

"Excuse me?" *Kneel? He expected me to kneel?*

"You heard me. Inside, on your knees. We have work to do."

"Listen, you're hot and all, but I'm not getting on my knees for you. I hardly know you."

And he was hot. God, was he ever. Tall and broad, but not bulky with exaggerated muscle. His understated black shirt and pants molded to his body just enough that I could easily watch the play of his *assets* as he walked in front of me. I'd never understood the desire to bounce a quarter off a man's ass, but I'll admit, he made me curious.

Suddenly embarrassed by the direction my thoughts had taken regarding a man who'd married the Lord, I cleared my throat and forced myself to lift my gaze.

Father Gallagher was staring at me. His nostrils flared angrily, and his intense, sapphire eyes bore deep into mine. "Well?" he demanded.

I blinked, having completely lost the thread of our conversation. He must have kept going while I'd been lost to my musings. What had we been talking about? Oh, right. He wanted to get me on my knees. Frankly, in a different situation, I might have considered it. All that smoldering intensity wrapped up in a delicious, completely forbidden package? That's an altar I could worship at.

"I was just wondering where your collar was," I lied, making my feet resume their hurried steps as I moved into what I'd assumed was his office, but turned out to be a little chapel.

"Only priests wear collars."

My steps faltered again. "But I thought . . . he called you Priest?"

"That was a long time ago."

I gestured to the flickering candles and the not-insubstantial crucifix hanging on the wall. "So what's all this, then? Sort of a weird decorating choice for a vampire, don't you think?"

His jaw tensed, and I could tell the time for questions had passed. Not that I thought it had ever actually started.

"I gave you an order, Miss Fallon. Obey it."

"I'm not in the habit of taking orders from bloodsucking leeches."

Oops. Wrong thing to say.

His eyes flashed dangerously. "And I am not in the habit of repeating myself." He grabbed me by the back of the neck and forced me to the cold tile. "On. Your. Knees."

My body obeyed without question, folding easily under the pressure of his vise-like grip. I'm not sure what it said about me that I pressed my thighs a little tighter together, his rough manhandling and the dangerous cast of his voice setting off a low throb in my core.

He released me at once, moving to stand just off to the left. "Your problem, Miss Fallon, is that you are undisciplined."

"You could tell all that after just a few minutes in my presence, huh?"

His eyes tightened, but he didn't rise to the bait.

"I am going to teach you mastery over yourself. Once you learn how to quiet your mind and focus, it should be no problem for you to summon your wolf."

"You think meditation is the answer to the last twenty-three years of my life? Just like that?" I laughed, a low scathing rumble that bounced around the room. "Let me save you a lot of time and frustration, preacher. Been there. Done that." I shifted on my knees, intending to rise, but he was there, his hand on my shoulder, holding me in place.

"I never said it would be easy, Miss Fallon. Clearly you lack the mental fortitude required for such introspection. But lucky for you, I am well-versed in all matters of self-control and self-discipline. I have no doubt we will persevere with time and intense study. Your grandfather has paid handsomely to ensure it."

His insults were delivered so silkily I could almost mistake them for casual conversation. Especially since my mind wanted to focus on the idea of what discipline at Father Gallagher's hand might look like. But the mention of my grandfather sent those thoughts scattering.

There it was again. The reminder of why I was here. Of what a consummate failure I was.

This guy—this priest—thought he could succeed where literally everyone else had failed? Fine. Let him try. What's the worst that could happen? Eventually he'd admit defeat, and I'd just be right back where I started. But, if by some miracle he was right and there was some little trick he could teach me, I'd finally get the one thing I'd been fiercely wishing for since I was old enough to understand what wishes were.

My wolf. My birthright.

I shifted uncomfortably. Kneeling was hardly the most demanding thing I've had to do, but the tile was unyielding beneath my kneecaps, and there was already a little ache building at the base of my spine.

"A little pain is good for the body. It keeps the mind sharp."

I raised a brow. "If you think I'm going to let you start beating me—"

"That won't be necessary."

Why did I get the feeling he'd omitted the word *yet*? And why did my protestation sound like such a lie?

"So what am I supposed to do now?"

"Now you will close your eyes and—"

"Pray?" I quipped. "Sorry, Father. I don't think the big guy is going to listen to a heathen like me."

"Miss Fallon, you are going to shut your mouth and do as you're told. Do I make myself clear? If that proves to be challenging for you, I will have no problem removing the temptation."

"How? You going to gag me, Father? I didn't realize priests were so kinky—"

"Silence!" he snarled, his movements so fast I didn't realize he'd put his hand over my mouth until the delicious scent of him wafted up my nose.

If I'd thought the tile was unforgiving, it had nothing on the steel of Father Gallagher's hand fused over my mouth. I couldn't open it if I wanted to. And I did. But whether to bite him or lick him, I wasn't sure. Both ideas were equally tempting.

He tilted my chin back so I was looking up at him. The dominance of his position, combined with the barely restrained power of his grip and the vulnerable bearing of my throat, had unease and something else skittering through my veins. Something I wasn't ready to examine too closely.

"You will not speak until I tell you to. Blink if you understand."

Once again, I obeyed, my body hardwired to follow his commands when delivered in that deep, resonant tone.

"Good, Miss Fallon. Now, when I let you go, you're going to close your eyes and empty your mind. Errant thoughts will try to distract you. You will silence them. You will embrace the discomfort of your body and dismiss it. For the next ninety minutes, you will focus only on the sound of your breathing."

I wanted to snort. My mind was not a quiet place. I wouldn't last nine minutes, let alone ninety. But he wouldn't let me up until I at least pretended to try. So I blinked.

"It's good to see that you're a fast learner, Miss Fallon. That bodes well."

He released me. I wasn't sure if it was my imagination when I felt his hand slide down the front of my throat and hesitate a little longer than necessary at my collarbone before he returned to his position in front of me.

"Now, close your eyes . . ." he said, his voice still holding the edge of command, but lower and more soothing this time, "and breathe."

"I CAN'T," I whispered.

"You can and you will."

Sweat trickled down the back of my neck, between my shoulder blades, and slid all the way down until it reached my bra. Could he tell? Did he know I was about to break? This was the third night in a row I'd been on my knees, *meditating*.

Something about Father Gallagher being present had me hyperaware of his focus on me, even if my eyes were closed. I knew he was watching. Judging.

Breaths came in short gasps as the intensity of my focus left me trembling. I fought the urge to sob from the effort of holding this position. Pain spiked up from my knees, needles stabbing me over and over with every slight twitch of my muscles. Then his scent overwhelmed me as his palm rested on the crown of my head. "Quiet your mind, *a stor*. You are tense and fighting your own thoughts."

On instinct, I opened my eyes and locked gazes with deep sapphire blue pools. He was close. So close I could have kissed him if I'd wanted to. "How do you know what I'm doing? You're not in here with me."

A rumble rolled through the room, coming from his throat, but he didn't look away. "Fall into my gaze and let me in."

"No."

"You'll do as I say, Miss Fallon. If you know what's good for you."

"Maybe I don't."

"You're reckless. A petulant child, just like your grandfather said you'd be."

Anger burst through me, a fireball escaping from the depths of my chest. "Fucking right. Petulant. A disappointment. A waste of space. You name it, he's hurled it at me."

My gaze flicked away from his because I couldn't take another second being a prisoner of his focus. But he gripped my face with both large palms and forced my attention back to him.

"Let go of me, Father."

"Caleb," he said, his voice rough. Those dark brows were furrowed, pulled together in a pained expression as confusion and conflict warred for control of his face. "Call me Caleb when my hands are on you."

I swallowed hard, unsure of what exactly was happening here. "Caleb. Let me go."

He did, his hands falling away as though I'd burned him. "Now. Close your eyes and take hold of all of that anger. Harness it. Open yourself."

I did. I took a long, slow breath, and even though he wasn't touching me anymore, my skin burned from where his fingers had pressed against my cheeks. In all the time we'd been working on this, he had resisted touching me, save for that first time when he'd forced me to the ground and held his hand over my mouth. Until tonight. The darkness that greeted me when my eyes were shut faded away and gradually lightened to a soft blue before fading further until it turned a brilliant white. I gasped.

"What are you doing to me, Caleb?"

He had to clear his throat before he answered. "It's not me, Miss Fallon. This is you."

"Can you see it?"

"No."

The light behind my eyes flashed so bright I was afraid I'd go blind if I didn't look away, but I couldn't. There was no way to escape what was in my own mind. I whimpered and fell forward, Caleb catching me before I hit the hard stone floor.

Resting my forehead on his chest, I forced myself to control my breathing and stop the tremors racking my body before I finally backed away. "What did you do to me?"

"You're opening to your wolf." He stiffened and shot to standing faster than I could track. I reached for him, but he blurred across the room before I could close the distance between us.

"What?"

"You . . . your knees are bloodied."

"That's what happens when you force a girl to spend ninety minutes on her knees while wearing a skirt three nights in a row."

He clenched his jaw and forced his gaze away from the blood. And then I understood. "Oh. You want to taste me. Is that what this is, Father?"

He was murmuring something softly, eyes closed, a deep line between his eyebrows, forged in concentration. Then he stopped and flicked his focus back to me. "That'll be all for tonight, Miss Fallon. Tomorrow night we will resume."

"But—"

"That's enough! Leave me."

His shout startled me. All this time, even when he'd been angry with me, he'd kept his tone measured and soft. This was a man on the edge.

"You know, you might be hot, but I'm not really a fan of being abused and treated like shit, so I think I'm done with these sessions, Padre. Have a nice eternity. See you never."

I brushed past him, reaching for the door, but his fingers encircled my wrist and pulled me close. "You'll see me when I tell you. You want to be rid of me? Do the work. Find your wolf. Then I'll free you from my attentions."

I rolled my eyes and broke the hold he had on me, though I knew with his strength he could've shattered every bone in my wrist with one squeeze if he wanted. "What will you do if I don't show up? Spank me, Daddy?"

No reaction. The man was a statue carved of stone. Except for that slight twitch in the fingers of his left hand. Barely noticeable, but there. I opened the door and strode outside, but not before he whispered, "Don't tempt me."

THAT NIGHT I fell into my bed in an exhausted heap, my downy blanket and pillows cradling my aching body like the softest cloud. I vaguely heard Moira saying goodbye as she snuck out to meet up with some witch named Casey.

"Don't forget to use protection," I called half-heartedly.

Moira's laughter chased her out of the door as my eyes lost the battle to stay open.

Usually, I needed to run at least a few miles to wear myself out enough to even try to sleep. My mind was always too active at night, my body restless. Not tonight. But my exhaustion wasn't due to running my limbs so hard they burned. This was my entire being. My soul. Caleb and what he'd helped me unlock. Whenever I'd mention my insomnia to my grandfather, he just blamed the absence of my wolf. I never thought he was right until now.

As if triggered by the reminder, his gruff voice reverberated in my mind, *"Find her, Sunday, and you'll sleep like a pup."*

Cool, Gramps. Thanks for that heartwarming and inspiring chat. I never actually said that part out loud, of course. That would have earned me a world of hurt and humiliation. And I'd already had more than enough of that to go around. But seriously, did everybody just assume I wasn't trying?

What shifter in their right mind wants to be the lone member of the pack that can't manage to do what they were born to do? I was left alone when the rest of them went out to run under the full moon. I was forced to sit by myself and remain on the outskirts because others thought my defect might be catching. I was the one whose mother didn't even love her enough to keep her in the first place.

Yeah, being wolfless was fucking great. A real treat.

Here she is, everybody. Sunday No-Wolf Fallon. Take a good look at the freak. Pity her. Mock her. Hate her for something completely out of her control.

I whimpered on the bed, the old pains and familiar taunts closer to the surface than they had been in years. It was like whatever had happened while I was back in that chapel had shaken loose the stronghold I tried to keep around that part of myself. The sad little girl who didn't understand what she'd done so wrong to make her mommy leave and get her daddy sent away.

My grandfather's voice continued to echo in my mind, even as I tried to push it away. *"Find her, Sunday. Find her."*

The transition between waking and dreaming was

seamless. My thoughts blurred and melded, the feel of the bed fading away until I simply floated in a sea of consciousness. Gone was the pain from my body. The hurt in my heart. Everything was suddenly, blissfully quiet.

Until it wasn't.

At first, I didn't register the stirrings. The little rumbles that sounded like thunder, or maybe a bunch of wild horses galloping in the distance. But then they grew closer until they were impossible to ignore. They tugged at me. Demanded my attention. Forced me to listen.

My consciousness narrowed, focusing on the sound until it was no longer rumbling but a voice brushing against the barrier of my mind. It drew across my skin like raw silk. Unsettling and wonderful at the same time.

"There you are."

"W-wolf?" I guessed.

"No, my daughter."

"Mom?" The impossibility of it should have torn me straight out of the dream, but there was a truth, a heaviness to the words that lies never quite matched. More than that, there was a familiarity in that warm, husky tone that called to me on a fundamental level. I'd never heard the voice before, but part of me recognized it.

"I've tried to reach you, but the shields around you were too strong until now."

"What shields?"

"Oh, my daughter, there are so many things I wish to tell you. But I haven't much time. Know that I tried to protect you. To place you in the care of those who could keep you safe. But they've found you. They're coming for you. You need to unlock your power; it is the only way you will survive. Embrace what makes you feel strong. Give into

41

it. Do not let them deny you your birthright. Do not let them make you weak."

"What are you talking about?"

"They hate you, daughter, for what you are. They will kill you if given the chance. Do not let them. Do not fight the pull of who you were born to be."

"Who? Who wants to kill me?"

"I must go."

"No. Don't go. Wait. I have so many questions."

The rumbles returned, this time the dull roars fading until I was once more floating in that sea of consciousness. Drifting. Existing.

Fading away until I was nothing at all.

"**B**loody hell," I muttered as the mouthwatering scent of Sunday Fallon filled my nose and overwhelmed me yet again.

Night after night she'd gone for a run, and night after night I'd kept to myself, stalked her from the shadows, made sure she didn't see me. Avoiding her notice during the day hadn't been as easy, but I'd managed. She didn't need to have any reason to be in my orbit. Not if she wanted to keep breathing. Not with the way her blood called me home.

But tonight was different. Sunday wasn't out for a midnight run. I'd watched and waited just like every evening. She hadn't left her room. How had I missed this?

My heart lurched as I rounded the corner of the trail in the woods and found her in nothing but a thin nightgown, her body crumpled on the ground.

No.

Rage boiled inside me.

No. This couldn't have happened. Someone else got to her before I did. Someone ruined everything. I rushed to

45

her, desperate to catch the scent of the creature who'd hurt her, who I'd be killing as soon as I could trace him. Except she wasn't dead or hurt. She was curled up and fast asleep, her dark hair strewn across the path.

"What the fuck are you doing out here?" I whispered the question even as I knelt next to her, fingers itching to touch skin I knew I'd find warm and soft.

She moaned, and her lips turned down in a frown. "No. Don't go. Wait. I have so many questions."

Stomach twisting, I almost answered her before it hit me. She was dreaming. She was a sleepwalker. Someone was going to have to bolt her door at night to keep our little wolf princess from wandering.

"You may be more trouble than you're worth," I grumbled.

I couldn't leave her out here, vulnerable, alone, scantily clad. No one else could see her like this, not if I had anything to say about it. I scooped her into my arms and had to fight the groan that built in my chest at the feel of her skin against mine. My cock throbbed and fangs descended, ready to take her as they always were, every night. But this time? This time she was within reach.

"Wh-what are you doing?" she asked, her eyelids fluttering open as I headed toward Blackthorne Hall.

"Shh, dove, I'll get you home. Get you safe."

Her sleepy nod was the only answer I got, but it was all the affirmation I needed. I had her. She was in my arms and at my disposal. The elevator opened the moment I pressed my thumb to the scanner. There were definite perks to being vampire royalty, privacy chief among them. I should have taken her back to her room, where I was sure her flatmate would be sleeping, unaware of Sunday's nocturnal venture through the forest. Instead, I took her straight to mine, not even bothering to pretend I was going to stop on her floor. I had her now. She couldn't get away. I'd been hunting her for the last two weeks, and I was only so strong.

Kicking open my door, I strode through the living room of my suite and straight to my bedroom. I needed to see her splayed out on my bed, to get her scent all over my sheets, so when I have to let her go, I can remember she was here. Her soft moan when I placed her on the mattress went straight to my cock again, and I had to force myself not to press my lips to her throat, bite down, and drink deep. God, but I wanted to mark her skin so everyone knew where she belonged. And *who* she belonged to.

I bared my fangs in a soundless snarl, maddened by the reminder that others were already sniffing around, coveting what was mine. I'd noted each of the offenders, already planning on repaying each transgression tenfold. Kingston was the worst among them, his wild gaze too focused on her whenever she entered the room. His attention was unwavering, his intent clear. He wanted her, my wolf princess. But he'd never have her.

It was a lesson he needed to learn, and soon. But not tonight. Tonight, Sunday was here. In my bed. And there was nothing anyone could do about it.

CHAPTER
SEVEN
SUNDAY

T he sound of birdsong woke me. I cracked my eyes open with a groan. "Moira, you forgot to close the window—"

As I took in my surroundings, my words stopped short, and I scrambled to an upright position.

This was not my room. And this was definitely not my bed. It was way too big and way too comfy.

Sleek, modern furniture filled the space. A pewter gray chaise lounge sat beneath the window, while the walls on either side were made up entirely of bookshelves stuffed to the gills with leather-bound tomes.

I lifted a hand to my aching head, feeling like I'd consumed an entire case of my grandfather's moonshine, but the last thing I remembered was passing out in bed after getting back from my session with Caleb. So what the hell happened? How had I ended up here? I groaned, trying to put together the pieces of the night before when the dream came back to me.

'*Unlock your power . . . Embrace what makes you feel*

strong . . . They're coming for you . . . They will kill you if given the chance.'

My mind twisted as it tried to make sense of my mother's cryptic warnings, but then a sudden, much more terrifying thought gripped me.

What if 'they' already found me? What if they were still here?

I let out a soft gasp, my gaze immediately dropping and relief crashing through me when I saw I was still wearing the nightgown I'd pulled on the night before, and I didn't seem to have any fresh injuries or bindings. Nothing to indicate I'd been harmed in any way or that I was being kept against my will. Then I held my breath, willing myself not to make a peep as I listened hard for the sound of somebody else moving around. After several racing heartbeats, I finally relaxed, breathing normally and allowing some of the tension in my shoulders to seep away. I was alone, but who knew for how long.

Okay. We can work with this. Maybe things aren't quite as fucked as they seem. So what if you woke up in a stranger's bed? These things happen, right? It's so common they'd named it. So let's just walk our ass on out of here.

Pep talk finished, I kicked my legs over the edge of the king-size bed, intent on doing just that. One of the silky black sheets was wrapped around my thigh, and I had to untangle myself before I was free. The act brought a fresh wave of bergamot to my nose. Citrus mingled with spice and dredged up an image of warm, amber eyes.

Instead of frightening me, the memory of them soothed me. Made me feel safe, protected even. But that was absurd, right? Because I'd definitely fallen asleep in my own bed last night and couldn't recall a single thing between then and now. Which meant I'd ended up in this bed without my consent and whoever brought me here was the furthest thing from a protector.

Right. Time to go.

I scrambled toward the door, heart racing in my throat as I half expected it to fly open before I reached it. Or worse, find it barred from the outside. But no, it was unlocked. I could have wept, so great was my relief as I flung the door open without issue, spotting an elevator just a few feet away. I ran toward it, my finger jamming the button several times as I cast my eyes around the little waiting area.

It was decorated in the same style as the rest of Blackthorne Hall, answering one of my many questions at least. I was still on campus. Still in my dorm. Just on a different floor, it seemed.

"Come on, come on," I urged, slamming my finger into the button again, only to stop and peer closer. It wasn't a button in the usual sense. It was some kind of scanner. Likely coded to whoever lived up here.

Fuck.

I spun around, looking for some other means of escape. But there wasn't one. The only two doors on this floor were the one behind me that would lead me back into the sprawling room and those that led to the elevator I couldn't seem to access.

Fuck!

Just as my panic really started to climb, there was a soft, electronic chime and the elevator doors peeled open. My heart slammed in my chest as they revealed the man within.

Tall, pale, dangerous, with thick wavy black hair and disarming eyes the color of molten amber. He took my breath away in that this-guy-is-bad-news-guard-your-virtue kind of way. I couldn't tear my gaze from him, needing to inspect him and make sure he was real.

Full lips? Check.

Penetrating stare? Check.

Chiseled jawline? Check.

Vampire, able to kill me with the flick of his wrist? Check.

He stepped out, making no move to walk around me, just crowding my personal space until I was forced to step back.

"Where do you think you're going?" His voice was smooth and skin-tingling, like he was whispering dirty nothings into my ear when all he'd done was ask a question. I blamed the British accent.

"Better question, asshole, is who the hell are you?"

"Noah." He extended an index finger to point to the door I'd left wide open in my harried escape. "The man whose bed you slept in."

"Ha, that's cute. Because I was in my bed when I went to sleep last night. Which makes you a creepy psycho kidnapper. Now if you'll excuse me, I'm going to go report you and then shower for about ten years to get the scent of you off me."

"Why don't we just go back inside—"

"Absolutely not. If you don't let me into that elevator right now, I am going to scream."

He seemed to read something in my face because he took a few backward steps into the elevator and gestured for me to join him.

I narrowed my eyes suspiciously, not trusting him, and yet unable to deny he didn't seem to be making any threatening advances. The knowledge gave me courage as I stepped inside and pressed the button marked '3.'

"So, Noah, do you make a habit out of kidnapping women from their beds?"

"No." He said it so simply, and just that one word annoyed the living hell out of me.

"Ah, I see. I was your first. Looks like you're not a very good serial killer then. You should probably give it up."

His lips turned up in a slight smirk. "You weren't."

"Wasn't what?"

"In your bed. I found you in the forest and brought you back here since I didn't know where you belonged."

His words caused my stomach to clench painfully. *The forest? What the hell happened last night?*

"And I'm just supposed to believe you swooped in like some sort of gallant knight and didn't lay a finger on me? Yeah, right. I was in your bed."

His eyes flashed, and he took two steps forward, closing the space between us and crowding me until I had no choice but to press up against the corner of the elevator. Was this the slowest lift in the entire world? I needed space, for the doors to open, for something to give. If only so I could breathe and stop toying with my kidnapper.

No part of us was touching, but I could feel him everywhere, my traitorous body responding to his magnetic pull. The air between us crackled with energy as he lowered his head until his lips hovered just above mine.

"Trust me, dove. Had I touched you last night, you'd not only remember it, you'd be begging me for an encore."

My mouth went dry, and it took me a second to recover from the undeniably sexy images he'd summoned in my mind. I managed to shove the images away, crossing my arms to force some space between us—even though the move only brought us into direct contact as my arm brushed along his chest.

"I'm just supposed to take your word for it, am I?"

"I can prove it if you'd like?"

My breath caught as he reached out and skimmed his knuckles down my cheek and then further, along the side of my throat. I finally knocked his hand away when it had drifted down to my collarbone—though I had the feeling the only reason his hand actually stopped its pursuit was because he allowed me to stop it.

"I'll pass, thanks."

He shrugged and stepped back. "Suit yourself."

Then, because I couldn't help myself, I asked, "So you were a perfect gentleman?"

He threw me a cocky smirk. "I never said that."

The chime of the elevator reaching my floor saved me before I could say anything further. As the doors slid open, I tossed him a final fleeting look over my shoulder. "Well, thanks for coming to my rescue, I guess, Noah."

His eyes flared again, the side of his mouth lifting in a slow, sexy smile. "My pleasure, Sunday."

EIGHT

SUNDAY

T he sun's rays beamed in through the window at the end of the hall, bathing me in light and casting my walk of shame in stark relief as I skulked down the hallway and reached the door to my room.

"Oh, my God, there you are. We've been looking all over." Moira's voice caught me off guard as my fingers touched the doorknob.

My head snapped to the right, where I stared down the hall. She stood, her acid green asymmetrical bob nearly glowing in the light spilling through the window. A hulking god of a man stood next to her. His eyes were framed by full, dark lashes, the irises blue, vibrant, and piercing even from a distance. His complexion was tanned from hours spent in the sun, and his dirty blond hair was pulled up into a bun, with a thick, full beard lining his chiseled jaw. He looked like sin and sex and every fantasy I'd ever had about being rescued by a handsome warrior.

"I . . . had a nightmare. Went for a walk."

I opened the door and stepped inside my room, where I

found our small space ransacked. Clothes were strewn around, drawers hanging open, papers everywhere. "What the hell happened in here? You really are a slob."

Moira shook her head, hands on her hips as she followed me inside. "I didn't do this. Do you really think I would treat vintage Chanel like this?"

I stared her down, the argument on my lips before she finished.

She had the grace to look embarrassed. "Except for that first day. That doesn't count."

"And who are you?" I jerked my chin toward the Viking man leaning against the open door.

Smirking in a way that made his ice-blue eyes sparkle, he said, "Alek Nordson. And you're the famous Sunday Fallon. You've got the whole university buzzing, you know?"

His accent was hard to place. It sounded British, but with occasionally clipped words that reminded me of the time a Norwegian shifter pack came to my grandfather's house for a visit.

"Nordson? Scandinavian?"

That smirk widened. "Novasgardian."

Interesting. Very interesting. I'd heard of them. Norse gods came from Novasgard, but they didn't leave. They kept to themselves for the most part. If Alek was here, making contacts, learning to be an ambassador, that meant things were shifting. The thought of Norse gods joining our world, taking a more active role, made me nervous. There was already plenty of supernatural dick swinging going on between the vampires, shifters, witches, and fae. We didn't need to add gods to the mix.

"Don't tell me you're the God of Thunder."

Laughter rumbled from deep in his chest, making me feel foolish immediately. "Not thunder, no."

"Wait, are you a god of something?"

"I suppose you'll have to figure that out on your own, won't you, Sunny?"

Moira tossed a shoe at him, missing by about a mile. "Leave her alone, Alek." She turned her gaze on me. "I'm glad you're not kidnapped. When we came home and saw the place was ransacked, I freaked."

"Aw, you worried? You do care after all," I teased.

She pretended to be unaffected, but couldn't hide her grin. "It's bad luck to be the one with the murdered roomie."

I held out my hands. "Not murdered."

"So where were you?"

"In a creepy vampire's lair."

Alek's brows rose. "By choice?"

"Apparently he found me unconscious in the forest." My voice was low as I fought the mortification of admitting I'd been asleep in the woods—and not on purpose.

"Oh, you can't be serious. Sleepwalking wasn't one of the categories I checked when selecting my roommate." Moira flopped down on her clothes-covered bed.

"Well, smart-ass wasn't one of the ones I checked, so it looks like we're even," I shot back.

"Do you two want me to leave you alone to fight it out, or . . ." Alek offered.

"Wait," I said. "I thought you were into girls." I locked my gaze on Moira.

Moira nodded. "I am."

"But you're out with this guy all night?"

"I'm an equal opportunity companion. Have you taken a good look at him?"

Alek crossed his arms over his broad chest and snickered as I let my gaze drift over his form. He was handsome as hell. They grew them strong and beautiful in Novasgard.

Moira laughed. "We aren't together. Alek and I are training. Late-night hand-to-hand combat. He's a warrior. I'm failing weapons and defense already, and we're only a month into the year."

"Fighting comes naturally. It's in my blood," Alek offered, then he shoved off the doorframe and strode closer to where I stood. "I could help you, if you need it."

I swallowed hard and had to work to keep my heart rate even. "I'm good. Thanks."

"Let me know if you change your mind. I'm available."

"Alek, stop flirting. She's too sweet for you. She wouldn't know what to do with you."

That got my back up a bit. "I'm not *that* sweet."

"I'd like the chance to find out just how sweet you are," he said.

"Don't get your hopes up. She's already been claimed by Kingston."

My chest tightened. "No, I haven't. No one has or *will* be doing any claiming. I'm not here for that."

"We'll see," Alek murmured before heading for the door. "See you around, Sunny. I'm sure of it."

Moira shook her head and tossed an arm over her eyes. "Get out of here, Viking. Some of us need sleep before we head to class."

Alek licked his lips before cocking his head at me. "Don't be shy, little fighter. If you need a real challenge, you know where to find me."

I couldn't help myself. I watched him leave, and my stupid heart fluttered when he winked—he fucking *winked* —as he closed the door behind him.

Moira snorted.

"What?"

"Apparently, your milkshake brings all the supernatural boys to the yard, Sunday. But which one gets the cherry?"

"None of them." Even as I said it, thoughts of four very different men ran through my mind. Each image more scandalous and tantalizing than the last. I knew Moira noticed the little shiver my mental peepshow caused because she snorted again.

"Keep telling yourself that, Fallon."

GETTING through the day had been a special sort of hell. Between my bruised knees and aching back from my sessions with Father Gallagher and the low-grade headache which had persisted since waking up in Noah's bed, I was so over this being conscious thing. I just wanted to sleep. Which was exactly what I was planning to do—just as soon as I finished catching up on some of the reading Caleb had assigned to me for our next session. I had no desire to end up on his shit list.

As curious as I was about what represented the good priest's idea of discipline, another part of me was pretty sure I didn't want to find out. Not when his teaching methods already left me bloody and battered.

I groaned as I flipped through the book, internally weeping at how many pages of this chapter were left.

"That's it," Moira declared. "We're going out. One of the fairies in my study group is DJing tonight, and those guys know how to throw a party."

The book in front of me closed with a loud snap, and I

jumped, nearly falling out of my chair in surprise. "Shit, Moira. How did you do that?"

"Uh, sweetie. It's called magic."

I made a face. "Yeah, I got that part. But *how*? I thought this place was warded or spelled or whatever? So grumpy shifters can't just wolf out in the middle of class when a vamp looks at them sideways, and to prevent a pissy witch from setting fire to her cheating ex's dorm room."

"First, that's oddly specific, and there are non-magical ways of starting a fire if said witch was so inclined. Second, I've already said this, but you clearly weren't listening. Only the classrooms are warded. And third, you're not giving me enough credit. I'm a Belladonna, remember?"

My cheeks burned at being chastised by her.

Moira rolled her eyes. "You're focusing on the wrong things here, Sunday. As your roommate, you get to benefit from my awesomeness. You should be taking advantage of it, not asking stupid questions. Come on, get your ass up."

"Moira," I whined half-heartedly. I'd already learned it was impossible to sway her from her path once she'd decided something. "I'm not in the mood for big crowds and loud music. I have a headache."

"Which is what the alcohol is for. Trust me. You need this. Hell, *I* need this just being around you. Now get up and start stripping. Here," she reached into her closet and threw something at me. "Put this on."

I held up the scrap of fabric I assumed was supposed to be a dress between my thumb and forefinger. "Uh, Moira. My ass will never fit in this."

She was petite and willowy with the body of a ballet dancer. I was . . . not. Which I was more than okay with, actually. I loved my curves, but how she thought we'd be able to share clothes was beyond me.

"Would you stop your bitching and just put it on? I know what I'm doing."

I gave her another dubious glance but stood with a groan.

"That's my girl!"

While she started rooting around for whatever she was going to wear, I pulled my T-shirt off and shimmied out of my jeans. I'd just started pulling the red dress over my head when I heard Moira's gasp.

"Shit, Sunday. What the hell did you do to your knees?"

Hands still awkwardly lifted above my head, I peered down, likely looking like some kind of demented scarecrow as I checked to see what she was referring to. The purple and black bruises on my knees made me wince. It looked even worse than it felt, which was saying a lot.

"I must have fallen when I was sleepwalking."

I'm not sure why I lied. I just didn't want to get into my kneeling sessions with Caleb. They felt private somehow. Like what happened in that room when he helped me access my wolf was just between us. Which was stupid. He was my teacher, and I was sure he'd had similar sessions with other students, but there it was.

"I thought shifters were supposed to have super healing?"

I tugged the dress down, grunting a little as I pulled it over my hips. "You have to be able to shift to be a shifter, remember?"

"Oh. Right. I didn't realize you didn't have access to any of the good stuff without your wolf."

"The wolf is the good stuff."

She shrugged. "Eh. I'd take the healing and enhanced senses over the furry smelly dog any day."

I should have been insulted, and coming from anyone

else, I probably would have been. Calling a shifter a dog never ended well, but from Moira, it wasn't insulting, just . . . Moira. Even so, I probably shouldn't have confirmed my complete lack of supernatural ability. She'd already known about the wolf, but no one outside of my pack knew about the other stuff. I hadn't intended for her to find out, but when she'd seen the truth with her own eyes, I couldn't exactly hide it.

"Hey Moira, can we just keep that between us? I don't really need—"

"Say no more. My lips are sealed."

I gave her a relieved grin, going to stand in front of the full-length mirror once I smoothed the material of my dress down my thighs. Moira came to join me, her wavy violet hair spilling over her shoulder as she studied me.

"Totally fuckable," she announced. "But you're going to need to add some tights if you want to hide those bruises." She moved behind me, lifting the chocolaty length of my hair up, holding it in her fist in a makeshift ponytail. "Oh yeah, definitely up. If the men aren't imagining the things they want to do to your neck, they'll be thinking about how good it'll feel to tug on this while they're fucking you from behind."

"Moira!"

"What?" She blinked innocently at me. "I should know. It's what I'd be thinking about."

"Is it even possible for you to fuck me from behind?"

She gave me a sad, pitying look. "You poor, vanilla virgin." Moira didn't give me a chance to respond to that before pushing me toward her desk chair. "All right, now let's do something about your makeup."

Forty-five minutes later, I was groomed, painted, and polished to within an inch of my life. We'd paired a chic leather jacket with my clingy dress, as well as some heeled ankle boots. She'd rubbed something rose-scented through my hair that made it silky and shiny and gave it a subtle shimmer. Then she gave me something else from her endless beauty supply to rub into my skin, which did the same for my body. All of that had been topped off with more bottles and tubes of makeup than I could count. Though the bold, red lipstick she playfully informed me was named 'Don't Stop' and the winged black liner around my eyes were my personal favorites.

"Wow," I breathed when she was finished, barely recognizing myself.

Moira grinned at me. "I won't even say I told you so."

She looked equally amazing in her black leather microskirt and sheer long-sleeved blouse. She'd done her makeup similar to mine, though she'd opted for a glossy black lip instead of red. And I still wasn't sure how she planned to dance, let alone walk, in her thigh-high heeled boots.

"Come on, now we're ready for a night of bad decision-making."

She took my hand and pulled me toward the door. This time I didn't even feign a protest. If I was being honest, I was already feeling better and sort of looking forward to it. I couldn't remember the last time I'd gone out and partied with a friend. Hell, I could barely remember friends. Being the pack outcast had really put a damper on my social calendar.

"Fuck it. What's the worst that could happen?"

CHAPTER
NINE
SUNDAY

"**A**re you sure this is allowed?" I asked as Moira led the way down a dark corridor.

"Don't be afraid. Nothing will happen to you while you're with me." Alek's voice was a caress as he leaned in from his place behind me.

"Why's he here again?" I asked, trying to suppress the involuntary tingles the puff of his breath sent racing down the back of my neck.

"Because I'm the muscle. And a damned good time," he added, the invitation to play evident in his voice.

"Stop flirting with her, Viking. Give her a chance to get used to the place before you start pissing on her to mark your territory." Moira stopped at a dead end and turned to stare at us. "Now prepare to be wowed." She held out both hands like a magician about to do a trick.

"Now who's flirting?" Alek teased.

Moira returned her focus to the blank wall before waving her palm across the brick. A faint green glow began to emanate from the mortar lines, the shape of a door appearing as the verdant shade spread. I knew witches existed, but I never really spent time with them. Our kind didn't really . . . intermingle. Seeing Moira in action was astonishing.

"Apres vous, mes amis," she offered in flawless French.

I hesitated, just for an instant. Walking through a glowing green door to parts unknown wasn't the brightest idea. Not with the warning from my dream still bouncing around in my head. But Alek took my hand in his and squeezed.

"Together then?"

Letting my gaze travel up, up, up, his large frame, I allowed his piercing eyes to calm me. "Okay."

"Ugh," Moira scoffed. "I'm dying to dance. Come on, you're acting practically human."

Together, Alek and I crossed through the doorway. My skin prickled, pins and needles breaking out across my entire body as magic coated us then snapped away as we passed the barrier. My ears popped the instant we crossed from school grounds to the exterior of a nightclub. The red neon script over the door said *Iniquity*.

"Are you sure this is a nightclub and not a strip club?" I asked.

Alek laughed. "Afraid of a little nudity?"

"No, but I like to know what I'm walking into."

Moira shoved past the two guys standing at the door. "Hi, fellas."

"Miss Belladonna," one of them said before pushing open the door for us.

Thumping bass spilled out of the club, low and loud, commanding attention, almost its own being. Moira took my hand and tugged me out of Alek's grip as we walked down a set of stairs and into *Iniquity*.

The dim lighting was just bright enough for me to see

the path mapped out by the hallway, and when we reached the end of the walkway, I saw yet another staircase to my left. I moved to head down, now eager to let loose and dance my ass off with Moira, but Alek's large palm encircled my arm.

"Not that way, Sunny. That's the true den of *Iniquity*. You're not ready for what lies beneath the surface."

My stomach clenched. What kind of sinful delights were hidden down there? And did I want to find out? He turned me in the opposite direction, tugging me to the right and into a club filled with people.

"Wow, this is . . ." I started, but my voice faltered as I took in the massive space, lit in greens and blues with purple spilling out from under the bar and DJ's booth. The dance floor was full of couples grinding together. A vampire in the corner had his fangs buried in the neck of a human woman who looked like she was on the verge of orgasm or maybe in the throes of one.

"Intense?" Moira asked.

"Yeah."

"I forget how sheltered you've been. Don't worry. No one will bite you tonight."

"They'd better not." Alek leaned in, and a shiver ran down my spine as his lips brushed the shell of my ear. "It'll be the last thing they do."

Wowza. He really had the whole sexy, murdery smolder thing down. And I liked it. A lot. Definitely more than I should. Not that I was about to admit it, especially not to him. Alek didn't seem like the kind of guy who needed any ego stroking.

"I can take care of myself," I protested.

"I don't doubt it."

"Leave her alone. She's my date tonight. And I need her

to dance with me," Moira said. "Don't make me turn you into a toad."

Alek laughed. "You know as well as I you don't have that power. I, however, do." He smirked and snapped his fingers, a spark of green filling the room as Moira transformed into a cute little tree frog. She gave an annoyed croak before he snapped again, and she returned to her normal form.

The free use of magic had my eyes flaring wide. I glanced around, wondering what everyone else thought about the random club toad, but no one batted an eye. I guess it was just a typical Friday night as far as they were concerned. Looked like Moira was right; my life was definitely sheltered compared to theirs.

"I'm going to have your balls for that." An orb of fire sat in her palm, and matching flames filled her eyes.

"Oh, I'm so scared." He held up his palms and pretended to shake.

"You should be."

I laughed. I couldn't help myself. "You'd better sleep with both eyes open tonight."

"It would take more than a whole coven of Belladonnas to faze me." He tossed me another of his panty-melting winks and walked away. "If you need me, I'll be over there," he called over his shoulder as he headed for a corner booth where a few other people I recognized from school were sitting.

"Jackass," Moira called to his retreating back. Then she sighed and added, "But goddess, is he pretty."

She was not wrong. I couldn't seem to make myself look away from him, my eyes trailing down his muscled back and locking on his ass. Man, did he wear the hell out of those jeans.

Moira cackled when she caught me drooling. "Come on, let's cool you down before you combust."

Moira and I snagged drinks and strolled around the large space together, scoping out the best places to dance, stopping to talk to a few of our classmates. The music changed to a song both of us loved, so we downed our drinks and headed for the dance floor. We laughed and moved to the music, the lights flashing, changing colors and making it look like we moved in slow motion as we spun and writhed.

I closed my eyes as the song morphed again to something a little slower and a lot dirtier. Moira had found a girl to dance with and abandoned me two songs ago. I didn't care. I loved the freedom of swaying to a beat and giving myself over to music.

"You're indecent. Do you know that, dove?" The scent of bergamot washed over me as Noah slipped his palms over my waist and pulled me against him from behind.

My heart lurched, then my pulse began racing, a dangerous reaction to have around a vampire. He recognized it too, if the way his fingers dug into my hips, pressing me even closer against him, was any indication.

"I didn't say you could dance with me."

His lips slid over my neck, trailing up until he nipped my ear. "You haven't stopped me yet."

"I like dancing."

"You like me."

"Don't be so sure."

"I can feel it in your pulse. I can taste it on your skin. You're just as drawn to me as I am to you, little wolf."

He spun me around to face him, those amber eyes locking onto mine and making my nipples pebble as arousal gripped me.

"Don't you dare try to use your vampire powers on me."

"I would never. Not with you."

"That's what you say now, but how do I know it's not exactly how I ended up in your bed? You could have easily glamoured me and made me forget the whole thing."

His low chuckle covered me like a soft blanket. It was safety and comfort I felt then, not menace. It may prove to be the stupidest thing I'd ever done, but in that moment, I trusted him when he repeated his earlier words.

"Not with you. I'll have you, dove. One day soon. But not until you beg for me to take you."

An insistent flutter took up residence low in my belly, making me achy with need and oh-so-aware of the way he was holding me. The grip he had around my waist was strong enough I couldn't get away even if I'd wanted to, and the hard length of his cock pressed against my belly, persistent and ready.

"Why do you suddenly want me so bad?"

His dark brows lifted. "Suddenly? I've been running from your scent since the day you arrived."

"Running? From me?" The thought of someone as strong and obviously powerful as him trying to escape me made me want to laugh. No one ever considered me a threat. Certainly not enough of one to run from.

He brought his head close to mine, ensuring I was staring deep into his molten gaze. "Yes, little wolf. You. All the while, my instincts demanded I hunt you. But I've given up. I shouldn't want you, but I can't help myself."

"Why shouldn't you want me?" Even under the heavy beat of the music, I could hear the breathless quality of my voice. I was far more invested in his answer to the question than I should be.

He laughed. "Have you paid any attention in class?

Pacts and treaties are the backbone of our society. The Blackthornes and Fallons have sworn to never join. The risk of our species mixing is too great."

"You're a Blackthorne?" I went rigid in his arms. I knew exactly what he was talking about. The abominations created when a shifter and vampire joined usually died. Not because one killed the other, but because usually, the vampire turned their mate, and the shifter blood rejected it.

Instead of releasing me, he held me tighter, his eyes laser-focused on my throat. "I am. My father is Cashel Blackthorne, and I am the heir to the Blackthorne bloodline. I'm sorry, I should've told you."

"Then you shouldn't be spending time with me."

He swallowed hard. "No. I shouldn't. But that won't stop me. I need you, even if I never taste your blood."

"Slumming it with the corpse, Sunshine? That's pretty pathetic, even for you." Kingston's voice slithered between us, stealing my attention from Noah. "Thorne, what business do you have with my castoff? She's off-limits, and you know it."

The lusty little bubble Noah had woven around us popped. For a second there, I'd forgotten where we were. I'd been so wrapped up in him, no one else had existed but the two of us. And then Kingston had to go and ruin it. And, as they always did when Kingston was near, shame and anger were quick to follow.

Somewhere between Moira's makeover and dancing with Noah, I'd forgotten why I'd come to Ravenscroft. For a little while, I'd gotten to be a normal twenty-three-year-old flirting with hot guys and dancing the night away. But Kingston brought reality crashing back down.

Before I could ask Kingston why he even cared, Noah tensed around me. Part of me expected him to tear into

Kingston, but he surprised me by laughing. His cold, cruel rumble conveyed just how insignificant he thought the shifter was. That was when I actually saw Noah as the Blackthorne heir, and not just as the dangerous, albeit incredibly sexy vampire I'd been so shamelessly dancing with.

"*Your* castoff? That's not how I heard it. Correct me if I'm wrong, dove. But weren't you the one who rejected him?"

Some of my embarrassment faded away at hearing Noah come to my defense. I smiled. "I did."

Noah slid his arm around my shoulder and pulled me close, cocooning me in his scent and wordlessly laying claim. "Sounds like you're the castoff, mate. Maybe it's time you learn to accept the fact that she never has been, nor will she ever be, yours."

Kingston growled. "She belongs to me more than she could ever belong to a bloodsucker like you."

The back of my neck prickled, warning me we were starting to gather attention. I could feel eyes on me from across the room, and despite the altercation unfolding in front of me, I craned my neck and found Alek staring intently in my direction. His icy eyes were narrowed, his lips flattened in something that looked a lot like anger, as his gaze shifted to Kingston.

Jesus. This was getting out of hand.

"Listen, Kingston, I'm not going to pretend to know what all of this is about, but you need to let this weird obsession you have with me go. It's been seven years. Rejection sucks. I get it. You've made it abundantly clear you think I'm a worthless piece of shit. Can't we just leave it at that?"

"No, Sunday. We can't 'just leave it at that.'"

"Why not? It's not like you want me anyway. I'm defective, remember? Nothing but an embarrassment. Why do you care who I spend my time with so long as it's not you?"

"Because you're my—" His eyes flashed, hinting at the beast within as he caught himself, not finishing his sentence. And in that brief span of time, there was something other than anger in his gaze. He looked . . . hurt. But that didn't make any sense. And his next words proved just how off base I was.

"Oh, I don't care. But you should. What's your grandfather going to say when he finds out about this?"

"Finds out about what? We were just dancing. Last I checked, that's not a crime."

"No, not that you were out dancing. That you're whoring yourself out for some leech."

I gasped, feeling like he'd punched me right in the stomach. Noah blurred as he stepped forward, his voice downright scary as he got into the shifter's face.

"Enough. You will not speak to her that way. In fact, you will not speak to her at all. Leave, before I make you. And trust me, pup, you do not want to find out what happens if I have to make you."

Kingston laughed. "I'd love to see you try, Thorne."

Noah smiled, and it was a cold, terrible thing. None of the sexy, playful vampire I'd been dancing with could be found in his menacing expression. "If you've a death wish, Farrell, I'm more than happy to assist with that. If you don't, I encourage you to walk away. Now. Last warning."

Kingston looked between the two of us, a muscle feathering wildly in his jaw before he snarled. "I don't know why I bothered. You're not worth it."

"Bothered doing what? Pick a fight?" I snapped.

"Tried to save you."

I reacted like I'd been slapped. "Save me? This is what saving me looks like? Calling me a whore?"

He ran a hand through his hair, looking frustrated. "Just forget it."

"No, actually, I think I want you to explain it to me."

"This guy, the one you're practically dry humping like a bitch in heat? He's a monster, Sunday. One of the worst. He's also the enemy. Or does the fact that you can't shift mean you've lost all loyalty to your kind?"

Noah grasped Kingston by the front of his shirt and shoved him hard. Kingston went flying, knocking over a table and spilling drinks everywhere. The two bouncers stepped into action, but instead of going after Noah, they went to Kingston, lifting him off the floor and escorting him to the exit.

"Good riddance to bad rubbish," Noah said, wiping his hands together before turning back to look at me. His eyes roamed over my face, his lips tilting in a frown at whatever he found there. He cupped my cheek, his voice gentle. "Are you okay?"

I wrapped my arms around my stomach, feeling cold despite the warmth of the crowded club. "Peachy."

His frown deepened. "Come on, let's get you something to drink."

In typical Noah fashion, he didn't give me a chance to respond before wrapping his arm around me and pulling me close. He led me in the direction he wanted me to go and just expected me to follow. For once, I didn't fight it. There was something comforting about letting someone else take control. Even if only for a little while.

I wish I could say the night took a turn for the better after that. But it didn't.

Not even close.

CHAPTER
TEN
ALEK

"What the hell is wrong with me?" This tightening in my chest wouldn't ease, no matter how many shots I downed or women I flirted with.

"Your guess is as good as mine," Moira said, holding up two crystal goblets and a bottle of expensive-looking mead. "I brought reinforcements," she said, flopping down next to me.

I hadn't had a proper flagon of mead since I'd left home, but one whiff as I cracked open the bottle told me she'd gotten her hands on the genuine product. My mouth watered, craving the smoke and honey taste.

Picking up one of the glasses, I splashed some of the amber liquid into it and handed it to her. Then, holding the bottle up to my lips, I toasted, "Skål," before knocking it back and draining it completely.

Once it was empty, I threw the bottle down on the floor beside me, causing a few of the patrons nearby to jump out of the way as the glass shattered. "I require more of this nectar!" I shouted at one of the waitresses in the loud, obnoxious fashion of my ancestors. Then I threw in a wink for good measure, and the pretty blonde turned a sweet shade of red before rushing off to do as I'd asked.

Moira was watching me with an amused quirk of her brow. "Was that really necessary?"

Stealing the drink she'd yet to sample, I downed that too. "Yes. Vikings don't fuck around when it comes to mead."

"Clearly," she said with a snort.

The waitress was quick to return with a fresh bottle, and I settled in to enjoy the club's atmosphere. I wasn't in the mood for dancing, but I was always up for a party. The mischief that could be made when a little alcohol was mixed with hot, sweaty bodies and raging pheromones was too tempting to resist.

"So what are you doing here, witch? Don't you have someone to keep you occupied? I know I don't have the right equipment to entice you."

She kicked her feet up on the low table in front of the oversized leather couch we were seated on. Instead of answering, she said, "I think I have you pegged. It took me a while, but I think I know now."

I lifted a brow, curious whether she'd finally put it all together. "Go on."

"Fenrir."

Before I could stop myself, a harsh bark of laughter escaped me. "You think I'm a fucking dog?"

"He's a wolf."

"I'm no animal."

She rolled her eyes. "That's debatable."

Opening the fresh bottle of Mannaölgr, I poured us each a glass. I raised mine, staring at her pointedly until she did the same. Then clinking them together, I shouted, "Skål."

When Moira started to lift her glass to her lips without repeating the toast, I put my hand on top of her goblet, preventing her from sipping.

"What the hell?"

"If you're going to drink with a Viking, sweetheart, you have to do it right."

"Oh fine," she groaned. "Skål."

I moved my hand, grinning at her before knocking my drink back. We continued on in this fashion until the bottle was nearly empty.

It took a lot to get me drunk. A lot. But Moira, however fierce she liked to pretend to be, was a cheap date. The woman swayed in her seat, then turned a little green. "Oh, goddess. I'll be right back."

Clamping a hand over her mouth, she ran for the bathroom, and I chuckled, shaking my head. "Fucking lightweight."

I poured another, and my gaze trailed over the crowd as I brought the heavenly liquid to my lips. My focus zeroed in on *her*. Sunday. The woman I had no intention of lusting over. She wasn't mine, wasn't even interested in me. But there it was again, that strange tightness, that curl in my belly that spoke of an intense draw to keep her safe.

Thorne was all over her as they stood together at the bar, his hands roaming her body, lips moving as he whispered in her ear and made her blush. I shouldn't care. I didn't. But she was, for some reason, my responsibility. If that vampire flashed any hint of fang, I'd take him down and pull those teeth out of his skull myself.

What the fucking hell was wrong with me?

My hands ached from the force of the fists I was making as Thorne abandoned her in favor of conversation with two of his bloodsucking minions. The three of them left the main bar area, likely heading for one of the private meeting rooms downstairs. The bastard couldn't even bother to stay with her once he had her?

I downed my drink and slammed the glass onto the table before standing and slowly weaving my way through the crowd toward her.

Kingston beat me to her. That gods-damned alphahole wolf.

He grabbed her by the elbow, jerking her roughly away from the bar before pushing her up against a table. It was aggressive, and the pain that flashed in her eyes when her back connected with the corner of the table was enough to send me running toward them. I didn't care that she had a vampire in her corner or that she was a grown woman who said she could take care of herself. This arse was hurting her, and no one hurt what was mine and lived.

I was so consumed by my anger, I didn't even stop to question the possessive claim I'd just staked. The only thing driving me was the need to draw blood. A whole fucking lot of it.

"Get your fucking hands off her."

I shoved him hard, but Kingston barely moved, his eyes a dull, lifeless brown. But then everything in him hardened. Rage and hatred boiled behind his irises, and though he snarled, there wasn't a whiff of wolf on him. Something wasn't right.

"I'm not done with her," he said, his voice unusually thin and tight.

He lunged, knocking Sunday to the ground and landing on top of her. Then she screamed and the world stopped. Everything froze around me as I moved with more speed and power than I'd ever known. Kingston's throat was in my grip, and I had him pinned to the floor, choking and gasping, clawing at my fingers.

"You won't keep her," he croaked out. "No matter how hard you try."

"Yeah, well, neither will you."

He continued to thrash beneath my grip, a wicked smile twisting his lips despite the fact that he was clearly outpowered and I had no intention of easing my grasp. The wolf was completely fucking unhinged, and it was my job to put him down.

"I don't want her. She's already as good as dead." Then, with one hand, he grabbed hold of the amulet around his neck and crushed it.

Kingston gasped, and his eyes rolled back in his head. He began to convulse, his body morphing and transforming until his features shifted into those of a different person entirely. Instead of the young alpha wolf I'd thought I'd been fighting, there was a man old enough to be my grandfather lifeless in my grasp. His heart still, eyes open and glazed over, and that fucking smile still stretched across his face.

"Alek?" Sunday's voice was a thready whisper, weak and filled with fear.

I turned to her, relieved she was up and talking. "Sunday. Are you all right?"

Her lower lip trembled. "I don't think so."

Then my gaze traveled down her body to the rapidly blooming stain on her abdomen and the jagged, broken blade sticking out of her.

"All right gentlemen, I believe that concludes our business for the evening," I announced, eager to be done with this conversation and return to Sunday. If I hadn't promised my father I'd meet with his men tonight, I would have told them to kindly go fuck themselves when they'd dared to interrupt my fervent seduction of the luscious Sunday Fallon.

As it was, my skin crawled at the thought of leaving her out there alone. Unprotected while so many other men circled like vultures. I'd seen the way they looked at her, lusted after her. And while I'd be a hypocrite if I blamed them for it, I'd sure as hell drain them dry if they so much as laid a finger on her.

"And what should we tell your father about the pretty little bird?" The thick cockney accent of his was rough and menacing. A remnant of his human life on the streets of London long ago.

Everything in me stilled. The only part of my body that moved were my eyes as they slid to Alrik's smirking face.

"You will not tell him a bloody thing because there is nothing to tell."

Alrik's smile faded, and he exchanged a nervous look with Peter. *Smart man.*

"Guess I was mistaken."

"It would seem so. Now if that's all—"

My words broke off at the sound of a commotion outside. While not unheard of at *Iniquity*—because any time the Families were thrown together like this, you were asking for trouble—they were rare. Lilith Duval, the dominatrix succubus who owned the club, ensured it. And as a woman who not only encouraged her patrons to indulge in their favorite sins but provided them with the means to do it, no one wanted to risk ending up on her blacklist.

"What was that?" I asked, on high alert.

"Sounds like a fight," Peter answered with a shrug. "Not our problem."

Usually, I'd be inclined to agree. But this was no ordinary nightclub, and when tempers flared, people had a habit of dying, so my first thought was for Sunday. I didn't want her to accidentally get caught up in the scuffle.

Without another word, I pushed open the door. The sound of the music was overshot by a few panicked shouts.

I had no trouble catching snippets of the ongoing conversations, and with each one, my anxiety grew.

". . . that wolf has lost his damn mind . . . two fights in one night . . ."

"Did you see how fast he moved?"

". . . the girl didn't stand a chance . . ."

That's when I caught the scent of blood in the air. Her blood. My fangs snapped down, and my mouth watered with the urge to feed.

Behind me, Alrik and Peter surged forward, their

hunger infusing them with strength as they tried to shove past me and toward the source of the blood. My muscles tensed as I fought against my own need, and I shoved them back.

"Stand down."

Alrik licked his fangs as he pushed to his feet. "If she's no one to you, what's it matter if I have myself a little taste?" He rearranged himself as he made his way to the door—and me—a second time.

He started running then, thinking to slip past me, but I was far faster. By the time he'd taken two steps, I'd already gripped his head in my hands, breaking his neck with a satisfying crack. As he slid to the ground, I growled, "I said. Stand. Down."

Peter's eyes grew wild as I stalked toward him. "No . . . wait, I—"

"Shh . . ."I said, my fingers gripping the sides of his face. "You'll only be dead for a little while. It's nothing personal." And then I snapped his as well.

No one would be feeding on my little wolf tonight. And though my fangs ached with need, I swore to myself that included me.

Threat handled for now, I raced down the hallway and back into the main room where the crowd had shifted to stand around a trio of bodies. One was dead, so I dismissed him, my eyes zeroing in on the Novasgardian who'd taken Sunday in his arms and was gently lowering her to the ground.

"What the bloody hell happened?" I snarled, shoving him out of the way so I could cradle her trembling form.

"A hunter, I think," he said, barely sparing me a glance as he moved to press his hands into the wound at her side.

"Hunters? What do they want with her?"

"I don't know."

"Why isn't she healing?" I asked.

"I don't know," he gritted out. "Can you just shut up and let me take care of her?"

"Because you did such a bang-up job of it in the first place? If this is you taking care of her, I think I'll just take it from here."

Though there wasn't a hint of animal on him, he bared his teeth, and a low rumble sounded warningly in his chest. "You were the one who left her alone."

The blow landed, though I did my best to keep it from showing. Before I could respond, a shadow fell over us, followed by the soft sound of a woman clearing her throat.

"Mr. Nordson, if you'd come with me."

I glanced up only long enough to confirm my suspicion. Lilith had come to deal with the rule breaker in person. The demon would barely reach the Novasgardian's chest, but there was no mistaking the aura of authority rolling off her. Or the way she held the enchanted length of chain across her palms. Either he'd follow her willingly, or she'd force the point.

He flicked his blue eyes between us, his anger palpable. "This filth stabs one of your patrons, and I'm the one you seek to chastise."

"The rules are the rules, Aleksandr. He merely attempted murder. You succeeded. Now, if you don't mind, the natives are getting a little restless. I'd like to put this unfortunate matter behind as quickly as possible. I promise to take your motives into consideration while setting the terms of your punishment."

Alek's brows flew up at that. "My what?"

"Your punishment, darling. Now come with me. I have

some people who will be thrilled to learn you'll be part of tonight's show."

Alek looked at me and then down at Sunday. The veins in his neck pulsed, and he clenched his jaw, but he seemed to make up his mind to obey.

"She better be alive when I come back, Thorne. Or there will be hell to pay."

I nodded, not really caring what he said. My full attention returned to Sunday. Her pulse was weak, barely more than a delicate flutter.

"Stay with me, little wolf."

"Noah?" she croaked, her eyes opening with considerable effort. "Wha—"

"Shh. Save your strength."

"It hurts," she admitted, and it felt like *I'd* been the one run through with a blade.

The scent of her overwhelmed me. It was the battle of my life resisting the urge to lean down and sink my fangs into her. To lap up every last drop.

"Why aren't you healing?" I repeated, though the question was mostly for my benefit. Speaking gave me something to focus on other than how badly I wanted to taste her.

"Can't," she whispered, her voice barely more than a rasp. If not for my vampire senses, I wouldn't have heard her at all.

My gaze dropped to the wound at her side, spotting the glint of blood-stained silver. The metal must be preventing her from accessing her gifts. With a low grunt, I grasped the jagged edge between two fingers and pulled it free.

But instead of her flesh knitting itself together, blood seeped from the wound, coating my fingers and sending a fresh wave of need crashing through me until I was shaking with it. Like the weakling I was, I brought my fingertips to my mouth and took the barest taste.

"You idiot!" Kingston snarled, pushing me out of the way. "Get away from her."

"Who let you back in here?"

"I'm a Farrell, they can't keep me out. Now, get the fuck out of the way, can't you see she's dying?"

"Dying? Don't be dramatic. It's—" but I snapped my mouth shut because the insolent little pup was right. Her heartbeat wasn't strong and steady anymore. It was weak, thready, and with every pump of the organ, her skin paled. "I don't understand—"

He pressed one of his meaty paws to her face. "Sunshine, I need you to listen to me. You need to find your wolf. Look at me."

Her eyes fluttered, but remained closed.

Kingston infused his voice with the growl of his beast, taking on the unmistakable edge of an alpha issuing a command. "Look at me, Sunday. That's it. Good girl."

"K-Kingston?" Her brows knit together in a mix of pain and confusion. "What are you doing here?"

"Don't worry about that right now. Call on your wolf."

"C-can't," she whispered.

Panic laced his features, and he shook her, causing her head to loll. "Yes you can. You can do this. She's in there waiting for you to let her free. Here, let me help you draw her out."

Sunday swallowed, trying to keep her eyes open. "How?"

"Wolves respond to their mate."

"Not . . . my mate."

It was a struggle for her to talk through the pain, and even more of one for me to stand by and watch it. I was a hairsbreadth from flinging the wolf away from her, but if there was any truth to his words, he might be the only one who could save her.

Kingston's expression shuttered for a second, but he kept his voice low and even as he asked her, "Do you trust me?"

"No," she croaked.

The ghost of a smile flitted over his mouth. "Do you at least trust that I'm not trying to hurt you worse than you already are?"

"Yes."

That one word broke something in me. She knew he could help her where I couldn't.

"Okay," he breathed, his eyes glowing amber as he began to partially shift.

It was impossible to understand what was happening because, from the outside, all I could see was Kingston stroking her hair and staring intently into her eyes. Their breaths mingled and seemed to align so when he exhaled, she inhaled, drawing it in.

As I watched, the flow of blood slowed. I released a shuddering breath, staring at the knife wound intently, willing it to close. But it didn't. Whatever Kingston was doing, it wasn't enough.

Sunday's eyelids drooped once more.

"No. Stay with me, Sunshine," Kingston pleaded.

I had to do something. She was mine, and there was no way she could leave me. I hadn't given her permission. "Get out of the way," I snarled, fangs already tearing through the skin on my wrist.

"What the hell do you think you're doing?"

"Saving her life." Holding my dripping wrist above her

lips, I held my breath as the crimson drops splashed down. "Drink, little wolf."

Her eyes were barely more than creases as she peered up at me. "No."

"You don't have a choice, dove."

Her tongue darted out, and my body couldn't help but respond to the sight of her tasting me. The rush of desire, inappropriate and undeniable, had my cock thick behind my fly in an instant.

"That's it," I whispered, pressing my wrist against her mouth. "Drink up."

A firm hand gripped my arm and tore me away from Sunday, causing a harsh growl to escape my chest in response. Who the fuck had the gall to interrupt me when I was in the middle of something so vital?

"Thorne, stop!"

Eyes wide as panic ricocheted through me, I backed away, hands shaking. Father Gallagher scooped Sunday into his arms, shooting me a reproachful look.

"You do realize you've done something you can't take back." His gaze rooted me to the spot as his focus drifted to my mouth, where I still tasted her blood on my lips. "What in God's name have you done?"

Oh, fuck, we'd exchanged blood. Not much, but enough. What *had* I done?

If I had room left to feel anything else, I might have been surprised to see the good priest here, but all I could manage was a wary reply.

"What I had to."

CHAPTER TWELVE

CALEB

Something was wrong. The rushing pulse in my ears sent panic stealing through me. What was happening to me? My heart hadn't beat since the night I was killed and changed irrevocably. Was this hunger? Was it her pulse I was feeling, hearing? It had to be.

Blood swirled in the bowl of the sink, the rich crimson contrasting starkly with the white porcelain. Hunger twisted my gut, burned through my body, made me close my eyes and will away the need to taste Sunday's essence. I had to get clean. Get her off me. If only so I could keep my wits about me and stop this wild monster inside me from breaking free.

Even as the water ran clear, I knew that alone would not be enough to purge myself. I needed a different sort of absolution. One that would cleanse my mind as well as my body. It would be the only way to cast the monster back to the darkest recesses of my mind. As always, thoughts of a session in my ritual chamber, making use of the tools I kept there, eased some of the restless yearning. With their aid, I would find my way back to a righteous path.

Purification through pain. I'd been taught this was the only way once upon a time, back before my life was altered, my soul stolen. Sunday moaned from where I'd settled her in my bedroom. The sound woke an altogether different kind of sin in my head.

Lust.

I was a glutton for blood because of something I didn't choose, but the lust I felt for her was something I had no one to blame for but myself. Gritting my teeth against the urge to be with her, I stalked to the center of the room where I pulled up the old faded rug, revealing a trap door. My hands shook as I lifted the latch and tugged until the stone staircase was revealed. I was so close to the only kind of confession I could give anymore.

My steps were hurried, my body trembling from the opposing forces seeking to overtake me. I needed release. Any release. But this was the only one still afforded to me. The only way I could cage my demons and purge my soul.

Lights flickered to life as I descended the staircase on my way down to the small antechamber. The room was sparse, free from adornment save a simple wooden cross and a series of floggers hanging from the wall.

Running my fingertips over the implements I preferred when participating in mortification of the flesh, I selected a cat-o'-nine-tails complete with barbs at the base of each leather strip. Intended for pain, not pleasure. Made to draw blood and bring my focus to a God who had forsaken me. As he should have.

Even now, I heard that heartbeat loud in my ears. Was Sunday my ultimate test? I still wanted her, even though I worked to keep her at a distance while watching over her. Fecking hell, everything in me throbbed at the thought of her lying there in my bed.

I fell to my knees and tore my thin shirt to shreds, the tattered fabric hanging from my waist.

As I adjusted my grip on the whip, I closed my eyes and began to mouth the familiar words of prayer.

"*Deus meus, ex toto corde poenitet me omnium meorum peccatorum,*" I began.

With each line, I brought the whip around to score my back. Each burst of pain caused my mind to clear and made the hunger recede. Over and over, I spoke the words, begging for forgiveness until my skin was slick with blood and I felt nothing but emptiness. Heard nothing but my own breaths.

Breathing heavily, I struck my flesh one final time and uttered a shaky, "Amen."

The whip fell from my limp fingers, and I pressed my trembling hands to my thighs as I came back down from the rush of adrenaline coursing through me in response to the pain. Mind clear, chest loose, I took my first easy breath, feeling in control of myself once more. Just as I was about to revel in the silence of the aftermath of my session, the heavy thump of a heart beating echoed once again.

My eyes snapped open, and I staggered to my feet.

No. No!

It should have worked. Why hadn't it worked?

What the fecking hell was wrong with me? Was I so lost that even my most sacred forms of repentance were useless against temptation?

It didn't matter. I had a job to do, and that was to keep Sunday Fallon alive and out of trouble. So far, I was failing.

After a cold shower to wash away the blood on my back, the wounds already healed thanks to my vampiric nature, I dressed and readied myself to face her again. To control my urges, my hunger, my lust, and do the one thing required of me: Save her soul and mine along with it.

I stared at her sleeping form, my devil of a cock thickening behind my trousers. She was beauty personified, leading me directly into temptation. Except I would be precisely the evil she needed to be delivered from if I couldn't stop myself from wanting her.

Standing in the corner, my tension eased as the pulse that had been incessantly thrumming in my ears became calmer, steady, and suddenly stopped feeling so foreign.

Her soft moan called me closer, and it took everything in me not to touch her when she let out a whimpered groan and said, "Oh, God."

THIRTEEN

SUNDAY

"Oh, God," I murmured before opening my eyes. Sitting up slowly, I blinked through hazy vision, willing my gaze to focus.

A simple bedroom, one plain oak dresser, dark curtains covering the window. This was a far cry from the luxurious room where Noah had brought me. The only thing in this space that was luxe by any stretch of the imagination was the bed I woke up on. Large and soft. Like resting on a cloud. Except I didn't know where I was. God, I had to stop waking up in strange places.

"Stay still, Miss Fallon." Caleb's voice tickled its way up my spine, sending an unwanted shiver through me. "You'll tear your stitches."

Stitches?

"What happened? Where am I?" The pain in my side brought it all back. "Kingston. Kingston tried to kill me. I knew he hated me, but not this much." Panic had my voice tight and high.

"Calm down, Sunday. He's not here. He's gone." Caleb sat on the side of the bed but didn't touch me.

"Where is he?"

"Dead."

"Kingston is dead?" Why did that make my heart ache?

Caleb shook his head. "No. He tried to save you."

Why did I feel like I needed a roadmap to follow this conversation? "That doesn't make any sense. He's the one who stabbed me."

"That wasn't him. It was a hunter."

I shook my head, trying to sit higher, to level the playing field as this priest loomed over me. "A hunter? But . . . I saw him." The memory of Kingston shoving me back and driving the blade into my stomach flooded my mind. Along with another, fuzzier image of him on his knees beside me. His face tight with fear . . . for me. But even if he wasn't the one who actually stabbed me, Kingston still hated me. Why would he care enough to come back and make sure I was okay? I shoved the questions away, in no state to sort through all the conflicting emotions they stirred to life, let alone try to answer them.

"How was he able to change his appearance? I thought hunters didn't have abilities."

"This one had some help." He pulled something out of the pocket of his suit jacket and held his palm out to me. In the center of his hand was an amulet, the amethyst crystal now clouded with dark smoky residue.

"Witches? Why would they do this?"

"I'm not sure. But they were most certainly after you." He tucked the necklace back into his pocket as he casually spoke. Like he hadn't just dropped a bomb in my lap.

"Me?"

Intense gaze trained on me, he licked his lips, and I forced myself not to squirm under his stare. I could barely breathe, but not due to pain. Father Caleb Gallagher was hungry.

"You."

"Why would anyone want me? I'm a freak. A shifter who can't shift. A joke."

"We all want you."

What did he mean by *we*? I needed some time to unpack what he just said, but he reached out, the gesture making me flinch away on instinct. Pain sliced through my side, and I cried out before I could stop myself.

"Dammit, I said stay still." Caleb's palm rested on my shoulder, pushing me to my back, pinning me there as he pulled the sheet away and lifted the edge of the white T-shirt I was wearing.

"Caleb, where's my dress? Did you undress me?"

He wouldn't look me in the eye. "I had to. You were covered in . . ." He swallowed and took a shuddering breath. "Blood. It was everywhere. I'm surprised Thorne stopped when he did."

The man next to me tensed as he focused on the gauze dressing on my abdomen. Blood seeped through, and the whole area was red and inflamed, even past the bandage.

"It's infected," he muttered. "You should heal faster than this. He gave you his blood."

The mention of Noah's blood sparked a burst of flavor in my memory. Not like blood at all, but like a kaleidoscope of tastes from the most decadent wine in existence. Spice and sweetness, salt and smoke, berries and apples, all blended together. My uncontrolled moan caused Caleb to stop what he was doing and snap his focus to my eyes.

"Do not make those noises around me. We're all sinners here."

His warning pebbled my nipples and made me grip the

sheet to keep from reaching out to brush away a stray lock of hair that had fallen over his forehead. "Sorry," I whispered.

Fingers gently peeling away my bandage, he frowned, the concentration on his face not boding well for me. "What was on this blade?"

The wound was red and angry, and blood welled to the surface despite the neat, tiny sutures. Caleb's hands shook as he used a clean cloth to dab the blood off my skin.

"Are you okay?" I asked. "Maybe someone else—"

"No! I will care for you. You're a risk for the rest of them."

My head throbbed along with the deep ache in my muscles. Honestly, I felt like shit. Like I'd been . . . well, stabbed. "Caleb, something's wrong."

"Of course it is. You were nearly killed."

"No. I feel . . . I'm not sure. I think . . ." The room spun, the edges of my vision going dark before I faded into unconsciousness.

LIKE THE FIRST time she came to me, rumbles preceded her arrival.

"Daughter."

My consciousness shifted, solidified. Instead of floating in a sea of nothing, I stood on an empty field, rustling grass and a cloudless sky all I could see for miles in every direction. And her.

My mother.

The similarity between us was striking and unmistakable. Same chocolate hair, wide ocean-blue eyes, and identical full lips. The only true difference was in our height and build. She was slightly taller, her muscles leaner and more defined. Whereas I had more of that traditional hourglass figure. No wonder I'd never fit in with the Fallons. Where they were all flaming hair and green eyes, I looked nothing like them. I stood out like a sore thumb. Never seeing myself in anyone. Until now.

Her expression was more curious than anything remotely nurturing. As if she was studying and dissecting a foreign creature instead of reuniting with the daughter she'd abandoned. Then again, she'd sort of proven that she didn't have a whole lot going on in the maternal department when she walked away without so much as a forwarding address or even a name.

Any affection I might have felt for the woman who'd given birth to me shriveled and died. "Two times in less than a week. Is this becoming a habit?"

It was nice to know that even though I was technically unconscious and dreaming, I still retained my favorite defense mechanism: my smart mouth. People didn't seem to realize they'd hurt you if you'd perfected the art of sarcasm. And though she was my mother, I didn't want to appear any more vulnerable than absolutely necessary.

Her head canted to the side, and her expression softened. It still wasn't affectionate by a long shot, but it was certainly more understanding. In a lot of ways, she reminded me of one of those angel statutes. Not the cute little cherubs with their sweet curls and fluffy wings. The other ones. The warriors holding swords and shields, decked head to toe in armor with their eyes blazing with divine retribution.

So, in other words, my mother was mildly terrifying. And she managed all of that in a simple maroon dress and leather belt. That almost made it scarier. If she could be that intimidating in a dress, what would she be like if she had actually been battle-ready?

"Your thoughts are troubled."

"Uh, yeah. Can you blame me? My mom keeps popping in on my dreams uninvited after twenty-three years, and I just got stabbed by a hunter wearing my ex's skin like a Halloween costume. What do you expect? A tearful family reunion?"

"I tried to warn you."

"Maybe next time you could go with something a little more direct, like 'Sunday, hunters have placed a bounty on your head. Don't leave school grounds.' Or, I don't know, send me names and addresses."

She pressed her lips together. "I've already told you what you have to do. You need to find that which makes you strong and harness it. It's the only way to unlock your full potential."

"That sounds like a whole lot of vague bullshit. I've been trying to find my wolf for *years*. You want to help, Mommy Dearest? Give me something more specific to work with."

"Your wolf is not the answer."

"What? You just said—"

My mom glanced over her shoulder, her eyes narrowing. When she returned her gaze to me, her irises seemed to swirl like galaxies before she blinked and they became twins of my own once more. "There is only so much I can reveal. Even here, we are being watched."

"Watched? By who? The hunters?"

"And those who wish to see you fail. Nothing short of your death will appease them."

Well, that sounded ominous as fuck.

"Super."

"The only way to protect yourself is to find the source of your power. Remember, the things that feed you will leave a mark. Embrace them no matter the consequences. They are the answer to the riddle of your birthright."

"What?"

She glanced over her shoulder again, and this time, the galaxies in her eyes did not fade. "Hurry, daughter. It will not be long before they make another attempt. You need to ready yourself. Remember what I've said."

"Wait, hold on! How will I know—"

But she was gone, the sound heralding her departure a series of ceaseless bangs instead of galloping horses. As I drifted, the field rippled outward like lights on the surface of a stormy sea, and I lost my sense of self.

Once again I was alone, adrift, with nothing more than the echo of her words chasing each other in the abyss.

Embrace them.

They are the answer.

Embrace.

Them.

~

"LET ME SEE HER."

Alek's voice broke through the haze of my . . . vision? Dream? Whatever you called it.

"I've already told your friends. She's not well. None of you can see her right now. Not until she's out of danger," Caleb said.

"Move aside, Priest. You've had her in your lair for the last seventy-two hours. It's time for proof of life. How can we be sure you've kept your control?"

"I'm keeping her alive. I haven't given in. That's more

than Thorne can say. If I hadn't taken her from him, she'd be dead by now."

The energy in the air radiated tension and aggression. I was sure if this came to blows, there'd be honest to God lightning and thunder.

Alek's voice grew colder, more intense and threatening. "You can attempt to keep me away. Vampire or not, you will fail."

Pain radiated through me, running the length of my side, down my hip to my thigh, but I forced myself to my feet. I regretted that choice instantly. The room tilted, and a wave of nausea hit me with the force of a tsunami. Something was very wrong with me.

Lifting my shirt, I couldn't help the little whimper of shock that escaped at the sight of my wound. Sickly black tendrils reached out under my skin, starting at the bandage and creeping across my body. A strange taste, bitter and metallic, filled my mouth. I was going to die here. How could I find my inner power or whatever if I was dead?

I stumbled forward, catching myself on the wall next to the door. "Go me. I didn't fall."

"What was that?" Caleb asked.

Before I could turn the doorknob, the door opened, and both of them stood there, expressions grim. I let out a hysterical giggle and pitched forward, but Alek caught me against him.

"What have you done to her, vampire?"

"I've cared for her. She was recovering. I don't understand how she's worse."

"She's dying. Can't you smell it on her? Death has one hand curled around her throat."

My skin crawled as Alek's words echoed my own fears.

"I'm fine. I just need to get out of here." Were my words slurring?

Alek held me to him, his large palm spanning most of my back. It felt good. Better. Something about being with him, in his presence, was like a healing balm.

"Let me see the wound, Sunny. I brought something that might help."

"How can *you* know what will help her?" Caleb spat. "Even Blackthorne blood hasn't fully healed her."

"The blade."

"Yes?"

My knees buckled, and Alek scooped me into his arms like I weighed nothing. "Thanks, big boy. I used to say I didn't like a man with too many muscles, but you just changed my mind."

A deep rumble rolled from his chest. "I'll hold you in my arms whenever you wish."

"You make me feel . . . delicate."

"You are."

I shook my head, loving the scent of him even as I knew this could all be fever delirium talking. He settled me on the hard leather couch near the fireplace and carefully lifted the shirt Caleb had given me. The worry lines etched across his forehead had my heart racing. So it was as bad as I thought. I wasn't hallucinating.

"The blade was laced with wolfsbane. I analyzed it after you took her." Alek spoke to Caleb but stared hard at me while doing so.

"Wolfsbane?" I whispered.

I'd seen a wolf die from a wound like this. Hunters were ruthless, out to end all of us, but wolfsbane was hard to come by, and even harder to make into a potent, concentrated form. They'd really wanted me dead.

"I have a cure. If you'll allow it."

"Yes," Caleb said before I could speak.

"I'm not asking you, Father Gallagher." Alek turned a tight gaze to me.

"I trust you."

He nodded, jaw clenched, before he gripped the T-shirt at the hem and tore it completely in two, baring my body to him and Caleb both. I'd never been more thankful that I'd chosen to wear panties. But that dress I'd worn to the club? That was a no-bra situation, so now, my tits were right there, literally in his face.

He swallowed hard but didn't stare down at my breasts. "I have to touch you."

"Okay."

His warm palm pressed gently to my belly, just below my sternum, before he slid it up to my chest, right between my breasts. The other hovered directly over the wound on my side.

"Your heart is hammering like a frightened bird's."

"Well, I *have* been poisoned."

A slight smirk turned up his lips. "We'll see to that. Close your eyes."

I did as he asked and instantly felt him inside me. His essence flowed from his palm and outward, racing through every cell and nerve ending. The pain in my body built and reached an unbearable peak, the overwhelming sensation making me whimper, but he whispered soft, comforting words in a language I couldn't understand.

"What are you doing to her?" Caleb asked. His voice was rough and breathless, and when I risked a glance at him, there was a feral hunger in his eyes.

"Healing her."

The pain crested again, a burning heat centering in my

wound, causing tears to leak from my eyes before turning to warmth, then pleasure. Pleasure I shouldn't have been feeling but *definitely* was. I moaned, my nipples tightening to desperate peaks, begging for attention.

"Alek, oh, my God. What are you doing to me?"

My eyes fluttered open again and locked with his. The same pleasure radiated from him, uncertainty flickering in the depths of his ice-blue irises.

"I don't know. Fuck, Sunday."

My whole body was alight with euphoria, desire, and rampant need for him to claim me and make me his. It was primal and undeniable. Reaching up, I gripped him by the nape of his neck and used a strength I didn't know I possessed to pull his big frame down until our lips met and that burning need was given fuel.

Power and strength flowed from him to me, and as my mouth opened to accept his deepening of our kiss, I threaded my fingers in his hair. Alek was giving me more than his healing abilities. He was feeding me his Novasgardian strength—and it felt *incredible*. Primal, ancient, wild. I'd never experienced anything like it.

Even though we hadn't moved, except to press closer to each other, my nose filled with the scent of snowy pine and my mouth the somewhat incongruous taste of the sea. Images of snow-capped mountains and crystal blue glaciers raced through my mind—which made no sense given how I'd never seen either in person. But laced through all of it was the absolutely delicious feel of *him*. Alek. His essence rolled through me, filling me, merging with mine, and it felt so utterly right.

For the first time in my life, I knew what it was like to feel powerful. Unstoppable.

And I wanted more.

A crack sounded in the room, breaking us apart and drawing my attention from the Viking currently ravishing me on the couch to the vampire priest standing at the small table fifteen feet away. The *remnants* of the small table, anyway. Caleb's eyes were wild, fangs extended and fists clenched by his sides near the rubble that once was his table. His gaze wasn't on Alek; it was completely focused on me.

"Your wound is healed," he bit out. "You need to leave here."

"Caleb—"

"I think it best if you call me Father Gallagher from now on, Miss Fallon."

I sat up, the tattered remains of Caleb's T-shirt falling off me. But Alek was there, pulling his black tee off his back and helping me slip it over my head without me saying a word. It smelled like him, which sent arousal careening through me once more.

"Come on, Sunny. I'll walk you back to your dorm. Moira will be glad to see you're safe."

I stood and took his offered hand, turning my head to thank Caleb for his help, but the priest was gone, the door to the room next to his bedroom clicking shut before I could get a word out.

CHAPTER
FOURTEEN
SUNDAY

Apparently, being stabbed and almost poisoned to death wasn't enough to get me out of another day of class. Caleb—correction, Father Gallagher—knew me well enough to anticipate I might try to use that as an excuse because he'd emailed me and copied all my professors, letting all of us know I would be back in class beginning that afternoon. And that if I missed one for any reason short of literal death, I would be spending the next two weeks paying for my insolence.

Real peach of a guy, that priest—ex-priest? I was still a little fuzzy on the details, seeing as how he was a vampire and all. It had to be pretty difficult to be a good shepherd to his flock when he wanted to eat them all. As far as I could tell, his vamp status made it impossible to participate in the ministries for which he'd been ordained.

Priest or not, you'd think spending three days in and out of consciousness half-naked in a guy's bed would earn you some leniency, but nope. If anything, he seemed even more uptight than usual. Which was not boding well at all

115

for me, considering that we had a session scheduled for this evening.

I groaned and snapped my laptop closed. Moira looked over with a concerned lift of her brow.

"Something wrong, sweetpea?"

She'd been momming me ever since Alek brought me back clad in only his T-shirt. I'm not gonna lie; it was pretty nice having someone tuck me into bed and keep refilling my water or bringing me warm tea. I was totally fine, physically, after Alek sent what felt like the force of the Norse gods raging through my bloodstream. But I think letting Moira take care of me made us both feel better about what happened.

She'd been really upset with herself for getting so drunk she'd ended up in one of *Iniquity's* private rooms to sleep it off, leaving me unprotected. And I . . . well, I just wasn't used to anyone caring for me like that.

I gestured to my computer. "Is the good father always this much of an asshole?"

Her second brow lifted to join the first. "Generally speaking, yes. Though, you'd have to tell me what he's done to give you a more thorough assessment. I will say that he does seem a lot more snarly around you. Then again, so do most people."

"Yeah, yeah. So you keep telling me." I sighed and scrubbed my hands over my face. "He just said I have to go back to class today. Threatened me with punishment if I failed to obey."

Moira moved to stand behind me, affectionately rumpling my already listing ponytail. "Sounds like we should get you dressed and fed, then. You have weapons and defense with me this afternoon, and word on the street is Sanderson transformed the grove for drills and sparring training. Welcome to hell week, sweet cheeks."

I groaned, folding my arms on my desk and dumping my head on top of them.

She stopped twirling my hair and chuckled.

"Are you really laughing at my misery?"

"No. Well, yes. I just realized your lover boy is in class with us."

"Lover boy?" I asked, peeking over my arm. I hadn't told her what happened with Alek the night before—I was still trying to figure out what the hell happened there for myself.

"I should say boys, plural. As in, all of them."

That had me straightening and twisting around to look at her. "Excuse me?"

She started counting on her fingers. "Wolf, Viking, and Vamp. You're going to be in a sandwich with the whole sexy trifecta."

The thought of having to deal with one of them, let alone all of them, had my stomach twisting in knots.

"Is it too early to start drinking?" I asked, not totally kidding.

She tugged my ponytail, then stole my rubber band to tie her own navy-colored locks up. "Unfortunately, the dining hall doesn't do alcohol, so yes. But if you hurry up and hop in the shower, I can braid your hair before we eat."

Even though I groaned as I stood, there was no heat behind it. If I had to spend the day sparring with supernatural sex gods and listening to lectures on the tenuous nature of our Families' politics, at least I'd have Moira to do it with.

We'd just finished up with our meal—no buffet style

here, Ravenscroft had an actual waitstaff and daily menu for its students—when Noah walked in.

My steps faltered, and Moira immediately craned her neck to see what had brought me up short.

"Oh hello, Prince of Darkness," she whispered under her breath.

"Don't call him that."

"Do you have a better name for him? Dark lover, perhaps?"

I tried to elbow her in the ribs, making her laugh as she sidestepped my blow. It almost distracted me from the fact that Noah's presence caused crackling energy to snap through the room.

I hadn't seen him since the stabbing. I remembered dancing with him. How his hands had wandered, and the way he kept trying to steal kisses but would purposely miss my lips until I'd been crazy with the need for him to just do it already. I remembered the taste of his blood as he forced me to drink, and how after the first taste, he hadn't had to force me at all. And then . . . nothing.

Crickets.

He'd totally ghosted me.

I mean, we weren't exactly dating or anything. But I thought maybe we were starting something. He'd made it pretty clear he was interested in me and then completely fell off the face of the earth. Granted, I'd been unconscious, and Caleb had mentioned how he'd told everyone to stay away. Still, I thought Noah might care enough to wonder how I was doing, at the very least.

Our eyes locked across the room, and for a second, I thought maybe I'd misunderstood everything. Maybe he was just respecting Caleb's rules. I started to smile, my hand lifting in a little wave.

Then *she* walked in, and all my naïve musings exploded right in my face.

Any hint of emotion I'd thought I'd found in his eyes was gone. Hidden behind a mask of bored indifference as a stunning redhead, her skin creamy and perfect, slid her arm through his. Noah barely spared her a glance, but the mystery girl gave him an adoring look as she trailed her other hand up his arm, leaving no doubts as to the claim she was making.

"Who is that?" I growled, not recognizing the sick, twisty feeling in my stomach.

Moira's eyes narrowed. "Callista Donoghue. Resident queen bee and spoiled little bitch. Heir to the Donoghue family fortune, and—if she's to be believed—fated mate of the one and only vampire prince himself, Mr. Noah Black-thorne." Moira's expression shifted, and she gave me an appraising once-over. "You might want to steer clear of her until you get your wolf thing sorted. Callie can be a real piece of work."

My brain was still stuck on the part about Noah having a fated mate he'd never mentioned. He was promised to someone, and all the while, he'd been running around with me, doing what exactly? Making a fool of the new girl? Playing with the broken little wolf? What could he have possibly hoped to gain by starting something with me?

Maybe you were just supposed to be another notch on his bedpost. Why does it have to be any more complicated than that?

Thinking myself the world's biggest fool, I forced my lungs to exhale and shook off the sense of betrayal that I had no right to feel. Then I tucked my arm through Moira's and said firmly, "Come on, we're going to be late."

~

MEG ANNE & K. LORAINE

So far, weapons and defense class had turned out to be nothing but boring lectures about politics, peacekeeping, and the history of conflict between species. Vampires can turn nearly any creature into one of them but, unless they were human first, their victims rarely survive. Shifters can change at will, not just with the moon—spoiler alert, I knew that one. The fae can't lie but are masters at bending the truth to fit their needs. Witches use elemental magic to harness their power and are thought to be the most dangerous of all. This wasn't news to me, but it seemed to be important for Professor Sanderson to drive the reminder home, so we all were forced to listen. Until today.

"Where is Sanderson?" I asked as Moira and I took our usual seats in the third row of the large auditorium-style lecture hall. Close enough to be seen and counted but far enough away to avoid the professor's flailing arms during one of her impassioned speeches.

"Maybe she's given up on us." Alek's voice came from behind, the feel of his breath on my nape sending a spark of attraction through me.

I couldn't forget that kiss we shared, even if it was simply because we were locked in the heat of the moment, our combined energy needing something—somewhere to go. He trailed one finger across the bare skin of my neck and leaned close before whispering, "As much as I like it when you wear your hair up, you should reconsider. You're vampire bait, showing off that pretty throat of yours."

My gaze traveled across the room, as if pulled by a magnet, before it landed on Noah. The vampire prince sat with one arm draped over the back of the chair next to him, legs spread, posture casual and sexy. His focus wasn't on Callie, who sat next to him, nor was it on the other vampire talking to him. No. Noah Blackthorne was staring daggers at *me*.

Heat blossomed between my thighs, and I had to clench them together in an effort to control the arousal I didn't want to feel. The vampire's nostrils flared, eyes burning as a slight smirk twitched the corner of his mouth.

"Fuck, if I was into dudes, I'd be so turned on right now," Moira muttered.

I swallowed past the lump in my throat and forced myself to look away from Noah, especially when Callie slid her gaze to me and then ran her palm up his thigh. I didn't know what drew me to him, aside from his vampire magnetism, but I had a literal Norse god next to me who made me smile and kissed me like I was the only thing he needed. What did it say about me that I was attracted to them both?

Before I could examine that any further, the door to the lecture hall opened, and Professor Sanderson strode in, her wild red curls resembling a fiery halo that frizzed out around her head.

"Oooh-weee, it must be mating season in here. You can smell the pheromones a mile away," she said in her strong southern accent. She had to be from Texas or one of the other southern states in America. There was no denying her roots with that twang. "Now, come on, y'all. There's fixin' to be a serious fight brewing in these parts, and I need you ready. That means you need to be on your feet and heading for the locker rooms so you can change for some hand-to-hand training today."

"Excuse me, professor?" Callie raised her hand, putting so much sugar in her voice I nearly gagged.

"Miss Donoghue?"

"What do you mean, change?"

Professor Sanderson looked her up and down, tutting as she took in Callie's patent leather spike-heeled Mary Janes and tightly fitting, extremely short dress that was a parody of a schoolgirl uniform.

"You won't get far in that, girlie. Vamp or not, your classmates will have the upper hand. Now, everyone go change. Your lockers are already set up with everything you need. Put on each piece you find in your locker, y'all."

The class let out a unanimous groan, but we filed out, heading for the locker rooms. There wasn't much different from a typical human school when it came to this space. Rows of benches, gray lockers, bad lighting, showers. Pretty much your standard fare. It actually left me with a sense of comfort. It leveled the playing field a little.

Callie walked past me with her bitches in waiting trailing behind. She huffed but didn't say a word to me.

"What's her problem?" I whispered as Moira placed her palm on the center of the locker in front of her. A white glow emanated from inside before fading.

She opened the door and pulled out a black long-sleeved high-performance shirt, matching cargo pants, and a pair of combat boots. "She's jealous. Thorne wants you, and he's supposed to want her."

"He wants to eat me. There's a difference."

"Oh, he wants to eat you, all right. That's the problem."

I blushed at the wave of heat that thought sent spiraling straight through me and shook my head. Following her lead, I placed my palm on the metal door in front of me, and the same thing happened. Opening the door, I found the same outfit Moira was wearing waiting for me. We dressed quickly before folding our original clothes and placing them inside the lockers. Before I closed mine, Moira stopped me.

"Don't forget the amulet. Sanderson told us to wear everything." She pointed to the pendant hanging inside the door. A simple disc suspended from a braided leather necklace.

Affixing the clasp, I instantly felt a weight on my chest and gasped at the heat coming from the pendant. "What is this?"

"I'm sure it's got something to do with our assignment." Moira hooked her arm with mine. "Come on. Back to class. Let's see what the old hillbilly has in store for us today."

CHAPTER
FIFTEEN
KINGSTON

I trailed out of the locker room after my classmates, filled with the same restless energy I'd lived with since my wolf caught her scent again. Sunday. My mate. The one who rejected me in front of both of our packs. Technically, that meant she wasn't *my* anything. But my wolf didn't give a shit about technicalities. As far as he was concerned, Sunday belonged to us. And her getting attacked at the club and nearly dying only intensified my wolf's protective instincts.

It was a damned pain in my ass if I was being honest. Because me, the man, didn't want anything to do with her. She humiliated me in the most public arena that existed for shifters. I'm the Alpha's son, future Alpha of the Farrell pack. Only one other pack in North America matches us in size. The Fallons.

A union between our two Families would have been some real Romeo and Juliet shit, bringing together two rival packs to create the largest wolf pack seen in centuries. But she sent any talk of peace right up in flames with her outright dismissal of me. As if *I* was the one unworthy here.

She couldn't even find her damn wolf. What right did she have rejecting *me*?

Sunday would be *lucky* to be my mate. Bitches have been sniffing around, practically begging me to mount and claim them since I was old enough to understand what it meant.

Except for her.

Just like always when it came to Sunday, all the old insecurities and hurt came roaring to the surface. And right on their heels, the anger. Seeing her again, after all this time . . . I hadn't been prepared for just how fucking angry I still was.

It was easier to pretend when I didn't have to look at— or smell—her. Fuck, that scent. It haunted me. Worse, it went straight to my dick. Every. Fucking. Time.

Just the memory of it was enough to have me adjusting myself as I found a spot to wait outside the grove for Sanderson to let us in on whatever game she had planned for today. Usually wolves were social, but as a rule, we didn't fraternize much outside of our home packs. As a result, I found myself sticking to the outskirts in mixed classes such as this one.

My eyes trailed over the other students milling around, my wolf snarling as my gaze landed on Thorne and his little red-haired skank. God, they deserved each other. If Sunday and I were the shifter version of Romeo and Juliet, they were the vampires' very own Ken and Barbie. Richer than God and blood bluer than the Atlantic. Pampered. Spoiled. Utterly insufferable. He probably had to consult her day planner when he wanted to schedule time to get his dick wet.

I laughed at the thought of Thorne pounding away while Callie snapped at him to hurry and finish while scrolling through her social media feeds. Personally, I wouldn't trust my dick near the chick. I'm pretty sure she could make it shrivel up and die with a single look. Her voice alone made my skin crawl, and her scent was toxic. Like huffing nail polish and gasoline.

"She doesn't actually expect us to go in there, does she? I mean . . . the sun's out." Callie's high-pitched voice grated even from where I stood.

"Do you listen to a word anyone else says?" Thorne snapped. "This isn't real. It's an illusion."

Callie pouted. "It feels real. It's warm."

I rolled my eyes at Callie's whining, wishing the artificial rays pouring out of the grove were enough to turn the bloodsucker into a pillar of ash. It'd be one hell of an improvement.

The name was misleading. It wasn't actually a grove, per se, but a magical antechamber that professors could modify as needed. Right now, Sanderson had it converted into a daytime woodland. But, just like the rest of the campus, there were all sorts of magical fail-safes in place to prevent any of its students from coming into contact with something that would cause them harm. Case in point, the sun. Most vampire classes took place in the evening hours for that reason, but there were some exceptions to the rule. And in those cases, Ravenscroft was magically equipped to ensure their safety.

Furthermore, the grove was one of the few places on campus where said fail-safes—such as shifting—could be lifted. I doubted such a modification had been made for today; it was rare in mixed-species classes. But, it wasn't unheard of during species-specific training.

My wolf let out a low rumble, secretly hoping for a chance to be let off his leash. He was dying to run. And if he happened to come across a certain vampire prince in the process, well . . . what was the harm in a little bite?

Sunday and that Belladonna roommate of hers were the last to join the class. My wolf—and other parts of my anatomy—came jerking to attention at the sight of her. It was no wonder, what with her skintight black outfit and the long sable braid hanging down her back just begging to be wrapped around my fist and—

Down boy.

Sanderson noted their arrival and clapped her hands together to call everyone back to attention.

"All right! Y'all want to hear this before you go inside. See those little discs you're wearing? Those are your beacons. They're spelled to help you find your partners, which will be randomly selected once you're inside. I'm going to have you go in one at a time so that you'll be nice and spread out before the beacons are triggered. Your goal will be to hunt down your partner and get them to submit without drawing blood."

My ears perked up at that. Sounded like they might be letting the training wheels off today after all.

"Without using your species' gifts, of course. That means no biting. No shifting. No spell casting. You'll have to overpower your opponent using brains and brawn only."

I, along with everyone else, groaned. Well, almost everyone. The Novasgardian smirked, his arms crossed over his chest, muscles bulging obscenely. I almost felt sorry for the poor schmuck that got paired with him. They didn't stand a chance.

"All right. In you go. Who's first? Ah, yes, Mr. Black-thorne, very good."

Thorne strode into the grove without a backward glance. Callie lasted all of five seconds before trotting in after him. The rest of us queued up, some more eager to get inside than others. I was somewhere in the middle, excited about the opportunity to do something physical, but not necessarily in a hurry. I couldn't help but look over my shoulder, feeling Sunday in line behind me.

Her lip was caught in her teeth, and her cheeks flushed with color when she realized she'd been caught staring. She dropped her gaze, and my eyes narrowed. Now, what was that all about? Was it possible the little wolf wasn't as disinterested as she let on?

Before I could consider the question further, a warlock behind me gave me a little push.

"Your turn, man."

I jutted my chin in acknowledgment before sprinting off into the grove. I could feel the magic take hold as soon as I crossed the threshold. It ran down my back like a cool trickle of water, agitating my wolf with the foreign sensation, but not enough to send me into high alert. Just enough that my senses sharpened.

Just because I couldn't shift didn't mean I couldn't draw on my wolf. That was the whole point of exercises such as this. Hone the strengths of your species, no matter your form. The vamps would definitely be using their super speed and strength. I'd be damned if I wasn't going to make use of my superior tracking abilities. There was no way my partner would get the jump on me.

With that thought in mind, I worked my way through the magic-made forest, climbing over fallen logs and heading deeper into the dense vegetation. Maybe ten minutes after I entered, there was a low bugle, and then a tendril of warmth tickled my chest where the pendant rested. The last of the students were inside.

The hunt was on.

I let my wolf take over, directing my steps and leading us around and through, always working our way closer to my prey. The pendant was buzzing with warmth now, not enough to burn, but definitely letting me know I had to be getting close.

The snap of a branch to my left drew my attention. Someone else was closing in, but when I turned in their direction, my pendant went cold.

Not mine.

When I turned back the way I'd been heading, my pendant flared to life again. I lifted my nose to the air, inhaling deeply.

If they were nearby, I should be able to smell them. And if I could catch their scent, I should also be able to sort out what species they were, which would help me sneak up on them. A witch, for example, would require no subtlety. Out of all of us, they were the weakest without their gifts. A vampire or shifter, however, would require me to stay upwind so they couldn't catch my scent.

I knew it was her the moment the breeze carried soft notes of lilac and honey to me. Picking up my pace, I zeroed in on the trail, focused on my target. My wolf howled as her scent exploded in my nose.

The need to possess my mate ran through me, hot and fierce.

I started running then. Silently moving through the woods like the creature whose nature I shared.

I found her not a minute later, peering around a tree into the empty clearing. She was right in front of me, and I was downwind enough the pretty little shifter didn't have a clue. The pendant flared white-hot and then faded out. The warning that our target had been located.

Sunday tensed, but I was on her before she could move.

Pouncing from behind her, I sent both of us flying out into the small clearing. I tackled her, knocking us to the moss and leaf-strewn ground, protecting her even as I pinned her. She squirmed in my arms, inadvertently grinding that perfect ass of hers right into my crotch.

She gasped, and the slight hitch in her breath told me she knew exactly what that did to me.

"Let me go," she growled.

I gave just enough space for her to roll over onto her back before I caught her wrists in my hands and flattened my body over hers. "Submit," I snarled, my voice more wolf than man.

She swallowed. "To you? Never."

As an Alpha, the act of defiance should have pissed me off. But coming from her, all it did was turn me on. My dick was already thick and heavy between us. I couldn't get much harder if I tried.

My beast's instincts took hold, overriding my own as my wolf gave in to the need to get closer to his mate. I nuzzled into her neck, drawing her addictive scent deep into my lungs until I thought I may never get rid of it.

Fuck, she felt good splayed out beneath me like this. All those soft curves cradling my hardness. My hips rocked into hers without my conscious thought, and I let out a hiss. It was good. So fucking good. And nowhere near enough.

"Wh-what are you doing?"

"Taking what's mine," I growled, scraping my jaw along her neck, marking that soft skin with my scruff.

She whimpered, and the sound burrowed deep into me, setting my blood on fire. I wanted more.

I lowered my mouth, my lips hovering just over the place where her mate mark should be. My teeth ached with the need to claim her. As my lips grazed her skin, I growled, my intention clear. If given half the chance, I'd have her right here and now. I didn't give a fuck who saw us. In fact, I *wanted* them to see the proof of my claim on her.

Instead of fighting me, Sunday arched her body into mine, her chin shifting ever so slightly to the side. As if she wanted the same thing I did. As if she craved it.

And then her breath hitched, and she stuttered, "N-Noah?"

"It seems you've found something that belongs to me, dog." Noah's voice was calm and unaffected, but I sensed the rage boiling under the surface of the leech's skin.

I rolled my hips one more time, smirking when Sunday moaned softly as my cock ground into her, right where she needed me. "Doesn't look like she's yours."

"Kingston," she gritted out. "Get off me."

"You weren't saying that just a minute ago."

Her small hands pressed against my chest, nails digging into my skin through the fabric of my shirt. "I am now."

A low growl of warning escaped the vampire's chest, but I stayed focused on my mate. She belonged here, submitting to me. "Submit, Sunday."

"No."

"Submit to your Alpha." I stared into her eyes, searching for the connection I knew was there. Shock sent ice through my veins as I saw it. Her wolf. Just a shadow. A promise. "So, you aren't broken after all."

"Fuck you, Kingston."

"That's the plan."

She blinked and then smiled sweetly, her expression going sultry and hungry. I had her right where I wanted her. She'd see. Denying what was between us wouldn't make her happy in the end. She wanted me. Maybe even as much as I wanted her.

Blinding pain shot through me, starting with my already aching balls, as her knee connected with my unprotected crotch. Nausea rolled through me as the pain radiated outward. She shoved me off her, and all I could do was curl up in the fetal position, coughing and fighting the urge to throw up.

"Well played, dove. It seems you didn't need a rescue after all."

That fucker Thorne's voice grated on my every nerve. When I wasn't focused on simply trying to breathe normally again, he'd pay for interrupting us. She would be mine. She wanted this. I could smell her desire even as she walked into his arms.

Sunday glanced back at me and smirked. "Now be a good boy and stay."

I maginary twigs broke under our feet as Noah and I walked away from Kingston. Kingston, who'd seen my wolf, proven she existed, and whose own beast called to mine like a siren lured sailors to the rocks. I hated how turned on I still was, how hard my nipples were under my bra. Noah didn't say anything as we continued down the path together. His clenched jaw and stiff posture said it all for him. He was pissed.

"It was just a wolf thing, that's all." Using every ounce of strength I had, I kept my voice from wobbling. I'm not sure why I felt the need to explain myself. He was the one who pulled the disappearing act. I didn't owe him a damn thing.

He stopped, turned those amber eyes on me, and raised one eyebrow. "A wolf thing." Each word came out clear and slow. Like he was trying them on to see how they fit. "Did you like this wolf thing?"

How could I answer him truthfully and not be admitting something out loud I didn't want to hear? "My wolf did."

"And how does your wolf feel about vampires?"

I sucked in a tight breath, the weight of his gaze affecting me just as much as Kingston's attention, maybe more. "I don't know about her, but I like them. Except when they ghost me."

"You don't understand."

Flinching when he reached for me, I powered past him. "I understand plenty. You can't be with me. Your family forbids it. So you moved on to someone more suitable, but you can't deal with me showing anyone else attention. Well, newsflash, Fang Boy, I kissed Alek *and* let him see my boobs. What do you have to say about that?"

He was on me before I could process he'd moved. Fuck, vampires were fast. Noah's cool hand encircled my throat as he pinned me to a wide tree and stared hard at my mouth. "I should put you over my knee for your insolence, little wolf. Show you exactly why your body craves my touch, my gaze. It kills me that I can't."

"Does it? Because from where I'm standing, you had your chance and blew it. At least I had the courage to reject the mate my family chose for me. I'm sure you and Callie will be sublimely happy together."

He dipped his head, breathing hard as he released my neck. Then those perfect lips of his trailed along my throat until he reached my ear. "But it'll be you I'm thinking of if I'm forced to be inside her. How does that make you feel? Knowing that I'll fuck her like a good little heir but fantasize about you while doing it?"

I shivered from the rough husk of his voice rasping over my skin. "It doesn't matter how I feel."

His large palm that was gripping my waist moved up my belly until he cupped the weight of my breast. "Oh, but it does. I want you to ache for me as I do you."

God, I did. I burned for him, and I couldn't answer because if I did, I'd lie to him.

"I feel it in my bones. You're meant for me," he whispered.

"Is this because you gave me your blood?"

"Maybe. I can't be sure. But all I can tell you is, if you choose him over me, it'll be the biggest mistake you've ever made."

The beacon hanging between my breasts heated rapidly, burning through my shirt and glowing bright white. Noah pulled his hand away, the skin there now red and angry as he swore.

Behind him stood Callie, a wicked smile on her too-perfect face, her own beacon glowing to match mine. "Oh, good, darling. You've found my next plaything."

Standing up straighter, I steeled myself for a fight. My wolf was riled up, awake but not released from her prison yet, and I was horny as hell. If I couldn't get my release by fucking, I might as well get it by fighting. And there was just something about the idea of smashing in that pert little upturned nose that seemed endlessly appealing. Sure, it wouldn't do permanent damage, but it'd hurt, and it'd shut her up for a little while.

Noah placed himself in front of me, posture protective even though this was part of our lesson. "Move, Noah. I need to do this."

"You don't know how strong she is. She's a vampire."

I rolled my shoulders and sighed. "And I'm a shifter. I can take her. Give me a chance. I don't want to fail this assignment."

Though it was obvious in every move he made that he didn't want to, he acquiesced and moved aside. His beacon held a faint glow, a reminder he had his own partner to find and spar with. A rustle in the brush behind me had me turning toward the sound, and when Kingston broke through, eyes feral and burning with determined anger, I flinched.

He wouldn't really try to hurt me, would he? I'd won our match. But Noah snarled and leaped from where he stood, his beacon glowing white and Kingston's matching.

"Noah!" Fear sprang to the forefront of my mind, worry that he'd be hurt, that Kingston would rip him to shreds, overwhelming me.

My wolf stirred, pacing and pushing at her restraints, restraints neither of us knew how to break. She wanted to defend her mate. Kingston. Oh, hell, this was going to be impossible to deal with. Fuck Kingston for waking her up.

Without warning, something crashed into me, laying me out and leaving me gasping for air as the wind was knocked from my lungs. Callie clawed at my face, her nails sharp and deadly.

"I can smell your fear. It's delicious. At least you're smart enough to recognize when you're outmatched."

I didn't realize it was possible to hate someone so quickly and so completely. Until now. "I'm not afraid of you. You're nothing but a blow-up doll with fangs for Noah to distract himself with since he can't have the woman he really wants. Why do you think he came back to find me?"

I kicked out, launching her into the air with all my strength. She hit a tree hard enough to shake loose a few large branches. As they rained down on us, I did my best to dodge them while she let out a low, menacing laugh.

"Oh, good. I was afraid you were going to make this easy on me."

"You're the only one who is easy around here."

"Says the bitch spreading her legs for every wolf, vamp, and Viking she can get her horny little hands on."

We took up fighting stances, both of us tensed and ready to attack as we circled the clearing under the tree cover. "So is that all you've got? One good surprise attack, and you're done? No wonder Noah is bored with you. I could go all night."

"It's no wonder, with all that practice you're getting. But I'll tell you one thing, he might be having his fun with you now, but I'm the one he'll be taking home to his parents. You'll never be anything more than his dirty little secret."

Something in me snapped as she spat the words that so closely echoed my own deepest fears. My jaw clenched, my nails sinking into my palms as I balled my hands into even tighter fists, wishing it was Callie's throat they were closing around. I stalked forward, my energy building, gathering in my center, fueling my strength as I pushed her back. Loose tendrils of hair that had escaped my braid whirled around my face even though there was no wind to move them.

Callie's eyes widened, fear sparking in them. "What the hell are you?"

"Your worst fucking nightmare."

Before she could escape, I snagged her throat in one hand, my grip tighter than I thought I was capable of. She panicked, her fingers scraping at mine, desperate to get me to release her because, vampire or not, if I tore her head clean off her body, she'd be nothing but a pile of dust.

"Do you submit?" I snarled, barely recognizing my own voice.

Her face was turning purple, mottled with fear and rage. But I saw my victory in her eyes.

"Y-yes," she gasped.

"Say. It."

She closed her eyes and released every ounce of fight left in her. "I submit."

I squeezed her throat just a bit tighter, not a big enough person to win gracefully, before I flung her to the ground. Callie connected with the forest floor hard enough the ground beneath my feet tremored. Dust and pine needles lifted into a cloud, and when the air cleared, she was there, in a crater made by her own body.

The shock of it was enough to pull me out of whatever dark, unrecognizable fugue I'd been lost to.

The clapping came first, just loud and obnoxious enough to be heard over the roar of my blood through my veins.

"Brava, little wolf. Seems you were right. You didn't need my help, after all." Noah smirked. "You certainly put her right where she belongs."

My gaze snapped to the place where Noah and Kingston stood. Noah barely looked rumpled past the smudge of dirt on his cheek and uncharacteristically tousled hair. Kingston was worse for wear, leaves clinging to his hair and shirt. A dark bruise bloomed across his cheek. Part of me was surprised to learn the Alpha-to-be had submitted to the vampire. The other part wondered if that had more to do with an unlikely truce while they watched the chick fight taking place right beside them.

Callie was alive; I was sure of it. She was bleeding from her mouth but breathing slowly. She remained unconscious as the scene we were immersed in melted away and became nothing more than a cold, sterile space made of four walls and gray paint. Everyone else in the class came into view, all disheveled and many sporting bruises, sweat stains, and torn clothing.

Professor Sanderson appeared in a cloud of purple mist, her gaze trained on me. "Everyone stop. Remove your beacons and place them at your feet at once."

Oh, no. What had I done to earn that look of reproach?

"Sunday Fallon, shower, collect your belongings, and return to your dormitory. You spilled blood during this exercise even though you were instructed not to. Following instructions is paramount for the safety of all students when we are in mixed-species classes. You'll attend sessions with Father Gallagher Saturday at sundown. Do you understand?"

Callie sat up and stretched, a saccharine smile on her face as she wiped away the blood that had trickled from the corner of her lips. Lips I never once hit.

"Professor, I didn't—"

"Don't argue with me, sugar. You did what you did. Now get out of my sight."

As I tossed my beacon on the floor, I looked back at the two men I'd been in the middle of before my fight with Callie. They both stood with their arms crossed over their chests, frowns on their faces. I wondered if they knew just how much they resembled a pair of faithful guards.

Callie got to her feet and offered me a little wave. "See you around, Sunday."

She'd marked me with a target that all but said, *watch your back*. She might not have said the words, but her message couldn't have been any clearer.

This wasn't over, not by a long shot.

CHAPTER

SEVENTEEN

THORNE

I slammed my locker closed, loathing the necessity of such a mortal convenience. I had a private shower and changing area, perks of the family name, but in times such as these—when I was intent on 'bumping into' a certain pretty dove—convenience trumped indulgence. Thus my willing use of the men's changing room.

Our conversation had been interrupted, and I intended to finish it. A mission that would be much easier to accomplish from here. Ideally, by intercepting her on her way back to her flat and locating a nearby alcove to pull her into until I had her moaning my name in defeat. She thought I'd let her go easily? Not a fucking chance. I may be a prince, but I was far from a gentleman.

I may not be able to sink my teeth—or my cock, for that matter—into her, but that didn't mean I was about to let her go off seeking pleasure in the hands of any other man, either. Sunday Fallon was mine. And it was well past time she realized it.

My thoughts were interrupted by the hum of dozens of whispered conversations and an unfamiliar twinge in my chest. I'd worked hard over the years to control my ability to read the thoughts of others, to insert myself into their minds. Here at Ravenscroft, it was part of the code of conduct agreement to respect the privacy of all students and staff. But this was different. This was . . .

Sunday.

I'm not sure why I was certain she was at the center of whatever was going on, but I just *knew*. Rising, I crossed the room in a few ground-eating strides, stepping out of the men's locker room the same moment Callie vacated the women's.

She was wearing her cat-that-caught-the-canary smile when her gaze found me, looking far more poised than she had the last time I'd seen her.

"What did you do?"

"Who, me?" she asked, pressing a nearly perfect, manicured hand to her chest. The polish was chipped and one of her nails jagged from her sparring match with Sunday.

I allowed myself a small smile at the visible evidence of her resounding loss. Donoghues, like Blackthornes, rarely lost anything. To do so in such a public fashion could not be sitting well.

"Answer the question, Callista."

Her eyes narrowed, and her lips thinned. "No, I don't think I will."

I raised a brow. Not at all used to such outright defiance from her. She was usually all simpering sweetness and ready to bend over backward to please me. I wondered if she finally realized I wasn't planning on touching her with a ten-foot-pole.

There wasn't anything Callista Donoghue could offer that I was interested in. Our parents might have negotiated a marriage contract, but I had no intention of seeing it through. Not before Sunday had entered the picture, and certainly not now. Though, I *would* use the relationship when it suited my needs. Which it did to drive a wedge between me and the creature of my obsession. Not that it worked.

Seeing that flare of jealous possessiveness in Sunday's eyes when she saw Callie claim me was burned into my memory. My cock thickened at just the thought of her desire for me. And the proof of it only fueled my own need.

I stalked forward, grasping Callie's chin in my hand and jerking her head up. "Yes," I snarled. "You will."

Her breath hitched, and her pupils flared. Apparently, Callie had a thing for pain. I could work with that.

Her tongue darted out, wetting her lips. "You saw what she did to me. I couldn't let that wolf bitch get away with it. No one insults us like that, Noah—"

"Do *not* call me that," I growled, my voice ice cold and deadly serious.

She blanched. "But, Sunday—"

"Yes. She did. But you may not. Ever. I am Thorne to you. That's all I'll ever be. Now . . . what did you do to Sunday?"

Anger flared in her dark eyes, and she sneered up at me. "Exactly what she deserved. An eye for an eye and all that."

"You bit your own cheek, didn't you? Sunday never drew your blood."

She sniffed. "As if she could. But getting her kicked out of class was only the beginning."

Panic buzzed through my veins. It felt off . . . too real to ignore and yet not wholly mine. I shoved it away, wanting answers. Still gripping her jaw, I shook her. "What. Did. You. Do?"

Callie winced as my fingers bit into her cheeks. "See for yourself."

Sweet lilac wine filled my senses before I saw her. And then, Sunday emerged from the women's locker room, completely nude, cheeks flushed red with anger and embarrassment she was working to control. My breath caught in my chest at the sight of her, lush curves, tight pink nipples, wet hair trailing down her shoulders, the ends stopping just before the tips of her breasts. The most perfect creature I'd ever seen, and yet, instead of appreciating her beauty, I was witnessing the brunt of Callie's cruelty.

"Bloody fucking hell, Callie. You're more childish than I gave you credit for," I muttered as I tore my shirt over my head.

I reached Sunday in a few long strides, handing her my shirt without a word. The gratitude in her eyes told me she was near her breaking point, but she held her head high and covered herself without a glance at Callie. Anyone who looked at her sideways got a death glare from me, and without hesitation, they trained their gazes elsewhere. All except for Kingston. The arse stood at the archway leading to the courtyard between this building and our dorm.

"Glad I stayed for the show."

I wanted to knock his teeth out, but Sunday threaded our fingers and squeezed, a silent plea echoing in my mind, then.

Don't.

It was just a single word, but her voice came through clear and present in my head. Fuck. I had my shields up. I couldn't hear anyone else. What the devil was happening?

"Bugger off and lick your wounds, dog."

"Maybe I need to lick hers."

I stiffened at Kingston's words. If he so much as touched her I'd rip his arms from his body and beat him to a bloody pulp, risk of war or no.

"Touch me, and I'll bite your dick off," Sunday snarled. "Try it. I dare you."

Kingston leaned against the arch, a satisfied smirk on his face. "Oh, there it is. The fire you were missing before I found your wolf. Sooner or later, she'll make her appearance, and you won't be able to resist me. I'm your mate, like it or not."

It took everything in me not to end his life right then. But something in her changed. She was fighting with her wolf, at war with the beast inside her that, fuck, that wanted *him*.

"Come on, dove. Let's get you back to your room before we both end up in Father Gallagher's office for the rest of the year. If we're going to spend time on our knees, I'd rather it be doing something much more enjoyable than his damned introspective exercises."

She shook with rage and frustration by the time we got to her door. "That fucking bitch. She stole my clothes and set them on fire in the showers. What is this, high school?"

"She's a spoiled, pampered princess. A petulant little twat. And you, my beautiful little wolf, are a goddess."

Her soft smile had me desperate for a taste. "Am I?"

"Fuck yes. And if you let me into your room, I'll show you exactly what a willing disciple looks like."

My voice was a low growl of need. She was too tempting, and I'd been tested time and time again, my will only so strong. The connection between us screamed for me to give in.

Her breath caught, that slight hitch drawing my attention to the hollow at the base of her throat, then lower, to the tight nipples pressing through the fabric of my shirt. *My* shirt protecting and covering her skin. My scent would be all over her, marking her as mine so no one else would dare attempt to make a claim.

A flicker of her indecision ran through my thoughts until she bit her lower lip and nodded. I couldn't stop. Not now. I gripped her nape and bent down, lowering my head until my lips brushed hers. Fuck, she was warm and soft and delicious.

Opening her mouth on a soft sigh, she wrapped her arms around my ribs, fingers digging into my back, urging me closer.

"Noah," she whispered.

"Let me in, Sunday. Please, let me in."

Into her room. Into her body. Into her heart. I wanted it all.

She reached behind her and opened the bedroom door, the two of us falling inside in a tangle of limbs. We were frantic, desperate, starving creatures. Thank fuck her room-mate was nowhere to be found.

"Lock the door." Sunday's breathless command had my dick rock hard and aching.

I did, throwing the deadbolt and moving a dresser in front of the door for good measure. "Ready yourself, dove. I'm going to make you scream."

Her pulse leaped at the warning, and I could hear the frantic tattoo echoing in my ears. Beckoning me. My fangs ached nearly as bad as my cock. I had to have her. I was mad with need.

I was on her in an instant, my lips sealing over hers as our tongues twisted together. Lifting her in my arms, I walked us back until my shins hit her bed, and then I dropped her.

"Take it off," I demanded, my hands already working on pulling my belt free.

As much as I loved the sight of her in my shirt, I wanted all barriers between us gone. I wanted to feel that silky soft skin pressed against my hardness. Usually, it was no issue to restrain myself, to draw it out. But I'd been craving her for too long, and I couldn't stop myself now if I wanted to. Not until she filled the room with the sound of her ecstasy.

She whipped the shirt off, as desperate for my touch as I was to provide it.

I studied her, taking the time to appreciate the perfection of her body, now that the vision she painted was for my eyes alone. All that flushed skin, delectable curves, the taut peaks of her breasts, begging for my mouth.

"Please, Noah." That breathy whimper, the sound of my name, one only she used, was my undoing.

I peeled off my pants, my thick length jutting forward as I crawled over to her. The look in Sunday's eyes as she stared down at what I had to offer proof positive she'd never seen a cock as big as mine before. She swallowed.

"Oh yes, dove. You won't walk straight for a week by the time I'm through defiling you." I leaned down, brushing a kiss to her collarbone, letting my hips settle between the welcoming vee of her thighs, then kissing up higher over the perfect column of her throat. "In case it wasn't obvious, little wolf, I mean to destroy you."

Her pulse fluttered against my lips, and I got the first echo of nerves rolling through me. I pulled back, settling my weight on my elbow so I could look at her.

"This might be a good time to mention that I . . ." She licked her lips. "I haven't done this before."

A groan ripped through me. My cock wept at the thought of being her first. The only one who could ever claim the title. Kingston might claim she was his mate, but this . . . this would be mine.

I ran my hand down the side of her face, staring into those beautiful ocean-blue eyes currently dark with desire.

"Your confession should make me want to be gentle. But the truth is, it only makes the monster in me that much more desperate for your screams. I want to utterly ruin you for anyone else."

"I want that too."

I grinned at her, though there was nothing kind or sweet about it. "You don't know what you're asking for, dove. But you will. I'll see to it."

I claimed her mouth after that, the arm not bearing my weight trailing down her body, pausing at her breast to grasp and lightly twist that taut bud.

She gasped beneath me, and I ran my hand lower, sliding between her legs and parting her slick folds.

Fuck, she was already drenched for me. I had to know what she tasted like.

I pressed down with my middle finger, which was currently resting right on top of her swollen bundle. She arched up with a wanton moan.

"Do you ever touch yourself, Sunday?"

"Y-yes," she admitted, her eyes closed, her cheeks stained red.

Something in the way she said it made me narrow my eyes and ask, "What do you think about?"

"Recently? You."

Fuck, I loved the breathy sound of her voice. I was doing that to her. Making her come apart slowly. Piece by fucking piece.

"Right answer."

I slid my hand lower, my fingers delving into her sweet, delicious heat. She was so damn tight.

Sunday groaned, her body clamping down around my fingers. "Yes, dove. I can feel how much you want me. But I need a taste. I need you to come on my tongue."

I slid my fingers free, and when I didn't immediately touch her, Sunday opened her eyes. "Noah?"

Holding her gaze, I lifted my hand to my mouth and sucked her off my fingers. Now I was the one who was moaning, my fangs bursting free at the promise of more than just her arousal on my tongue. I could feed from her, here and now. Sink my teeth into her femoral artery while I fucked her with my fingers. Give myself everything I craved. Her pleasure, her blood, and then . . . her virginity.

"Noah, your eyes . . ." she whispered.

Hunger. That was what she'd seen. There was no other possibility. Her fear coated my skin like oil, slick and impossible to shake. She feared me in the moment she should be begging me to take her. But I'd let my monster win. I'd given in to my instincts as a vampire and was about to do the one thing I shouldn't. Take her blood without her consent. Fuck her and claim her without making sure she was really ready for what that would mean. Set something in motion that could bring down the tremulous treaty between my kind and hers.

In the space between one heartbeat and the next, I was on the other side of the room, breaths coming in heavy pants as I pulled on my clothes and worked to control myself. "I can't do this. I'm sorry."

She sat up, hair wild and wavy around her face, a blanket pulled over her naked body. "Excuse me?"

"I'm so sorry, dove. I . . . I don't have the control I need to be with you like this. No matter how much I want to."

Her gaze traveled my body until it rested on my aching shaft. "Can I at least help you take care of *that* problem?"

God, but I wanted her to. She had no idea. Closing my eyes and taking a deep breath, I said, "It's best that I'm not within touching distance of you right now. I'll fuck you silly and do something stupid like knock you up. Then you'd be stuck with me."

She laughed. "Shifters and vampires don't procreate."

I cocked a brow. "Don't they?"

Shaking her head, she bit her lower lip, and I had to fight a groan at the sight of the flush on her skin.

"Tell that to my uncle's mate. She's helped more than one shifter bring a hybrid into the world."

Her mouth dropped open. "What?"

This was a safer topic. One that helped me focus on the real reason we shouldn't be together. And one that had the added benefit of helping me control my raging desire. "They used to be called abominations. Sometimes they still are. Hunted by humans and the vampire and shifter councils alike. No one talks about them to keep them safe."

"I thought they couldn't survive. That the shifter or the vampire side always killed off the other, and they ended up dying in the process."

"Not always."

I shouldn't have told her this. It was a risk. But I trusted Sunday Fallon in a way I'd never trusted anyone else.

That wasn't the only reason we shouldn't be together, but I didn't want to remind her of the fact that our union would likely lead to consequences that would result in war. She was already an outcast. Being with me like this would only make things worse for her.

"I have to go. Until I know how to control myself around you, we can't do this again."

She nodded, the disappointment so heavy in her eyes I could practically taste it. Or perhaps that was my own.

"Bye, Noah. Thank you for what you did earlier."

"That was purely selfish, little wolf. I don't want anyone seeing you naked but me. At least, not when it's against your will. But enough talk of unpleasant things. I have something I want you to do for me after I leave. Something that will make leaving you now more bearable."

"Oh?"

"When you touch yourself, I want it to be my name on your lips as you shudder out your release."

What I didn't tell her as I fled before her desire-hooded gaze or the sweet 'o' of her lips could lure me back into her bed—and into all kinds of trouble I couldn't afford—was that I would be doing the same for her.

CHAPTER
EIGHTEEN
THORNE

B y the time I reached my dorm apartment, my dick throbbed so intensely it was near painful. I was aching for her, my balls so blue I was afraid to find release because it might hurt just as much as it felt good.

After I was safe behind the thick, soundproof door, I gave in to the wave of confusing emotions swirling through my brain. Why was I so bloody drawn to her? She was beautiful, dazzling even, but so were plenty of other women. By all rights, Sunday Fallon shouldn't be the object of my affection. But here we were.

Here *I* was.

Rock hard and edgy.

I'd been so close to fucking her, to marking her flawless skin with my teeth and filling her with my cock. She deserved better than the feral beast I became when my hunger took over, especially for her first time.

"Bloody hell, Sunday, what are you doing to me?" I groaned into the empty flat as I stripped and made my way to the shower.

Once under the cool water, my raging hard-on finally

eased, still stiff and thick, but no longer painful. Until a tendril of *her* raced through my brain, filling it with the echoes of her soft moans and harsh breaths. And then a whisper of her voice calling my name in pleasure.

Noah, yes, more.

I closed my eyes, letting the rush wash over me. Was this what it was like to be hunting someone and draw it out? I didn't think so. I'd hunted before, toyed with their hearts before I fed from them and left them none the wiser. This was something else. Something more.

Pleasure ghosted across my senses, making my knees weak and my cock jerk as it intensified.

Yes, inside me. I need you. God, Noah.

Was this her? Was she . . . touching herself and calling for me? I closed my eyes and let down my guard, allowing her fully into my head. The onslaught of her building climax buckled my knees and had me reaching out to hold myself up on the shower wall. I may have been at half-mast before, but now? I was straining and dripping for her. I fisted my length and gave a slow stroke from base to crown, letting out a pained groan as I did.

Give me your pleasure, Sunday. Let me feel it.

I sensed alarm racing through her, but she was too far gone to hide it. Her orgasm washed through her, and I felt every golden burst of pleasure as I moaned and spilled my release against the tile wall.

The connection between us snapped, a barricade appearing and sealing me from her. Had I done that, or had she?

I'd been able to communicate with my family telepathically from a young age. It was something most of the vampires in my family could do. We talked to each other, annoyed each other, and my sister regularly invaded my thoughts when we were younger just to torture me. We'd been trained to protect ourselves from hearing things we didn't want to know, a warning from our father that privacy was a gift and we were not to squander it.

He'd taken me aside one night after one of our yearly Blackthorne masked balls, where shifters, witches, and vampires alike gathered to scold me for my clumsy attempt to read the thoughts of a witch I'd been toying with. She'd been easy to read but never had it gone both ways. She hadn't heard me, been as present in my mind as Sunday had. This was a two-way street, and that was . . . troubling.

"Fuck. What the bloody hell just happened?"

After cleaning up and wrapping a towel around my waist, I stalked through the flat in search of the pants I'd discarded in my rush to get a handle on my situation. Something was wrong with me. That had to be the answer. I'd never been so focused on a single creature, so conflicted about whether she was prey or meant to amuse me. But the feelings in my chest when I thought of Sunday didn't add up to either of those categories.

I was loyal to her.

I cared about her.

I wanted her safety, her security, her love.

But she was a wolf.

I fished my cell out of a pocket and scrolled until I found my uncle Lucas's name. Dialing, I paced the floor as the phone rang.

"Ah, nephew, what have you been up to that warrants a call at this hour?"

I swallowed past the lump in my throat. "Tell me how you knew Briar was your mate."

"Stupid asshole vampire and your stupid perfect face," I grumbled to myself as I stormed my way around the deserted campus.

It was the middle of the night. The light of the moon bathed everything in a pale glow, buildings casting shadows across the grounds. Noah Blackthorne might've vanished without a trace three days ago when he ran from my room like a bat out of hell, but he still did dirty things to me in my dreams. Night after night, I woke with the memory of his lips on me, leaving me swollen, aching, desperate, and with no choice but to take matters into my own hands.

Thankfully, these Noah fever dreams happened *after* my initial nightly rendezvous with my mother, who told me everything and nothing all over again. I was keyed up. Wound tight. Ready to snap. If I kept going like this, I'd die of exhaustion and dehydration before I ever had a chance to live.

"Something troubling you, Miss Fallon?"

Caleb's—no, *Father Gallagher's* voice curled around me

from somewhere to my left. "Skulking in the shadows? How fitting for a vampire."

"I'm not skulking. I'm patrolling. And you're supposed to be in bed, Miss Fallon, so what's your excuse?" He stepped from the trees and halfway into a shaft of moonlight.

His face, even partially obscured, was ruggedly handsome. I imagined he would've been the object of desire of anyone he wanted if he hadn't devoted himself to God.

"I didn't realize the school needed someone to patrol. Aren't there protective wards set all around the grounds?"

His lips twitched in the barest hint of a smile. "Who do you think set them off?" Then his smile faded. "Although, with the recent hunter attack on one of our students, I admit I've been cautious. Never hurts to be careful."

My side gave a dull throb, a reminder of the very attack he mentioned. The one he'd saved me from. A spark of fear ignited in my chest. "I can't sleep. That's all. I needed to blow off some steam and get my thoughts under control."

His gaze sharpened, and a flicker of something . . . concern, perhaps, flashed in his eyes. "Have you been practicing what I taught you?"

"Yes, I get down on my knees every night, *Father*." I couldn't help but poke at him a little. I loved watching the set of his jaw change at my insolence. So sue me, I had daddy issues.

"Apparently not correctly if you're forced to resort to nightly wandering and putting yourself at risk. I'd feel much better if you allowed me to join you."

I had to fight the urge to tease him again with another dig about me being on my knees. Instead, I sighed and nodded. "If you want."

He didn't say a word, simply fell into step beside me, his warm earthy scent of incense and spice filling my senses.

We walked together in silence, around the well-kept path through the wooded area on the property, then stopped at a clearing that overlooked a small lake. The moon glowed across the water, a sky of twinkling stars our canopy, the air thick with the aroma of night-blooming jasmine and a symphony of crickets chirping our sound-track. If I didn't know better, I'd say this setting was almost romantic, and this little midnight stroll of ours was a perfect first date.

But I did.

The awkward silence between us was the most telling thing of all. Finally, when I couldn't take it anymore, I asked, "So were you hired to be the resident lurker, or do you actually *do* something here? Besides tormenting me?"

"Contrary to what you might believe, my world doesn't revolve around you, Miss Fallon. I teach theology and an upper-level rituals and relics class, neither of which you're ready to attend."

"Relics. How fitting."

He glared at me. So I decided to keep on going with my gentle ribbing.

"Speaking of relics, how does a vampire become a priest?"

"He doesn't. A priest being turned into a vampire, however, is a different story."

So, he was a made vampire, not born like Noah. "I'm all ears. It sounds like a story worth telling."

He gave me a look tinged with exasperation, one I was intimately familiar with after all our sessions. "Oh, I'm sure it does. Religion. Politics. A man of God being denied the life he swore himself to? It practically writes itself, doesn't it?"

He gave a dramatic shudder, making me laugh. Who knew the priest had a sense of humor? Self-deprecating though it was. "There's not much to tell. A vampire wanted me. I declined. She didn't like that very much. Thought she could sway me once I was turned. She couldn't. The end."

"She sounds like a real bitch. Consent is way sexier than coercion."

"She is."

Something twisted inside me. She was still alive. That meant one day, Caleb could get his vengeance, because from the haunted look in his eyes, I knew there was more to that story than he was sharing.

"So you still live life as a priest even though you can't be one anymore? Isn't that a special kind of torture?"

"Technically, I stopped being a priest the day my heart ceased beating and I woke without a soul. Some habits . . ." He sighed, looking uncomfortable. "There's solace in habits. More in pain. Perhaps it is my destiny to be tortured. For what punishments of God are not gifts?"

"We've gone this long without you spouting scripture at me. Let's keep it that way."

His lips twitched, and the sight of his amusement made my stomach flutter.

"What would you like me to spout at you, then?"

Was he . . . flirting? On the heels of that thought came another. One I was desperate to know the answer to.

"Are you still . . . you know . . . celibate?" My cheeks burned from the deeply personal question I had dared to ask, but I had to know.

He turned slowly to look at me, his expression unreadable, and I found myself getting lost in eyes so blue they appeared black in the darkness.

Before he could answer—assuming he ever intended to

—three wolves sprang from the trees on our left. I recognized Kingston's scent instantly, the pull of my wolf to his strong. He stopped and stared at us, eyes glowing, intensely focused on me, as though asking me to shed my human form and join them as they ran.

"Do you want to join them?" Caleb's voice was low and measured. I couldn't tell if he wanted me to say yes or no.

I shook my head, and Kingston must've seen it as rejection because he let out a low growl. "No. Even if I wanted to, I still can't shift."

"Have you made any progress with your wolf?"

"I have, a little. Kingston did something when we were paired during Sanderson's class. He unlocked the cage my wolf was in, but she still can't get out."

Caleb pressed his lips together, giving me a shrewd look before turning his attention on Kingston, who was still staring in our direction. "Perhaps the two of you should spend more time together? It sounds like being around a dominant wolf is good practice for you."

I glanced at Kingston and then back at Caleb. As much as I didn't want to admit it, he was right. "Set it up."

Caleb's hands balled into tight fists, as though something about me being with Kingston bothered him. But he'd been the one to suggest it. Men were so complicated. Kingston gave a little huff before bounding away in the direction of the rest of his pack, leaving me to walk back to my dorm with a former priest who may or may not be celibate. Either way, Father Caleb Gallagher definitely gave more sinner vibes than saint every time I saw him.

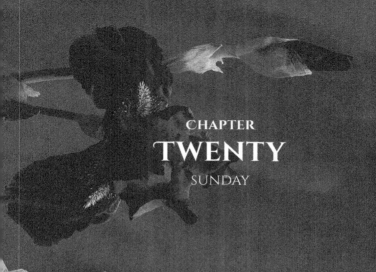

CHAPTER
TWENTY
SUNDAY

"Hmm ... I'm not sure silver is your color," Moira mused, staring at my hair like it was some kind of science project.

"I told you," I said with a laugh.

She narrowed her eyes. "Maybe if we go with something a little more unconventional."

"More unconventional than silver? Go nuts, but I'm drawing the line at shaving it off, okay? On you, it's sexy as hell. On me? Not so much."

Moira smirked, and I already knew her well enough to know that's exactly what she'd been planning. But since she'd been sporting a series of pixie cuts with various designs shaved into them for the past couple of days, it hadn't been much of a mental leap.

"Don't you want to look all badass for your date with the priest? I could give you a crucifix? Or ... how 'bout we really make him go wild and I give you the mark of the beast? I think you'd look like hot shit with a 666 along the back of your head. It could be like your version of a tramp stamp. Something for him to stare at while your head is bowed in supplication. And then he could . . . *exorcise* your demons."

"Oh, my God, Moira. He's not going to exorcise anything." I rolled my eyes, trying to cover my snorts of laughter. "It's not a date. It's punishment. And you're supposed to be helping me get it off my mind."

"But if we do it my way, maybe he'll help you get *off* instead."

"Stop it." I already had enough inappropriate thoughts about him all on my own. I didn't need Moira to give me any new ideas.

"I'm just trying to make you feel better since the Prince of Darkness has left you high and dry again."

High maybe . . . but not dry. The fucker.

She'd caught me moping around our room and declared a mandatory roommate makeover session. What that really meant was Moira wanted an excuse to turn me into her real-life doll so she could play around with various hair and makeup styles. All I had to do was sit there and look pretty. She always set me back to rights after she was done having her fun. Which was fine with me. At least it gave me something more productive to do than think about my upcoming session or that panty-melting asshole Noah.

He'd ghosted me. Again.

We'd been T-minus ten seconds away from him claiming my V-card, only for him to all but flee from my room and leave me with no choice but to take care of myself. Not to mention whatever the hell *that* had been when I'd come so hard I could have sworn I heard his thoughts in my mind. So much build up and then . . . nothing.

God, I was such an idiot.

"You're doing it again," Moira chided.

"I can't help it."

I'd filled Moira in on the whole humiliating tragedy. From Callie's stupid prank right up to Noah's disappearing act.

"What I want to know is why are you worrying about him when you have that Norse beefcake just waiting on the sidelines? Or, hell, you could have Kingston here with the crook of your little finger."

Her comment should have made me smile, but it only made me groan louder. My feelings for these guys were so complicated. I was going to need a damn murder board to make sense of them.

"I thought you liked Alek?" she asked with a frown.

"I do. A lot. I mean, the guy saved my life, and there's something about being around him that makes me feel strong and powerful. But I also have these crazy feelings for Noah I can't just wish away. Like there's something that happens when I'm with him. I feel safe and in control . . . like he calms the chaos inside me. I've never responded like this to anyone, except—"

"Except?" she prompted when I didn't immediately continue.

"Kingston. As much as it kills me to admit it, my wolf has it bad for that Alpha asshole. She only showed up once she was around him. I . . . I think I need him to find her."

That had been a rather uncomfortable lesson I'd learned during our match-up in class the other day. When his wolf had growled, signaling his intent to mark mine . . . Fuck, just the memory of it had my blood heating and my core tightening. After everything Kingston had said about me over the years, there was absolutely no reason for me to feel this way. But my wolf had other ideas. And now that she was scratching at whatever barrier had been keeping us apart, it was not so easy to deny her.

"All right, so what you're telling me is you need a harem."

I laughed. "Yeah, right. Okay. Because I'll be able to convince not one but three alpha males to just set their instincts aside and share me."

Even as I said the number, my brain automatically corrected me. *Four.* There were four men I couldn't get off my mind. But it may as well be one hundred for as likely as it was any of them, let alone all of them, would agree to such an arrangement.

Moira looked at me like I was stupid. "Why wouldn't they? You're a snack, in case you haven't realized it. You have this whole sexy alpha female just discovering her power thing going on. Men eat that shit up. They might beat their chests and claim to be dominant, but at the end of the day, they want a woman to serve. You, Sunday, could bring men to their knees."

I was pretty sure my mouth was hanging open at that point, but Moira stopped and cocked her head, her eyes narrowing. "Sunday, you've been with a man before, haven't you?"

My cheeks burned. "Kind of hard to lose your virginity when you're locked away most of your life. I never had a chance to be tempted before now. The only men I came into contact with were the few assigned to guard me, and they kept their distance. But now, when I'm around Kingston, Noah, and Alek"—*and Caleb,* I whispered in my head—"it feels like something inside me has finally woken up."

"Oh, my God, you really are a virgin princess. No wonder they're all sniffing around like this."

"It's only them. None of the other guys on campus even exist to me. But what does it say about me that there is more than one on my mind?"

Moira smirked, more than a little tickled by my admission. "Well, harems aren't that uncommon. I mean, the fae do it all the time. Haven't you heard about the Shadow Queen and her men? And I'm pretty sure I've run into a few poly groups at *Iniquity*. They like to make use of the private rooms when they're in the mood to play. Maybe you should chat with one of them next time. See what the whole dynamic is about. But I'll give you this little nugget for free. Whatever you do, you don't want a group scene for your first time."

"I . . . how would that even work?"

Moira lifted one shoulder in a shrug. "That's the kind of thing you guys would have to figure out for yourselves. But I'm pretty sure admitting to your feelings is the first step. And if you really do have it bad for the Prince of Darkness—"

"I told you not to call him that."

"—then you're going to have to strap on your lady balls and tell him."

I tipped my head back and groaned again, which only made Moira laugh.

"You don't have to decide anything now. Play the field for a while. You certainly have enough options. Just know that being with all of them is . . . *one* of your choices. The only opinions that matter, Sunday, are yours and whoever you give your heart to. No matter how many *someones* that might be. Just make sure they're worthy of it first."

"Aw, that was actually sweet. Maybe you should be part of my harem."

She grinned at me. "Tempting, but the thought of all that man meat flapping around makes my skin crawl. I'll stick to being your bestie."

Moira moved over, using her hands instead of her magic to play with my hair, making me think the conversation was over. But she surprised me by asking, "What was that thing the lady in your dreams keeps telling you? Embrace them? Maybe she's talking about the guys. You said each of them makes you feel stronger and in control. What if they're the key to unlocking your power?"

A current of electricity buzzed through me. The kind that made my hair stand up on end and my body go hot and cold at the same time. It felt like . . . premonition.

"I told you about the dreams because they were weird. Not so you could make sense out of them."

I'd finally caved and told Moira about my recurring dreams the other morning after she'd heard me muttering to myself in my sleep. While I hadn't had any more sleep-walking episodes, I'd been having the same dream almost every night since my sessions with Caleb started. Unfortunately, I hadn't gotten any closer to deciphering it. Leave it to my mother to keep things vague and confusing.

But what if Moira was right? What if 'my guys,' as she called them, were the answer to discovering who I really was? Kingston had already woken my wolf, and all he'd done was annoy and arouse the hell out of me. And as mad as I was at Noah for once again disappearing, I couldn't deny the peace I gained when he was around. And Alek? Power pulsed inside me just thinking of him.

If I had them all . . .

The thought was both terrifying and enthralling, like

the promise of something forbidden but oh-so-sweet. Because if Moira was right, maybe, just maybe, I really could have everything I wanted.

I guess the real question was, would I be brave enough to find out?

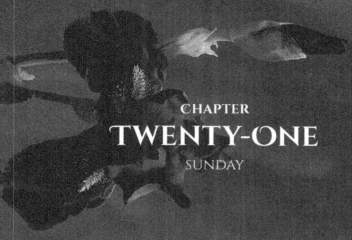

CHAPTER
TWENTY-ONE
SUNDAY

My steps were slow and measured as I trailed down the hallway to Father Gallagher's office. Unfortunately, slow steps or no, there was no getting around what waited for me behind his closed door. If our sessions together were any indication, this was going to be a barrel of laughs.

I reached the door too soon, my hand poised to knock when his voice came from behind me, his breath tickling the little hairs on the back of my neck.

"You're late, Miss Fallon. Not a good way to start out our evening. What do you have to say for yourself?"

Shame washed over my cheeks as I thought about what exactly I'd been doing while fantasies of Noah Blackthorne played out in my mind only minutes earlier. I'd needed something good to help take the edge off before coming down to face my unwarranted punishment.

Since it wasn't like I could go with the truth, I stalled. "Um . . ." I bit my lip. "I got lost?" As far as lies went, it was beyond weak. I'd been down here every night for almost two weeks now.

He snagged my wrist and brought the fingers of my right hand to his nose, inhaling deeply. Those dark eyes locked on mine, intense and needy. "In your panties?"

Hearing the good priest talk about my panties shouldn't send all sorts of wicked butterflies swirling around my stomach, should it? I probably should have been a little more embarrassed that he could smell exactly what I'd been up to, but if he was going to be a dick and mention it, then I was going to own it.

"Jealous, Daddy?"

"Caleb. I'm not your priest, nor your father. And definitely not your daddy, Miss Fallon. I'm here to keep you in line, and if you're going to be late because your hormones are so out of control you have to abuse yourself before you can meet your obligations, we'll add extra time to your punishment."

"Goodie. Just what I always wanted. More time on my knees with you."

His jaw went tight, and he leaned in close. For a moment I thought he might kiss me, but he reached past me for the doorknob instead. "As you wish, Miss Fallon."

I brushed past him, trying to ignore the delicious and smoky scent of him that reminded me of sin and all the things we could do in a confessional booth. *Man . . . this priest has really brought my undiscovered fetishes to light.*

"Shall I assume the position, then?" I asked as I breezed into the space.

He swallowed, and the tightly balled fists at his sides told me everything I needed to know. "As much as I enjoy seeing you on your knees before me, I'm afraid we have other matters to tend to before we get there."

"And will the other sinners be joining us tonight? Or will this 'matter' be for my benefit alone?"

The slight twitch of his lips sent a zing of arousal through me. How could I be so completely turned on by Noah, consumed by thoughts of what had almost happened between us, and then turn around and get wet for Caleb? *Don't forget what almost happened with Kingston . . . and what* did *happen with Alek.* Maybe Moira was right about all this. I shoved the reminders away. Thinking about them when I was already feeling some kind of way was not going to help me get through whatever Caleb had in store.

"Your punishment is yours to serve and benefit from alone."

"Can't wait. So . . . if I'm not going to be kneeling, what am I going to do?" I glanced around to see if I could get a hint of what to expect.

He gestured to the simple chair in the center of the sparsely decorated room. "You may choose your punishment tonight. You put the safety of everyone in your class at risk by spilling the blood of Callie Donoghue. As challenging as she may be, you broke a cardinal rule. Blood is a trigger for many of us. And some are less controlled than others."

"But I didn't—" I broke off, frustration leaking through my voice. Then I sighed. "Never mind. It's not like you're going to believe me anyway. No one else ever does. What are my choices? Polish a crucifix? Write lines from the Bible? How does one repent for something they never did?"

A flash of something like tenderness passed over his features. "You may choose tedium or something more . . . direct." His gaze flicked to a large bowl on his desk. "This bowl contains fifty-nine glass beads mixed in with identical beads of pure silver. Pick out every silver bead until only the glass ones remain. Endure the pain, and our session will be done sooner."

175

I wasn't known for my patience, so having to do such tedious menial work sounded like absolute torture. I wasn't afraid of the silver burning my flesh, but what the hell was the point of sorting beads? What was it going to teach me, besides more creative ways to curse as the stupid things slipped through my fingers, making me have to fish them out over and over again?

"What's behind door number two?" I asked, glancing over at him.

"Corporal punishment."

"Wait what? You're going to beat me?"

I swear to God, his palm twitched. "Spank. Not beat."

Why . . . why did that make my insides flutter? "I'm sorry, I think I just had a stroke. Did you say you were going to spank me? Like I've been a naughty girl? What the hell kind of university is this?"

"You have been. And, yes, if you choose this punishment, I'll put you over my knee and spank your insolent arse until you can't sit down without a reminder of what my palm felt like on your skin."

I had to look away; the intense searing heat of his gaze had me all twisted up inside. Made me want exactly what he was offering. *Wait. Was I actually considering this? Did I want to feel Father Gallagher's hand smacking my behind?*

Yes. Yes, I did.

What did that say about me?

Fuck it. It would be over faster than bead counting, and while everyone would see the welts silver would leave on my fingers, no one would be the wiser if he left marks on my ass. He probably didn't think I would ever even consider it. Well, the joke was on him. He wanted to spank me? Fine.

"I await your decision, Miss Fallon."

"Do it." I jerked my chin up, infusing my gaze with as

much defiance as I could muster. "Shall I bend over the desk, or . . ."

He took in a sharp breath, loud in the cavernous office, then with carefully controlled steps, made his way to the chair and sank down. "Over my knee."

I stared at him for a long, drawn-out moment, still not entirely sure this was happening. His chest rose and fell, his nostrils flaring slightly as he fought to control his own breathing. He raised a challenging brow. Like he was calling my bluff.

But I wasn't bluffing.

I walked over, my hands twitching slightly with nerves. Standing in front of him, I moved to bend over his lap, humiliation rearing its ugly head. I fought through the emotion because I'd be damned if he'd see what this cost me.

"Bare bottom, Sunday. That's the only way this works. Purification through pain. Skin to skin is more painful."

I snapped my head up to look at him. "You've got to be kidding me! There's no way people actually let you do this."

"You're the first to choose my hand over the beads. Would you care to change your decision? I could also get a paddle if you'd like?"

It was on the tip of my tongue to tell him to go to hell, but for some reason, it was more important to me to prove something to him. Or maybe to myself. I'd picked this path. It was time to see it through.

"Just get on with it," I gritted out, shimmying out of my compression tights until they were around my thighs.

A low rumble curled from his chest, and he reached for me, grabbing my wrist and tugging until I was laid across his lap, my feet barely touching the ground, hands bracing myself on the exposed portion of the chair. I could feel every rigid muscle in his thighs. Could smell his dark and deadly scent. Could feel the tension between us snap tight as piano wire.

His large, cool palm brushed across the back of my thigh before caressing my ass cheek. "Brace yourself, and with every strike, own your mistake."

I didn't know how I was supposed to think about anything other than the feel of his skin pressing against mine. But sure. I'd think about my mistakes. Namely, this one right here. How the hell was I supposed to hide what he was doing to my body if the evidence was dripping down my thighs?

And why was I reacting like this? He was punishing me, for God's sake, and here I was practically panting in his lap, begging for it.

When the crack of his palm against my flesh sounded, I jerked in his lap, a soft gasp exploding out of me.

It hurt. More than I thought it would. But I also liked it far more than I expected to. That must be at least part of the reason I couldn't help the urge to be disobedient, because just one taste of Caleb's hand on me and I was addicted. I wanted more.

"Do you repent?"

"No," I growled.

"So be it."

His hand found me again, this time raining down on the other cheek. I could feel the impression of his palm searing my flesh, the sting sharp and then fading away to a warm glow. I was tingling everywhere. I'd never been so aware of the air on my skin.

He didn't lift his hand this time. Instead, he circled the place he'd connected with and squeezed.

"God give me strength to deal with you, Sunday Fallon."

Then his palm was gone, but I felt the air shift as he landed another blow on my already stinging cheek.

I grunted, the sound low and needy. *More. I needed more.* "Harder, Daddy."

His sharp gasp followed by a growl of, "I told you not to call me that," echoed through to my core, making me clench my thighs. Then he shifted his hips, and oh, my fucking God, was that an erection?

When his next blow landed, I nearly went cross-eyed from the pain. He'd been holding back, but he really let me have it that time. The part of me that couldn't resist goading him whispered through my mind, *He's getting off on this.* Spoiler, so am I.

"Is that all you've got?"

I lifted my hips as he raised his hand once more, shifting just enough that his blow landed, not on my ass, but on the drenched lips of my pussy. This time, I cried out, but not from pain. Fuck, he was going to make me come.

The twitch below my breasts told me I might not be the only one.

"More," I groaned, begging now for something far different than his hand against my ass. I wanted friction between my legs to send the buzz coursing through my veins straight to my clit, building up to sweet relief.

"You like this? You like what I'm doing to you?" His words were colored with rough desire, tight and low.

"Yes. And so do you." I rubbed against his lap, feeling him grow thicker and longer as I did. "Admit it."

"Repent," he said, smacking my pussy again, this time on purpose, bringing me within an inch of the precipice.

"Never."

Not when being bad means I get to feel you doing this, I thought.

"Stubborn girl." This time his finger circled my throbbing clit, and I bucked against him, his own hips kicking up enough to tell me he was searching for more too.

I was so close. So fucking close. Just a little more and I'd be . . .

"Please," I begged. "More. Make me repent, Caleb."

"Yes," he hissed.

"God, who knew punishment could be so much fun?"

He shuddered under me, but his finger disappeared, his whole body tightening. "You're a lost cause. Get out of here."

My skin went cold, the warm tingles racing through me fleeing, leaving me numb and utterly humiliated. I pushed off him with shaking limbs, pulling my pants up and taking a step back. "Yeah, well, it takes one to know one, Father. And fuck you very much, by the way."

He didn't turn to watch me leave. He remained stoic and still as a statue, and I wondered if this had been his plan all along. Torture in the form of edging me to near insanity.

If so, well played.

TWENTY-TWO

"Ugh, this is ridiculous." I slammed shut the dusty old tome in front of me, very aware of the people around me and their disapproving stares. "What?" I shot them dirty looks, annoyed that no one would come near me after the incident with Callie.

It had been this way since I arrived at Ravenscroft. The students—aside from Moira, Alek, and Noah—avoided me and whispered behind my back. But since I nearly killed Callie with my bare hands in Sanderson's class, it was worse. Now, instead of hushed conversations and stolen glances, it was outright fear and avoidance. I was used to that kind of treatment at home, my grandfather being disgusted by my inability to shift, my father abandoning me in favor of numbing his issues with alcohol, but I'd truly hoped it would be different here. Naively, I'd thought this would be my fresh start. Guess I was wrong. As usual.

A low voice whispered in my ear, nearly sending me skyrocketing out of my chair. "A woman as beautiful as you should never wear such a tragic frown."

I turned my head to see Alek leaning over me, my braid

grasped in between his thick fingers. He booped me on the nose with the end of it, tickling me and making me laugh despite the heaviness of my thoughts.

"Do they send you to some kind of Viking charm school as children? That was smooth."

"No. My brother and I are special. Our parents and their love story are a bit legendary where I come from. My father ensured we were well equipped to live up to the rumors he and my mother inspired. He's a notoriously swoony moth-erfucker. I learned from the best."

I wondered for a moment what it must've been like growing up with a loving family. Parents who cared about what happened to me, about who I became without it being something that served them. In my case, all I was good for was my family legacy. If I couldn't be who they wanted, they didn't want *me*.

"If I ever meet your parents, I'll be sure to let them know they did a good job."

"Oh, they would love that. My mother and aunt have been obsessing over my brother and me settling down since we were ten. Ever since they got their happily ever afters, they're determined we all need them." He rolled his eyes like it was a nuisance and then grinned. "Can't say they don't make an impression, though. Once you've seen the real thing, there's no way you'll settle for anything less."

"So you have a brother? That means there are *two* of you running around breaking hearts. Why isn't he here?"

Alek's grin turned mischievous, and he straddled the seat next to me, leaning close. "Can I let you in on a little secret?"

Intrigued, I closed the distance between us until our faces were an inch apart. "Always."

He narrowed his eyes playfully and then held up his

hand, his pinky finger extended. "Swear yourself to secrecy first, Sunny. I have to know you can be trusted."

Butterflies fluttered in my belly at the thought of sharing something with him. I wrapped my pinky around his and whispered, "I swear."

As soon as our skin connected, Alek jerked back as if he'd been shocked, his eyes flaring wide. "Allfather above, I haven't felt that much power raging through someone since I left home. Are you all right? That has to be a lot to keep under control."

"You can feel that? I thought it was just me."

He gripped my face between both large palms and stared deep into my eyes as though he was searching for something. "Untamed. That's what you are."

"That's how it feels. I don't know how to control it. I feel like there are these weird surges through me. You saw what happened with Callie. I nearly killed her and then got punished for it." I had to fight a shiver at the memory of Caleb's hand on my ass . . . and between my legs. Shoving the thought away, I asked, "What if next time I don't stop?"

His eyes searched mine, considering. "What if I help you learn? Then next time, you won't have to worry."

"How could you possibly understand what this feels like? You're a Viking mage, a demi-god."

"I have berserker blood running through my veins. They're not exactly the most level-headed bunch, and while I didn't inherit their gifts, I did inherit their tempers. I had to learn from an early age how to control my emotions, else they'd play havoc with my power. And, well, not to brag, but when you're as strong as me . . . that's problematic, to say the least."

I studied him, his rugged, handsome features making my heart beat fast. He was a warrior, even without the berserker bloodline. Stronger than most, built to fight. Maybe he could help me. "I've been working with Father Gallagher to find my wolf, center myself, but maybe this is something else. Maybe you could teach me how to rein in this need I have for war all the time?"

"Absolutely. I'm sure the priest has been helpful with the more mental things, but what you need is physical."

A shiver worked its way through me, and it took everything in me not to make it obvious how his words affected me.

"When you learn to control your body, you can control all parts of yourself. Think of it like a muscle. You have to work it out, build it up, and once you learn how to isolate that part of yourself, you can call on it at will."

"A muscle. Okay." I thought back to the gym we had on the Fallon estate, trainers there working with the pack members who were our security. They pushed and trained hard so they'd be able to respond if there was a threat, not so they could fight whenever they were angry. Focus and determination ruled them. Control. That was what I needed. "So . . . you'll be like my trainer. You'll whip me into shape."

His lips curled up in a sexy grin. "If it's whips you want, I'm your man."

I had to tear my gaze from his mouth. I wasn't sure about whips, but I was sure about him. "Okay, let's do it. Caleb trains my mind. You train my body."

"When do you want to start?"

"Start what?"

I heard him before I saw him. Kingston. My wolf stretched and pushed at her confines the moment his voice brushed over my skin.

Rolling my eyes, I turned in my chair to find him seated on my other side, leering. "Training."

"That's my job. Father Gallagher set it up, remember? You were there when he suggested it."

I bristled. "That's not what this is. You're supposed to help with my wolf, not my control. Not fighting."

"It's the same thing. You'd understand that if you could shift. But since you can't, you'll have to trust the expert."

Expert? The gall of this asshole.

"And who's that?" Alek asked dryly. "You?"

"I'm certainly more of an expert on the topic of who she is. Who she's meant to be."

Alek scoffed, his eyes turning an electric shade of blue. "Down boy," he commanded, right as the chair Kingston was sitting on disappeared and he crashed down hard on the library floor. His mouth opened to protest, but no sound came out. "And why don't you keep quiet while you're at it?"

The laugh escaped me involuntarily, prompting a withering glare from Kingston. "Alek, let him talk. It's all he has."

"Are you sure? He's so much more pleasant to be around like this."

The commotion had called the attention of other students and the librarian. Soon, we'd be caught, and Alek would likely end up punished because of his abuse of magic. There was no reason both of us needed to be in the doghouse. "Yeah. He's right anyway. I need to work on both things at the same time. Controlling my anger and my wolf."

Alek looked at Kingston with a severe expression. "That mouth of yours is going to get you in trouble one day. Be thankful she's here to protect you. I won't be so tolerant the next time you piss me off." Then his eyes flared that brilliant azure color once more, and the library was filled with the sound of Kingston's tirade.

Profanity, loud and plentiful, flew from Kingston, warranting a strong word of warning from the librarian. Kingston gritted his teeth and clenched his fists, his whole body trembling from the effort to restrain himself.

"My goodness, Kingston. I thought you had more *control* in you than that," I teased. "Maybe you and I should both work with Alek to get better at it."

Alek's brows lifted in amusement. "Always happy to help. I'd gladly offer my services to you both. But I should warn you, Kingston. I can be a bit of an arsehole. You might not enjoy it."

"Fuck your services." Kingston turned his focus to me. "Sunday, I'll expect you to join me in the clearing by the lake tonight for our first session. If you don't show up, I'll come get you, toss your ass over my shoulder, and cart you out to your lesson. Understood?"

"How 'bout this," Alek drawled. "We'll both be there. And if you have a problem with that, you can air your grievances with my fist in your face."

Kingston's eyes glowed a deep amber, a feral growl building in his chest. But before he could answer, the librarian approached.

"Whatever . . . this is," she gestured between us. "Needs to end. Here and now. I don't care for pissing matches, and certainly not in my library. Take it outside, or you three can visit the headmistress."

Realizing the only one who could put an end to this was me, I sighed. "Sorry. We're leaving."

She glared at us over her half-moon spectacles once

more for good measure before adding. "See that you do. With haste." Then she turned on her heel and stomped off.

"Tonight. Both of you. At the clearing. But for now? Leave me the fuck alone. I'm already in enough trouble as it is."

T he tension rolling off Sunday was strong enough to set my blood boiling as we stood together in the clearing. There was definitely something going on between her and the shifter, though it was unclear if either of them knew exactly what it was. All I knew was he set her on edge, and it made me want to knock his teeth down his throat.

"So . . . this isn't awkward at all," Sunday said, looking between us.

I realized Kingston and I had been sizing each other up for the better part of the last few minutes, both waiting to see which of us would cave first. I wouldn't give him the satisfaction. Instead, I'd teach him exactly who he was dealing with. They didn't call my father the Warrior of Odin for nothing. And I was every inch my father's son.

"Here's how this is going to work," I said.

"Oh, so you're in charge now?" Kingston snapped.

"Yup."

"Put your dicks away. I'm in charge here. This is my

training session, and I'm the ticking time bomb, so handle with fucking care."

Sunday stepped between us, her anger and frustration palpable as she spoke.

I could feel power crackling through her. A storm about to break. Recalling a technique my brother and I put into practice regularly, I summoned my magic and created a target for Sunday . . . using Kingston as the dummy. Something about him taking on the form of Sunday's rival seemed fitting. From arsehole to bitch. Appropriate for a wolf.

"Seriously? Her?" Sunday stared at the fake Callie I'd conjured, disgust plain on her face.

"Do I threaten you so much you can't even deal with my likeness?" I made the conjured image of Callie sneer in her voice. Kingston pushed back against my magic, clearly not liking the sounds coming from his mouth. Maybe I'd gone too far, but Sunday needed to be poked and prodded if we were going to learn anything about her triggers.

"How exactly is this supposed to help her with her wolf?" Kingston asked, clearly unimpressed with his new body. You think he'd be thankful I at least gave him use of his own voice.

"The idea is to test her limits. Sunday wants to learn control, so we need to push her to her breaking point. The only way to do that in a safe scenario is to make it feel as real as possible. Thus . . . her nemesis."

"Why do I have to wear the chick suit? You already have the man bun. You wear the tits."

"Just be thankful I only made you look like her. I could change your voice permanently if I wanted to."

"Hello, I'm right here, and I can tell you right now, we don't need to turn Kingston into Callie for me to kick his ass. Just say the word, and I'll have him on the ground in no time," Sunday huffed.

My lips twitched, and I moved to stand behind her, placing one hand on each of her shoulders. "You told me you felt most out of control during your fight with Callie. We're going to recreate the scenario, and you're going to harness and use your anger without letting it overtake you."

Taking a long, slow breath, she nodded. "Okay. Lemme at her."

Kingston growled. "I'm not going to forget this, Nordson."

"Good. Maybe next time you'll remember who you're dealing with. Because if you think *that* is the extent of what I can do, you clearly need to freshen up on your Norse mythology."

Sunday shrugged. "Or watch a Marvel movie."

This time I was the one who growled. "The number of liberties they took with those fucking movies . . . do not get me started, Sunday. Trust me, it's not remotely the same thing."

"Aw, does the big bad Viking have issues with Thor and Loki? Give me five minutes alone with Tom Hiddleston and I—"

"Enough," I grunted. "Get to work."

"What am I supposed to do? Just stand here like this?" Kingston asked, twirling a piece of hair on his finger. He glanced down at the curvy frame he sported. "On second thought . . ."

"Attack."

Sunday narrowed her focus on Callie's doppelgänger and balled her hands into fists. "I don't want to kill him."

"You won't," I promised. "Focus on your movements,

not your emotions. When your anger pushes you to react, I want you to ignore it. At least for now. The purpose of this exercise is to subdue, not harm. Just like in class."

I ran my fingers up the sides of her neck, working the muscles to center her. I could feel her pulse beating like a caged bird fluttering in vain for freedom, but she nodded. "Subdue, not harm. Got it."

Kingston seemed to settle into his role after my little speech. He began taunting her with a surprisingly good impression of the vampire. "You pathetic little nobody. You think you're remotely on my level? On my worst day, you aren't even close. Thorne's taking pity on you. All he wants you for is your blood."

The air around Sunday crackled with energy, a feeling akin to the atmosphere just before lightning struck. The ends of her hair lifted, just enough I noticed, and with a calming palm between her shoulders, I murmured against the shell of her ear, "You can do this, *Kærasta*."

Everything stopped the moment the endearment fell from my lips. Why was I calling her that? It wasn't a word used lightly. For the men in my family, hailing all the way back to my grandfather's time, it was the term reserved for their true mates. The woman who called to their soul. I had absolutely no business using it with Sunday. Did I?

Her rage didn't ease as it should have because I lost my damned focus and had taken my hand off her. Before I could fix what I'd broken, she lunged, a wild growl tearing from her chest. I released the magic keeping Kingston in the form of Callie to give him a fighting chance at subduing Sunday.

Kingston, thankfully, seemed to realize something had changed because he dropped all pretense, his body language shifting as he prepared to intercept her. Amber flashed in his eyes as his beast merged with his human form.

"Sunday," he growled, his voice lower and filled with authority, "stop."

He'd used an Alpha's command, I realized. But he wasn't Sunday's Alpha. And she wasn't obeying.

"No. I'll never stop fighting you. All you want is to command me, control me." Sunday pinned him, possessing a strength she shouldn't have. Kingston was the next in line to take the position of prime Alpha of his pack. He was more powerful than most wolves, built to defend and protect. But the small, curvaceous woman straddled him and held him down. "I can't stop."

Well, this didn't go as expected.

TWENTY-FOUR

SUNDAY

Anger boiled in my veins, uncontainable and near painful. My skin felt like a live wire had touched it, an electric current racing across every exposed inch. All I knew was I needed to dominate this threat in front of me. Kingston was here to take my freedom, just like everyone else in my life had done from the time I was born. I wouldn't cave to him.

A growl ripped from somewhere deep in my chest as I gripped his shoulders and pinned him to the ground. Searing pain burned through my fingertips where they dug into his skin, making his eyes widen.

"Sunday!" Alek shouted in panic.

"Stop. I've got this," Kingston said. "Just go. You've done enough."

Alek's palm hovered over my shoulder. I could feel his energy even though he didn't touch me, wasn't in my line of sight. It should've unnerved me that I knew he was right there without seeing him. But I was too focused on the wannabe Alpha in my grasp.

"You're still a cocky asshole, Kingston. Even when I've got you beat."

Kingston's eyes narrowed, that powerful jaw clenching before he closed his eyes and took a long breath. One tattoo-covered arm lifted, and I tensed, ready to tear him to shreds if he tried anything, but he cupped my cheek gently, making me uneasy. Then his eyes flicked open, and that penetrating gaze of his locked onto me, his wolf talking to mine. I relaxed just a fraction, my nipples doing the opposite, responding to my wolf's call to take him as hers. His large palm slid down my body, between my breasts, until he rested at the curve of my waist. When he brought up the other hand and rested them both on my hips, I couldn't help but take in a sharp breath.

"That's it," he whispered encouragingly. "Focus on my wolf. You don't want to hurt us, Sunshine."

He was right. The haze of rage and the need to fight began trickling out of me. But I still couldn't let him win.

Kingston must have read it in my body language. A shudder ran through him, as if he'd reached a decision he wasn't entirely sure about. Then, still holding my gaze, he slowly tipped his chin up, baring his throat to me in submission.

My heart fluttered, frantic and wild. He'd submitted. Wait. He'd *submitted*? Holy shit.

"Only for you, Sunday." His words were breathy, as though this had cost him everything.

"What the hell just happened?" Alek asked, his voice low and cautious. "You just let her dominate you? You're an Alpha. I've never seen it done."

Kingston looked over my shoulder at Alek, a growl working its way up his throat. "You can leave now. I don't have to explain anything to you."

Alek hesitated behind me. I could still feel his presence looming.

"It's okay," I told him. "We'll be fine."

The weight of Kingston's hands on me, the way his fingers dug into my flesh, paired with the obvious erection in his jeans, had me wondering if what I'd just said was true. Would we be fine? Or would I do something I'd regret?

"If you're sure . . ."

"He won't hurt me."

Emotion flickered in Kingston's eyes, there and then gone. "I would never hurt you, Sunday. You're my mate. All I've ever wanted to do was protect you."

Why did that strike such a chord inside me? I hadn't ever let the idea of him as my mate take hold because it wasn't going to happen. I was damaged goods, and once he realized it, he'd send me away. Replaced and disgraced. But now? Every word he'd just said rang with absolute truth and honesty.

I opened my mouth to speak, but no words escaped. I was too swept up in my confusion.

Alek must have realized he was definitely intruding on something more than wolf dynamics because I heard his footsteps as he walked off. "I'll check in on you later," he called. But it felt more like a warning for Kingston than a promise to me.

"Alone at last," Kingston murmured, rolling his hips a fraction.

I was ashamed to admit how much my wolf wanted to respond, to let him claim me as his mate.

"As much as I enjoy the experience of you on top of me, maybe you could do something about those claws? I have plenty of body piercings already."

Glancing down to where my fingers were dug into his

chest, I gasped at the sight of his blood seeping through the thin gray Henley he wore. How the hell had I done that?

I pulled my hands away, my heart racing when instead of fingers I saw long, sharp claws.

"What the fuck?"

"You know what it means. Only Alphas can partially shift."

No. I wasn't an Alpha. While I'd been born a beta, I'd been treated as little more than breeding stock and political fodder once my wolf refused to appear. "But I didn't know I was doing it."

He sat up, me still straddled across his lap, one arm around my waist, holding me close.

"Doesn't matter. Your wolf knew what she was doing. She's trying to come out. You need to free her. She wants me to help her . . . to make her mine."

He leaned in and ran his nose along the side of my neck, pulling a shiver through me. Those lips brushed my skin, followed by the flick of his tongue and a distinctly round metal ball which had to be one of the piercings he'd mentioned.

"You want it too, Sunday. Just give in. Why are you fighting it?" A low growl escaped him on the last word. "Why toy with the vampire's emotions? You're wasting his time. You belong to me. You've *always* belonged to me."

He was rocking us back and forth, his hand now knotted in my hair, teeth grazing my shoulder as he ground his hard cock against my crotch. Thank God I was wearing pants, or he'd know what he was doing to me.

"Say. You're. Mine." That fucking growl again.

"Don't tell me what to do."

My protest was weak even to my own ears, my wolf begging for what she wanted.

200

"Just give in. You know I'll make it good for you. I'll take care of you."

He nipped my neck, right where he'd give me a mating mark if I'd let him. I nearly came on the spot. Damn pheromones. They were clouding my judgment.

"I don't need you to take care of me. I can make it good on my own."

He licked his way up my neck to my ear. "Think about how much better it'd feel if I were buried inside you. Giving you my knot."

Jesus, what was wrong with me? My thighs clenched, and I had to grit my teeth to stop the wave of need that sent through me. Primal. That was what this was between us. Different from anything with Noah or Alek . . . hell, even Caleb. I couldn't deny it even if I wanted to. Even if I should.

He tore his shirt off his body with one hand, revealing thick muscles and swirling tattoos. His chest was a work of art, accentuated by barbell piercings in his nipples. God, he was hot, but had that been a question I'd ever had? No. There was no denying how sexy Kingston Farrell was.

Then his big hand slipped down and under the waistband of my yoga pants, delving between my legs to where I was slick with desire. I couldn't fight my moan or the way my hips rolled forward, my clit begging for attention.

"Fuck, Sunday. I knew it. I could smell how badly you want this." His fingers slid deeper, teasing my entrance. "Say the word, and I'll mount you here and now."

I wanted it. God, I wanted it so badly. It would be so easy to give in. To let myself be his and finally feel the connection everyone said was there when a mate bond was formed. I whimpered when one finger sank inside me.

"Fuck, you're tight. Saving yourself for me? God, that's so fucking sexy." He nuzzled deeper into my neck, the warmth of his breath pebbling my skin. When he spoke again, his voice was a deep growl I felt straight in my core. "Good girl."

His mouth pressed to my shoulder, followed by the pressure of teeth as he carefully bit down. Panic shot through me. If I let him do this, bond with me, mark me there, it would be something I couldn't come back from. I'd be his.

Shoving with all my might, I pushed him away. I landed on my ass in the dirt and must've caught him off guard because he stared in shock.

"No. You don't get to mark me."

His eyes flashed with frustration as I got to my feet. "Dammit, Sunday. Why the fuck not? We were born for each other. This is our destiny."

"I'm meant for more than being your breeding bitch, and that's all a mate is good for in my pack."

"Who the hell said that's what I expect? It doesn't have to be that way."

I propped a hand on my hip. "Oh really? *Giving you my knot.*" I did an impression of him that brought a flash of amusement to his eyes. "You want to breed me just like any Alpha wants to breed their mate. It's who you are."

He pushed to his feet. "Of course I do. That's our nature. It doesn't mean I expect you to stay at home barefoot and pregnant. We can have fun practicing before we start reproducing. Imagine me taking care of you during your heat."

My wolf said yes, but my heart said run. "No. I am not here to let you claim me. Either help me with my wolf or leave me alone. No more of . . . this."

"Maybe *this*"—he gestured between us—"is exactly what you need. Maybe your stubborn refusal to give in is the only thing standing in your way. Ever think about that, Sunshine?"

I had to grit my teeth against the bitter retort I wanted to hurl his way. Instead, I shook my head. "Maybe. But it's not your call to make. I get to decide. And right now, I need more time before I'm ready to take that step. You won't give me that, so we're done here."

I didn't give him a chance to respond. I walked away without looking back, but my wolf was angry, growling at me all the way to the dorm.

CHAPTER
TWENTY-FIVE
SUNDAY

"And then he got all snarly and possessive about it, trying to mark me. And being all 'You know you want me, Sunday.'"

Moira flicked her gaze to me through the mirror as she finished applying her massive batwing eyeliner. Somehow that woman made it look amazing, but I knew if I tried, I'd look like Harley Quinn got left out in the rain.

"Wait a minute, you're saying he tried to *force* a mate mark on you?" Her eyes flashed with violet sparks of power. "I'll kill him."

Her threat of violence on my behalf made me feel oddly squishy inside. Though, in this case, her anger wasn't warranted. "Down, girl. I didn't say he forced me. He just forced the issue. He stopped when I told him to."

She turned around on the stool in front of the vanity and assessed me. Her hair fell in long platinum waves all the way to her waist today. It made her look like a faerie.

"Ooookay, I guess I don't really understand the problem then. He was helping you. He stopped when you asked him to. You said he even brought out more of your wolf. Why are you mad?"

"Because I—" I stopped. Why *was* I so upset? "Because he—" A growl of frustration slipped out. "Because I don't want to feel that way about him." And *I'm already feeling that way about someone else. Several someones.*

"Do you think he's not your mate? That they were wrong when you were matched?"

I wanted to say yes. That would certainly make things easier. But the truth was, there was very clearly something between us. There had been even on the night we'd been brought together by our packs.

"No. It's just. After I rejected him, Kingston went out of his way to make my life hell. We weren't in the same pack, but that didn't matter. Our community rallied around him, and he did nothing to lessen their reaction. After that night, I was completely ostracized and never got to set foot off pack land again. Until now. It's hard to just put all that aside because of some cosmic bond."

Moira twirled a lock of hair around her finger, then released it, over and over as she let my words sink in. "Remind me why you rejected him? I've always heard it was nearly impossible for mates to avoid the pull."

Memories of that day swirled through my mind, filling me with guilt and shame once more. "Because in order to accept the bond, you have to shift. And I couldn't. Rejecting him was the only way to protect my family's legacy. Not that it mattered in the end. Word got out anyway, but it was the only thing I could do to try and prevent that from happening."

"I see. And what happens once your wolf finally appears? Will you reject him again?"

No, my wolf vehemently protested. She wanted our mate. If she was the one to choose, it wasn't a choice at all.

"I never really thought about it, to be honest. I mean, I didn't expect him to want me after that, so what did it matter?"

She shrugged and got to her feet, her layers upon layers of bracelets filling the air with a metallic jangle. "I suppose if I knew someone was my mate, even though I rejected them once . . . or in your case, eleventy-billion times, I'd want to be on good terms with them. Because it sounds like he's never going to *not* be yours."

I opened my mouth to argue and then immediately closed it again. I hated to admit it, but the witch had a point. "There's just so much bad blood between us now. Can we really just pretend all that never happened?"

"No. I never said you should pretend it didn't happen. That part of your story is written. But the rest is still blank, and you are in charge of where it goes." She winked. "To a point. There are some things fate has sway over. He's acting like a wounded animal. Lashing out, protecting himself from a threat. I wouldn't let what happened when he was hurt keep you from giving him a chance to prove himself worthy of you now. You were teenagers then. A lot can happen to change someone over the years."

I hadn't ever stopped to consider the reason Kingston had said such awful things. I assumed, perhaps naively, that it was bruised pride. But was it possible he'd been hurt? Something shifted in me at the possibility. Was I the bad guy here? All this time, I'd painted Kingston as the villain, but maybe it was me.

Fuck. And then I had to go rub salt in the wound time and time again when all he was doing was listening to the instincts of his wolf trying to repair things with his mate.

Guilt started to eat at me. I worried at my bottom lip, casting Moira a sideways glance. "I think I, uh, might have overreacted. Maybe. Just a little."

"I'd be inclined to agree."

Ouch. Couldn't she sugarcoat it, even just to spare my feelings? Then an even worse thought took hold. *Crap.*

"I'm going to have to apologize to him, aren't I?"

"Sorry, but yeah."

She murmured a soft incantation under her breath, and a small kitchen appeared in the corner of our room. I swear she made the space bigger somehow. The countertop was filled with containers of sugar, flour, cocoa, butter, and anything else someone might need for baking.

"Um, did I just step into an episode of Bake Off? What's happening?"

"Oh, hush, babycakes. The way to a man's heart is through his stomach. Especially a wolf. Make him lick the icing off your cupcakes, and he'll come around."

"And by cupcakes, are you speaking figuratively, or . . ."

Moira winked. "Maybe if you're lucky, he'll lick both. Now get that sweet ass over here and start measuring."

TWO HOURS LATER, I strolled down the hall on the second floor, where I knew his room was. My palms were sweaty as I held the platter filled with chocolate cupcakes, complete with a cherry center. He might laugh in my face or throw the cupcakes in the trash, but at least I tried. When I reached his dorm room door, I forced myself to take a deep breath and shore up my confidence. I was a strong, capable, badass bitch. I could do this.

The door swung open before I could knock a third time,

revealing a shifter I'd seen Kingston with before. I believed his name was Derek. He gave me a lazy grin, his white teeth bright and perfectly straight. I bet his dad was a dentist or something.

"Hello there, princess. What in the world brings you here?" He took a long sniff of the air around me. "Mmmm, you smell delicious." His pitch dark eyes flashed with mischief.

Since the last thing I needed was another eager male sniffing around my lady parts, I glanced around him, trying to peer over his wide shoulders. "Is Kingston here? I baked these for him."

He leaned against the doorframe, crossing his insanely large arms over his chest. The dark tattoos swirling around his biceps and shoulder nearly blended in with his warm brown skin. "He's not here. He went out to the clearing to work off some . . . tension. Maybe you should come in, and we can pretend you baked them for me. I'm much more fun."

Even though he could give Michael B. Jordan a run for his money in the looks department, there wasn't even the flicker of a spark. Which was a bit of a relief. I had my hands full enough trying to juggle the men I already had in my life. I didn't need to add anyone else to the roster.

"That's probably true, but I'm not interested." I gave him a sweet but firm smile. "Can you just make sure he gets these?"

"Will do, doll."

I offered him a pointed stare. "Don't eat them."

He gave me a suspicious look. "Why? Whatcha do to them? Poison 'em or something?"

"Missed opportunity. If I was trying to get back at him

MEG ANNE & K. LORAINE

for something, don't think for one second I'd hesitate to have Moira hex them with a hair loss spell."

He ran a hand over his smooth head. "Guess I'm safe then. Might be worth the risk."

"At least wait until Kingston gets one. He should have the first bite. After all, they're cherry. His favorite."

"What'd he do to get you to give him your cherry?" he asked with a wink.

"He hasn't gotten it yet."

Derek let out a low whistle. "Damn, girl. It's not too late to change your mind and come inside. I could help you out with that. I like my girls feisty."

"Pass. Thanks." I handed him the cupcakes and turned on my heels, needing to get to Kingston so I could apologize before his roommate ate all the treats I'd made.

"Well, you know where to find me," he called after me.

I held up my hand in a noncommittal wave, beelining for the clearing. I wanted this over with. Apologizing to Kingston would be about as pleasant as swallowing a box of knives. Come to think of it, the knives might hurt less.

As I reached the path that would lead me to the clearing we'd used for our training the night before, I caught his scent, the air punctuated by Kingston's heavy grunts.

Bingo.

"Take it, Sunshine. Take it and love it." His voice was tight, and it was then I realized the grunts weren't him working out. Not at all. Arousal coursed through me at the thought of him taking care of his needs out here, thinking of me.

How should I handle this? Should I leave him alone until he . . . finished? Do I offer a helping hand? My cheeks burned at the thought. I knew what he was packing. I might need both hands.

But as I stepped into the clearing, a cold pit formed in my stomach. He was working out his tension, all right. Balls deep inside some shifter girl he'd bent over a fallen log, his fingers tangled in her hair, other hand gripping her waist.

A soft gasp escaped my lips, and Kingston's eyes snapped to mine. Before I could even decide what to think or feel about the sight of him pounding into her, his face twisted in panic and pleasure, and he came with a loud growl.

"Sunday—"

The girl under him sighed. "My name is Heather."

I felt sick. This asshole wasn't different. He was still just as much of a dick as ever. "Fuck you, Kingston."

He pulled out of Hester, taking a step as if he was going to come after me. His shaft thick and glistening and . . . pierced.

Jesus, how many of those things were in there? Wait, no. Focus, Sunday. This is not the time.

"Wait, Sunday. This isn't what—okay, it is, but—"

I forced my gaze back to his face, fury replacing all other emotion. "And to think, I was here to apologize. You sonofabitch. You just couldn't wait to stick your dick in someone, anyone. It didn't matter if it was me or Hailey."

"Heather," the girl said again.

"Shut up," I growled. "Get out of here, Heidi."

Harley stood, righting her skirt and slinking off without another word. Smarter than I gave her credit for. Kingston strode toward me, cock swinging, still hard, still huge. The thing was a weapon of mass destruction, jutting from his hips. He needed to put it away before he hurt someone.

"You're the one who rejected me. What the fuck right do you have getting pissed at me? You can't have it both ways, Sunday. Either I'm yours, or I'm not. Make up your damn mind."

"Weren't you the one trying to complete our bond yesterday? How do you go from that to railing some random chick less than twenty-four hours later?"

"You. Left. Me." He came closer with every shouted word. "How I choose to drown my sorrows isn't your concern. If I want to bend Hannah over a tree and think about you while I fuck her, I will."

"Heather!" I automatically corrected, my stomach twisting at his words. But I was too angry to focus on any other emotion. He was the one in the wrong here, not me. "Don't even try to make this my fault. It was your dick inside her—"

"It could have been inside you, but you didn't want it. Remember?"

My wolf rallied inside me, just as angry as I was that her mate betrayed her. Fingers turning to claws, I forced myself to control the need to lash out. "You know what? I hope you choke on your cupcakes."

He blinked, confusion coloring his expression. "What?"

But I was already gone, running before he could see the tears threatening to fall from my eyes. I hated this. Hated that he made me feel this way. I just wanted to go back to regular old hating him, but I couldn't. That's why it hurt so much. He made me care. He told me he'd take care of me. Protect me. And then he turned around and rejected me right back.

So which one of us was the villain now?

TWENTY-SIX

THORNE

My skin crawled with unease. Everything felt off, like a song just slightly out of tune, my world disrupted by the lack of . . . something. No. Not something.

Someone.

My return to Ravenscroft was met with little fanfare. Not that I'd expected any. After dropping off my luggage in my room, I immediately set out in search of the one person I wanted to see more than anything. My Sunday.

This time of night, there was only one place she'd be, so I followed her scent deep into the part of the forest she preferred to use for her midnight runs. The time away had dulled my connection to her, raising a barrier between my thoughts and hers. Necessary, but that didn't mean I had to like it.

When I found her, she stood bathed in moonlight, the wind blowing tendrils of her hair free of the bun she'd piled on top of her head. Even with a diminished bond, I could sense the heaviness of her thoughts and taste her sadness in the air. I wanted to lick a line up her nape before dragging my teeth across her earlobe and whispering my devotion to her. To tell her exactly what I'd done for her.

As I neared the clearing, I purposely allowed my arms to brush against some branches to give her notice of my approach.

"Is that you, Caleb?"

My anticipation soured, coiling into jealousy. *The priest? Just what has my little dove been up to while I've been off burning bridges and ensuring the matter of our future was settled?*

"I'm about the furthest thing from a man of God you might find, I'm afraid," I said, stepping out into the soft moonlight.

"Noah." The elation in her eyes didn't last nearly long enough for me to appreciate. Those ocean-blue orbs narrowed, flashing with anger. "Where the hell have you been this past week?"

The venom in her tone took me aback. So my wolf had found her claws. "I had some important business to take care of. Unavoidable, I'm afraid."

"And you don't know how to pick up a phone? Or use a pen? Or a computer? Or fucking smoke signals? Maybe even a carrier bat . . . I think that's more your style than a pigeon."

I smirked at her undisguised jab. "Your tongue is sharp when you're angry." Crossing the clearing, I closed the distance between us, giving in to the itch under my skin, the need to touch her. "I'm sorry. I never intended to upset you. I had to leave unexpectedly, and telling anyone where I was going was out of the question."

"Oh. Well . . . is everything okay now?" Her body language and tone changed, softening as if my apology had taken some of the wind out of her sails. She'd obviously been prepared for a fight and hadn't expected it.

Even though she was no longer on the offensive, there was still some residual anger in the furrowed cast of her brows and lines bracketing her full lips. It was obvious my disappearance had hurt her, leaving a mark that would require more than words to soothe. The realization bolstered me because it meant she cared, making me even more confident I could repair any damage I'd inadvertently caused. Especially once she knew the reason I'd been away.

"It will be. But I have to do something first."

"What's that?"

Locking gazes with her, I cupped the back of her head and pulled her into me before bringing our lips together. The contact set my body ablaze with need and the powerful sense I was home. Right where I belonged.

Her palms rested on my chest as she moaned into my mouth, opening for me, letting my tongue dance with hers. I kissed her like a man might kiss the love of his life before going off to war, like she was the only thing keeping me alive. Because after what I'd done while I was gone, nothing was ever going to be the same. Life as I knew it was over, but life with Sunday was just beginning.

"Noah," she whispered, pulling back. "What's going on? You're so intense."

I laughed, feeling practically euphoric now that she was in my arms once more. "Comes with the territory. Vampires aren't known for their warm and snuggly personalities."

She shoved at my chest, but I didn't budge. I had no intention of letting her go any time soon. "You know what I mean. You're even *more* intense than usual. What has got you all riled up?"

Her fingers trailed up my arm, hand resting over the

traitor mark cuffing my bicep. The burn was deep and searing as the silver embedded in my skin shifted. One day, it would be nothing more than an annoyance, but as of now, it felt akin to a branding iron digging into my muscle. I hissed involuntarily and pulled back.

"What was that?" Her eyes widened, concern flashing in her gaze. "Are you hurt?"

The only way I could explain was to show her. With nimble fingers, I unbuttoned my shirt, deliberately keeping my movements slow because I'd never been so nervous. As certain as I was in my actions, I had no way of knowing how she'd react to the news.

My impromptu striptease also had the unintended side effect of distracting Sunday. Her eyes were drawn from my face to my chest as my shirt peeled away. Heat sparked in her expression. Hunger too. My body responded in kind. There was no universe in which I wouldn't want her, especially not when she looked at me like that.

"Right here? Now?" Then, instead of lodging the protest I'd expected to follow, she asked, "What if we get caught?" The excitement in her voice had me tucking that little display of kink away for later use. She wanted to be watched. I could make that happen for her. But now wasn't the time for sex.

"No, dove. I'm showing you why I was gone."

The lust heating her gaze fled as curiosity returned. "By getting naked?"

My shirt fluttered to the ground, and before I could direct her gaze to my mark, she gasped.

"A tattoo?"

I shook my head. "A brand."

She moved closer, her hand hovering just above the mark seared into my skin. It had taken days for my uncle

Lucas to etch the silver into my flesh. And twice as many more for it to heal enough for me to wear anything over it.

"Does it hurt?" she whispered, glancing from the angry red skin and back up to my face.

"Yes. But it's supposed to. It's the mark of a traitor."

"What? Why would you have that?"

"Because, my little wolf," I said, lifting my hand to cup her cheek. "I chose you."

Her brows drew together. "I don't understand."

"You're my mate. I feel it in my bones. After what happened the other day, when the barriers between our minds fell away, I know it beyond all doubt. And in my world, it's still a crime for royals to mate outside our own kind. My father murdered my grandfather to save the human he loved, to take her as his mate. His traitor mark is even bigger than mine because the Council views his crime as more egregious. But I'd rather be a traitor than give you up."

"But your father is king. How did that happen?"

I took a deep breath, not wanting to rehash the past. "It was a long time ago before I was born and a story for another night. But the end result is I am not going to live a life without my mate because the Council thinks they can dictate my life. I refuse to deny myself the only thing I've ever truly wanted."

She bit down on her lip, looking both hopeful and wary. "Okay . . . but I still don't understand how I can be both yours and Kingston's mate. How is it even possible?"

"Sunday," I said with a sigh, "what you don't realize is it doesn't matter. I chose you. That's it for me. You might have other mates, but I am yours. Wherever you go from here, I'll follow. I'm not going to run from it."

She smiled weakly. "I . . . I don't know what to say."

"Say I can be yours."

"I . . ."

I leaned down, my lips nearly touching hers. "It's true whether you say it or not . . . if it makes it easier for you to give in."

"Noah," she breathed, closing the distance between our lips and claiming mine in a spine-tingling kiss. She backed away just a fraction, her eyes staring into mine. "You're mine."

Her palm skated down my torso until she found my belt. My breath caught as she slipped her fingers over the obvious bulge at my crotch. I was aching for her. I always was, but now that she'd claimed me, I was desperate.

"So does this mean we need to go make things official in your bed?" she asked.

"I have a better idea."

Noah's fingers tightened in mine as we approached the doors of *Iniquity*, the bass thumping through the walls. It was nearing the witching hour, the prime time for creatures of the night to come out and play. "*Iniquity*? Really? I thought we were going to need something more . . . private."

"This is as private as it gets. Trust me." His smooth voice with that posh accent brushed over me like velvet, and I leaned against him in response. "You've only seen the surface level of this place. It's a whole new world downstairs."

"If you've brought me to some sort of sex dungeon for our first time together, I might like it too much, and then what are you going to do? What if this is the only thing that does it for me?"

"I'll give you whatever it is you need, dove. Wherever you need it."

Heat unfurled within me, the words and his dark voice weaving the same seductive spell as his lips or hands on my

223

body. I wanted everything he promised and more. Right the hell now.

"Do you trust me?"

"I've been told to never trust a vampire."

"I'm not asking you to trust any vampire. I'm asking if you trust *me*."

Taking a deep breath, I stared into molten amber eyes and knew he was telling the truth. I did trust him. "Lead the way."

He took me by the hand, lifting it to his mouth and pressing a kiss between my knuckles. Before pulling away, his tongue flicked the tender flesh where my index and middle fingers met. The action, while perfectly innocuous, left absolutely zero doubt about his intentions. The caress shot straight between my legs, and I gasped as my clit pulsed with need. I was on fire for this man, and he'd barely touched me. What would happen when he was inside me?

We walked through the doors, the air in the club heavy with the energy of the many powerful occupants. Witches, shifters, even some fae. All of them stretched their magic freely here. It was a safe space—except for that one time a hunter tried to kill me.

"Are we going to dance?" I asked.

"Not on the dance floor. I planned on a different kind of dance tonight."

I shivered with longing, already so aroused my thighs were slick, and I was regretting changing into a dress before we left the school.

We'd only navigated halfway around the dance floor when we were intercepted by a Bettie Page look-alike. Complete with a sexy leather corset dress, fishnets, and a whip.

"Why, Mr. Blackthorne, what a surprise." She turned

her blue eyes my way, her nostrils flaring slightly before a wide smile stretched across scarlet lips. "Ah, Ms. Fallon. I've heard so much about you."

"You have?" I asked, blinking away an unexpected wave of lust as her eyes swept down my body.

"Sunday, this is Lilith, the owner of *Iniquity*."

The crazy heightened lust fog hadn't cleared; every word from Noah made my thighs clench. He must've sensed the change in my body because his eyes darkened, and he let out a low growl.

Lilith laughed. "Seems like you two are in need of a room. Any special requests?"

"Room? Like . . . a sex room?"

She had to be a demon. The scent of brimstone tickled my nose as she looked at me, her eyes sparkling with amusement. "Oh, sweetheart. You have no idea, do you? I created *Iniquity* so that supernaturals could be free to explore their deepest desires in a safe and completely non-judgmental space. Here, sin isn't only allowed, it's encouraged." She winked, sending a bolt of lust spearing through me. "If you'll allow me . . ."

She reached out with black-tipped fingers and ran her hands down my shoulders and over my arms, sending tingles sparking across my skin until she finally wove our fingers together.

"Let me give you what you need. After all, your first time should be special."

My heart raced as the demon leaned close and pressed her lips to mine, inhaling deeply. It was just the barest touch, and yet sensation rolled through me, starting in my mouth and washing through my veins in a warm, soothing rush. When she backed away, I swayed on my feet, a state of euphoria enveloping me. It reminded me of the deep relaxation I felt after a massage.

"Ah, the gray room, I think. It will meet every desire the two of you share, and some you may not yet realize exist."

"I'm sure it will be perfect," Noah said, a secret smile playing about his mouth. "Thank you, Lilith."

Lilith didn't even glance his way, her eyes remaining trained on mine. "The pleasure will be entirely yours, Sunday."

She vanished before I could say anything in response, her body dissolving into a deep red mist. I turned toward Noah, mouth agape. "What the hell was that?"

He smirked and chuckled darkly. "That was Lilith. Legendary succubus and owner of this fine establishment."

"A succubus? Those are incredibly rare creatures. She's brilliant, hiding here in plain sight."

"She isn't in hiding. Lilith won *Iniquity* from Lucifer in a bet. But that's her story to tell."

"Don't Succubi feed off sexual energy?"

"Feed, induce, create . . . though, they will settle for any extreme emotion when hungry. Sex is their preferred love language, so to speak." He leaned in and nuzzled my neck. "It's why there is no monetary cost to utilize the rooms here. One night spent at *Iniquity* can give her enough energy to survive an entire month. It's a small price to pay."

"Smart woman, setting her business up that way."

"No arguments here. But enough about her. Let's focus on you and me."

He ran his tongue up my neck before nipping the tender flesh just below my jaw. My skin pebbled as fresh arousal that had nothing to do with Lilith hit me. "Yes."

"Come, dove, we have a room waiting for us."

Noah led me through a dark hallway, down a set of

stairs, and to an entire sublevel I hadn't known existed. While I'd expected a basement to be musty and dank, what I found was something completely different. Walls padded in leather-covered panels dampened the sound, making the space feel incredibly intimate. Red lights illuminated the area, creating a warm, inviting atmosphere, and velvet couches nestled in the corners were covered with lush pillows and soft-looking blankets. The couples who milled around seemed entirely focused on each other, none of them paying attention to us. But it was the soft, sensual music that filled the air that gave this place the ambiance that lived up to *Iniquity's* name.

This was a place where people did dark, dirty things without being judged. A place where you could give in to your fantasies and live out every scene you could dream of. A place where you could be wholly yourself. I was already more than a little infatuated.

Noah and I walked together, fingers twined, down a hall lined with doors, all identical and missing one key detail.

"Noah, there aren't any knobs on these doors. How are we supposed to get in?"

"Don't worry. We'll know which room is meant for us. Just keep going."

I nodded, my heart pounding as we kept moving forward. Until a door to my right swung open, revealing an empty room. "Bingo," I whispered.

Noah ushered me inside, the door gliding closed behind us. Once it clicked shut, the interior flickered into being. It was like stepping out of a luxurious hotel and straight into a castle from the most beloved fairy tale. A large—three times larger than normal—bed took up the center of the room with a canopy of gauzy curtains. Candles littered every surface, flickering merrily while offering subtle illumination. A fireplace roared to life as we moved deeper into the room, the flames casting dancing shadows on the rest of the space.

Something soft fluttered from the ceiling and landed on my arm. I frowned, staring down at the . . . petal? I plucked the velvet-soft red rose petal off my arm and tipped my face up. A gentle shower of red petals fell from the sky, slowly carpeting the ground and scenting the air with the bite of rose.

The only thing that felt out of place in the romantic setting Lilith provided for us was the frosted window cut into one of the four walls.

"What do you think that's for?"

Noah looked at me, his lips curling up in a sexy, secretive smile. "It would seem one of us has an exhibition kink."

The thought of being watched, of someone witnessing these most private, intimate moments, sent a thrill hurtling through me. I guess it wasn't much of a surprise which one of us he was referring to. "I think it's me."

"Or both of us."

"Is someone watching us now?" My mouth ran dry at the possibility.

Noah glanced to our left. "Doesn't look like anybody's there at the moment. But that could change at any time."

Swallowing past the lump in my throat, I pulled together all my courage and released his hand before I reached behind me and unzipped my dress, thankful for the low back and easy access. Noah sucked in a tight breath and brushed my hair over my shoulder so he could help me out of my clothes.

"Perfect and smooth," he murmured from behind me as he slipped one strap of my dress off my shoulder.

I shuddered with pure need when his lips brushed the space between my shoulders.

"Made for me." His voice was the barest whisper, but it seemed loud in the quiet of the room.

In that moment, with nothing but the warmth of the flames and the heat of his hands resting on me, I knew it to be absolutely, one hundred percent true. "Yes," I agreed.

"Are you going to let me have what's mine, little wolf?"

"Yes," I whispered, my heart racing at the thought of what was to come. "Please, Noah."

He slipped the other strap off my shoulder, and my dress fell to the floor in a puddle of fabric, revealing that I hadn't worn a bra, but something told me he didn't care. His palms trailed around my ribcage until he cupped the weight of my breasts in his hands, and I moaned at the contact.

Somewhere during this little show, he'd taken off his shirt. I'd been so focused on what he was doing to me, I missed that detail. Part of me was sad I hadn't had the opportunity to do it myself until his strong, muscled chest pressed fully against my back.

He wrapped his arms around me, holding me against him until the heat of the fire was nothing but a distant memory compared to the feel of his skin pressed against mine. Our hearts beat together, a steady tandem pulse.

He kissed his way up the back of my neck, his mouth brushing over my ear as he asked, "Do you remember what I told you the other night? About how I intended to ruin you for anyone else?"

"Are you ready to live up to your warning?"

He laughed, his low, throaty chuckle echoing inside me. "I think the more pertinent question is, are *you*?"

"Shut up and fuck me, Noah. I've been ready for too long."

His hands whispered over my body, starting with my breasts and trailing over my stomach until his fingers reached the lace of my panties. He stepped away, my heart protesting the distance. The only place he touched me was where his fingers curled around my underwear.

"Brace yourself, dove. My control isn't what it should be."

Sliding to his knees behind me, he peppered kisses over the base of my spine as he used his fingers to tug the fabric down my thighs. He followed the path, teeth nipping one of my cheeks playfully as he went.

"Step out of these silly little things, then get on the bed."

A tingle worked its way up my body at his words. I'd never been so eager to obey a command in my life. I think I wanted what he was offering more than he did.

Shimmying out of the scrap of lace I'd selected with Noah in mind, it took almost more restraint than I had to ignore the hungry look in his eyes as I rushed over to the bed. Climbing up onto the thick mattress, I positioned myself on all fours and tossed a coy look over my shoulder.

"Like this?"

If the low groan that came from him was any indication, he liked what he saw. He moved so fast he was a blur as he whipped his belt open and tore at the zipper of his trousers. Then he stood in front of me, long, thick, and hard. Ready to make me his.

I'd thought I would be nervous, this being my first time and all, but as I stared into Noah Blackthorne's hungry eyes, I knew he was the one. This was the man I was meant to share this moment with.

"I don't want you on your knees while I'm inside you, Sunday. Not this first time. I need to watch your eyes as I take you. I need . . ." he faltered, his voice breaking as clear emotion overwhelmed him. "I've never felt like this."

I spun around, lifting on my knees and scooting closer so I could wrap my arms around him. His eyes were wild, his expression so intense it seared me, warming me from the inside out. "Then take me, Noah. I'm yours."

That statement hung in the air between us, powerful, meaningful, and exactly what my vampire prince needed. He threaded his fingers in my hair and tugged hard until my face was tipped up and he could crush his lips to mine in a frantic kiss.

We were moans and harsh grunts as he used his free hand to support me, and the two of us fell to the bed. I don't know how we managed to position ourselves the way we did without someone getting hurt, but before I knew it, I was under him, my knees bent, legs spread, and he was there, his cock nudging at my entrance.

"Last chance, little wolf. Are you sure this is what you desire?"

I grasped his hips, my nails digging into his firm skin. "If you don't fuck me right now, Noah Blackthorne, I may—"

"Don't you dare finish that sentence."

His harsh warning was underscored by the press of his crown barely breaching my opening. Pressure, the delicious promise of being filled, teased me. I knew it was going to hurt. There was no way it wouldn't, but God, I wanted this.

"Noah," I whined, squirming and desperate for him to put me out of my misery.

His eyes met mine, his jaw clenched, sweat peppering his brow as his arms trembled on either side of my head.

"God, do you have any idea what you do to me, dove? I could tear you in half if I gave in to the monster inside me."

"You think you're so strong? I'm not a human. Don't forget that. I don't break easily."

He huffed out a laugh that sounded pained as he slid slightly deeper. "Perhaps not, but gentleness doesn't come easily to me. I want to make this good for you."

"Then touch me."

Closing his eyes, he took a shuddering breath and reached between us, fingers finding my clit as he shallowly thrust into me, controlled, steady, and wonderful. I felt myself open up as I got wetter with each circle of his fingers, each roll of his hips. What could have been painful blossomed into deep, agonizing pleasure.

"More," I gasped. "Noah, please. I need more."

"Fuck, Sunday. Stop begging like that. I'll give you what you want before you're ready if you don't stop."

"I know what I'm asking for. I know what I want. I need you, Noah. Please. Make me yours."

With a feral growl, he slammed home, the pinch of my hymen breaking noticeable, but veiled by the orgasm his fingers coaxed from me at the same time. I cried out, my back arching, eyes locked onto his own desperate ones.

"Yes," he groaned, his hips pistoning as he rode out wave after wave of my climax. "I want your pleasure. I love the sounds you make when you come. The way your cunt flutters around my cock."

The dirty words whispered in his low, throaty voice sent aftershocks coursing through me. *Fuck. Who knew orgasms could be so much better when you didn't have to work for them?*

Come again for me, my mate. Come all over me. Let me feel it. His words echoed in my head, that connection I'd thought I felt after he walked me to my room and kissed every inch of my body blazing back to life.

Just like last time, I was helpless to do anything but obey his demand. My body detonated, my back lifting off the mattress as I clung to him and rode out wave after relentless wave of ecstasy. He followed, his cock jerking and a deep, pained groan leaving him as he held me close and shuddered through his orgasm.

I opened my eyes, staring at the window beyond us, my heart racing as the distinct silhouette of a man moved behind the now illuminated glass. It was just obscured enough I couldn't make out what he was doing, but there was no mistaking the palm pressed against the glass or the bowed angle of his head.

I don't know when he showed up or how long he'd been watching, but knowing that he could see everything, that he'd likely witnessed me falling apart for Noah, was enough. A third even more intense climax rippled through me, and my inner muscles clamped down around Noah as I cried out.

"Shit, Sunday," he groaned as my body milked him, his forehead dropping to my shoulder.

He thrust his hips in time with the pulses of my release, but my gaze never left the man in the window, and I could swear his eyes were locked on mine even though I couldn't see him. My focus on the shadowy figure finally broke when Noah slammed me back onto the bed and began frantically pounding into me until I saw stars.

Noah came again, barking out my name, fangs extended, eyes dark and hungry for more than sex. He closed his eyes and regained control, pulling out of me and staring down at his cock, glistening with a mixture of our come and my virgin blood.

"Are you okay?" I asked.

"I am so much more than okay. I don't know if a word has been invented to express it." He crawled up the bed and settled next to me, lazily trailing a finger around my nipple. "Are you okay? I couldn't stop myself there at the end. I might've been too rough."

I curled my arms around him, wanting to be close and feeling the need to kiss him. "Not too rough. It was perfect."

The warm trickle between my legs sent my heart pounding. Fuck. We hadn't used protection. He'd come inside me twice. "Noah, we didn't use anything."

His hand ran down the side of my face, his fingers coming to rest at the place where my pulse thrummed in my neck. "I already told you, mate. I will always protect you. It's not your fertile time; I can smell it. We're safe." He slipped his other hand between my legs and pushed his cum back inside me slowly, his finger gliding in and curling sending little shock waves through me. "I belong inside you."

The words did something to me. Settled something and made me glow with absolute joy. I tightened my hold on him, urging him down until his ear was at my lips. Nipping his earlobe, I whispered, "When can we do that again?"

CHAPTER
TWENTY-EIGHT
SUNDAY

"Sunday, wake up!" Noah's voice reached me like a lifeline, tearing me from the horrific scene I'd been trapped inside.

I gasped for breath, bolting to a sitting position, my throat raw, limbs shaking. "I couldn't save you."

He reached for me, and I jerked out of his grasp, chest still heavy as I tried to draw air into my lungs. His expression clouded, hurt mixing with confusion at my instinctive reaction.

"Don't touch me," I hissed.

"Sunday . . . what's this all about? I won't be so rough again. I'm so sorry if I hurt you."

"No. It's not that," I started, my head still filled with the images of a world on fire.

I could still feel the heat in my palms and taste the soot in my mouth as, one by one, the people I tried to save caught flame. Orange and red flickered in my vision as their horrified gazes latched onto mine, their screams overwhelming me almost as badly as the acrid scent of charred flesh in my nose. All because they touched me. I wasn't

237

their saving grace. I was their death. And throughout this nightmare, I'd laughed with wicked glee at the destruction I'd wrought.

"Then tell me what it is. Or better yet, let me inside your mind and show me."

I cringed away, not wanting to relive how awful the nightmare had been. I didn't want Noah to have the image of the monster I'd become living inside his mind. How could he ever look at me the same if he knew what I might be capable of?

"I could never fear you."

He must have read my expression, or perhaps even my thoughts. While comforting, his words still weren't enough to make me want to share the horrors of my dream. I squeezed my eyes together and let out a ragged sigh. "How can you say that when you don't know what I've done?"

"It was a dream, dove. You haven't done anything wrong. If you knew the things I dreamt of doing, you'd run screaming for the hills. The vengeance I've craved against those who wronged my family has been played out time and time again in my subconscious. If we could be judged on our thoughts alone, I'd have been damned a long time ago."

"Aren't you already?" I lifted my lips in the ghost of a smile. "Vampire and all?"

He reached out again, stopping himself just before his fingers brushed against my skin. Then he gave me an apologetic smile and dropped his hand. "Probably. Though if I am, it has more to do with my other sins, not being born a beast."

My pulse slowed to a normal pace, the panic ebbing, and now all I wanted was for him to touch me again. I needed to feel normal. To be reminded I wasn't the monster the dream had portrayed. A shudder ran through me at the memory of my mother atop a blood-red horse at the crest of a hill, watching with a stoic expression as I'd lain waste to anyone who touched me.

Noah tensed, his eyes falling closed as he took a deep breath and slowly released it. "Is that all?"

I knew exactly what he was asking. He'd been inside my head. He'd seen it even though I didn't want him to. "Not by a long shot."

His eyes opened, his gaze warm and free of judgment as it met mine. "Show me. Let me see the worst, so you'll know it's nowhere near as bad as it seems. The dream will only hold power over you if you let it."

I shook my head. "I don't want to think about it anymore. Make me forget it, Noah. Take it away."

He didn't hesitate, my request the only permission he needed before he crossed the bed and pulled me into him. Rolling our bodies so I was straddled across his hips, he grinned, his smirk sexy and entirely unrepentant. "By all means, Sunday. Take what you need. I'm more than happy to provide you with a distraction."

We were still fully nude, and my body, although recovering from the nightmare, was more than primed for him. There was something about Noah, about being near the man, that made me hot and slick, ready at the drop of a hat. I rocked my hips, rubbing my pussy across his hard length as it pressed to his lower stomach.

"Yes," he groaned, his hands roaming up my legs to rest on my hips. "Just like that. Take me inside you and ride me."

I shivered from head to toe, reaching down and notching him at my opening. Then, in purposefully slow motion, I sank down on him until he was buried to the hilt.

"Fuuuck, Sunday. You fit like a fucking dream. So tight and deliciously warm. I could live buried inside you. In fact, I think I will."

I giggled. "We'll have to separate sometime."

His fingers spasmed on my hips, biting into my skin and holding me just tight enough to bruise. "Never. You're stuck with me. Always. I'll never leave you by choice. Now fuck me."

"I don't know what to do. What if I hurt you?"

"You're not going to hurt me. Just chase your own pleasure. Be selfish and move in ways that feel good for you. I promise you'll do it right."

I planted my palms on his chest, digging sharp nails into his skin as I circled my hips, then rolled them back and forth, dragging his cock over the perfect spot inside me. Stars dotted my vision, and my breath caught as I rode him to the crest of perfect pleasure. He held on tighter, grunting and lifting his hips in time with my motions.

"Open your eyes, Sunday. We aren't alone."

His voice was tight with need and desperate lust, gaze trained on the window once more where our mystery voyeur had returned.

Once again, the stranger had one hand pressed to the fogged glass, and there was no missing the furious pump of his other arm.

"I think he wants a show," I whispered, my heart picking up again at the thought.

"Then let's fucking give him one," Noah said with a slow grin, sitting up and wrapping his arms around me, holding me tight.

Before I could register what was happening, his legs were over the side of the bed, and he was moving us across the room. My back pressed into the cool stone wall, directly across from our guest, and again, something drew my focus to where his eyes would be if I could see him better. I knew beyond the shadow of a doubt, we were connected somehow. He was getting more than arousal from this. But I didn't know what.

Noah's hands were pressed against the wall on either side of my head, his face lowered to my neck as he trailed kisses down my throat. "Are you ready, dove?" he whispered.

"For? You're already railing me harder than I thought you could."

He chuckled, low and deep, the sound rumbling through me and sending tingles racing across my skin. "We're putting on a show, remember? Let's make sure our friend gets a good look at you. I want him to covet this pretty pink pussy and wish he was able to taste it any time he wanted just like I can."

He pushed away, his hands gripping me beneath my thighs, almost high enough to grasp my ass. Then he pulled out, spreading me wide and holding me up against the wall as he dropped to his knees. The cool air hit my oversensitive flesh, making me cry out and squirm. Noah had such a strong hold on me, though, I would have been less stable on a chair. I should have been concerned that a stranger had front row seats to a detailed examination of my lady bits, but I didn't have time to think about it before Noah buried his face between my thighs and ate me like a starving man.

"Fuck, Noah," I cried as overwhelming sensations careened through me. I grabbed him by the back of the head and pushed him closer, needing him to give me more, to help me reach the crest. My climax exploded through every nerve ending I had, making me come so hard my eyes rolled back in my head.

Noah continued sucking and nibbling my clit, drawing out my pleasure. Then he looked up my body, his eyes flashing with a different kind of hunger. My breath caught in my chest as understanding dawned.

"Just don't take too much," I whispered.

Nuzzling his face in the crook of my inner thigh, he struck. Deep pressure, a sharp burn, and then indescribable euphoria hit me all at once.

"Noah." His name came out as a barely intelligible moan.

He made a rumbling sound low in his throat, taking one last swallow before pulling back. He lifted his hand to his mouth, pricking his thumb with one of his fangs and smearing a drop of blood over the wounds to heal them. Noah held me up with one hand as though I weighed nothing, and as soon as he was sure I'd healed, he lowered me to my feet, a proud smirk on his kissable lips. Lips still coated in my arousal and stained with my blood.

I ran my hand through Noah's hair, my heart still pounding wildly in my chest as I glanced up and back to the window. I would have sworn the stranger's eyes caught mine just a second before the light behind the glass flickered out.

"Do you think we scared him off?" I asked.

"Not a chance in hell. If he frequents *Iniquity,* this is far from the worst of his sins. In fact, I'll bet we run into him again the next time we're here."

"Next time?"

"Didn't you warn me you'd acquire a taste for the club if your first time was here?"

That brought up an entire world of possibility. Noah and I could explore my darkest desires here . . . *his* darkest desires. I had to know every detail about him and what he wanted, what stirred his need besides vanilla missionary sex. He'd given up so much to be with me. I'd give him everything he craved.

The reminder of what brought us here, his confession about his traitor's mark and my role in it, had me turning my head and pressing a soft kiss just above the darkened silver, wondering if it still hurt. If it had, he'd not let on. Before I could say anything further, my stomach let out a loud grumble.

He chuckled. "I guess now that we've seen to one of your hungers, we should take care of the other. Come on, dove. Let's get dressed and get you fed."

CHAPTER
TWENTY-NINE
THORNE

E ven though it was the wee hours of the morning, the party upstairs hadn't lessened. *Iniquity* was made for this time, when day and night fought for dominance, when people's inhibitions were at their lowest. With Sunday's hand firmly grasped in mine, I led her through the bodies grinding against each other on the dance floor, the seductive bassline of the song humming through my chest, begging for us to join the throng. But I had other plans, ones that included taking her for something to eat and then back to my flat so I could get her back into my bed.

"Wait," she called, giving my hand a tug. "I think that's Moira."

I turned back, curling my body protectively around hers, eyes scanning the crowd but not finding her flatmate. "Where?"

"Right there. She's dancing with that hot as fuck Indian girl." Sunday pointed toward the two women practically fucking on the dance floor.

I barely recognized Moira. The woman was worse than

245

a bloody chameleon with her ever-changing hairstyles. Tonight she was full-on sex appeal. Hair cropped short, shaved on one side, a white button-down shirt I might've found in my own closet, open at the throat and down to her sternum, and red leather pants that fit her like a second skin. She was dominant and deadly and had the woman in her arms completely enthralled.

"She looks like she's about to seal the deal. Maybe it's best not to interrupt—"

Even her head lifted, and she spotted us. For a second, there was a flash of worry in her lavender gaze, but it vanished when Sunday gave her an eager wave. Moira dipped her head, whispering something in the other woman's ear before taking her hand and leading her to where we stood.

"Hey guys," she said. "I didn't realize you two were here tonight."

God help me, but Sunday blushed. Her cheeks blazed, and the thought of what memories were flashing through her mind made my cock thicken.

"We . . . needed some time together. I've been away."

Moira narrowed her eyes. "I know, you dick. We all know. We should call you Casper instead of Thorne." Then she glanced back at Sunday, pulling the woman beside her forward. "Sunday, this is Ash. Ash, my roommate Sunday, and," she cut me an annoyed glare, "Noah Blackthorne. Ash is a friend from back home."

There was no mistaking the softening of her gaze or the flood of joy that ran through the petite witch as she introduced her—unless I was reading this wrong—lover.

"Moira, you should have told me you had a guest coming. I would've made some plans to be out of the room more so you two could be alone," Sunday said.

Ash's relieved smile said it all. She had been worried what Sunday would say about their obvious relationship. "My parents had to fly to Mumbai to visit my grandmother unexpectedly. Mo didn't know I was coming."

The expression on Moira's face was just as relieved, if not slightly emotional. I got the feeling neither witch was used to open acceptance. This was probably one of the few, if not the first, times they'd been out together in public.

"You don't have to do—" Moira started.

"For what it's worth, Sunday will be occupied in my room for the foreseeable future. You'll have the place to yourselves until after class on Monday, at the very least."

Challenge sparked in Sunday's eyes as she trained them on me. "Oh, will I?"

I flashed her a grin with more than a little fang. "Oh yes. And if you're able to so much as walk by the end of it, I'll consider it a distinct failure on my part and be forced to continue until I remedy the situation."

"Somebody definitely just got fucked," Moira whispered to Ash. Then the little witch offered Sunday a high five, which my wolf begrudgingly returned.

"Leave her alone," Ash said. "She's a new soul. Can't you sense it? She's never been here before. She's not as worldly as either of us."

"Ash can see and read auras. The things she can pick up about a person . . ." Moira's voice was brimming with pride.

"The things I know about *you*, you mean." A teasing smile turned up Ash's lips.

"It has its uses," Moira said with a bit of a purr.

The beautifully curvy woman let out a throaty, sexy laugh. "I'll use it tonight then."

"I hate to break up a party, but we were about to go get a bite. There's a pub just 'round the corner, open all night and friendly to supernaturals. Would you ladies care to join us?"

They exchanged a glance.

"I could do with a snack. I've never been to a proper pub," Ash said.

"It's settled then," I decided for them. "Follow me. It's not the fanciest, but you won't find a better meat pie this side of London."

Squeezing Sunday's hand, I led the women out of the club and into the brisk early morning air. "You warm enough?" I asked, glancing down at Sunday.

She shivered. "I didn't really dress for a walk."

I wrapped my arm around her shoulder and tugged her close. "Better stick by me then. I'll warm you up."

The sky was a shade of deep blue that warned sunrise was nearing. This was the time for drunks to stumble home, lovers to fall into bed, and the world to just begin stirring.

"Hang on, he's a vampire. It's almost sunrise. Aren't you going to burst into flames or something?" Ash asked.

I shook my head. "No. My mother has the blood of the sun running through her veins, as do I. I can enjoy the day and night."

Ash's deep brown complexion faded a shade as the reality of what that meant hit her. I sensed it in her energy. "You? Are there more of you?"

"Two. I have a younger sister and brother. And yes, we can all walk in the sun. But Ash, we're not the bloodthirsty monsters my grandfather would've had us become."

Her look turned appraising. "You expect me to believe *that* after what the Blackthornes did to the witches of Salem?"

"Trust me," Moira said with a put-upon sigh, casting

me a look that told me I owed her one. "He's practically tame compared to their ancestors. But enough about dirty blood suckers."

The two witches fell a bit behind, their low voices and breathy giggles telling me they were enjoying themselves just as much as they had been at the club.

We'd made it perhaps a block, Sunday snuggled beneath my arm, her head resting on my shoulder, when Moira swooped in between us.

"Oh! Sunday, I need to speak to you about something," Moira said, weaving her arm through Sunday's. A protest was on the tip of my tongue, but she winked at me. "Official roommate business, you understand. We'll just be a second."

Sunday giggled, and that sealed it for me. Anything that made her happy was impossible to refuse. I let that sink in a moment, an unfamiliar sense of calm settling in my chest. I truly cared if she was happy. Until now, I'd never cared about anyone who wasn't family. Not like this.

Moira pulled Sunday back, leaving Ash and me to amble along beside one another.

"Do you know why Dracula doesn't have any friends?" Ash started after we'd walked about halfway down the next block in silence.

"Please don't."

Her lips turned up in a smile as she tried and failed to hold in her laughter. "Because he's a pain in the neck!"

"Jesus . . . and there it is."

She poked me in the ribs. "Admit it. You thought it was funny."

"No. No, I didn't."

I fought a laugh despite myself as I made eye contact with the witch, and then everything stopped as her eyes rolled back in her head and she fell to the ground. My skin was on fire as a woven net of pure silver landed on me from above. The pain was like nothing I'd ever felt. Not even my traitor mark could compare. Sunday let out a panicked cry, and from the corner of my eye, I saw her and Moira being tugged into the alley by two hooded figures.

The pain was excruciating, my muscles locking up and preventing me from going after her. As I watched, helpless to do anything to stop it, my mate vanished into the alley. The only thing I could do was vow to get her back as I shouted her name.

They'd taken her. She was gone and all because I had failed at my one job. To protect her at all costs.

CHAPTER
THIRTY
SUNDAY

My breath came in thready gasps as I tried to draw in air through the thick black hood tied over my head. By the sounds of Moira struggling beside me and the steady stream of creative insults she hurled at our assailants, I could tell her head was also covered. But she was alive, and knowing that gave me hope. If we were together, we could get out of this.

The van we'd been shoved into before they blinded us came to a rough stop, and I jerked forward, unable to catch myself since my hands were bound behind my back. The silver cuffs burned every time they rubbed against the tender skin of my wrists. I collided with something cool and flat, my head throbbing at the bone-jarring impact. Shit, I was going to have a bruise.

Whoever was driving cut the engine, and the vehicle jostled before two doors slammed shut. This might be our only chance to speak without being overheard. I blinked away the pain and whispered urgently, "Can you get any sense of where we are?"

"No. Whatever they put on my hands is keeping my magic contained. Fucking asshole hunters."

"Fuck, mine too. We're going to have to brute squad this, then."

"You're on the brute squad?"

"I *am* the brute squad."

"Since when?"

"Just follow my lead, okay?"

"What lead? I can't see a damn thing. How am I supposed to follow you?"

"Moira—" but there wasn't time for anything further. Cool air rushed over my skin as our captors threw open the sliding door.

"Lookie what we got here, a bitch and a witch." The man's deep cockney accented voice covered me like a layer of dirty oil. "I just wanted one, but you brought me two."

"Touch me, and I'll bite it off, I swear," Moira growled.

I inwardly groaned. *So much for following my lead.*

"Oh, I like 'em feisty. This is going to be more fun than I thought."

Rustling sounded to my left, like clothes and skin brushing against each other. There was a soft grunt followed by the unmistakable sound of a boot meeting bone.

"Fuckin' bitch," he snarled.

"No, I'm the witch, remember?" Moira said, her voice dripping with false sweetness.

"Take them inside and lock the door. I don't want to see them until it's time to torture the information we need out of 'em. I'm gonna enjoy this one."

"You always enjoy the torture part, boss." A male voice came from somewhere to my left.

"True, but this is going to be sweeter. I got dibs on the witch."

A hand grasped me hard about the arm, pulling me unceremoniously out of the van. I stumbled as I tried to catch my balance, tripping over my feet as I was pulled forward. Part of me was shouting to fight, to break free, but attempting to fight while blinded, with my hands bound, was hardly ideal. And there was Moira to think about. I couldn't just leave her here. We were going to need to wait until their guard was down.

Still, I made a show of resisting, trying to tug out of the man's grasp. Pain exploded from the side of my face as his free hand cracked across my cheek. I tasted the copper tang of blood in my mouth where my lip had split.

"You don't want to do that, love."

"Touch me again, and I'll tear your balls out through your mouth," I snarled.

He laughed. "And how you gonna do that without your hands, dearie? If you think I'm afraid of some wolf bitch who can't even shift, you got another think coming. I've taken shits bigger than you."

A fist connected with my stomach, doubling me over and making me gag as the wind was knocked out of me. My wolf clawed inside her cage, desperate to break free and lay waste to them, but even if I *could* shift, the silver binding me would keep that from happening.

Forcing myself to calm the useless rage inside me, I put into practice what I'd worked on with Alek and Kingston. I needed to be controlled, strategic, and beat these fuckers at their own game. I let my shoulders slump, feigning defeat and willing them to believe I'd given up fighting. With each step we took, I trained my focus on keeping count—twelve steps, right turn, seven steps, left turn, twenty steps, right turn, and then we were inside a cold, dank space.

I could hear Moira faring about as well as I had. Unlike me, however, she didn't bother to pretend to be cowed. The girl just didn't have it in her, which only made me love her more. She wasn't going to stop fighting, and neither was I. There was no way we were dying here tonight. I wouldn't allow it.

Moira continued to curse the entire way from the car right until they were shoving us down onto icy concrete and wrapping a heavy chain around our stomachs, tying us to some kind of pole. Then they ripped off our hoods. I blinked rapidly, my eyes trying to adjust to the sudden light.

The space was barren, nothing but a hole in the ground in the corner that smelled of shit and piss. A concrete box. A cell. The door slammed shut, and the click of the lock engaging echoed in the room. At the top of the heavy metal door, a small panel slid open, revealing a pair of glittering green eyes.

"This can go easy for you, or we can draw it out and make it hurt. You decide. But either way, we're going to get what we want from you."

That cockney bastard would die first, I decided. "Oh, it's going to hurt all right. For you, that is."

The window closed with an ominous clank, and the sound of his gravely chuckle as he walked away had my gut churning.

"We have to get out of here. Right now." My voice shook, betraying the bravado I'd put on to try and intimidate our captors.

Moira rattled her chains. "I'm all ears, but unless you have a plan to deal with these, we're fucked."

"What if . . ." I squirmed, trying to find her hands with mine. It took a second, but I managed to wriggle my fingers between one of her wrists and the cuff clamped around it.

"Ouch!"

"Sorry, I just need a little room." The silver on my fingertips sizzled, itching and burning all at the same time. I knew it was worse for vampires, but shifters avoided the precious metal for the same reason.

"Where the hell do you expect me to go? These don't exactly have any give. They aren't a damn pair of leggings."

"Moira," I snapped, pain turning to impatience. "Just work with me here."

She huffed, but I could feel the roll of her shoulders as she attempted to slide her arm up and provide me with a better angle.

"Okay, try to keep quiet and move your wrist free as I spread this cuff."

I took a deep breath, steeling myself for the pain I knew was coming. I let my wolf come roaring to the surface, picturing the fight with Callie, the attack at the club, the bastards who'd taken us. With every ounce of strength I could muster, I pried apart the cuff, pushing through the agonizing burn until Moira's hand slid free.

"Holy shit, girl. Do you have vampire strength now, or is that a wolf thing?"

Breaths coming in gasps, I said, "I have no fucking clue."

"Well, whatever it is, do you think you can do it again?"

"I sure hope so. We need you to be able to magic us out of this shithole."

"I'm all over it just as soon as you get me free."

This time, it was a little easier to maneuver our bodies so I could wedge my fingers between Moira's hand and the second cuff. Even though the rage was still roaring through me, the pain caused my arms and fingers to shake as blisters appeared from the repeated exposure to the silver, making it hard for me to get a good grasp on the metal.

"Come on, Sunday. You can do this."

I closed my eyes, sucking in air through my nose and forcing myself to fight past the pain. This was nothing. If those fuckers got their hands on us, it would be so much worse. Once I felt settled, I adjusted my grip and yanked at the metal, a low scream building in my throat and growing in volume even as I tried to swallow it. Tears dripped from the corners of my eyes, but a flood of relief washed over me when the metal hit the ground with a soft clink.

"You're a fucking savage, Sunday Fallon. Now, stay still while I do my part, okay?" Metallic clinking echoed as Moira dealt with the chain around our bellies. I couldn't see what she was doing, only that it worked when the chain fell to the ground.

"No problem," I mumbled, my heart thundering in my chest and spots dancing in my eyes. It'd taken a lot out of me, but I couldn't relax. Not yet. Not until we were both free of this place.

I couldn't see what Moira was doing, but her hands wrapped over the cuffs at my wrists, the metal rapidly cooling until it frosted over and became brittle as it froze.

"Moira—"

"Just give it one more second," she urged.

There was a crack, the sound of metal breaking, and then my cuffs fell to the ground on top of hers.

Moira moved to help me stand, and we spared only a second to hug each other. Both of us were shaking, but the feel of her arms wrapping around my body, holding me tight, steadied me. We could do this. We *were* doing this.

I pulled away, my hands resting on her shoulders as I searched her eyes. "I memorized the route they took. If you can do something about the door, I can get us out of here."

Moira smirked. "I'll do you one better. I'll handle the door *and* the security system."

Her eyes began to glow as her lips whispered the words of her spell. I knew better than to interrupt her while she was casting, but curiosity tugged at me. I wasn't familiar enough with witchcraft to know exactly what she was doing, but as she continued to speak, the air grew warm and thick around us. If it was possible for air to be malleable, that's what it felt like. As if Moira had found a way to shape and bend it to her will.

Just when the heat began to feel unpleasant, it evaporated as quickly as a bubble being popped, leaving absolutely nothing to suggest it had ever been there at all.

"Okay," she murmured. Faint blue smudges marred the pale skin beneath her eyes, alluding to how much it had taken out of her to cast her spell. "The glamour should hold until we get out of here."

"Glamour?"

"I created a time-loop, essentially. Anyone who comes to check on us will see the two of us sleeping in our cell like a couple of good little prisoners. But we should hurry, just to be safe."

Shock washed over me. The Belladonna coven was insanely powerful, but seeing Moira in action and hearing the extent of what she could do . . . I was finally starting to understand just how powerful they actually were.

"Of course you did. Okay, let's do this."

Moira pressed her palm to the door, whispering under her breath as she magicked the lock open. The red welts around her wrist were hard to miss. Together the two of us made our way out into the hall.

Closing my eyes, I called up the map of the maze of hallways in my mind as I snagged her hand and led her back the way we'd been brought inside.

Left turn, twenty steps, right turn, seven steps, left turn ...

We were almost there. It was too quiet. Too easy. Twelve more steps.

"Where do you two think you're going?" The low, gravelly voice belonged to a man I hadn't heard before. His rough London accent and the scent of stale beer and grease on his skin had me on edge. This was a man who didn't care what he had to do to get by. He had Moira by the arm, his eyes glazed and dark.

"Get your hands off her," I snarled.

His laugh morphed into a smoker's cough, deep in his chest, wheezing. Moira's frantic gaze locked on mine, and I could sense her plea from here. *Do something.* So I did. I let go of all the control I'd worked so hard for and let as much of my wolf out to play as possible. My vision ran red, fingers shifting to razor-sharp claws. He didn't see me coming until his guts hung outside his body.

"You?" he gasped, releasing Moira in a feeble attempt to use both hands to hold his entrails in place. To put them back where they belonged.

"Me." From the massive amount of blood pooling on the floor, I definitely hit an artery. Even the best surgeon in London wouldn't be able to put him back together in time to save his life. "You've got something ... just there," I said, pointing to the bit of intestine that had escaped his hold as he crumpled to the floor in a twitching heap.

"If I wasn't so disgusted, I'd be turned on right now," Moira whispered. "You're a beast."

I shrugged, flipping my hair over my shoulder. "He had it coming."

Moira pulled open the door, and the two of us walked into the early morning light. "God, girl, you're gonna need a shower . . . maybe two. I think you have blood in your hair."

"Worth it," I said with a grin, taking her hand and giving it a squeeze. "Thanks for your help in there. I couldn't have done it without you."

She raised a brow. "Me? Did you see *you* in there? You're a one-woman weapon of mass destruction. You killed that guy in like, two seconds flat."

I grinned. "Yeah, I was pretty awesome, wasn't I?"

For someone who'd been treated like a useless waste of space her whole life, being able to take him down, get us out of there, and not fall apart made me feel like maybe coming to Ravenscroft was a good thing after all.

Footsteps pounded down the alley, sending my adrenaline spiking once more. I shoved Moira behind me, already prepared to defend her when two familiar faces came around the corner, staggering to a halt.

"Noah?"

"Sunday? What the hell happened to you?" He raced forward, his eyes dark with fury. "Where the fuck are they? I'll kill them."

"Already taken care of," I assured him.

"You should've seen her, Thorne. She was like an animal. She diced him up without flinching," Moira said as Ash wrapped her in an embrace.

Noah's eyes remained wild as he looked from my blood-splattered body to Moira and back again. "Did she now?"

"She did," I confirmed with a nod. "I have plans with my boyfriend this weekend. I wasn't about to miss them."

Without warning, my limbs began trembling with fierce intensity, teeth chattering as adrenaline finally left my system. Oh, shit. I was lightheaded, nauseated, and there was no chance I'd be upright much longer.

Noah seemed to sense my shift in attitude, concern flickering across his face before he scooped me into the cradle of his arms.

"Well, my little warrior. Your boyfriend has plans for you as well, and they start right bloody now."

CHAPTER

THIRTY-ONE

SUNNDAY

N ight had just begun to fall when urgent knocking sounded from Noah's front door.

"Expecting someone?" I asked, glancing away from the sunset I hadn't really noticed, my thoughts too filled with the events of the night before to appreciate the pink and orange hues. I didn't want to deal with anyone or be interrupted. Noah and I were simply enjoying our time together. Couldn't I just have a normal night for once?

He hadn't strayed too far from me since we returned to his penthouse that morning. Currently, he was pretending to read while I snuggled into him, my head resting on his shoulder while he used the fingers of his free hand to draw lazy circles up and down my arm.

The knocking sounded again, this time harsher and angrier, rattling the door. Noah's posture changed from relaxed to tense, and he grumbled under his breath as he closed his book and set it on the small end table.

"Nosy fucking priest."

That got my attention. *What's Caleb doing here?* I

straightened, my eyes following Noah as he walked across the room toward the door.

"What do you want?" Noah snapped, angling his body so he blocked my view of Caleb.

Or his view of me.

"I know she's in there."

"And? What business is it of yours who I entertain in my own home?"

"Need I remind you this is not, in fact, your home, but a university."

"My name's on the building, Priest. I think that counts." Noah began closing the door. "Now, if you don't mind. We were in the middle of something."

Caleb shoved his shoulder between the door and the frame, stopping Noah before he could close it in his face. His next words were gritted out, temper leaking into his tone. "One of my students was attacked last night. I need to ensure her well-being."

"Sunday is no longer your responsibility. I have matters well in hand."

"Is that so?"

"Quite."

"Then perhaps you can explain to me just how it happened that the woman you claim to be guarding so successfully was kidnapped while under your protection?"

Oh . . . low blow, Caleb.

Noah's back went rigid, his knuckles turning white and the wood groaning beneath his hand. Fierce energy seeped into the air, crackling with possessive anger, but I couldn't tell which one of them it belonged to. Caleb's beautiful, heart-stopping eyes found mine, concern, contempt, and guilt all swimming in their depths.

"Come with me, *a stor*. We have a session scheduled, and you cannot miss it tonight. I need you to provide me with every detail of your attack. The headmistress will need to know."

"I don't think so. What she needs right now is to rest, not be interrogated. You can resume your session on Monday."

Caleb let out a low snarl, shoving his way into the flat. Strength radiated from him, and Noah's fatigue was evident on his face. Noah hadn't slept, likely since the night before last. Dark circles ringed his eyes, and something about our connection told me my instinct was correct. He needed rest.

"Your name might be on the building, but I am the one in charge here. Not you. Now, step aside before I make you, Blackthorne."

Noah's fists clenched, fight passing across his features. "Please, go ahead and make me, Priest. One call to my father, and you'll be the one sent to the well for punishment."

"Your hand would be out the window before you finished dialing," Caleb growled.

I'd never seen him quite so aggressive before. Intense, without a doubt. Angry? Pretty much every time we interacted. But never this dominant. Of the two vampires, I would have said Noah was more likely to out-alpha Caleb, but now . . . I wasn't as certain.

Realizing their dick-swinging would only escalate unless I intervened, I pushed to my feet and moved to where they stood, sneering at each other in the doorway. Resting my arm lightly on Noah's back, I murmured, "It's okay. I'll go with him."

"Sunday—"

I brushed my lips over his cheek, which made Noah soften but Caleb tense. "It's fine, really. You should get some rest, anyway. And I'll come straight back once we're finished."

"I really can't condone—" Caleb started, but Noah cut him off.

"Unless you're planning on enforcing that rule for every single student in residence here, I suggest you don't even bother finishing your sentence. Sunday will be staying with me for the foreseeable future, and there's nothing you can do about it."

"You certainly have earned your title of brat prince, haven't you? I've been a vampire longer than you've existed. Before you were a twitch in your father's pants, I was roaming this earth with the power to raze entire towns to the ground. Don't test me, lad. You might think your name protects you, but it doesn't."

Noah stepped forward, his fangs bared and his eyes flashing with venom. I shoved at his chest, putting myself between him and Caleb.

"That's enough, both of you. I already said I would go with you. There's no reason to antagonize him further." Then I glanced back at Noah. "Rest up while I'm gone so that you're not too tired for other things when I get back."

He smiled at that, curling an arm around my waist and pulling me close so he could drop a kiss on my lips. "Well, when you put it that way . . ." His gaze left mine and flicked to Caleb, a wicked smirk on Noah's tempting lips. "Looks like I'm the winner either way, Priest."

I sighed and removed myself from his grasp, trying to keep from letting my face show the amusement I felt. "I'll see you when I'm done, Noah." Turning to Caleb, I said, "Lead the way, boss man."

His nostrils flared with annoyance, but he merely turned on his heel and strode toward the elevator.

"Wait, that won't work for you."

Instead of responding, Caleb pressed his finger to the panel, which caused the doors to slide open.

"How come you can open it, and I can't?" I grumbled, following him into the small space.

"I work here. There are few places I cannot get to. I'm surprised Noah hasn't allowed you access. He seems taken with you."

"It must have slipped his mind," I said, crossing my arms. Despite my innocuous reply, annoyance simmered. If I was boning the guy, the least he could do was let me use his elevator, but no . . . I was stuck in stair city. Oh well, at least it was good for my ass.

As soon as the doors slid shut, Caleb positioned himself as far away from me as possible, his gaze trained on the panel straight ahead. The vampire was clearly uncomfortable, but was that due to being in an enclosed space or because I was here?

"So does this session include more punishment? Because I didn't really dress to be fondled." My nipples tightened at the memory of him spanking me. We hadn't seen each other since the incident, but I'd thought of it . . . fondly . . . many times since.

Something shifted in Caleb's eyes, a muscle feathering in his jaw. He glanced at me, seeming to weigh his words carefully. "No more punishments."

"Oh?" Disappointment hit me hard and fast. Because I'd liked the punishment. A whole hell of a lot.

"I think last time proved well enough that I cannot be

trusted when it comes to you, Miss Fallon. Things never should have progressed to that point. I was there to be the implement of your repentance, nothing further. And yet, I crossed a line that never should have been crossed."

"Because you're a priest?"

"Because I am your mentor. But also because of the vows I have made, yes. It's inappropriate, and it will not happen again."

"I'm willing to bet I'll do something to land myself back in your office one of these days. Are you saying I have a get out of jail free pass now?" I cocked a brow. "Or does someone else get to spank me?"

His eyes narrowed, and he clenched his fists, a small tremor working its way down his rigid frame. "No. No one else will touch you. You'll simply serve your time with the headmistress in the future."

"Oh, lucky me. She's a joy."

"She is more powerful than almost anyone I have ever known. The only being who eclipses her in power is The White Lady. Madame le Blanc has lived many lives, seen and done a great many things. Her being here with us means there is something in motion we will all have to face."

"So she's here to help us?"

"She's here to make sure everything that must happen does happen. Whether that helps or harms is of no consequence to her."

"Well, that's appropriately terrifying."

His lips quirked.

"What's so funny?"

"I was starting to believe I'd never live to see the night you'd be appropriately terrified of anything."

The elevator stopped, the doors sliding open silently

and shattering the privacy of our conversation. Just like that, we weren't two people sharing information; we were student and teacher, distant once again.

"Come along, Miss Fallon. You have a story to recall for me."

THIRTY-TWO

ALEK

I climbed up the stairs to the second floor of the stacks in the Satori library, my mind wandering as I moved without hurry. I still had a few minutes before I needed to settle in. It was quiet up here, the bulk of the students choosing to remain downstairs closer to the well-lit study area and the more popular reference materials.

As for me, I enjoyed the hushed calm that only solitude and books could provide. The tightly packed shelves dampened the sound of the whispered conversations below while cocooning me in the warm scent of hundred-year-old leather and the sharp bite of ink.

My route was familiar, having come up here at least once a week since the semester began, and I was able to wind through the labyrinth of stacks without getting lost on my way to a small reading nook set just beneath a mosaic of the Satori sphinx. It was both familiar and ancient and reminded me of home, which is why I'd chosen it for these weekly meetings.

Glancing up at the enormous clock suspended in the

air, magic keeping it visible to all from nearly any vantage point, I noted I had one minute left. Just enough time to make sure I was ready for her.

I pulled the pocket mirror from my, well . . . my pocket and smiled, thinking of the day my aunt Quinn gave it to me. My mother had laughed at the sight of the familiar trinket and then spelled it. She insisted I bring it with me before allowing my uncle Finley to open the portal that sent me to Ravenscroft.

Just as the clock announced the top of the hour, the small mirror in my hand began to glow with vibrant blue light, and tingles shot up my arm as it vibrated. I flicked the lid open, my mother's smiling face greeting me as I held the mirror up.

"Right on time," I said with a grin.

"You look pale. Are you eating?"

I couldn't help but roll my eyes. "Yes, mother. I'm eating. You look beautiful as always."

"Your father would be so proud. His lines rubbed off on you. But I can see right through your charm, young man. What's wrong?"

A cool trickle of unease ran down my spine. My mom was surrounded by too many seers for me to ignore her warnings, especially if she was sensing something I could not. "What do you mean? Why would anything be wrong?"

"Your eyes are haunted by something."

"Is that all? Maybe I just need more sleep. And how's Astrid?"

"Don't try and change the subject by asking about your little sister. She's fine, running your father ragged, as usual. Now back to you. Have you been partying too much?"

"That's like asking if Vikings drink mead."

She sighed and propped her chin on her free hand. "Maybe I was wrong to listen to Cora. Maybe Tor should've taken this spot at Ravenscroft instead of you. I don't like seeing this look in your eyes."

The mention of my twin taking my place had my hackles rising. Technically I'd stolen his, but that was neither here nor there. "Just because Tor hasn't figured out how to remove the stick he shoved up his own arse doesn't mean he's the better candidate for this mission. I simply know how to enjoy myself while working hard at the same time."

"I'm going to ignore your tone and pretend you didn't just talk to me that way because if your father hears about it, he'll have Fin send him there right now so he can haul you back by your ear to apologize."

She wasn't wrong. My father was an 'act first, ask questions later' kind of guy. His temper was notoriously short, as was the case for most berserkers. And being raised by one was no picnic. I was exhausted just thinking about the never-ending training sessions he'd subjected us to.

A warm glow built in my chest, calling my attention from where my mother's face gazed at me through the mirror and to the shelves in the periphery.

Sunday.

My heart fluttered, erratic and wild, as her focus landed on mine, and she smiled sweetly, lifting one hand and giving me a slight wave.

"What are you doing hiding over here?" she asked, stepping into the prism of light cast by the window above. Her eyes flicked to the mirror in my palm, and her lips twitched with laughter. "Doing your makeup?"

I sat up straighter, tempted to close the mirror and end

the call with my mother, but knowing if I did that, she'd make good on her promise to send my father after me. "No. Just a bit of magic. I come up here every week to check in back home."

Her eyes widened, and she moved closer. "Are you talking to someone right now?" she asked, tipping her face down so that her lilac and honey scent washed over me. I could not get an erection right now with my mother staring at the two of us.

"My mother."

She turned her face, bringing our mouths mere inches apart. *Odin's beard, she was trying to kill me.*

"That is just the sweetest thing I think I've ever heard. Who knew big bad Novasgardians were mama's boys?" Then she turned back to the mirror and gave my mother a cheerful wave. "Hi, I'm Sunday. And there's no way you're old enough to be anyone's mom."

Mother offered her a sweet and somehow knowing smile. "Magic can do a lot for a girl's complexion. It's nice to meet you, Sunday. I'm Lina. Is my boy taking good care of you?"

My heart flipped in my chest, and I had to swallow back a groan. "Mother—"

Sunday rested her hand on my shoulder. "He's an absolute doll. He saved my life, in fact. So I guess I should thank you for that. I may not be here right now if not for your son."

Mother's perfectly arched brows rose nearly into her hairline. Fuck. "Aleksander Alistair . . . You've never looked more like your father than you do at this exact moment. Maybe I was right to take Cora's advice after all."

"Who's Cora?" Sunday asked.

"And that's all the time we have. Sorry, Mother, I have to go. Love you." I snapped the mirror shut and closed our connection before any more awkward conversation could happen.

"I didn't mean to ruin your family time."

"You didn't. I'll call her back later."

My fingers itched to touch her, to feel her silky smooth skin. And then there was the memory of her lips on mine. What I wouldn't give to get to kiss her again when she wasn't on death's door. She straightened, and I immediately resented the distance between us.

"So you come up here every week to chat with her? I really didn't peg you as the kind of guy who would indulge his mom that way. She must really miss you."

"Family is everything."

It was simple but true. Even when we hated each other, we loved each other. My parents had fought too hard to be together not to instill the same core values in the rest of us.

Her eyes flashed with remembered pain. "Must be nice."

I almost reached for her until Thorne made his way from the depths of the stacks, eyes laser-focused on us. Staking his claim, as usual. Bloodsucking prick.

"There you are, dove. Get lost?"

She glanced over her shoulder at him, her smile soft and her eyes warm and only for him. A dagger to the heart would have hurt less. It was then I realized just how fucked I was. Because I wanted that smile for myself, but she wasn't meant for me. She'd already chosen someone else.

"Nope. I just stumbled upon a Viking in a reading nook and couldn't pass up the opportunity to have a chat."

"Thorne," I said, offering him a curt nod.

"Alek."

Sunday glanced between us and shivered dramatically. "Brrr, is it chilly in here, or is that just more alpha male posturing I'm picking up on?" Then she rolled her eyes. "It was really nice chatting with you, Alek. See you for our next lesson, yeah?"

"Of course."

"Lesson?" Thorne asked, one brow cocked.

"He's teaching me how to control my . . . warriorness."

I laughed. "That's not a word."

"I used it in a sentence, didn't I? And you knew exactly what I meant. Therefore, it's *totally* a word."

"I stand corrected. I'll see you next time. Though I don't think we'll need Kingston to be anyone but himself to get you to attack."

Her lip pulled back in a snarl at the mention of his name. "No. Definitely not."

My brow quirked. *What'd the asshat do now?*

Thorne leaned in and murmured against her ear, something so low I couldn't hear it, but from the way her cheeks turned a deep pink, it wasn't something I wanted to know. He ushered her away from me, one hand on the small of her back in that possessive way alpha assholes had of walking with their women. I hated him on instinct. But was it because of how he was behaving with her? Or because *he* was with her and I wasn't?

Pocketing the mirror, I flopped back in the chair and released a heavy groan. Women had never been complicated. They'd always been fun, and we'd enjoyed a shared release together with no strings attached. The time I'd spent with other women was casual and entertaining, and while I'd felt affection for them, I'd never experienced . . .

well, definitely not whatever this was twisting me up inside.

I threw my arm over my face, not ready to admit just what those feelings might mean. It wasn't like I could act on them anyway. She wasn't mine. Thorne had all but marked her as his mate. And then there was Kingston, her actual wolf mate. Stolen kiss or not, I wasn't even on her radar.

A buzzing at my hip forced me to drop my arm and pull out my phone, tearing me from my wallow. Why the hell was Moira Belladonna texting me rather than just coming to find me?

I opened her message, my eyebrows raising further with each word I read.

Correction. Why the hell was Moira Belladonna *summoning* me?

This should be interesting.

~

I STRODE down the winding path through the witch garden in the southernmost part of the grounds. Of course the witch would ask to meet here. Herbs of all kinds grew in neatly planted rows, the scent of rosemary hitting my nose first, followed shortly by the distinct aroma of sage. My steps crunched on the gravel path, louder than I'd like when approaching someone I wasn't sure meant to scold or praise me for something I'd done.

Low voices reached me first, ratcheting up my confusion. I thought Moira had intended for us to meet alone, but apparently I'd assumed incorrectly. Even more curious as to her intentions, I walked a little faster, finding her standing in the circular center of the garden, benches strategically placed at the points of the pentacle etched into the earth with stone. She was scowling at Kingston, impossible to miss with her hair a vibrant, cornea searing shade of highlighter yellow with neon-green roots.

"What is *he* doing here?" Kingston spat, his eyes hard and annoyed.

"I could ask the same of you."

"Shut up, both of you. You're here because I asked you to be, and that's all you need to know right now." Moira's amethyst gaze flashed with warning as she muttered, "What is it about the devil's eggplant that makes you all act like a bunch of spoiled assholes?"

"The devil's what now?" I asked, unable to stop my grin. "I've heard of the devil's doorbell, but this is a new one."

"Your dick, Nordson. I'm talking about your dicks. Everyone knows what the eggplant emoji is. Surely you have emojis in Novasgard."

I chuckled. "Oh, I know. I just wanted to make you say dick."

"Since you know I am severely allergic to dick, that means you owe me my next ten rounds at *Iniquity,* you ass."

"That's two now."

She glared at me, hands on her hips.

Kingston let out a frustrated groan. "Come on with it, witch. I have places to be that don't involve you or your ragtag team of misfits. What is this all about?"

"Calm your teats, dog boy. We're waiting on one . . ."

Thorne came through the clearing at the mouth of the path to my left, the rumpled state of his shirt and hair leaving little doubt about what he'd been doing before receiving Moira's text. My jaw clenched, and I tore my gaze away from him, but not before I caught sight of the obvious hickey on his throat.

"Oh, good, he's here." Moira clapped her hands together. "Take a seat so we can get started."

Thorne looked first to me and then to Kingston before his brows shot together. "What the bloody hell are you up to, Belladonna?"

"We need to have a talk about Sunday."

Thorne's posture stiffened. "She's fine. I just left her, and I can assure you, *all* her needs are being met."

The low growl that came from Kingston was matched only by my own involuntary snarl. Freya's heaving bosoms, where had *that* come from?

"I said calm your fucking teats, wolf," Moira said, pure venom in her voice. "This is exactly why we're here. The three of you."

"What about us?" I asked.

"I'm sure at least one of you is going to try to deny it, but it goes without saying that all of you are drawn to my roomie."

"I'm not part of this." Even as I said it, the argument fell flat.

Moira rolled her eyes. "Thanks for proving my point, Viking. But yes, you are. All of you are. And after what happened the other night, it's pretty obvious to me that Sunday is going to need all three of you if she has any chance of staying safe."

Alarm shot through my chest, leaving me cold and on edge. "What about the other night? What haven't you told me?"

Moira's eyes flared, anger making them glitter like jewels. "We were taken by hunters."

"What?" Kingston snarled, his body trembling, eyes glowing deep amber as he and his wolf battled for control.

Wrath unlike anything I'd felt before uncoiled in my chest, something untamed and feral rattling through me. "Where?" I demanded.

Moira fought against a smile. "Easy, tiger. Sunday and I took care of it. Mostly Sunday, but you don't need to worry about running off and ripping heads from bodies. I just meant that they've come after her twice now. Clearly these guys are after something, and I think all of us would feel a lot better if we knew she wasn't going to find herself in a situation where she had to deal with them on her own."

"And so you summoned all of us here and left her on her own?" Kingston's voice was an inhuman growl.

Moira narrowed her eyes at the shifter. "I hoped she'd remain safe while on campus, but after today, if you idiots follow the plan, we won't need to worry about that again."

Thorne crossed his arms over his chest. "I can protect her."

"Can you? You did a bang-up job of it the other night. Real hero stuff there, buddy."

I rounded on him. "You were there and let her get taken? What the hell is wrong with you?"

"The bastards used silver. They came out of nowhere."

"So what's to keep them from doing it again? Clearly you can't be trusted with her safety on your own," I snapped, fury still surging through my veins.

"Oh, and you think you can, is that it?"

"I sure as shit wouldn't be taken out by a bit of fucking metal. If that's what you're asking."

Kingston took a step toward me. "It's my job to keep her safe. If she'd just accept the truth and let me claim her, she wouldn't be out roaming the streets with a leech."

OBSESSION

"Silver would stop you just as easily," I pointed out. "I'm the only one here unaffected."

"And you think you can stay with her twenty-four hours a day? I bet you'd love that. Having her all to yourself so you could convince her to finally give you the time of day." Kingston's words hit home, and rage boiled in my blood.

"Just give it a break, you three," Moira said, holding her hands out. "We get it. You all have massively big tree trunk dicks. No one cares. We aren't impressed. This is about Sunday and her well-being. I thought you could all be grown-ups long enough to admit she would be safer if all of us work together. But if I was wrong about you—"

"Enough, häxa. You've made your point." She startled, her eyes going wide as the words she'd been about to say died on her tongue at my harsh tone.

"You're proposing we all care for her?" Thorne asked, his question hesitant. "She's my mate."

"Mine," Kingston growled. "She. Is. Mine."

Another ripple of possessive anger rose in my chest, and I had to fight to keep myself from biting out *mine* as well. My hands balled into tight fists, clenching so hard my knuckles cracked.

Moira smirked at us. "It's hardly unheard of for a strong woman to have multiple protectors and/or lovers. The fae have been working together successfully for ages. I'm sure you can figure it out."

"Multiple lovers?" I asked.

"Absolutely not." Kingston stared at me, the promise of pain in his eyes if I so much as touched her.

If only he knew just how much of her I had already touched.

Thorne, surprisingly, didn't protest.

"And you?" I pressed, curious as to his seeming acceptance. "Are you okay with this? You've practically marked her as yours already."

"I realized she was meant for me a while ago. The mate bond is strong even though we haven't completed the ritual. But I've already accepted that the wolf part of her is connected to Kingston. It's not out of the realm of possibility for her to have more than just the two of us."

"Don't get ahead of yourselves. It's Sunday's choice who she ultimately ends up with," Moira reminded us. "But if you all care for her as much as it seems you do, then this is a way for you all to have what you want. Devotion comes in many forms. Not all of them have to involve sex, you know."

"So you're not proposing to also be part of this . . . what do you call it, harem?" I asked.

"No. There's too much sausage at the table. I'm here for platonic moral support. You three are a lot to handle. Something tells me she'll need my help."

I smiled at that. If today's meeting proved anything, it was that she was right. "Fair enough." I made eye contact with each of the men. "Whatever happens, her safety is the most important thing. I think we can all agree on that."

"Agreed," Thorne said, turning his attention to Kingston. "Are you in?"

The wolf remained silent, a muscle in his jaw ticking furiously as he considered the question. "Fine," he spat, the words seeming to cost him. "Since you seem to already have been inside what's mine, I suppose I have to let you keep her safe."

I had to hand it to Thorne; he managed to keep his cool and not rise to the bait. He held out a palm, waiting for Kingston to shake on the agreement. When the shifter finally took the offer, Thorne then turned to me. "Viking?"

I took his hand in mine, surprised by the strength of his grasp as we shook on our pledge. "For Sunday."

"Aw, would you look at that? Miracles do happen. Can I get you to kiss and make up now?"

"Don't push your luck, witch."

She held up her hands. "Got it. This is a no swords crossing zone."

I laughed. "So what now? Do we draw straws and pick shifts?"

"If we're going to do this, we have to make it seem as normal as we can for her. Sunday Fallon doesn't like to be told what she can or can't do. Trust me, I know." Kingston's voice held a note of regret, which surprised me. "We'll need to put ourselves in her path and keep an eye out without letting her know we're working together."

"Do you really think she won't figure it out?" Thorne asked, his voice laced with amusement. "You must not know her as well as you think you do. She's no fool. She'll sniff you out the second you start paying attention to her."

"She may, but if we tell her the plan, she'll refuse. This way, we don't give her a choice. Wherever she is, one of us is there."

"Force her. Of course that's your tactic."

Kingston snarled a harsh, "At least I don't abandon her every single time I get scared."

"Oh, for fuck's sake," I sighed, stepping between them. "Let's just do our best to be discreet, and when the time comes to reveal our hand, we tell her the truth. Until then, it might be good if you two stay away from each other. You're about as pleasant to be around as a bare ass against a cactus."

"We take shifts. Communicate when we're taking her anywhere. More than one of us should be nearby if she's off

285

campus. That includes the club, Thorne. She can't be alone. Not ever." Kingston's posture was tense, ready to fight.

"And when you need to hunt, let one of us know," I told Thorne, noting the dark circles under his eyes. A clear sign the vampire hadn't been feeding. "I'm not going to take her from you. I swear it."

"As if you could," he drawled.

I didn't respond to that. "You are no good to her weak. And no matter how much you posture, you are weak. I can smell it on you."

"All I can smell is her pussy on him," Kingston bit out.

Moira glared at him. "Where her pussy has or hasn't been is none of your business, dog boy. Stop with the temper tantrum because she doesn't want to play with little Kingston."

"There's nothing little about him, I assure you."

Moira rolled her eyes. "Men," she sighed. "You all seem to forget the things I can do with my fist are far more impressive than what you can do with that piece of meat between your legs."

That shut us all up. I gaped at her, trying not to picture what she was describing.

"Thorne, you need to go hunt. There's no way around it. Kingston, you take the first shift. Don't you have a session with her today, anyway?" Moira asked.

He gave her a tight nod. "I do. I'm already late for it."

"Then off you go. No need to give her more reasons to hate you." As he turned away, she called, "But, Kingston? A word to the wise. You can't call her your mate and then turn around and shove your cock inside the first willing hole you find and expect her not to be upset. Keep that in mind for the future, will ya?"

"Looking out for her includes her emotional wellbeing,"

I told him, my voice hard. "You hurt her in any way, wolf, you answer to me."

"And me," Thorne echoed, solidifying our future as a team. From here on out, Sunday had at least two men pledged to remain at her side no matter what. Kingston would come around . . . or he'd be removed from the equation.

The choice was his.

CHAPTER
THIRTY-THREE
KINGSTON

Where the fuck was she? I paced along the shore of the lake, trying to catch Sunday's scent. Praying for there to be no trace of her because I couldn't handle it if she'd been there and left, or worse, been taken while I'd been preoccupied with the witch and her plot. All I smelled was earth and the slightly muddy aroma of stagnant water. Not a hint of the sweet lilac that called to me even when I was asleep. Even though I tried like hell to keep it out.

It had been worse ever since I'd seen the broken look in her eyes while I pounded into . . . what was her name . . . Hope?

The proof that Sunday had felt something, anything, more than lust and indifference had torn me apart. If I thought there was any chance she might actually care about me, I never would have done it. No matter how badly my balls ached and how desperate I'd been for release, there was no substitute for my mate. I sank myself willingly into the first girl who'd said yes, chasing the mind-numbing pleasure as a tool to push Sunday away.

MEG ANNE & K. LORAINE

But it hadn't worked.

The truth was, I'd all but lost my hard-on until Sunday burst through the clearing and I locked eyes with her. Without warning, that need, that primal desire to fuck and claim and mark her came roaring to the surface, and I couldn't have stopped the orgasm even though I wanted to. But it wasn't for the girl under me. It was all for *her*.

Sunday.

My mate.

Every single time, it was for her. Ever since the day I first laid eyes on her. She owned my body and my soul. Whether she wanted them or not.

And I wished I could hate her for it.

My phone buzzed in my pocket, dragging me back from the memory of my betrayal. Fucking Moira. How did she even have my number?

"Hello, witch. Miss me already?"

"Ha! Not likely. I was calling to inform you that you're failing already, asshole. Sunday is in our room when she's supposed to be with you."

"Goddammit. Stubborn wolf. Keep her there. Leave the door unlocked."

I hung up before she could respond, shoved my phone into my pocket, and stalked back the way I came. She had avoided me over the last week, and I wasn't letting it happen anymore. Her time for pouting was up.

I caught her scent as soon as I reached the stairwell, and my cock stood up and took notice as well. "Down, boy," I muttered, taking the stairs two at a time. I was on her floor in no time flat, not even bothering to knock as I sent the door to her room crashing open.

Sunday looked up at me in shock, her expression

shifting from surprise to anger in half a second. "What the hell do you think you're—"

I crossed the room and flung her over my shoulder. I wasn't here to listen to any more of her shit. She was coming one way or the other. We'd get to the good kind of coming eventually, but for now, this would have to do.

I chuckled as her tiny fists hammered on my back. My arm banded around her thighs held her tightly in place, her wolf already bending to the Alpha who had her in his grasp. It felt good to touch her, even if I was pissing her off.

And anger was sort of like foreplay for us at this point. Once we worked out all our shit, we would be explosive. I just knew it.

My wolf pushed at me, begging me to take her back to my room rather than the lake, asking me to give in to my instinct, which screamed to take her and make her mine. But I couldn't. I wouldn't touch her that way until she was begging me for it. That first time in the library, when I'd lost control and let my wolf take over, had been crossing a line I'd promised never to cross again. *I* was in control, not my beast.

"I swear to God, Kingston, put me down right this instant or—"

"Or you'll what, exactly?" People popped their heads out of their rooms as I hauled her down the hallway, my goal in sight, the stairs. "No one here is going to help you. They know you need training. They're all still afraid you're going to snap and kill them."

"That was a low blow, you sonofabitch."

"Oh, keep talking dirty. It turns me on."

That shut her up, which made me laugh. It shouldn't be so much fun getting her riled up.

"I'm sure one of your harem of willing women will be

thanking me then. Do you have someone lined up to bend over a rock after I leave?"

Her anger meant she still cared. It was her indifference —and her pain—that cut me apart. Anger I'd gladly face all day long. It meant there was a chance my wolf and I would get exactly what we wanted. And anything that ended with me sinking balls deep inside Sunday Fallon was worth the wait.

I stopped, dropping her so her body slid down the front of mine. Her shock held her still as I caught her gaze, holding her chin between my thumb and forefinger. "Listen up, Sunshine. I'm only going to say this once. From now on, the only woman I'm bending over anything is you."

"Well, I'm not interested."

"Liar. I can smell how much you want me right now. But that's all right. We'll get there. Once we free your wolf, you won't be able to resist the urge to present for your Alpha."

Her eyes flared wide as her breath hitched. Fuck, the sounds she made, even small like that, got to me. "Fuck you, Kingston."

"Patience. Like I said, we'll get there. Now come on. We have work to do."

Two hours later, we were both sweaty, out of breath, and more than a little dirty. Other than scratching the hell out of my shirt and chest with her claws, Sunday was no closer to fully shifting. I could sense her wolf, far closer to the surface than ever before, but there was still something caging her. Until we figured out just what that was, Sunday wouldn't be able to break free.

I was hard and aching, exhausted from using so much control and fighting my beast's natural instinct to mark my mate. But my job was far from over. More than that, with every passing moment I spent with Sunday, my desire to protect her grew stronger. I didn't just have to be with her; I fucking *wanted* to.

It was a hell of a revelation, especially after so many years of forcing myself to hate her.

Even as the need to claim her roared in my veins, there was no denying spending time with her also soothed something wild and broken inside me. It was right.

She was right.

We were meant to be. I just needed to make her see it too.

I followed close beside her as we walked through the courtyard, filled with students studying, chatting together, and laughing. I hadn't really laughed in far too long. I'd been too busy trying to drown my sorrows in booze and women who didn't matter. Or, if I wasn't doing that, I was in the music hall purging my pain on the keys of a piano.

She was so focused on getting away from me, she clearly didn't see the stepladder in her path as she made a beeline for the door that led inside. My hand twitched as I reached on instinct to press my palm to the small of her back and steer her toward safety.

"What are you doing?" she snapped, slapping my hand away.

Her vitriol instantly soured my mood. "Trying to keep you from eating shit in front of the entire campus. My bad. It won't happen again."

Glancing from me to the ladder in her way, then back again, her expression softened. "Oh. Thanks."

I immediately craned my neck up and scanned the sky.

"What are you looking for?"

"Checking to see if pigs randomly started to fly or if the world is coming to a sudden and fiery end. Because, as far as I know, those are the only two scenarios where you'd ever willingly thank me for anything."

Her lips twitched into a slight smile. "I'm not that bad."

"Yeah, you are. But I've earned it."

"No shit."

The words might have been harsh, but her tone wasn't. She was warming to me. I pointed to the posters recently affixed to the wall of the courtyard. "Did you see this?"

She glanced at the sign announcing the upcoming Midnight Masquerade with a frown. "Really? A ball? Aren't we a little . . . old for school dances?"

"This isn't just a dance. It's our first foray into political niceties. It's a test."

"What do you mean?"

"It's the first time everyone in attendance will have full access to their power without any limitations. We're . . . taken off our leashes, so to speak." I shrugged. "And if we make it through without killing each other, we get to continue through the remainder of the year."

Sunday's brows flew up. "Is that safe?"

"Not remotely. But life in our world rarely is." I smirked. "So far, only a handful of creatures have died."

"That's comforting." The sarcasm in her tone was impossible to miss.

I took a sharp breath and prepared myself to step out on a ledge I hadn't braved since she'd rejected me. "Sunday, would you—"

"There you are, dove," Thorne called from the other side of the courtyard, the bastard looking like he stepped out of the pages of motherfucking GQ magazine. "I've been looking everywhere for you."

"I bet you have," I muttered. The vampire had clearly fed, his eyes bright and no longer ringed by purple bruise-like circles. I hated that he could turn her head so easily. Like I didn't even exist to her anymore.

She went to him, nestling against his chest with a relieved smile on her lovely face. I wanted to make her smile like that.

Fuck.

"You're looking well," she murmured, pressing an innocent kiss to his cheek. A fucking brush of lips had jealousy gnawing on my insides. Any hope or wishful thinking I'd been nurturing died a swift death.

"I'm feeling well. I'm sorry I had to leave to feed. It's the nature of the beast, I'm afraid."

"You shouldn't go so long without. Especially not because of me."

Their display of togetherness had me barely resisting the urge to dry heave. Or start punching things. I needed to get the fuck out of here. Turning on my heel, I intended to do just that. My shift was over. The package transferred. Job done.

"Wait, Kingston. You were about to ask me something . . ."

Her voice sliced through me. There was a tenderness in the words I hadn't expected. Like it mattered to her, whatever I'd been about to ask.

"No. Don't worry about it. I already have my answer."

CHAPTER

THIRTY-FOUR

SUNDAY

"Is this what it's like in Novasgard?" I asked, annoyance coloring my tone.

Alek chuckled from his spot two steps behind me as we walked down the hall and toward my dorm. "I have no idea what you mean."

"Big bad Vikings shadowing their women? Giving them no space to breathe?"

He laughed again. "Definitely not. Our women carry axes and know how to use them. Strega, our jarl, would skin the man that tried to imply she couldn't take care of herself. All the women would."

I stopped so quickly he crashed into me, knocking me off balance. He reached to steady me, but I righted myself and jerked out of his hold, turning to face him, daggers in my stare. "Oh, I see."

The amusement in his expression fled, telling me he instantly realized his misstep. "That's not what I—"

"Isn't it? You should quit while you're ahead. You three think I haven't figured out what you're doing? God, it's so

297

obvious. You think I can't handle myself, that I'll hurt someone. You don't trust me."

My chest burned with embarrassment. I'd thought I was doing better. Gaining control. Even today in our session, Alek had told me how far I'd come. But if it wasn't him acting as my shadow, it was Noah, or worse, Kingston.

"No, Sunday. You misunderstand. Even the strongest women need someone to watch their backs. It's not about your control. It's about your safety."

"Safety? I'm safe here. I'm not sure how you missed it with as far up my ass as you've been lately, but I haven't left the campus since the hunters snatched me and Moira." I reached for the doorknob but stopped, sighing. "I just need some space to breathe. I can't believe I'm saying it, but I do."

Apology flickered in his eyes, but I could already tell by the determined cast of his face that he had no intention of backing off. His next words confirmed it.

"Are you going out again tonight?"

With a frustrated huff, I whipped around, tearing my gaze from him. My long braid connected with the stubborn Viking's broad chest, and for the briefest moment, I wished for his fist to catch me by my hair and tug me back against him. Instead, I entered the room and slammed the door before he could protest. Or piss me off further by trying some stupid alpha male maneuver like following me inside.

"Um. Hi?" Moira said from where she was perched on the edge of her bed.

"Men are stupid."

"Truth." She gave me a considering once-over and closed her book before setting it beside her. "I know why I think so. But what finally convinced you?"

"Them. All of them. They won't leave me alone."

"That's what happens when you have a magic pussy."

I dropped my jacket on my desk and peeled off my sweaty workout clothes to change into something more comfortable. "That would make sense if anyone other than Noah had access to it. But seeing as how even he's pissing me off right now, he's not getting it either. The only man *not* annoying the shit out of me these days is a hot priest. So what's your next excuse?"

Moira snickered. "Well, that was more information than I thought I'd be privy to. We're going to circle back to the priest in a minute." She stood and walked to the small cabinet where we kept a few bottles of wine, said a little spell under her breath, and the cork popped free. "This calls for some alcohol."

"God, yes," I groaned. "Seriously, Moira. It's like I haven't had a second to myself since the night with the hunters. And I can't believe I'm about to say this, but having three sexy men breathing down my neck nearly every second of the day is not as fun as you might think. It's infuriating. I swear to you, Kingston followed me straight into the bathroom this morning. It wasn't until I shoved him back out on his ass that he finally stayed put. Like, what the actual fuck? Did he think I needed his help peeing? Or is he so desperate to get into my pants that he thought coming in with me would get him closer?"

A guilty look flickered in her eyes.

"Moira . . . I know that face. That's the face of someone who needs to fess up."

"Guilty as charged," she admitted. "I may, uh, have something to do with your prison guards."

"What? Why? You were there. I kicked ass."

Pouring us both a glass of rich red wine, she motioned to my bed. "Sit down first."

I held my hand out for one of the glasses. "How about you wine me first? Seems like I'm going to need it." Once we both had our beverages, we settled on the bed, but she wouldn't look at me. "Moira, you're scaring me. What's going on?"

"Do you remember how I told you about my aunt Tabitha?"

"The one who has visions, right?"

"Yeah, well . . . surprise, Tabitha is me. I'm the one with the visions."

"So this is like an *asking for a friend* situation?"

She took a big gulp of her wine and nodded. "People freak out when they realize you get glimpses of the future. They either start demanding every little detail, or they want nothing to do with you."

"So, you had a vision?" I swallowed back the tension building in my gut. "About me?"

She bit her lip and nodded slowly. "Nothing specific. They don't work that way. It's just images and emotions. I saw enough to know something's coming for you, Sunday. I don't know what or who or when, but I know these men are part of it. My vision made one thing clear. You need them. So I asked them to keep you safe."

That changed things. A cold shard of fear sliced deep, lodging itself in my belly. She wouldn't have done this if it wasn't serious. "You asked them to watch over me? And even Kingston agreed?"

"Believe it or not, getting them to agree wasn't the hard part. They're all crazy about you. The second they realized you were in danger, they were all but demanding to be the one to save you. It was the working together part they struggled with. But, in the end, all of them came around." She frowned then, a shadow passing through her eyes.

"There's a fourth figure I sense around you. I didn't see a face, so I'm not sure who it's supposed to be, but he's out there."

I squirmed under her scrutiny. I knew who she saw. Who I tried—and failed—not to think about. Was she also a secret mind reader? I tried to bring up the mental shield Noah had been teaching me to use just in case. She didn't need to know my sordid fantasies about Caleb. No one did. Panic clutched my throat, causing my breaths to come in shallow gasps.

Moira reached out, her brows furrowed. "I'm so sorry, Sunday. If I'd realized how much it would upset you, I wouldn't have done it. I just wanted to protect you." As soon as her hand connected with mine, a frisson of electric energy shot up my arm, and a chill bolted down my spine. The world around me went gray, and my head swam.

"Moira, what—"

I stared at her, my vision clearing as she came into focus. Her eyes were clouded, a pale smoky white. Eerie and unnerving.

"Moira! Moira, are you okay?"

Her limbs trembled, eyes rolling back in her head. Holy fuck, was she having a seizure? What did I do? How could I help her? Her hand released mine, and she went still.

As quick as it had come over her, the fit or spell or whatever it had been was gone. Blinking rapidly, she shook her head, her hair changing from a vibrant indigo to a deep emerald green. When her eyes lifted back to mine, genuine fear shone in their depths.

"Moira, what is it?"

"I saw . . ." She licked her lips, her voice hoarse. "It was a vision. Sunday, the things I saw." She shook her head, refusing to elaborate on whatever had put that haunted look in her eyes. "You have a choice to make. They're with you for a reason. If you choose wrong, the consequences will be dire." The tremble in her words scared me. "It's worse than I thought."

"What consequences?"

"Death, Pestilence, Famine . . . and War."

"Like the apocalypse?"

Swallowing hard, she locked gazes with me. "I think so."

Jesus. If that wasn't enough to knock the wind out of you . . . I sat there, her words heavy in my mind . . . and my heart. I knew the idea of having them all was too good to be true.

"Are you saying that if I don't choose correctly, I'll start the end of the world?"

Moira nodded.

I let out a burst of hysterical laughter. "So . . . no pressure then."

CHAPTER
THIRTY-FIVE
SUNDAY

P rofessor Moriarty droned on, and it was a struggle to keep my eyes open. The man had a monotone that could have made an erotic novel sound positively boring. Add to that the history of a centuries-long blood feud, and he'd lost me the second his mouth opened.

The only positive thing about the history class was being sandwiched between Noah and Alek. I was overwhelmed by the way their scents seemed to complement each other. Even though I'd made a resolution to stop thinking about anyone other than Noah in *that* way. It was one thing to tell myself that and something else entirely to get my body on board.

Apparently, ending my twenty some odd year dry spell had turned me into a thirsty bitch. Noah took excellent care of me, often keeping me up through several toe-curling orgasms well into the wee hours of the morning. And yet, here I was, picturing what it would be like if Alek and I did the same. Or better yet, all three of us.

Stop. It.

I shifted restlessly in my seat, adjusting my torso so I

was positioned more toward Noah than Alek. Warm eyes the color of melted honey met mine, Noah's brows furrowing as he tried to get a read on me. I had my thoughts blocked in the hope I could focus, and even though he'd been teaching me to do it, I could tell he didn't like the separation.

Long fingers trailed across my wrist and up the underside of my forearm in seemingly mindless patterns. I loved the feel of his skin on mine, the clarity his touch brought me, the feeling of pure connection. We were supposed to be together. I was making the right choice. It was Noah.

Alek's arm brushed against my back, disrupting my attempt to behave. Almost as if he could sense me trying to keep him in his own little box and refused to play along. I straightened, subtly pulling away only for his thigh to press against mine. As frustrated as I wanted to be, I secretly loved that he was keeping the two of us connected.

Biting back a smile, I glanced at my notes, blinking a few times as the words on my notebook rearranged themselves, my distinctly bubbly print transforming into a much more masculine scrawl.

Alek's persistence suddenly made a lot more sense.

He'd just passed me a note. Or the Novasgardian equivalent.

My heart stuttered, and my insides turned to jelly as I scanned the words and the two little boxes at the bottom.

WILL YOU GO TO THE DANCE WITH ME? CHECK ONE.

Instead of supplying me with two options, both boxes said YES! in all caps and enthusiastically underlined.

I couldn't help myself. I giggled. It was ridiculous. And fucking adorable. And exactly what I needed.

"Miss Fallon? Something funny about the pixie geno-cide of the early 1800s?" Professor Moriarty snapped in his froggy voice. It matched his frog-like face.

"No, sir," I said, blushing furiously.

Noah's gaze dropped to my notebook, and he groaned softly. "Oh, come the fuck on, man. How old are you? We're not in bloody primary school."

Alek smirked at him over my head. "Old enough to recognize some things are always classic. Aren't they, Sunny?"

"Classically stupid," Noah muttered.

"It was sweet," I corrected automatically, sending Noah's brows flying upward.

"I see. So I guess it would be a waste of my time to ask you to attend the ball with me then?"

Oh, for fuck's sake.

What had started off as an insanely sweet gesture had just turned into my personal torture session. How the hell was I supposed to choose between them? Whoever said having grown men fighting over them was sexy had never lived through the experience. I'd rather swallow a bag of nails than have to make this decision.

My brain knew what I needed to do, mostly thanks to Moira's terrifying warning, but my heart was of an entirely different mind about the situation.

"Technically, I asked her first," Alek pointed out, wrapping one of his big arms around my shoulders and tugging me close.

Fury rolled off Noah in waves, and he hadn't stopped touching my arm since before this started. He opened his mouth to speak, but no sound escaped. That only made his anger more palpable as he tried again and failed to respond.

"That'll be enough from you, Mr. Blackthorne. In fact, I

believe it would be best for all parties if you three remained silent and enjoyed my lecture since you seem so desperate to participate." Professor Moriarty's wicked smile contrasted with the dry tone of his voice. "The three of you can have your voices back once class is over."

Snickers rippled through the class, one standing out over all the rest. My gaze landed on Kingston, sitting in the back row, legs spread like the royalty he was named for, a shit-eating grin across his lips.

Alek's thick finger tapped on my notebook, drawing my attention back to his message. I snorted, despite my mortification at being so publicly called out by our professor. Before I could do anything, Noah took my pen and scratched out both boxes.

Huffing, I tore the paper out of the book and crumbled it before shoving it into my bag. Then I crossed my arms over my chest and stared straight ahead at our toad of a teacher, desperate to look at anyone but the two men who both wanted something from me.

I had two invitations from two beautiful men I wanted, but it had never been more clear to me that I had to make a choice. Anxiety curled in my belly, forming a cold pit that gnawed incessantly.

Which would keep us safe, and which would end the world? How could I know who was the right choice?

I COULDN'T GET out of the room fast enough when Professor Moriarty dismissed the class. I wanted my voice back. But more than that, I wanted the pressure of their gazes, and their expectation, off me. How could I choose one of them over the other?

Even if I knew I had to.

"Sunday, wait," Noah called, following behind me.

I knew he could've been in front of me, blocking my path before I could even blink if he wanted. Still, he chased, his breath hot on the back of my neck. I was too frustrated to acknowledge him or Alek. I needed to breathe, to have some space to think.

"Leave me alone, Noah."

"Never going to happen, dove. You're mine, remember?"

"Mine," Alek said. "She belongs to both of us—"

I whirled around, my hair flying. "Excuse me? Belongs?"

Alek's eyes widened, the icy blue irises searing into my soul. "I . . . I don't know where that came from."

I narrowed my eyes but didn't sense anything but raw honesty rolling off the Novasgardian. Just to be clear, though, I took a step forward, poking him in the chest. "Good, because I'm the only one that gets to decide who I'm in a committed relationship with, and last time I checked, Noah is the only one who fits that bill."

Noah smirked, wrapping his arm around my shoulders. "So it's settled then. You'll attend the ball at my side."

I slapped his arm away. "No, it isn't, because I'm not going."

"What? You can't just *not* go. This is part of our—"

"I can do whatever the fuck I want, Noah Blackthorne. How are they going to know if I'm faking being sick? Spoiler alert, they won't."

"Father Gallagher will know," Alek butted in. "I don't like the way he watches you. He's possessive."

I snorted. "Says the man who just growled *mine* like a caveman."

He blushed. The big, strong Viking man *blushed*. "Um . . ."

309

"If you don't go, neither will I." Noah slid his palm over the small of my back, sending a shiver down my spine. "I'd rather spend the night in bed, anyway."

I opened and closed my mouth. It was a tempting offer, but he was missing the point. Just because I had feelings for him didn't mean I suddenly wanted someone else making decisions about *my* life or who I could or couldn't spend time with. That decision was my own, and since I didn't feel comfortable making it, I decided I wouldn't choose any of them. I'd choose myself instead.

"No. If I don't go, it's because I want to be alone."

"Not possible, *Kærasta*." The way Alek said that word had something in my chest warming. Like something was awakened in me.

"Why not?"

"You know why."

I released a heavy breath, some of the fight leaving me. Stupid Moira and her stupid visions. "Okay, then Moira can stay with me and babysit. Penis not required."

Alek leaned close, invading my space. "Maybe not, but in this, I will not be swayed. Your safety is my top priority, whether you like it or not. So either you go to the ball with one of us, or you stay home with one of us. It's the only way we can keep you safe until the threat is neutralized."

"I should have just stayed locked in my tower back home. This is ridiculous. Why does anyone want to kill me, anyway? I'm a defective shifter. Damaged goods."

Noah stiffened beside me, but Alek beat him to the protest. Curling his hand around my cheek, eyes warm with an emotion I was too scared to name, he shook his head. "No, Sunday. You are perfect. I've felt the power pouring through you. It consumes me. You're a lot of things.

Exquisite. Unique. Untamed. But damaged is not one of them."

There he went, being a swoony bastard again. This was why I couldn't stay mad at him. He did shit like that. "I don't want to choose."

"So don't. Take us both," Alek suggested.

"Both?" I snorted. "And what is Madame Moody going to say when she sees me walking in sandwiched between the two of you?"

"Do you really think a deity is going to care how many men you have at your side? Have you ever read mythology? The gods take new lovers as often as they change clothes. She wouldn't bat an eye at you arriving with both of us."

That gave me pause. Here it was again. More proof that polyamory wasn't just accepted in our society; in some instances, it was encouraged.

"You both really want to go with me?"

"You know there's no other choice for me, little wolf," Noah said, eyes blazing hot.

"Nor I," Alek admitted, his voice tender.

Slow clapping filled the air, and like a snake slithering from his hiding place, Kingston appeared out of the shadows. "Well done, Sunshine. You got them both to hand you their balls." He stepped closer and inhaled. "You must really have a magical cunt. I wasn't aware the Viking had gotten a taste too."

Anger curled in my belly, calling my wolf to the surface. "Don't be a little bitch because they have what you want."

"Who says I still want you? I don't like sloppy seconds."

"The way you always seem to pop up and metaphorically pull on my pigtails like a stupid schoolyard bully."

A wicked glint flashed in his eyes. "The only time I'll be

pulling your hair is when I'm deep inside you, fucking you so hard you forget all about these two."

I wasn't even going to point out that he was contradicting himself. "In your dreams."

"Are you sure you don't mean in yours?"

A bolt of arousal hit me, merging with my anger and sending my wolf howling with need. I hated that I wanted him, but there was no ignoring my body's reaction to his promise. Even if I had no intention of acting on it.

Noah stepped in front of me, shoulders tense. "The difference between us and you, dog, is that we are giving her what she wants. I'd rather share her and be given a place in her heart than spend my life on the outside looking in. You're too bloody selfish to do that, which means you'll never be hers."

Kingston scowled, but I caught the hint of pain Noah's words caused before he quickly covered the emotion with more posturing. "Keep her. I'm done fighting for a mate who doesn't want me."

Guilt and something that tasted a lot like sorrow tore at me. As childish as he could be, I never meant to hurt Kingston. Everything he'd done since the day of our mating ceremony had been a direct result of my rejection. It didn't forgive his awful behavior, but it put it in a new light.

Kingston stormed off, leaving me torn between wanting to punch him, hug him, and fuck him all at the same time. I hated it.

My shoulders slumped, and I turned away from the path he'd headed down. I needed to let go of him, but I couldn't. It hurt. Even though I had two strong, protective, gorgeous men at my side, Kingston's anger physically hurt me. My wolf mourned every second he was away from us.

Almost in unison, Alek and Noah took my hands,

infusing me with their strength and comforting me with their silent support.

"We're here with you. We always will be, Sunny. And one day, he'll realize what he did." Alek's deep voice soothed the ache in my chest, filling the wound Kingston's callous words had carved into my heart.

"And he'll regret not choosing you over himself," Noah added.

I hoped it was true. Lord knew a part of me regretted the moment I'd rejected him. And that part grew a little larger every single day.

THAT NIGHT I WAS RESTLESS, indecision and worry warring for top billing in my mind. Despite Alek and Noah's assurances, I couldn't help but feel that choosing someone would devastate those I left behind. The thought of hurting any of them was killing me inside. I needed someone to talk to, someone who wasn't going to just tell me to let the world burn, keep them all, and ride them to the finish line, like Moira.

A chill seeped into my bones as I stalked across the grounds in search of the only person I wanted to bare my soul to tonight. Rain hit me in icy drops, freezing my skin and raising goosebumps everywhere it touched. Normally I liked the rain, but not now. It only added to the melancholy in my heart.

I hesitated only for a moment as I stood outside the abandoned church Caleb had claimed as his classroom. It stood on the edge of the property, complete with a creepy graveyard. I shuddered as my focus landed on the spectral figure floating just above one of the tombstones. He was

dressed in what appeared to be wedding clothes, now tattered and moth-eaten. The skeletal man doffed his moldering top hat.

"Oh hell no," I muttered, throwing open the door as I noped straight inside the church. A cranky vampire priest was much better than Skeletor out there. Better the devil you know, and all that.

"Miss Fallon?" Caleb said as soon as I shut the huge doors behind me. The echo of the wood slamming shut filled the cavernous space.

"Did you know there's a ghost outside?"

"You mean Friedrich?"

"You *named* him? That's like adopting a trash panda. You're only encouraging him to stick around."

"His name is Friedrich, and he's been in that same spot for the last hundred years, waiting for his wife to join him. Sadly, when they were killed on their wedding night, she was turned into a vampire and has never come to find him."

Pity replaced my fear, and I found myself depressed on his behalf. "Well, damn, now I feel bad for ditching him."

Something soft shimmered in his eyes. "Don't worry, he's doing what he feels he must. We are all ruled by instinct and desire, even if we don't want to be."

"Have a lot of experience with that, do you, Padre?"

"A lifetime's worth. Now, tell me what brings you here in the middle of the night, Miss Fallon."

I looked around the sanctuary. Pews still filled the space, but instead of a pulpit, a large oak desk loomed at the end of the aisle. "This is where you teach? A church? Isn't that a bit on the nose?"

"I teach theology."

He said it so simply like he was telling me it was raining outside. Even so, I couldn't help but wonder if he merely

preferred being surrounded by the trappings of the life he'd intended to lead. Or if the reminder of what he'd lost was yet another way for him to torment himself.

"Fair enough." I trailed the tip of my index finger over the back of one of the pews. "I guess this does lend your class an air of . . . authenticity."

"I do try."

I'd never been in a Catholic church before, but there was no mistaking the ornate wooden structure situated on the right side of the sanctuary. "A confessional? Really?"

"You'd be surprised how freeing confession is."

The way he said it gave me pause. "You still confess?"

"I have no confessor to speak to, but I am penitent in my own way. I can only pray that God hears me, damned as I am." He strode down the aisle, not asking me to come with him, but I followed anyway. "What is weighing so heavily on your heart? I can feel the burden you're carrying tonight."

He'd given me the opening I needed, but now that the time was upon me, I found myself suddenly shy. How could I look at him when admitting to the things keeping me awake?

"Can you still hear my confession?"

He stopped, turning so swiftly I had to take several steps back to catch my balance. "You seek the Sacrament of Reconciliation?"

"I'm not Catholic or anything, but if it's all you chalked it up to be, why not?"

"I can't offer absolution. You understand that?"

"I don't care. I just need to talk to someone without them judging me."

His entire countenance softened, and for the first time,

real tenderness shone in his sapphire eyes. "I can give you that."

His admission showed me a kindness he hadn't revealed to me before. Instead of fire and brimstone, there was only understanding. For the first time, he wasn't just my mentor or punisher; he was offering to be my friend. It was . . . everything I hadn't realized I'd been hoping for when I blindly made my way through the storm to find him.

Taking my hand, he led me over to the structure and held open the deep purple curtain so I could step inside. I frowned, glancing between the small wooden bench and the kneeler.

"Am I supposed to get on my knees for you again?"

"It's your choice, but I find it helps with my mindset when I kneel. The discomfort brings with it focus."

"Knees it is then," I said with a heavy sigh.

He released the fabric, and the space went dim. I thanked my lucky stars I wasn't claustrophobic, because there wasn't much room in this antique confessional booth. It smelled of wood polish and age, but the scent quickly changed to incense and spice and everything Caleb as soon as he took his place on the other side of the lattice screen. For something that was supposed to be anonymous, this didn't do a very good job of hiding anyone's identity. Maybe that was because I knew it was him.

Either way, it was unexpectedly intimate, making me think of the other places you'd whisper your secrets in the dark.

Dropping to my knees, I positioned myself, my wet skin sticking to the leather kneeler and making a funny sucking sound as I got comfortable. Caleb didn't laugh, but I would

have sworn his lips lifted with amusement on the other side of the booth.

Clasping my hands, I took a deep breath and asked, "Okay, how do I start?"

"Typically, the penitent begins by saying, 'Bless me, father, for I have sinned, it's been however long since my last confession.' And then they lay out the sins their soul has collected since their previous unburdening."

I swallowed. "Okay." Then I repeated his words, adding that it had been twenty-three years since my last confession.

"I can't bless you, Sunday. But I can listen. Unburden yourself to me. Tell me why you look so sad."

Here we were. The part where I was supposed to admit to all the ugly, horrible things about myself. Instead of being scared, I was eager. I wanted to purge this poison from my heart. I surprised myself by beginning way further back than I'd intended.

"I've hurt everyone I've ever loved, and I'm afraid of ruining everything now. First was my father, who chose the bottle over dealing with me. Then my grandfather, when I couldn't be what he needed me to be. Then Kingston, when I couldn't accept him. And so on, and so on. I fear that I'm destined to be alone. How can I be with anyone when I bring them nothing but heartache?"

"Why do you think any of that is your fault, little one?"

"I mean . . . isn't it? I'm the common denominator here. All of them have been hurt because of me. Simply because of my existence."

"Forgive me for saying so, but that's pretty selfish of you."

"Beg your pardon? This is not very priest-like of you."

"Ah, but you forget. I'm not a priest. I'm simply playing

the part for you. And while I cannot absolve you, I can offer you the truth. Even if it hurts." He took a deep breath, then released it slowly. "Sunday, the decisions others make are not things you can be responsible for. You didn't put the bottle in your father's hands, nor did you set expectations for your grandfather to be anything other than what you are meant to be. As far as Mr. Farrell, I'm certain if you couldn't accept him, it was for a damned good reason. Your fate will lead you to where you belong. Trust and have faith."

"Do you believe fate brought me here? To you?"

"I know it."

His conviction stunned me. "Oh."

"Do you doubt it?"

I reflected on my time at Ravenscroft and how I felt more myself than I ever had back home. "No . . . I guess not."

"Then trust that you are here for a purpose, and everyone put in your path will be part of the plan."

"But what if the plan leads me to disaster?"

"I don't have that answer for you."

I let out a heavy sigh.

"There's more on your mind. Tell me."

"I have to choose, and I don't want to," I whispered.

"Choose what?"

"A mate."

"Kingston is your mate. What choice is there?"

My gut clenched. The thought of being Kingston's sent a thrill through me connected with my wolf, but the rest of me cried out for the loss of Noah, Alek, and . . . the one man I could never have. "You really want me to choose him?"

"No. But I don't have a say in the matter."

I snorted. "Neither do I."

"Choices are never easy. I've had to make many difficult decisions over the years."

"Oh yeah? Like what?"

"This is your confession, Miss Fallon. Not mine."

"Please tell me. You're not a priest, remember? You're just playing one on TV."

His soft laugh lightened something in my chest. "All right, if it will help. The hardest choice I ever had to make was the one to give myself to God. It meant leaving a family I loved, as well as a lass I cared for and could have married if not for my calling. It left a wound I never fully recovered from. Not even after I took my vows."

Irrational jealousy spiked through me. The woman was long since dead, and here I was, ready to claw her eyes out. "How long have you been a vampire, Caleb?"

"March 14, 1922. The day I took my place as pastor of my very own parish."

"How old were you?"

"Thirty-eight."

His voice was heavy with the recollection, telling me there was far more to the story than he was letting on, but my slut of a brain was stuck on the realization that Caleb might have gone thirty-eight years as a human man without ever touching a woman. Why did I like that idea so much?

"Caleb . . . have you always been . . . chaste?"

"Are you asking me if I'm still a virgin?"

"Yes?" I couldn't believe I had the audacity to ask him something so profoundly personal. I blamed it on the darkness of the booth. It made me far bolder than I'd be if we were face to face.

"I've never lain with a woman, Miss Fallon. Not that it's any business of yours."

"Have you ever been . . . tempted?"

He cleared his throat. "I believe you've collected enough of my secrets, Miss Fallon. Unless there's anything else you'd like to get off your chest, I think this confession is over."

"Sounds good to me. Isn't there some kind of . . . punishment you're supposed to assign me now?"

"The ache in your knees should suffice. And if it's not enough, we can address that in your next session. Wear a skirt."

His shadow shifted behind the lattice, and I knew the instant he was gone, taking the spicy scent of incense with him.

I sat back on my heels, my heart far lighter than it had been when I'd sought out my confessor. I wasn't any closer to finding answers to the questions hounding me, but my mind was quiet. My heart calm. Confession with Caleb had been exactly what I needed. I felt closer to him now. Like we'd shared something far more sacred than a couple of truths about ourselves.

Like we may just actually be . . . friends.

Rising, I stepped out of the booth and made my way out of the church, knowing while this had been my first confession, it certainly wouldn't be my last.

Until next time . . . my dark and twisted priest.

I shoved the doors of the headmistress' office open with such force they broke off their hinges. I couldn't believe what I'd just been told. Fury boiled under my skin, barely contained. Everything had been shot to hell with one conversation.

"Thorne, wait!" Callie called, trailing after me and yapping a bloody mile a minute like a damned rabid Chihuahua. "This is a good thing! It's the *right* thing. You'll see."

"Callie, do yourself a favor and shut the fuck up before I shut you up."

She pouted, batting her eyelashes at me like it would garner any ounce of sympathy. All it made me want to do was shove her into the lake and see if they'd double as flippers. "Thorne, you know how these things go. The Vampire Council makes edicts to keep us safe. This is the way things are supposed to be. You and me. Together. I mean, I even have your aunt's name. I was made to be a Blackthorne."

"Keep my aunt out of this. You and I are nothing,

Callista. You don't understand what you've done, calling attention to things this way."

"I didn't call attention to anything except that we haven't gotten a chance to spend the appropriate amount of time together because you're always running off. We're to be wed, Noah—"

"Do. Not. Call. Me. That," I snarled, baring my fangs and scenting her resulting fear. *Good.* Maybe the little fool had some sense after all.

"She's not good enough for you. Whatever this is, she's got some kind of spell cast on you. Don't you see? It's her and that witch friend of hers. They're trying to ruin everything."

She reached out, attempting to run her fingers through my hair, pressing her body against mine.

Before I could stop her and shove her away, her gaze locked on something behind me. "Oops," she whispered.

"What the hell is going on here?" Sunday's voice, filled with hurt, hit me like a bucket of ice poured down my back.

Callie sneered. "If you wanted to get frisky, *Noah,* you should've asked me to meet you somewhere more private. I know you're excited about the ball, but really . . ."

"Oh, piss off," I muttered, flinging her hand away and spinning toward my mate. "You know this isn't what it looks like."

Hurt still flickered in her gaze, Kingston's actions too fresh for her to immediately dismiss what she'd seen. "So what is it, then?" She cast a livid glance at Callie. " What does this dollar store Barbie doll mean about you being excited about the ball?"

"Oh, poor lamb, she doesn't know?" Callie put on an air of pure innocence. "The Council decreed like species must be paired for the ball. That means, unfortunately for you, our Noah can't lower himself to take a disaster like you."

Uncontrolled rage built in my chest, exploding before I could stop it. "Don't you dare speak of my mate that way, you pathetic little maggot."

Callie's pale skin leached of all color before two angry splotches of red stained her cheeks. "Your *what*?"

"You. Heard. Me." I stepped forward with each word, and she took careful steps away. Then I ripped the sleeve of my shirt free at the shoulder, exposing my voluntary traitor mark.

Callie lifted a shaking hand, gesturing in Sunday's direction. "This? This is what you choose when you could have had me? This low-born, half-breed, nothing of a reject shifter? Her own family doesn't even want her. She's not good for anything—"

Four red slashes opened up on her cheek, blood trailing down the porcelain skin, healing almost instantly.

Sunday stood at my side, her fingers shifted into razor-sharp claws, eyes glowing wild. "I didn't hurt you last time, and you blamed me anyway. Consider this payback."

"You little bitch!"

Sunday growled, a deep, violent rumble low in her throat. "Give me one reason, Callie. I fucking dare you."

"Enough!" The headmistress appeared in a cloud of black mist between them, and for the first time ever, I was relieved to see the powerful and terrifying woman. "Mademoiselle Fallon, come with me."

Callie smirked, crossing her arms over her chest, but Headmistress le Blanc shot her a disdainful glare. "You are clearly not innocent in this either, Mademoiselle Donoghue. We will be speaking about your choices shortly."

I hated how bloody powerless I was in this. Headmistress le Blanc could reduce any one of us to ashes if she so chose. She was the strongest being on this plane of existence. She'd been killed more times than history even knew, yet she always returned, unscathed, wiser than before.

She turned toward her office, not checking to see if Sunday was following her, and yet when I took my first step, she called over her shoulder, "That will be all, Mr. Blackthorne. Your mate will be safe with me and returned to you shortly."

All I could do was watch Sunday walk away. Every step killed me. But I had to trust le Blanc's word. And once I had Sunday in my arms again, I'd make this up to her. Ideas sparked to life in my mind, my lips curling up in anticipation.

Yes.

I'd make this a night she'd never forget. So when we had to attend the ball with others, she wouldn't doubt my love for her for a single moment.

CHAPTER
THIRTY-SEVEN
SUNDAY

The headmistress's office was bright and airy as I stepped inside. The light breeze that flowed through the space took me off guard. Where was it coming from? There were no windows, and the door was already closed behind me. Where I'd expected a stone floor, I found mossy earth and walls covered in flowering vines. The scent of jasmine and rain was all at once soothing and strange. This was like something out of a fairy tale. A stark contrast to the Gothic design of the rest of the university, which was better suited to a classic horror novel.

The headmistress walked around the flat-topped boulder that served as her desk and took a seat behind it. She gestured to the two small mounds of moss-covered ground in front of me. "Please, take a seat."

"On the ground?" I asked, confusion swirling through me as I assessed the space and searched for a chair.

"Do you have a problem with my office, Mademoiselle Fallon?"

"Nope," I said, falling into the same self-preservation mode I would turn to when summoned to my grandfather's office back home. Then I plopped myself on top of one of the mounds as gracefully as I could, which wasn't very considering how low to the floor they were.

I had to admit, this seat was comfier than I'd expected. I bounced a little, letting myself settle.

"Are you done?" Her gaze was sharp and unamused.

"Yes?" I wasn't sure what it was about this woman, but she terrified me.

"You know why I called you in here, I presume?"

I sighed, anger swirling up inside me, though it was far more muted now that the object of said anger wasn't smirking at me while running her filthy fucking hands all over my man. "Callie."

"That's only a small part of the reason. The girl is insufferable, I know, but you have to control yourself around her. She's picking at you on purpose, and you can't help but rise to take the bait. Father Gallagher said you've been working with Alek Nordson and Kingston Farrell to tame your temper. How is that going?"

"Well, this time I actually intended to draw blood whereas last time I didn't. So I think that shows significant progress." I sighed. "Also, she's still alive. That's a win."

This time, amusement twinkled in her eyes. "Yes. I'd say when a mate bond is threatened, it usually ends in death or severe injury, so she's quite lucky a few scratches were all she endured."

I hadn't realized it until she gave a name to it, but that's exactly how I'd felt. Threatened. Well, not me specifically, but Noah. Seeing Callie stare at him with unabashed hunger, touching and caressing what was mine. I couldn't stop the red-haze as it clouded my gaze or my claws as they snapped free. She really was lucky I hadn't killed her. My wolf certainly wanted far more in payment for her transgression.

"Miss Fallon, do control yourself." Madame Moody stared down at my hands, which had turned to claws with just the memory of Callie touching Noah.

"Sorry," I said, focusing hard to resheath them. "This is still pretty new to me. I've never felt this way before."

"It's understandable. Mate bonds can be tricky to navigate at first."

"But we aren't mated. At least, I don't think we are," I said, my brows furrowing. "I mean, Noah said I was his mate, but there was no blood exchange or biting or anything. Isn't that sort of a requirement?"

"I'm certain you will get there. The mating process for vampires differs greatly from that of wolves. Your bond has been growing since the first moment he saw you. Poor soul thought he was hunting you."

"How do you know that?"

She smirked. "I know everything."

Gulping, I thought of *everything* Caleb had done to me in his office. "Everything?"

"Most things."

Somehow that didn't make me feel any better. Not wanting to dwell on it, in case she could pick up on the direction of my thoughts, I changed the subject. "Okay, our Callie talk is out of the way. What else am I in trouble for?"

She quirked a brow. "Why would you assume you're in trouble?"

I winced. I could give her a list a mile long. "Because I'm in your office. That means trouble."

"While discipline is certainly the most common reason students find themselves here, your situation is more unique than most. I'm not usually one to get in the way of a woman and her harem, but unfortunately, the situation is out of even my hands. Twice now, you've injured another student. Our masquerade is the opportunity for our students to mingle and prove themselves. If I do not intervene, I fear that is a test you will fail, Mademoiselle Fallon. And so . . ." She clasped her hands, the pause nearly killing me. "You will attend with Mr. Farrell."

"Kingston? No. I can go with Alek. He's already asked me."

Her eyes flared an eerie acid green then returned to nearly black. "You will do as I direct, or you will spend the entirety of the ball in the well, unable to be reached by any of your men."

"The well? Is that some kind of joke or nickname or something?" I asked, even as fear pooled in my stomach. Whatever it was, it didn't sound good.

"No, dear one. The well is exactly what it sounds like. Before this was a university, it was home to Blackthorne vampire royalty. Centuries ago, before they left England, the Blackthornes ruled over much of this land. Their favorite method of punishment for wayward vampires was through isolation. In the well."

I shivered. An actual fucking well. I could only imagine what that would be like, and I never wanted to find out. "You *use* that?"

"Only when absolutely necessary. We haven't had to put a student in the well in fifty years. The threat is enough to keep them straight."

I could see why. Jesus. Another shiver raced down my spine. "Does it really have to be Kingston? I understand why I can't go with Noah, but you already know Alek helps keep me calm, so why Kingston?"

"Unless there is another wolf you'd rather be paired

with, you'll attend with Mr. Farrell. This has been handed down by both the Vampire Council and the High Council. All students must attend paired with their own species. The test is designed for you to work together to coexist in an environment where you might let your guard down. Where dancing and drink make lips loose and inhibitions lessened. That is where mistakes are made and wars begun. Being with one of your own will strengthen you in some ways and weaken you in others."

I balled my hands into fists. "So Alek is going alone, then? Doesn't that put him at a disadvantage?"

Her lips curled up in a cruel smile. "I doubt the Novasgardian would appreciate you suggesting he cannot defend himself. They're a god-touched people, you know. More than capable of fending off any threat he'd find on this campus. But, since you're so worried about his safety, it should appease you to learn that he'll be attending with the valkyrie Kara."

All I could picture was a screaming warrior woman with gold breastplates. And then I remembered her. Tall, blonde, fierce, and terrifying. Kara paired well with Alek. Jealousy bolted through my heart. What would he think of being with her? Would he realize she was a better match? More like him in every way?

I brushed that thought away and focused on the fact that I would have to spend my night in the well or with a man who hated me. The well was sounding better by the minute.

But no, I'd never backed down before. I wouldn't let what was sure to be an uncomfortable and awkward evening keep me from proving that I had learned to control myself. This was a test I wanted to pass.

Not for them, but for me.

And if I had to spend the night ignoring a pissed-off wolf, well, that was nothing new. Besides, we might have to be together for show, but there was nothing stopping me from finding a dark corner with Noah.

"Fine. I'll do it, but if Kingston ends up castrated by the end of the night, don't say I didn't warn you."

Amusement flickered in her eyes once more. "Fair enough, Mademoiselle Fallon. He'll likely have earned it if you have to resort to that."

"Any idea where I can get a dress?"

I stood outside *Iniquity*, my palms sweaty and nerves coiling in my belly. One of my ever-present shadows hovered nearby. I could sense whoever it was watching me, but they never crossed into my line of sight.

The short, slinky black dress I was wearing was so far out of my comfort zone, I had to fight the urge to tug on the hem with every passing moment. But how could I deny Noah this?

He'd left a package on my bed while I was in with the headmistress. The dress and ridiculously sexy lingerie inside spoke volumes about what he had planned for tonight. So did the note that simply read,

Iniquity. Our room. Sunset. - N

No questions, no polite requests. Just instructions.

Usually, it was the act of getting undressed that had my body quivering with need, but as I put on the items Noah had selected specifically for me, I found the opposite to be true. With each brush of silk between my thighs or scratch of lace over my nipples, my arousal grew. At this rate, he wouldn't have to do more than crook his finger to send me toppling over the edge.

The sensual roll of bass filtered to my ears as I stepped over the threshold and headed down the darkened hallway, my path a straight line to the staircase that led to the room I needed.

Excitement and anticipation hummed in my veins. Would we take another step toward a mate bond tonight? Was that something I wanted? If I accepted that from him, wouldn't that mean I'd chosen? The questions tumbled through my brain, pushing away the arousal I'd been feeling and replacing it with anxiety.

"Sweet Sunday, you look absolutely delectable this evening."

Lilith's sultry voice interrupted my thoughts, and I blinked, not realizing I'd been seconds away from running straight into her.

"So do you," I said, not having to force my smile as I took in her red leather dress and the whip coiled down her arm.

The succubus's eyes narrowed as she ran her gaze over me. "Everything okay, sweetheart? I'm sensing some fear, and not the fun kind. Anything I can do to help make your visit more comfortable? Do you want me to call Thorne? He's not here yet, but I know he's on his way. He reserved your room for you and left very specific instructions." She winked. "If it helps put you at ease, you're in for one hell of a night."

My nervous energy morphed into lust under the power of her gaze and whatever sexual energy she was putting off. I had to admit, I needed that. She dragged me out of my own head with no effort, and I appreciated that about her right now.

Taking a deep breath, I shook my head. "No. I'm fine. I'll just wait for him in the room."

She slid her fingers down my arm, the lust she exuded washing over me. "You do that. And just remember, that room is for *you* as much as it is for him. Use it as you need. There's nothing to say you have to wait for a partner."

As soon as the suggestion left her crimson lips, I knew I'd be taking her up on it. Maybe if I could relieve some of this tension, I'd feel more in control when Noah arrived.

I turned down the hallway that would take me to the gray room. Just like last time, the door swung open as I approached, inviting me in. Unlike last time, there was a small table just beside the door, a tiny bottle filled with iridescent swirling silver liquid placed in its center. A tag stating 'Drink Me' was the only clue as to its purpose.

"Who am I, Alice?" I muttered, fingers playing across the tag.

Nevertheless, my curiosity got the better of me. Noah had set this up for me. He wanted me to get out of my head and relax after the news of our forced dates to the masquerade. I picked up the vial and uncorked the top, giving the liquid inside a cursory sniff. It smelled sweet and rich, like some kind of nectar.

"When in Wonderland," I murmured, lifting it up and draining the contents.

Immediate, uncontrollable desire pooled between my thighs. Oh, shit. Maybe I should have waited.

I took one tentative step forward, but the tantalizing brush of material over my skin was almost too much. I stopped, reaching out and grasping the table as I let out a breathy moan. I squeezed my eyes shut, trying to control my racing heart and the surge of sensual heat pulsing through my veins. What the hell had I just done to myself?

Opening my eyes, I blinked a few times to clear my fuzzy vision. My heart lurched as the scene surrounding me became not the beautiful bedroom I'd expected but Caleb's office. It was sparsely decorated, cold and empty, although strangely laid out just like the room at *Iniquity*. His altar was still there, though instead of cool stone and wood, it was made up like a bed, complete with thick satin pillows and draped with a silky black sheet. Where the frosted window usually sat in the gray room, there was now a wide screen, reminiscent of what you might find in a confessional separating the penitent from the priest. I swear the shadow of a man moved behind that screen, and a dirty thrill ran through me.

I shouldn't be here. I should be with Noah. He was the vampire I was waiting for. But something built inside my chest, a magnetic pull toward the screen. Like I was being summoned.

"Have a seat, Miss Fallon." Fuck, that voice. I knew that voice. Caleb's Irish brogue rippled across my senses, raising the fine hairs at the back of my neck in anticipation.

"Caleb?" I whispered.

"In a manner of speaking."

The vague admission was enough to let the last of my inhibitions fall away. If it wasn't really Caleb, if this was just a fantasy, then it was okay. Why shouldn't I give into my subconscious's deepest desire? What was the harm in a little naughty roleplay with my imagination?

"Where do you want me?"

"In front of the confessional. Show me my sins."

"Show you? I thought I was supposed to tell you."

"Your body will speak for you. It reveals all you're too

ashamed to say out loud. Now do as you're told, Miss Fallon."

My legs shook as I approached the window, my gaze never leaving the silhouette of the man who'd haunted my fantasies without permission. I shouldn't want him, but clearly, my subconscious was a horny bitch. And I secretly loved her for it. Even as I tried to deny myself, I couldn't help but tremble with anticipation. I was finally going to experience what I'd been dreaming about.

I moved the chair from the center of the room to right in front of the window. Then I sat, knees together, ankles crossed. He might be my imagination, but he still had to work for it.

"Spread your knees."

"Yes, sir." My voice was tight and thin; need coiled in my belly as I complied.

He shifted, his shadow moving just enough I noticed, then he growled, "Wider."

A satisfied groan came from him as I did what he instructed.

"Good girl."

I stared hard at him, wishing I could see through the woven screen and thankful I couldn't all at the same time. If I saw those eyes lit with fire for me, I might not survive.

"Lift your skirt. Show me your world."

My hands were clumsy with desire as they bunched the material at my thighs and slowly tugged it up. My heart beat so loud in my ears, I wasn't sure if it was my imagination or if the shadow figure really did let out a whispered curse.

"Pink and perfect, exactly as I remember." He sucked in a sharp breath as though trying to get my scent. "Are you wet?"

"Y-yes."

"Show me."

I swallowed past the tightness in my throat. "Can't you see?"

"Touch yourself. Slide your fingers through your perfect cunt, and let me see them glisten."

I had to bite down on my lip as I slid my hand between my thighs. There was no stopping my moan as my fingers drifted past my swollen clit and down toward the place already dripping with desire. I swear to God, I heard a moan from inside his booth.

"Show them to me, *a stor*. Show me what I can do to you without even touching you."

My hand was visibly shaking when I held up the two digits slick with the proof of what he'd done to me.

"Suck them clean."

I balked. "Taste myself?"

"For me. Taste yourself and tell me what you taste like."

I almost didn't do it, but the urgency in his tone and the whatever the fuck I drank had my inhibitions all but non-existent at this point. Slipping my fingers between my lips, I sucked my arousal off them.

"Tell me what it tastes like, Sunday."

"It's . . . sweet. Like honey. Like the elixir I drank earlier."

His warm laugh spilled over me like a caress. "Of course you'd taste like honey."

"What do you want me to do now?" I asked, my voice betraying my need.

"Stand up. Take off your clothes and show me what's mine."

"I'm not yours."

"You are right now."

The shadow man had a point. I was so far gone I'd do just about anything he asked me to right now. Including strip down to the sexy silver and black lingerie Noah had selected for me. I tried to make a show of it, slowing my movements as I dragged the straps of my dress down my arms and then shimmied out of the rest of it, letting the material pool forgotten at my feet.

"Perfect. My God, you must've been sent by Lucifer himself to tempt me."

"Nope. Unless my grandfather isn't telling me something."

That fucking laugh again. I knew this wasn't real simply because Caleb never laughed like that. He was grumpy and intense. Hot as sin and made for fucking. But never even close to lighthearted or free.

"Take off the bra, but leave the garters. I love the way they frame your pussy."

Reaching behind me, I unhooked the row of clasps that started at the middle of my back and went all the way to my waist. The bustier fell free, my nipples tightening instantly in the chill of the room.

"Father, forgive me," he grumbled, the shadow of his arm moving slowly, just rhythmically enough that I got the picture of what he was doing clear as day. That was hotter than Hades, knowing he was touching himself while watching me. "Get on the bed."

I would have sworn I could feel his eyes on me as I made my way to the modified altar. It was just raised enough I had to climb up, exposing myself as I got to my knees on its flat surface.

"Fuck yes," he growled. "Would that I could sink inside you right the fuck now."

Just the thought was enough to set off little flutters

rippling inside me. I pressed my thighs together, but the friction was a sorry replacement for what I really wanted. "What's stopping you?"

His answering groan had me reaching between my legs and rubbing tight circles on my aching clit.

"Stop. Don't you fucking move until I say so."

It was the hardest thing I'd ever done, but somehow I managed to obey. I was panting hard, my breasts heavy and just as desperate for his touch as the rest of me as I breathed through the wave of lust.

"There's a blindfold on the pillow. Put it on, and no matter what happens, do not remove it. Do you understand me?"

"Yes, Caleb."

I crawled forward on the makeshift bed, spotting the red length of satin and pulling it toward me as I shifted to sit on my hip. One end of the fabric dipped between my legs, ghosting over my aching cunt and making me groan.

His voice was rough and thick when he gave me his next growled command. "Tie it and then lay down on your back with your legs spread wide."

I pulled the blindfold up, biting down hard on the inside of my cheek when the fabric rode back up. The whisper-soft touch was the worst sort of tease because it was nowhere near enough. I allowed myself a final glance at the shadowed figure behind the screen, his arm still moving in slow, measured strokes, and with that picture in mind, I tied it over my eyes and laid down.

As soon as my sight was taken from me, I was instantly more aware of every other sense. But more than anything, I was aware of how close to the edge I already was. One well-aimed breath on my clit would probably do it. Hell, the scrape of Caleb's scruff over my breasts would get the job done. Every nerve ending in my body screamed for him to get out of that godforsaken box and come fuck me. It was my fantasy, after all. Why did I have to be such a cock-blocker?

"Touch yourself, Sunday. Bring me to worship at the altar I can't have."

This command I obeyed without question, my hand slipping eagerly between my spread legs. I rolled my finger over my clit, my breath hitching, hips kicking as sensation exploded across my pussy. I was already so on edge, I was sure I'd be coming hard and fast if I kept this up.

"Don't you dare come without my permission."

It must have been the blindfold, but his voice sounded closer. Like it was right beside my ear. Were those footsteps? Alarm shot through me, and I moved to sit up. But then his scent, incense and spice, washed over me, giving me everything I craved and pushing aside my worry. It was then I remembered the room was designed to give me what I want . . . what I need.

"Don't worry, *a stor*. This will be our little secret. What happens within these walls is ours alone. No one will ever know."

"Caleb," I moaned, giving myself fully over to the fantasy. "I need you to touch me."

His groan was tortured, as if he was a man on the brink of losing control.

"Please," I begged.

"I don't have the strength to deny you any longer, Sunday. God help me, but I can't stop myself. Not now."

I tensed with expectant need. Waiting for the feel of his hand on my bare skin. When the touch came, it wasn't between my thighs or over my chest as I expected. No, it was the barest brush of his fingertips on the inside of my knee. Innocent . . . except that it was absolutely forbidden. Which made it so fucking perfect.

"Make yourself come," he gritted out. The sounds of a belt unbuckling and his zipper lowering were unmistakable in the silent room.

I pictured him sliding his palm over his long, rigid cock. The feel of it against my skin when he'd spanked me was a memory I'd never forget.

"Sunday," he scolded. "You're not listening."

"I want you to come too."

"Oh, fuck. You must be part succubus. That's the only explanation for why I want you so badly."

"Whatever you need to tell yourself, Padre. As long as I get to hear what it sounds like when you shoot your cum all over me, I don't care."

"Sunday. You're going to be the fecking death of me."

Our breaths mingled, the harsh pants fueling the furious pace of my fingers over my clit. He gripped my knee harder, not touching me beyond that one small spot, but I was burning for this man.

The tension in his fingers laced with his tight breaths told me he was close. So was I. "Caleb," I moaned. "Please."

"I can't stop."

"Who asked you to? Come for me, Caleb."

He grunted, his fingers digging into my skin as he gasped and ropes of his release spilled across my hand and lower belly. "Holy hell, Sunday. What have you done to me?"

I smiled and continued chasing my own climax, using his orgasm as my lubrication. The feel of his slick spend touching my clit sent me over the edge, and I cried out, back arching, intense pleasure spreading through me in an explosion of sensation. My damn toes curled.

I came down, panting, heart racing, my fingers still rubbing his cum into my skin. But I could tell things had shifted the moment I came. No longer did the scent of him linger in the air.

I opened my eyes, the blindfold gone, the room back to normal. I lay naked on the bed, thighs wet from my own orgasm, but no evidence of Caleb existed. Not even the release he'd spilled across me. Except for the bruises on my thigh in the shape of fingers. I must've been so deep in my desires I had been gripping my own knee in hopes of making it feel real.

Wow, what a fantasy. This room was more than I'd given it credit for.

My gaze flicked to the window where my shadow man usually stood. I half expected to see the confessional screen in place of the frosted pane. The space was empty. Nothing more than dark glass.

The sound of the door opening had me snapping my head to the side. Noah's heated gaze roamed over my body, his lips lifting with amusement. "You got started without me, I see."

I blushed, hoping if he had an inkling of what my fantasy had been he wouldn't be jealous. "It said *drink me*. I drank it."

"All of it?"

"Yes."

"Well, I had intended for us to share in your fantasy, but I suppose as long as you're ready for more, I can adjust the schedule."

"There's a schedule?" I said it with a British accent just to tease him.

"There was. I'd planned to make up for everything

347

Callie caused by proving to you no matter who I attended the ball with, my heart was yours."

"Well, we have all night, don't we?"

"Yes, we absolutely do." Then his amber eyes darkened with promise, and his fingers went to work on the buttons of his shirt. "Guess that means I'm just in time for round two."

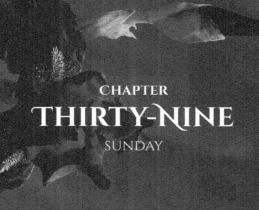

"I don't think we're going to find one," I huffed, staring down at my body, which was currently encased in a skintight sequined gown that weighed at least fifteen pounds.

"You look like a disco ball," Moira agreed.

"A bloody disco ball," I grunted, peering at the scratches the sequins left beneath my arms.

"This is not the one."

"I've tried on all of them. What am I supposed to do? Show up naked? Say I'm Lady Godiva?"

"Maybe? You could get Kingston to let you ride him into the ballroom."

I snorted at the mental image. "Now that would be a hell of an entrance. Callie would choke on her tongue."

"I think Thorne would go ballistic and kill every single guy who looked at you."

Heat crept up my cheeks as I recalled the last time Noah saw me naked in public. "Maybe. Or he'd wrap me up in his jacket and usher me off to some closet where he could fuck me senseless. You know, come to think of it, this idea really has some merit."

"No. I'm sorry. I can't participate in something that will end up getting Thorne locked in a cell for murder. Take that ghastly thing off. I can't believe my mother sent it here in the first place."

I glanced around our room at the number of discarded rainbow-colored dresses ranging from frosting-esque ballgowns straight out of a little girl's faerie princess fantasy to sexy little numbers more appropriate for private rooms at *Iniquity*.

"Hang on. I have an idea. I can't believe I didn't think of this before." Moira unzipped the back of the heavy, awful dress. "Shit," she muttered.

"Shit? That's not a good thing to hear." I tried to glance behind me to see what she was cursing about, but could barely move.

"The zipper is stuck."

"No. I am not going to wear this stupid torture device one more minute. Get it off me."

She cursed again, her hand smacking into my back as she lost purchase on the little piece of metal. "Oh, fuck it."

The gown heated against my skin as Moira did something to the fabric. Panic lanced my chest. In the tall mirror, I watched in horror as flames engulfed the entire dress, with me still wearing it.

"I'm on fire! Shit, Moira! Why am I on fire?"

"Oh, settle down. You're fine."

"No! I'm not fine. I'm on fucking fire, and the last time I checked, I was still fucking flammable. For a witch, you're pretty cavalier about setting innocent people on fire."

I began patting frantically at the flames, but they didn't burn me. Instead, as they disappeared, the gown underneath changed into a gauzy black fabric that covered a tight-fitting off-the-shoulder bodice. Sleeves reached down my arms, stopping in a point at my wrists, held in place by a tiny thread wrapped around my middle fingers. It reminded me of Sleeping Beauty's pink and blue ball gown . . . but a sexy Gothic version. The full skirt had an indecent slit, which stopped at my hip. I loved every inch of the dress. Especially the fact that the fabric underneath the black gossamer was blood red and made me think of Noah.

Moira caught me staring at my reflection in awe. She smiled at me over my shoulder, her expression teeming with smug satisfaction. "Bibbity bobbity boo, bitch."

I couldn't help but laugh. "Tell me we're sticking with this color, though, please. I don't look good in pink."

She gave a mock-horrified gasp. "Darling, as if. Red is your signature color." Her words took on an exaggerated southern drawl on the last.

Moira assessed me, her shrewd gaze zeroing in on my face. "Close your eyes. I'm not done yet."

"Well, you already set me on fire. What's the worst that could happen?"

She rolled her eyes, but I did as she asked. A warmth spread across my skin, tingling everywhere, but not in a bad way.

"Okay, open."

When I looked back at myself in the mirror, absolute beauty stared at me. I still looked like myself, just . . . a more sensual version. My hair fell over one shoulder in glossy waves, and a comb made with deep red jeweled rosettes kept one side away from my face. But the thing that stopped my breath in my chest was the choker around my neck. The chain was a network of twisting onyx-encrusted thorns that came to a point at the hollow of my throat where the thorns transformed into an upside-down rose made entirely of red diamonds.

"Moira," I breathed, my hand hovering above the beautiful flower. "This is too much."

"It's just right. This way, Thorne will know you're thinking of him even if you can't be with him."

"I thought you didn't like him."

"The Dark Prince has his uses. And he hasn't pissed me off lately. Besides, *you* like him, and I adore you, so . . ." She lifted one creamy shoulder in a shrug. "I'll tolerate him for your benefit. To that end, I actually have something else for you." She held out her hand where a blue vial rested in her palm.

"Where the hell did that come from?"

"Magic, dearie."

I rolled my eyes. "Of course. I should have known." I plucked the vial from her hand. "What is it?"

"Just a little something to help your vampire resist the urge to beat the shit out of everyone who looks at his mate. Trust me. It will make the night far easier on you both if you mask your scent."

"What do I do with it? Drink it?"

"If you want a serious case of the runs, sure." She took the bottle from me and opened it, pulling out a dropper filled with the liquid. The bite of freshly crushed roses tickled my nose. "One or two drops should do the trick. Put them behind your ears, down your cleavage, between your thighs, maybe. Wherever you like, but it's important to help him out here. A vampire with an unclaimed mate is dangerous, especially when there are other unmated vamps in the same space. Let's try our best to keep him out of trouble."

I was already dabbing the rose oil on before she finished speaking. Anything that would help Noah was A-OK with me. But if this was such an issue, why was this the first time anyone mentioned it to me? Seemed like something I should be wearing on the regular.

Moira must have sensed my question because she added, "I hadn't realized just how serious things had gotten between the two of you, or I would have made you a concentrated batch earlier. As it was, the spell takes at least two weeks to mature. This was the soonest I could provide you with any after I ran out of my supply."

"Does Noah expect me to be wearing this?"

"Doubtful. I know his mother had to bathe in rose oil before they sealed their bond because her scent was so tempting to the rest of the vampires at Blackthorne Manor, but that was a long time ago now. It's very likely he's never been told how to manage something like this."

Finished Noah-proofing myself, I set the little vial behind me on my desk. "How do you know all this about his family?"

"Who do you think supplied Cashel Blackthorne with the oil? My coven, of course."

"You Belladonnas are just always right in the middle of things, aren't you?"

She booped me on the nose. "And don't you forget it."

"So, you've faerie witch-mothered me this gorgeous dress, made me the most beautiful version of myself I've ever seen. What about my mask?"

"Way ahead of you, Cinders." Moira stepped forward, affixing something black and glittery over my eyes.

When she moved, I was finally able to see the intricate lace mask that mirrored the design of my choker. Dozens of twisty thorns rested against my skin, not quite poking me. It was beautiful and just this side of dangerous. I loved it.

"Wow. That's . . . a weapon?"

"Darling, everything's a weapon if you use it right. Just ask Alek."

My chest fluttered at the mention of the mischievous Viking. I wondered what his mask would be. "What about you? Who are you going with?"

Ash had returned home after her weekend visit, and I hadn't seen Moira with anyone else since. "Emilia. She and Ash are friends, so there are no worries of unwanted awkwardness. She's going to be Eve, and I'm her snake."

As she said it, green smoke swirled around her, replacing her yoga pants and drapey shirt with a body-hugging gown of the same color. A silver snake with bejeweled red eyes wrapped around her neck, acting as the clasp that held the clingy material together. But as I watched, the tail wriggled, and it dove into the fabric, moving languidly down her curves. It was hypnotic. Deadly. Absolutely sinful.

In a word, it was perfect.

"Shit," I whispered. "You make one sexy snake."

Moira smirked. "I know. Careful now, your harem is full. But if you want a bite of my apple, I'm willing to share."

Fuck if I didn't blush. I fanned my face. "Stop using your sexy voodoo on me, you temptress."

Moira winked. "As you wish."

"I love you, too."

The clock on Moira's desk chimed midnight, and her smirk took on a wicked edge. "Oh look, the witching hour is upon us. Time to go have some fun." She winked, pulling on her mask. "What do you say, Sunday? Ready to raise some hell?"

"As ready as I'll ever be."

Moira sighed. "All right, that was a little anticlimactic, but I'll take it." She wove her arm through mine. "Come on, kitten. Let's go break some hard-ons."

"I don't think that's what you're supposed to do with them."

"Then you're not doing it right. Even I know that."

I paused, staring at her. "Moira . . . one of these days you're going to tell me your secrets."

She batted her eyelashes at me. "Sweetie, you'd never survive it."

"Try me."

"Maybe when you're older," she said, her expression deadpan as she patted my hand.

I laughed so hard I worried I would ruin my makeup because I'd start crying. "I don't know. I already have more dick than I can handle. How much more experience do I really need?"

She opened the door, and all the lightheartedness was sucked from the room the moment I saw who waited outside. There he was. The biggest dick of them all, and not the fun kind.

Kingston stood there, his large frame covered in a fuck-hot tuxedo, his mask covering his eyes and pulling my attention to his full lips, hair slicked back, cheekbones on display. God damn him, I was wet already.

I hated him.

Almost as much as I wanted him.

And fuck if that wasn't the most annoying part of all.

F uck me, Sunday was the most stunning creature I'd ever seen. She didn't just take my breath away, she stopped my fucking heart. Everything in me begged to have her in my arms, against my chest, held tight and kept safe. Not just my wolf.

Me.

When had this shift happened? I'd been so determined to hold on to my hatred after her rejection, but somehow this woman had broken through the barrier I'd put up to protect myself. Instead of keeping her out, she'd managed to worm her way in deeper, proving I'd never be free of her or what she did to me.

Fuck.

"Well, you look . . . different," Sunday said, a slight smile on her perfect crimson lips. But the light that had been in her eyes when Moira opened the door dimmed the moment Sunday saw me.

Even though she and Moira seemed amused, I could feel the shift in their moods. Like when you're out for a walk and realize you just stepped in a pile of dog shit. And *I* was the proverbial shit in this equation.

It killed me to realize I was the one responsible for the change. Not that I could really blame either of them. I'd been a complete asshole. Why *would* Sunday be happy to see me? I hadn't given her a reason to want to be around me. I'd relied completely on my wolf's connection to hers while Noah Blackthorne swooped in and charmed her literal pants off.

"You're . . . fuck, Sunday, you're so pretty."

She sucked in a sharp gasp of surprise. "Why are you saying nice things to me?"

"Because a woman like you, looking like that, you deserve to hear the truth. And no matter how fucked things are between us, I've never lied to you. Not going to start now."

Moira shoved past me, her tiny frame bumping into mine. "Don't try to get cute, dog. You've been nothing but a dick to her, and she wouldn't be going with you if she could help it. Remember that."

I might be the one with the claws, but the witch's words gutted me, flaying me open.

"True. And even though I probably don't deserve it, I'm not going to waste an opportunity to set things right."

Something flared in Sunday's eyes as I spoke. Sure, I'd been responding to Moira, but my gaze never left my mate. That was for her benefit. A promise I wasn't going to break.

She swallowed and adjusted her mask before cutting eye contact with me. "We should go."

Moira sighed, her expression softening as she turned her attention back to her roommate. "Are you going to be okay? I need to swing by and pick up Emilia. I promised we'd walk in together, but if you need a referee, I can ask her to meet us there."

I couldn't wait for the little witch to get out of my fur.

"No, don't do that," Sunday said, her eyes narrowing slightly as she looked up at me. Though not with suspicion. "I think we'll manage to play nice for at least that long."

Oh, I'd play nice with her—and naughty if she'd let me. "I can behave. For now."

Moira pressed her hand to her chest. "Mercy, miracles do exist." Then she rolled her eyes and stepped right into my space, shoving one of her talon-like nails into my chest. "You fuck up tonight, dog, and I will rip your dick off and feed it to the fishes, you get me?"

The witch wasn't fucking around. I had zero doubt she intended to do just that. I made no effort to hide my movements as I cupped a hand protectively over my junk. "No thanks. I like Jacob right where he is."

Confusion flickered in the witch's eyes. "You . . . named your dick after the werewolf in Twilight? I've heard of hero worship, but that seems like you went a little too far, buddy."

I looked back at Sunday and the knowing flush blooming over her cheeks. "No. Sunday knows why."

I couldn't help myself. I winked.

Sunday's lips were pressed into a tight line. Clearly she wasn't going to share with the class.

"Jacob's ladder," I said, staring hard at Moira as she glanced down at my crotch. "I could have gone with Albert, but . . . Jake has a nice ring to it."

Understanding dawned. "Oh. Ugh . . . I could've gone my entire life without ever knowing that. And Sunday, I think we need to have a chat about why exactly *you* know.

But on that note, I'm going to head off." She pressed a chaste kiss to Sunday's cheek. "See you guys there."

"Alone at last," I said as she disappeared down the corridor.

I reached for Sunday, my fingers itching to touch her, to close the distance between us. But she flinched away from me, the distrust in her eyes something I'd earned.

"Those heels look dangerous to navigate. Just trying to keep you from falling on your ass in front of the whole world." I tried for what I hoped was a charming smile, but it felt more like a grimace. If I was ever going to repair the damage I'd done, I needed to start small. To prove myself.

I couldn't see it behind her mask, but I was pretty sure she raised a brow at that. "Are you trying to imply I don't know how to walk in these?"

"No. That's not . . ." I was fucking this up already. "I just want to keep you safe, Sunday. That's all I've ever wanted. But you won't let me."

She opened and closed her mouth, looking surprised by my honesty. Finally, she blew out a breath, pursing her lips for a moment as she studied me. "Look. Like it or not, we're stuck with each other tonight. I'm willing to call a truce if you are."

"Who says I don't like it?"

"Oh, I don't know, everything you've ever done?"

I closed my eyes, guilt washing over me at her words. "Look, Sunday. I can't pretend that I've been anything more than an absolute douche when it comes to you. But you haven't been entirely blameless in this either. I've been fucking in love with you since the day I saw you for the first time. It was out of my control, a goddamned lightning bolt straight to my soul, and you tore my fucking heart out in eight seconds flat. I was ready to give you everything just because you existed, but you rejected me before I had a chance. What the hell did you expect me to do? The only person I'd ever wanted didn't want me. I didn't know what to do with all that. I still don't," I added lamely, totally taken aback by my confession. I had never admitted, not even to myself, what my feelings for her meant. To do so now, on complete accident, threw me for a fucking loop.

"You aren't in love with me. I don't think you even know what love is."

Raw from my admission, my heart laid bare for her, those words burned as she shoved them back in my face.

Again.

I couldn't help it, I snarled, crowding her back against the wall. "Don't you fucking dare tell me what I feel for you." I grasped her wrist, holding it up against my heart. "Do you feel that? It beats for you. It has ever since I saw you and realized you were mine. Even when I wished it wouldn't. I can't get you out of my mind, no matter what I try. You're under my skin, in my fucking veins, and I don't know if you're a poison slowly killing me or the cure for everything."

The truth cost me. It turned my voice guttural and ragged with pain from her continued rejection of me and my heart. She was my mate. Fated for me by the moon goddess herself. So why wasn't I enough for her?

Why couldn't she just let me love her?

Her breaths came in sharp pants, eyes locked on mine, fire blazing behind them. I just needed one taste of those lips. Just one brush of her mouth on mine to show her what she was missing. Because there was no way I felt this ache alone.

Dipping my head down, I closed the distance between us, my forehead pressed to hers, lips a breath away. "If you don't want this, tell me now. I'm laying my heart at your feet."

Her breaths were ragged, her chest rising and falling. I fought a groan of frustration, my entire being desperate to just put us out of our misery and kiss her. Her tongue darted out to wet her lips, and if I were a weaker man, that would've been the moment I lost control. But then doubt flickered in her eyes.

No.

No.

No!

I'd been so close.

"No, Kingston. Not like this. I can't."

A feral growl escaped my chest. "You can."

"You don't understand."

"You're right. I don't. How can you deny what your wolf wants so badly?"

"It's my wolf, not me."

I cupped her face gently, even though my need was so great I was shaking. "You *are* your wolf, Sunday."

"If that was true, I'd be able to shift."

Something shattered in me, and I forced myself back even though everything in me rebelled against the distance. "Then I guess we'll just have to get you there. Because once you're out of excuses Sunday, I'll still be here. I'm not going anywhere. Not again. You can't just *dismiss* me. I am your mate. Period. And I will claim you."

I snagged her hand and tugged her behind me out of the room, forcing myself not to look back at her because everything fucking hurt. Knowing I'd failed as a mate, that she wanted someone else, that he'd *had* her, burned in my gut. But I wasn't going to sit around and brood about it any longer. It was time for me to man up and make her see how wrong she'd been to not choose me.

Because one way or another, Sunday Fallon would absolutely fucking choose me.

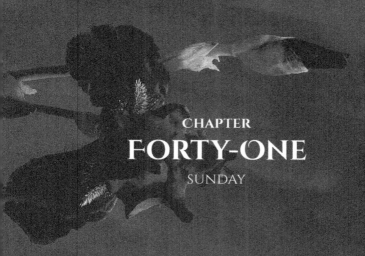

FORTY-ONE

SUNDAY

The hum of voices surrounded me as I stood in the ballroom, Kingston's arm around my waist, his scent tearing down my walls piece by piece. It was nearly impossible to focus on the room and people and everything we were supposed to be doing when the words he'd said still flickered through my mind, one by one, embedding themselves in my heart. I had broken him. He didn't hate me, he loved me, and I ruined us because I was afraid.

Denying his kiss had been physically painful. Everything in me was desperate to close the distance between our mouths and take what we both wanted. Everything except Moira's warning. That stupid vision fucking haunted me. Fear of choosing wrong had me terrified of choosing at all. But then, I'd already chosen Noah . . . hadn't I?

"Do you want to dance?" Kingston asked, his deep rumble mixed with vulnerability I wasn't used to cutting through my inner turmoil.

I blinked at him, staring into eyes that seared mine. In his wolf mask, he looked dangerous and sexy as sin, but it was that slight hesitance in his question that really got me. "I . . . I don't know how."

This was no human high school affair. Stepping into Ravenscroft's ballroom had been like stepping back in time. Instead of a DJ, there was a string quartet, their darkly beautiful melodies a perfect accompaniment to the couples swirling around the dance floor. They wove intricate patterns around each other as they participated in dances you'd expect to see in a Regency-era movie, not in the middle of a modern-day school dance. No matter how elaborate the ball or antiquated the establishment.

Kingston's eyes hardened, and his nostrils flared as he gave me a tight nod. It wasn't a stretch to see he'd taken my answer as yet another rejection. Spotting one of the cocktail servers, he waved her down and plucked two flutes of champagne off her tray, handing one to me without a word.

We stood in awkward silence, his confession racing through my mind. I felt horrible and confused, and even though I knew I had to prove myself to the powers that be by getting through this ridiculous test, I really just wanted to go home and crawl into bed.

"I could—" Kingston started, but Alek appeared out of nowhere and plucked the drink from my hand, passing it to Kingston with a cocky wink.

"Hold that, will you?"

He pulled me out onto the dance floor, his eyes twinkling with mischief.

"What in God's name are you dressed as?" I asked, laughing and forcing myself not to look back at what I was sure would be a fuming werewolf.

I glanced down Alek's form, my gaze trailing over the tightly fitting leather getup in shades of green, black, and gold. It was the horned mask that made me grin. It didn't cover any of his face, stopping just over his brows instead.

"I thought you hated the Marvel movies?"

He smirked. "Not when I have a glorious purpose to serve."

"What's that?"

Leaning close, he whispered, "You."

Heat crept into my cheeks and pooled low in my belly. Trying to play off my reaction, I slapped him lightly on the arm. "Okay, Loki. Good luck with that."

"I don't need luck. Trust me."

He spun me out and then pulled me back, my dress swirling around me in a graceful fall of fabric. I felt like a princess in that moment. For such a big man, Alek moved lithely, completely ignoring the choreographed steps of the dance as he pulled me against his body and we swayed to the music.

"I should get back to my date," I murmured, not wanting to cause any trouble between him and Kingston. We were supposed to keep our heads cool tonight, and Kingston was already strung tightly.

His focus flicked over my shoulder. "A little distance might be just what you both need." Then those blue eyes caught and held mine. "You know, things would be easier for you both if you stopped fighting so hard."

"What do you mean?" I was all innocence and naivety.

He smirked. "You'd have to be a fool to miss the way you two look at each other. He's yours every bit as much as we are."

"None of you are mine. Not really. I have to choose and if I choose wrong . . ." I trailed off, not wanting to get into the dirty details of Moira's vision.

Alek frowned, clearly not liking that I'd censored

myself. "I don't think you understand, *Kærasta*. We're yours whether you claim us back or not. There's no choice to be made, simply acceptance. Things will be far more enjoyable, not to mention pleasurable, when you give in."

I let out a disbelieving laugh. "You act like Kingston is going to roll over and accept the concept of sharing me with anyone. That's not going to happen."

He gave me a look tinged with sincerity. "You'd be surprised what a man would be willing to sacrifice for the woman who makes his soul cry out 'Mine.'"

"Is that something you have personal experience with?"

His lips curled up in a sensual smile. He leaned close, his mouth brushing against the shell of my ear as he whispered, "Perhaps."

"He hates me even though he says he loves me, Alek. I don't know what to do."

"If you're asking for advice, I don't have any. But I will say this. I know that I've not found my way into your heart yet, and that's okay because you still allow me in your orbit. You are that man's sun, and yet you refuse him any of your warmth. Shine for him, Sunny. See what happens when you give a dying man hope like you give me hope."

I closed my eyes against the overwhelming wave of rightness I couldn't deny when he was so close to me. Opening my mouth to respond, I stopped at the scent of bergamot and the pull of my heart toward Noah. I hadn't even seen the man, but I knew he was there. I opened my eyes, and sure enough, Noah stood at our side, gaze soft and expectant all at the same time.

"Mind if I cut in, Viking?" His smooth voice flowed over me, blanketing me in pure happiness.

Alek ran his warm palm down my spine, giving my ass a

cheeky squeeze before letting me go. "Not at all. She's just as much yours as she is mine, after all."

I expected Noah to deny it, but all he did was roll his eyes and offer me his hand. "Shall we, darling?"

"Are we allowed to?"

He swept me into his arms. "Who the bloody hell cares?"

My gaze traveled across the room until it landed on Callie, clad in a gown cut so low I could see her navel. Her mask was white feathers, tall enough she looked more like a stork than a woman. I chuckled. "Your bird."

"I only have one bird, dove. And she's in my arms right now."

Callie stared daggers at me, her lip curing up in a sneer as she stomped across the floor and headed straight for Kingston. Noah pulled me into a smooth waltz, leading me effortlessly around as though this was second nature to him.

"You look absolutely fucking edible right now," he whispered, his cheek pressed against mine. "Do you have any idea the things I want to do to you, seeing my thorns collar your beautiful throat?"

"Yours?"

"Yes. Those are Blackthorne jewels you're wearing."

My stomach flipped. Moira, you saucy little minx. I wondered if she knew exactly who I was supposed to choose, and instead of telling me, she'd been trying to show me all this time.

"How is it possible you're still this good-looking even when you're wearing a mask?" He was dressed in a perfectly tailored tuxedo, his dark hair slicked back, a plain white leather mask on half of his face. "You look kind of like the phantom of the opera, actually."

He twirled me around and then reeled me in so our bodies molded together. "Perhaps I'm here to lure you into the darkness where I plan to hold you captive and do unspeakable things to you."

And now I was so aroused I couldn't see straight. "If you're trying to get me to sneak off with you, it's working."

"Well, then. I'm never one to miss out on a perfect opportunity. How about you and I sneak off to the garden so I can ravish you properly."

"But, what if we get caught? I'll be ruined," I teased.

"Then I guess I'll just have to marry you and make an honest woman out of you," he said, utterly serious.

My breath caught in my throat. "Noah."

He dipped his head again, his smooth, smoky voice temptation itself as he whispered in my ear, "I'm ready if you are, Sunday. Meet me in the garden."

Then he released me and walked away, glancing back once as he left the ballroom. My heart thundered in my ears, possibility, desire, fear, and need all jumbled up inside me. I pressed a hand to my chest, willing myself to breathe and not chase after Noah then and there.

I scanned the dance floor, jealousy shooting through the happy glow both Alek and Noah had wrapped me in. Kingston was dancing . . . with Callie fucking Donoghue.

I knew exactly what he was doing. And why. The only time he ever seemed to get my attention was when he did something to make me jealous. Well, it wouldn't work. Not this time. If he wanted that plastic bitch's hands on him, he was welcome to her. I wasn't playing this game with him. Not anymore. One of us needed to break the cycle.

I met his gaze and gave him a slow shake of my head, letting him know that I saw straight through him. I knew it made me a hypocrite to be angry at him when I was with

Noah, flirting with Alek, and fantasizing about Caleb, but here we were. So I walked straight up to them and said, "Enjoy your night, Kingston."

Then I spun on my heel and followed after Noah. I was late for a ravishing.

I swear I still felt Kingston's burning gaze on me even after I entered the corridor outside of his line of sight. His focus was a weight I couldn't deny. It pulled me in and demanded my attention. But this wasn't about him now. Noah was waiting for me, and Moira had been pointing me in his direction all this time. I just hadn't seen it.

My hurried steps echoed in the cavernous hallway; any faster and I'd be full-on running. Now that my heart and mind were aligned, I didn't want to wait. All I wanted was to get to Noah so I could tell him I was ready for his mark.

Something that felt an awful lot like a cool hand wrapped around my wrist, tugging me into the darkened room to the left. A hard chest pressed against my back, warm breath tickling my neck.

"What happened to the garden?" I asked on a breathy laugh.

I shivered as his lips trailed across my bare shoulder and up to the tender skin of my throat. "What garden, *a stor?*"

Before I had time to process the sound of his voice or the knowledge of who he was, he spun me around and slammed me against the wall, his lips crushing mine with bruising force. I moaned on instinct, and he took that opportunity to slide his tongue into my mouth, his taste and the intensity of his kiss pushing away all else.

All that existed right now was me, him, and this one stolen moment in the dark. I couldn't see more than shadows, but I knew exactly who was touching me. The man I'd never thought would let himself have what he wanted so clearly.

Caleb pulled away, his breathing labored as he tucked his head and ran his fangs along the side of my neck. "I knew hunger before, but never like this. I will taste your honey."

"Caleb? What are you doing?" Even as the words left my lips, I knew I didn't care about the answer. He was giving me everything I'd wanted. It was my fantasy, but a hundred times better because it was real.

His palm drifted down my body, finding the high slit of my dress with ease. "Saints be praised. You're bare for me. Keep quiet, and when you can't, bite down on this." He handed me a neatly pressed scrap of fabric that smelled like him. "I'm going to make you scream."

His fingers slid between my thighs, and he groaned against me as he found my body slick and ready for him.

"Please," I moaned.

Instead of sinking into me, Caleb grabbed me roughly by the waist and set me down hard on a smooth, cool surface I could only assume was a desk. Then he dropped to his knees, his hands grasping my thighs and shoving them wide.

God, I was going to ruin this dress; I was so wet.

"Caleb," I whispered.

"Quiet, little one. Let me show you what it feels like when you allow me to worship you."

"God, yes."

He struck me between the legs, his fingers landing directly on my clit and sending a bolt of need zinging through me. "Blasphemer." There was no mistaking the amusement lacing the word.

"Again."

"Patience, Miss Fallon."

His lips burned my inner thigh as he kissed his way under my skirt until two thick fingers sank inside my cunt, and his mouth found my throbbing clit. I gripped the edges of the desk as I tensed and fought the urge to cry out. God, the orgasm was already here. I was going to die if he didn't let me come this time. When it was real.

The things the man could do with his tongue. Who knew an ex-priest would be so skilled?

"You know . . . you're really good at this," I moaned, one of my hands sinking into his hair and pressing his face closer, my hips rocking desperately against his mouth.

He gripped my thigh and pulled his head back. "Do you want to find release, or do you want to talk?"

"Fuck me, Father."

"I would if I could. My mouth will have to suffice. Now shut yours."

I wanted to ask why, but he was already on me, his tongue and fingers working me into a frenzy that had my entire body shaking. He curled his fingers in a beckoning motion, and then he sent me straight to the edge when he ran his fangs on either side of my clit, pressing down just hard enough I saw stars but not enough to draw blood.

I was so close I could practically see the golden edges of

my orgasm coming together into a beautiful explosion. And then it all came crashing through me as he latched onto my clit and hummed. The vibration, combined with the motion of his fingers, was too much and not enough at the same time. I barely had time to bring his handkerchief to my mouth to muffle my scream of release.

Caleb pulled his fingers free, but he wasn't quite done. He lapped at my arousal, licking me clean with his tongue and finishing with one languid lap straight up my seam. Then he pressed a final, almost chaste, kiss right on my clit before he stood and whispered, "Amen."

My body was trembling with aftershocks of pleasure. I wanted to feel him against me. I wanted to taste him and please him the same way he'd done for me, but when I reached for him, he stepped back. The only things visible in the darkness were his mouth and the two fingers he raised to his lips.

He sucked them clean, a low, rumbled moan coming from him. "Aye. Honey. That's exactly what you taste like. You were right."

What had he meant by that? Alarm shot through me as I recalled living out my solo fantasy at *Iniquity*. How could he know I'd said that?

Before I could ask, he left me alone in the room, shaking, desperate, and dying inside because now that he'd crossed this line, I wasn't sure how I was going to give only Noah my heart.

How could I when it was torn into four very different pieces?

CHAPTER
FORTY-THREE
SUNDAY

My knees still felt shaky when I finally summoned up the courage to leave the little nook Caleb had pulled me into. I was sure I smelled like sex and . . . him.

"There you are."

Noah's voice washed over me, dredging up more confusion and my new constant companion, guilt.

"Got lost, did you?" he asked with a wry smile.

"I got . . . distracted. I'm sorry." I couldn't lie to him, but how was I going to admit I'd just been tongue fucked by a priest while I was supposed to meet with him in the garden?

His gaze turned assessing. "Is that so? And here I thought I was the distraction."

"I have a few distractions in my life at this point. I'm a mess."

"A beautiful mess," he said, stepping close and feathering his lips over mine before growling, "*My* mess."

"Yes. I'm yours. I'm complicated as fuck, and yours."

He brushed a stray lock of my hair back into place. "I

wouldn't change a thing about you. I knew what I was getting myself into when I chose you, Sunday. And yet here I am. No stipulations. No conditions. Just yours."

"Even if I might be someone else's . . . or *several* other someones?"

His gaze was strong and steadfast, unwavering. "Even then."

"Noah, I have something I need to tell you—" A heavy explosion coming from the direction of the ballroom sent me crashing into Noah's chest, interrupting my confession. "What the hell was that?"

He looked over me, his expression wary and tense. "I'm not sure. Perhaps you should stay here while I check it out."

"No way. You aren't going in there without me."

"Right," he agreed, releasing a heavy breath. He took my hand in his, holding tightly as he led me back into the ballroom.

Smoke poured in from the windows, but students and instructors alike milled around. No one seemed to be doing anything, though the revelry had come to a halt.

"Do you think this is part of the test?" a pixie girl asked.

As soon as the question left her lips, I paused. It sounded like exactly the kind of sneaky, underhanded move I was coming to expect from Ravenscroft's professors. Some of my anxiety seeped away as I joined the others. The air hummed with tension as we collectively waited for something, anything to happen.

A bloodcurdling scream echoed from the hallway, and Callie burst through the doors and fell dramatically into Noah's arms. She was bloodied and battered, her dress torn, hair mussed, the feathers on her tattered mask splattered red with blood.

"Help me! Please, they're coming."

Noah gripped her arms, pushing her far enough away he could peer into her face. "Who's coming? Who did this to you?"

"Demons. They've broken through the wards."

"Demons?" I repeated, horror streaking through me.

There hasn't been a demon attack since the Siren coven stopped Lucifer from opening the gates of hell. Other than the handful, like Lilith, who had carved out little niches for themselves on the mortal plane, they'd stayed on their side of the underworld ever since.

"Get behind me, Sunday," Caleb said as he closed the doors and picked up one of the tall candelabras that decorated the entryway. I wondered if he could still taste me on his tongue. If Noah could smell me all over him.

I shook my head to clear my thoughts, watching as he snapped the base off the candelabra as easily as I could snap a twig. Then he slid the thick metal through the door handles, barricading the doors. Black wax candles fell to the floor, their flames still burning. Sanderson and several other witches stepped forward and quickly snuffed out the flames before we had another emergency on our hands.

"Come on, y'all, prepare the wards," Sanderson called, hands already outstretched as she wove her spell.

Witches and warlocks moved to the center of the room, and all joined hands as they took up Sanderson's chant. I spotted Moira's venom-green head and sighed in relief.

"Don't worry," Noah said, squeezing my hand. "The demons won't be able to pass the wards. We'll be safe in here."

Callie sobbed at Noah's feet where she'd fallen. That he was ignoring her made me happy in a way that proved just how petty I was.

A large, warm palm slid around my waist before

tugging me away from Noah and Caleb. Kingston stared down at me, his jaw clenched, eyes hard with unease. "You need to get out of here. This doesn't feel right."

"This is the safest place for her," Caleb contradicted.

"What the hell do you know, Priest?"

He cocked a brow, his expression pure condescension. "About demons? More than most, I assure you."

"Something is off. Can't you feel it?" Kingston asked, not releasing his hold on me.

"I agree. There's not a whiff of brimstone in the air." Some of the anxiety in my chest eased at the sound of Alek's deep rumble. He strode across the room, looking like a fucking god as he joined our little band of fighters.

"You're right," Noah said. He growled low in his chest and trained his focus on Callie. "Demons? Are you certain?"

She blinked her fake eyelashes rapidly. "Noah, you don't think I'd lie to you, do you?"

He took her face in his hands, squeezing tight as he lifted her up on the tips of her toes, snarling, "You will show me what you know." His voice pulsed with power, so there was no mistaking the order for anything but the compulsion that it was.

Callie's doe-eyes went hazy as she obeyed.

Noah hissed, shoving her back. "Hunters. You little bitch."

There was no time to react to Noah's warning. Glass shattered, shards raining from above as something was tossed down from the massive hole where the beautiful dome had once been.

Eyes wild, Callie tugged something free from beneath her skirt. Silver glinted dangerously as she lunged forward, stabbing Noah straight in the heart. "This all could have been avoided if you'd just done what you were told."

I screamed Noah's name just as someone else shouted, "Take cover!"

Before I could get to Noah, both Kingston and Alek shoved me to the ground as an explosion rocked the room. My ears rang, and terror washed over me in a cold wave. I couldn't lose them, none of them. But both Kingston and Alek climbed off me, helping me to my feet, taking protective stances.

"Are you all right?" Kingston asked.

I did a quick mental check. Other than feeling a little tender where my knees and palms collided with the ground, I felt fine. Shaken, but fine. "Yes. What happened?"

"The cowards threw a bomb into the witches' circle."

My gut clenched. "Moira?"

Alek offered a wary gaze in the direction of the blackened circle of downed figures. "I don't know."

Noah let out a pain-filled groan. "Sunday," he gasped.

My head shot to the side just in time to see him fall to his knees, blood pouring down his chest. "Noah!" I ran to him, but not before he hit the ground right beside Callie's headless body.

Caleb knelt beside me, his eyes locking with mine. "He's been run through by a silver dagger. He needs your blood if he has any chance, *a stor*."

I nodded, tearing my sleeve up my arm and holding my wrist to Noah's lips. His skin was gray and dull, eyes closed, and he wasn't breathing. He was a vampire. He'd be okay. He had to.

"Here, let me." Caleb carefully took my arm and pressed a tender kiss to my wrist before biting into my skin. His groan of pleasure sent a bolt of fear through me that he wouldn't stop now that he'd started.

"Let her go," Kingston growled, his voice more beast than man.

Caleb ripped his mouth away, lips stained red with my blood, pupils dilated with a hunger that had nothing to do with what happened between us earlier. I took a shuddering breath and laid my bleeding arm against Noah's cold mouth.

"Please, Noah. You have to stay with me." Tears clogged my throat and made my words shake.

Alek dropped to his knee beside me, curling one arm around my waist and holding me steady. Infusing me with his strength.

Kingston paced, fury causing him to tremble with the need to shift. I felt it, my own wolf wishing for freedom. He looked at me, eyes on fire. "I'll kill them all for you. I'll burn them to the fucking ground."

My heart stuttered, his promise of vengeance doing more for me than all his earlier declarations.

Not giving me a chance to respond, Kingston stood in front of me, facing the crowd and giving one sharp jerk of his chin before shifting into his wolf.

Caleb strode smoothly to the door he'd locked and tore the bar out of the handles, opening the tall doors and readying the exit for the wolves. Letting out one terrifying howl, Kingston took off. One by one, the rest of the shifters followed suit, their cries joining his.

Tears streamed down my cheeks as Noah's lips didn't move. I stared at Alek, pleading with him silently for help. "Can you do anything?"

"Like what? I don't . . ."

"Help him. Heal him like you did with me."

"That's not how my power works."

"How do you know?"

"I don't . . . feel for him the way I feel for you, Sunny."

I squeezed my eyes shut, too overwhelmed by my fear to process anything else. Tears splashed from my cheeks and onto Noah's too-still face, making him appear like some kind of weeping angel.

As I used my free hand to brush away the tears, I felt it. The first pull of his lips against my skin. If not for Alek's arm around me, I would have toppled over, so great was my relief.

"Noah?" I whispered.

One of his hands darted to my arm, gripping hard and holding me to his mouth. His brow furrowed, eyes still closed, and he groaned as his fangs bit into my skin and that gentle pull became a deep, desperate draw.

I wasn't expecting the pain. The last time he drank from me had been nearly orgasmic, but this time it burned, feeling like he was tearing through skin and vein and ripping me apart.

"Noah," I protested, trying to pull free. "Noah, you're hurting me."

Alek tensed, preparing himself for a fight. I could sense it in the way he moved. But Noah's eyes fluttered open, those amber irises clearing as he recognized me and came back to himself.

He released me as though I'd struck him, sitting up and running a hand over the place where he'd been stabbed. The skin was smooth and unmarred; not a trace of the deadly wound remained.

"You saved me, Sunday." His voice was filled with awe, as if he couldn't quite believe I'd do such a thing.

"Of course I did," I said with a watery laugh. "I fucking love you. I'm not ready to lose you yet. We're just getting to the good stuff."

He cupped my face and stared hard into my eyes. "I fucking love you too."

His tender fingers trailed down my neck and to the ruined sleeve of my dress before turning over my arm as he examined my wound. "Let me take care of you now," he whispered.

He raised his thumb to his mouth, pricking it with one razor-sharp fang and reverently wiping it over my wrist. Warmth spread across the torn flesh as it began to knit together, taking all lingering pain with it.

"You killed Callie?" I asked, my focus drifting to the beheaded vampire corpse at our feet.

"She had it coming. No one tries to harm my mate and lives to tell the tale."

"It wasn't me she was after. You're the one who had the hole in his chest."

"Make no mistake, dove. You were her true target. I saw it in her mind."

The thought sobered me. "I knew she hated me. The feeling was entirely mutual. But enough for this? Tonight could have ended so much worse. So many innocent people could have died. And for what? Petty jealousy?"

"Jealousy, the desire for power, status, take your pick. These are strong motivators." Alek held out a hand to help me to my feet. "But poorly executed attacks incited by these things never succeed."

I shook my head, still stunned by the revelation that tonight's chaos was my fault.

A triumphant howl came from outside. One I had no trouble interpreting after years of living on pack land during successful hunts. The wolves had been victorious. Yips and barks turned to deep male voices cheering and congratulating each other on kicking hunter ass as the shifters approached. I didn't let myself look away as Kingston appeared in the doorway, naked, proud, streaked with dirt and blood.

His gaze caught and held mine from across the room, not a single sign of shame or embarrassment as his body responded to me. Several women whistled and whispered at the impressive sight of my mate. My *other* mate.

"They're gone, either dead or scared off, but gone for sure," he said. "It's okay now. No one is going to hurt you."

It was over. Callie was gone, and all her meddling attempts to get rid of me were finished. I could finally start over. Free from the threat of her jealousy.

Noah moved to stand beside me, catching one of my hands in his. Alek stood on the other side, his palm resting on the small of my back. I turned my head slightly, catching Caleb's searing gaze, knowing it had been on me ever since he tasted my blood. And then I returned my focus back to Kingston. Proud. Regal. Head alphahole himself, Kingston.

My mates. All of them.

Something clicked in me as I finally let myself admit it. I needed these men. All four of them. I was stronger, faster, more in control—mentally and emotionally—when I was with them. They completed me. I couldn't choose between them. I needed each and every one of them.

"Sunday!" Moira burst from the crowd, her dress torn, lip split, but thank God she was alive.

She crashed into me, dislodging me from the connection I'd made with my men. "You're okay," I whispered, hugging her tight.

"I wouldn't be if Sanderson hadn't thrown herself on the bomb. She saved everyone."

My gut clenched. "Is she . . . did she survive?"

Nodding, she sighed. "She used a shield spell. Her recovery is going to take a long time, but she'll make it."

Relief cascaded through me. I didn't know how much more of this I could take.

Moira's hands dug into my flesh, her body spasming once.

Shit.

"Moira?"

She didn't respond right away, but when she did, ice water ran through my veins because the voice that came out wasn't hers.

It was my mother's.

"The Blackthorne heir is the only way."

FORTY-FOUR

THORNE

Three days after the attack on Ravenscroft, I was finally fully healed, inside and out. The silver blade had done more damage than Sunday's blood could cure, which had required me to hunt and feed until I was back to my old self. But tonight was ours. I had Sunday all to myself, and I planned to take full advantage.

I'd booked our room at *Iniquity*, needing to be completely alone, safe, and uninterrupted for what she wanted. My heart raced at the thought of the step we were about to take together. One that couldn't be undone.

Sunday moved in close behind me as we approached the door to the club, running her hands over my chest and trailing them down toward my already hard length.

I chuckled, grasping her wrist and stopping her exploration. "Why the hurry? We have all night, dove."

"I'm ready. I want to do this now. No more waiting."

I scented her arousal, but something was lying beneath the surface. There was an undercurrent of trepidation that concerned me, especially given her sudden urgency. She was forcing this, and while I should have just gone with it, I knew I'd never forgive myself if she regretted her decision.

Tugging on her wrist, I pulled her around to stand in front of me, my eyes scanning her face for answers. "Why?"

"Because I love you and want to be yours. Isn't that enough of a reason?"

"It's a perfect reason, but I don't think that's the whole truth. Don't lie to me. Not about this."

She bit down on her lush bottom lip. I cupped her cheek, using my thumb to free the pillowy flesh from her teeth.

"Stop trying to distract me."

"Oh, do you like it when I use my teeth?"

"Your teeth. Your tongue. Your hands. Name the body part, and I'm a fan."

"Same." Her voice was breathy and filled with desire, but her thoughts still hummed with anxious energy, and I hated that I couldn't piece them together through the block she'd raised.

We definitely needed to sit down and talk before things moved any further. I couldn't in good conscience allow this to happen without knowing her mind. But that kind of chat required privacy, and the sidewalk outside a supernatural sex club hardly qualified, especially with a certain wolf trailing us.

I wove my fingers through hers and led her into the club, laser-focused on our destination. I wanted her under me, but I also needed to set things straight before anything else. The club was quiet this time of evening before all the creatures of the night came out to play. It didn't take long for us to reach our special room, the door opening as soon as we arrived, revealing the romantic space we'd grown to love.

Sunday was on me the instant we stepped inside, her mouth crushing against mine as her fingers worked at the buttons of my shirt. Desire flared in me, hot and swift. It was only my concern for her that prevented me from giving in to the need she ignited.

"Wait," I breathed, pulling away.

"Noah, don't stop this." She tugged her hair away from her neck and bared her throat to me. "Make me yours. We have to do this. You have to give me your mating mark."

My fangs extended at the perfect offering on display for me. Fuck, I wanted her so badly. Everything in me ached to drive inside her slick cunt while my fangs were embedded in her vein and I claimed her fully.

"You already are mine," I gritted out. "The mating mark doesn't make that *more* true. Sunday, sweetheart, tell me why you really want this. Why now? There's no hurry. Because once we do this, there's no turning back. It can't be undone. A mate bond can't be broken without losing half of your soul."

Tears filled her eyes, and my heart broke. "I have to. Please. I have to do this."

"Why?"

Taking her hand, I walked her to the bed, and when she took a seat, I joined her.

"You almost died." Her voice was small and tremulous.

Her pain tore at me. I took her face in my hands, kissing away the tears that had slipped free. "I did. But you saved me, and I'm currently very much alive."

"It's my fault."

"No," I growled vehemently. "It was that stupid bitch's fault. Never yours."

"You don't understand. My dreams, Moira's visions . . . this happened because I was too selfish to choose between you. I made the wrong choice by not choosing at all."

My brows furrowed, her explanation heartfelt but not making sense. I vividly recalled the terror they'd induced but didn't understand what they had to do with this. "Who told you that you have to choose? Sunday, we've been over this. I don't expect that from you."

"She said if I choose wrong, the consequences will be dire. I watched you nearly die. It doesn't get more dire than that, Noah. I can't lose any of you. So that means I have to let go of everyone and choose. Even if . . ." she trailed off, her whole body shaking. Clearing her throat, she continued, "Moira had a vision after the attack. She told me it was you all along. I should've chosen you. You are the only way to keep everyone safe."

Instead of reassuring me, her words had the opposite effect, leaving me cold and hollowed out. I sat back, my hands dropping to my lap.

"Noah?"

"I don't want you to bond with me out of some mistaken sense of obligation. That's not what this should be about at all. I've never coerced a woman in my life, and I bloody well don't intend to start now."

Her expression fell as understanding dawned. "Noah, I'm sorry. That's not what I meant at all. I'm explaining this all wrong." She reached for me, taking my hand in hers and feathering kisses over my knuckles. "I do love you. So much. And I do want to bond with you. I was just confused for a minute. I thought I could have all of you, but the answer has been right here in front of me the whole time. It's you, Noah. You're the one I'm supposed to be with. I choose you."

"I'm . . . fuck, Sunday, I need a minute." I stood and

paced, raking my hands through my hair as I tried to come to terms with the wild rollercoaster of emotion she'd taken me on.

Sunday stood and came to me, resting her hands hesitantly on my shoulders. "Noah, what can I do to make you believe me?"

I shook my head, not sure how to answer her. I waited for a beat, taking a deep breath, when it came to me. "Drop your shields," I told her. "Let me in, so I know this is what your heart truly desires."

Fear flashed and then was gone as quickly as it had come. "Noah, there's something I need to tell you about first."

"I know about Father Gallagher."

"You . . . you do?"

"I smelled him all over you." I knew I had a right to be jealous, her connection with him was the only one she kept from me, but I also understood exactly why she couldn't tell me. There was too much at stake for both of them if it got out.

"I'm so sorry, I didn't want to keep it from you—"

I stopped her with a kiss. "Sunday, it doesn't matter. Not to me. But I can't do this with you if you're going to keep me out. I want everything. That means no shields, no barriers, nothing between us at all. Can you do that?"

Relief flooded her expression, her shoulders sagged, calling to attention exactly how tense she'd been. "I promise. No shields."

"Even when you're angry with me. When I drive you up a wall."

She nodded.

I ran my nose along hers, nibbling on her lower lip. "Even when you're fantasizing about them."

"Shouldn't I stop fantasizing about anyone but my mate?"

"You couldn't if you wanted to, dove. And I doubt that's what you want. As long as you allow me to be part of what brings you pleasure, to share in that journey with you, you can fantasize about fucking the queen herself. I don't give a damn what gets you off, as long as one of those things is me."

"I love you, Noah. I don't know what I did to get so lucky as to find you, but I'm really fucking glad I did."

She dropped her shield then, and the wave of her love washed over me, her thoughts brushing against and mingling with my own. *Fuck.* It felt so good to feel her, all of her, again. I craved more. I needed to be inside her.

Instinct guided me as I scooped her into my arms. This was the moment I'd give her my bond, mark her as mine. No shields between us, our thoughts melded, sensation shared, love connecting us and making us stronger together.

I stood her on her feet at the side of the bed, and slowly we undressed each other, nothing clouding this moment now that we'd talked through everything holding me back.

"How do we do this?" she asked, her gaze never leaving my eyes as she slipped her hand down my chest until she reached my jutting cock.

I smirked. "Well, love, we do it the same way we've done it before. I seem to recall you think I'm quite skilled in that arena."

Her cheeks turned pink. "I know that. I mean . . . the bond. The mating mark. Do you just bite me?"

"No. First, I will fill your body, and while we're joined, I'll take some of your blood, then I'll give you mine. Our bond should be established by my heart beating in tandem with yours."

"Should?"

Now it was my turn to blush as embarrassment heated my neck. "I've never done this before."

Her eyes went molten. "You mean I get to take your cherry just like you took mine? That's the hottest fucking thing I've ever heard."

"You are the hottest fucking thing I've ever seen, so I guess we're even. Now, lie back on the bed and let me make you mine in every single way."

She obeyed eagerly, her body flushed with desire as she moved up the bed and crooked her finger, summoning me. I crawled up her, leaving a trail of kisses and little love bites until I'd explored every inch of her perfect form. She was breathless and squirming by the time my lips met her throat.

A little gasp left her, and I stilled as my cock nudged her entrance. Following her gaze, I looked over my shoulder and chuckled as I saw the voyeur had joined us.

"I guess he enjoyed our last performance and is back for a repeat," I said with a chuckle, returning my attention to her.

"Do you care?" she asked. "This is supposed to be about us."

"If it turns you on this much, I have no problem with showing him what it looks like when I claim my mate."

"Then do it, Noah. Claim me."

I thrust deep, the sensation already overwhelming because of the link between our minds. I felt everything, the stretch, the burn, her absolute pleasure in addition to my own. "Oh, God, Sunday," I groaned.

"It's so intense. I can't believe we haven't been doing it like this all this time."

I stared hard at the woman I loved, watching her eyes glaze over as need took her closer to climax already. I was doing that to her. I was giving her everything I had. I'd never stop.

"Are you ready?"

"So fucking ready," she moaned, raking her nails down my back and pulling my hips deeper against hers.

"Slowly, dove. I need this to last." I rocked into her, then pulled out to the tip before sinking fully into her once more. Then, hovering over her, held up by my elbows, I lowered my lips to her throat and allowed myself to take from her. I fed deeply, her walls fluttering around me as she came, my own release charging forward, desperate to be given permission to crest. The sound of hoofbeats filled my mind, surprising me, but I was so far gone to the pleasure, I dismissed it as her heartbeat thundering in my ears. Intent only on the feel of her and staving off my release. I couldn't come yet. We weren't done.

Tearing my mouth from her neck, I reached for the bedside table where the room had provided exactly what I needed to finish this process. A small blade glinted in the candlelight. I grabbed the cool metal and sliced across my chest, just over my heart, blood immediately welling to the surface. The knife clattered to the floor as I brought her to a sitting position, the change bringing her onto my lap and pushing me even deeper inside her perfect warmth.

"Drink from me, Sunday. Be mine."

She licked her lips, her eyes shining with hunger that echoed through our bond. I'd feared she might not be into this part, but I shouldn't have worried. My little wolf had a taste for blood. She trailed her tongue up my torso, following the path of the blood that had spilled and driving me wild with need.

"Fuck yes, Sunday. Take me."

My hips drove up into hers as she latched onto the small wound, a moan of appreciation vibrating in her throat. Her thoughts reached me, her voice as clear in my mind as if she'd whispered in my ear.

Noah, you taste so good. Like a wine made from smoke and berries and spice. All of my favorite things.

And then the word that sent me careening over the edge.

Mine.

I roared her name, my hands fisting in her hair and holding her in place as my body shuddered with the intensity of my release. I poured myself into her, leaving every drop of my seed deep inside her, where it belonged. I felt it the instant the bond snapped into place. My heart swelled and linked to hers, our souls forever joined, and I knew nothing would ever be the same now.

Until this moment, I'd lived solely for myself. And now, I existed only for her.

We came down together, breathing heavily, and most importantly, hearts beating together. We lay still joined together in the bed, sheets stained with our blood, the air scented with sex and filled with more contentment than either of us had ever known.

"I felt it," she said. "The bond."

"So did I. You're mine forever, Sunday Fallon. I'm never letting you go."

Blood humming with anticipation, I stuck to the shadows as I forced myself to stride calmly down the stairs to *Inquity's* lower level. Lilith was waiting for me, her usual smirk in place as I reached her.

"Father."

"Demon spawn."

"Technically, I'm pure demon."

I let out a light chuckle at the oxymoron, plucked a few notes from the pocket of my trousers, and handed the money over to her. "Thank you for letting me know."

"Always a pleasure doing business with you. If you ever want to take me up on my other proposition, the offer is open."

I cast her a disdainful glance. "Never going to happen."

"A girl can dream." She raked her gaze over my form. "A hot priest at my disposal, ready for me to defile . . ." A little shiver raced through her, and she sucked in a sharp breath. "Succubi have fantasies too."

"None I'm interested in."

"No," she murmured thoughtfully. "You prefer to watch."

My jaw clenched, and any humor I'd felt at our interaction fled. I dismissed her with a wave and strolled down the hallway toward the room that had become my own private den of sin. I'd have to spend some quality time with my flogger after this, begging forgiveness for the weakness I couldn't conquer. But I'd resigned myself to the fact that no matter what vows I'd made, I was also a man, and God made us sinners. It was the only solace I could cling to.

The door to my room slowly creaked open, the darkness within absolute. My hand found the switch without effort. I'd done this enough times by now to operate by memory. I should have been ashamed; instead, I was hard as a fecking rock. She was already there and on display, just for me.

Well, not just for me. But my eyes were for her alone. It was easier to pretend I was the one touching her and responsible for those breathy little moans that fell from her lips. Even now, the scent of her cunt sparked in my mind, the taste of sweet honey and cream, the memory that I could've fucked her deep and hard on the desk in that study room during the ball fresh in my mind.

"Fecking hell, I am depraved," I muttered even as I took my seat and unbuckled my belt.

Her voice filtered in through the speakers, sweet and perfect, an angel sent from God to test me. I was a failure.

"Then do it, Noah. Claim me."

My hand snapped out, shutting off the speaker. I didn't need to hear how much she loved him. If I didn't have to listen to the words, I could believe they were for me as I read her lips. Her moans, the look on her face as she found pleasure. I could pretend she was in my arms, taking my cock, scoring her nails along my back. Not his.

When I was in here, I could pretend she was mine. And I did. I watched the forbidden fruit be plucked that first time, and every single time they were here thereafter. Only when she came in alone did I finally give in and join her in her sordid fantasy. Because it was about *me*.

How could I resist the angel of my darkest desires when she called out *my* name? I was only a man. I was weak. Broken. Soulless. But damn it all, in that moment, I was hers.

One soft gasp from her, and I'd thrown my resolve out the window. I'd lost my soul when I'd been made a vampire. What was I holding on to my vows for? I was damned already. Hellbound and lost. Forsaken by the very God I'd sought to serve. Why should I deny myself the only thing I'd wanted in decades?

So I let the sin of lust take me prisoner. As though observing a holy rite, I'd even anointed her with my seed. Marked her as mine. Watched as she'd rubbed the proof of it into her skin, branding herself in my scent.

Trails of crimson streaked down Sunday's neck as Noah drank from her. My fangs filled my mouth as a new kind of hunger joined the first.

Fuck, but I wanted to taste her again. Her blood was every bit as delicious as her sweet cunt. A groan tore from my chest, and I gave in, spitting into my palm before encircling my cock and stroking from crown to base, gripping hard enough to hurt. My hips kicked upward involuntarily as I searched for more friction, moving in time with the thrusts she was taking.

Sensation built at the base of my spine, but I needed more. I needed to be closer to her. Getting to my feet, I planted one hand against the cool surface of the glass, my other hand working furiously. I was already so close, desperate to ride out the orgasm along with her. Preparing myself to drown in the wave of shame and guilt after, but ready to accept it as penance for wanting her.

My thighs tensed, balls tight and heavy as the swell of pleasure built, ready for the dam to break. "Yes, Sunday, take my fucking cock," I murmured as precum dripped from the head. "It's all for you, my sweet girl."

As if she could hear me, Sunday threw her head back, her mouth opening on a scream. One last glide of my fist, and I was right there with her, grunting out her name as if she was both my salvation and my curse.

Because she was.

I bowed my head as though in prayer as I rode out the last pulses of my orgasm, the wall of glass painted with thick ropes of my release. God save me; I was weak for her. My stomach churned as I brought my gaze back to her, to where Blackthorne had lifted her onto his lap and latched her mouth to his chest.

No. She couldn't bond with him. If she did, I'd lose what little of her I had.

Tucking myself away, I tried to ignore the sight of her feeding from him, but as any masochist would be, I was drawn to the things which hurt me. And watching Sunday give herself to someone else was the most exquisite sort of agony. Perhaps witnessing this moment between them was my penance. No flogging came close to tearing me apart the way losing her did.

I felt it the moment it happened. Their bond snapped into place, locking me out, uniting them for all eternity. It was done. I'd lost her before I could accept that I wanted to take her.

Searing pain blossomed on my chest, the burn akin to a brand from a red-hot iron. I let out a harsh cry and tore at my shirt, wondering if this was the moment God sent me to hell. Had He been watching all this time? Waiting for me to earn my spot in torment?

But the pain receded, and clarity returned, a familiar unease curling in my gut as my mind stumbled upon a faint memory from twenty-three years ago. The very night Sunday Fallon was brought into this world.

My fingers traced the decades-old burn over my heart. The small circle barely the width of my fingertip had been there all this time. Signifying that the first seal broke open when she'd been born. A larger circle, raised and angry, ringed the first. Dread twisted through me as I traced the new, still raw scar that had appeared the moment Noah Blackthorne bonded with Sunday.

The second seal of the Apocalypse was broken, and I'd failed in my task to stop it.

An insistent vibration at my hip pulled my focus outward. I knew exactly who would be calling. The only one who had this number. With shaking hands, I flicked off the light and answered my phone.

"Yes?"

"What the hell did you do? The second seal has been broken."

"She just bonded with Blackthorne. He must have been one of the seals."

"Well, Priest . . . what are you going to do about it?"

Clenching my jaw, I took a deep breath. "Don't worry," I said, casting my gaze into the room where two naked figures curled around each other. "I'll take care of him."

To be continued in Rejection . . . keep reading for a sneak peek!

SNEAK PEEK
REJECTION: CHAPTER 1
KINGSTON

Seven years ago

Tonight my fate would be sealed forever with Sunday Fallon. I'd never met the girl, but my father had assured me she'd be the perfect mate, that she was meant for me. It had been agreed by our packs from the time she was born that she was destined to be mine, and now that we were nearly of age, we'd solidify our betrothal with this ritual run.

My nerves sang with anticipation as I caught her tantalizing scent on the air. It had to be her. Nothing had ever smelled so good. My wolf howled happily inside of me, eager to be free and to chase his mate through the meadow.

"What do I do?" I asked, staring at my father, who stood next to me at the base of the hill beyond.

He placed his large palm on my shoulder, and I knew it was the Alpha and not my father who answered. "Now you go and claim what's yours. But go slow. She might be skittish."

I didn't want to scare her. I never wanted to do anything but care for her and make her feel safe. As her future Alpha, it was my job to protect her and the family we'd make together. I wouldn't let her down.

My hands shook as I readied myself to climb the hill and meet her at the top. Nervous energy burned through me at all the possibilities that lay ahead. What would she look like? How would her skin feel on mine? Would she be proud to call me hers?

I had no reason to believe she wouldn't. Girls had been coming around trying to get me to go for midnight runs with them since I'd hit my growth spurt a few years back. But knowing I had a mate, that she was waiting for me, I'd turned them all down, saving myself for her. Why give my attention to anyone else when the one fated for me was waiting?

My parents were fated mates, destined for each other, twin halves of the same soul. They told me the same was true for Sunday and me. The Seer had prophesied it.

Releasing a deep breath, I took the first step that would lead me to her. My heart raced with each stride until it felt like it had crawled up into my throat. I'd never been so nervous in my entire life.

She was already waiting for me when I reached the top, her chocolate hair falling in big loose waves down to shoulders bared by the thin straps of her white sundress. She must have caught my scent because her body stiffened and then she slowly turned her head toward me, her ocean-blue eyes widening as they met mine. My entire being called to her, the pull between us already intense and untameable. I'd never wanted anyone the way I wanted this creature.

"Sunday?" I asked stupidly because I had no other word left in my brain.

She nodded, her tongue darting out to wet her lips. "And you must be Kingston."

Her tone was sweet, innocent, and it caught me totally by surprise. I rubbed a hand over the back of my neck. "My parents weren't exactly subtle, were they?"

Her smile damn near knocked me on my ass. "I like it. Not just any guy could pull off a name like that, but it suits you."

Was it wrong of me to want to pull her into my arms right now and kiss her? That was exactly what I wanted. Not just to feel her soft body pressed against mine, but to taste those berry-colored lips. She was so fucking beautiful. More perfect than I'd even dared imagine . . . and I'd imagined a lot over the last seventeen years.

"You're so pretty," I whispered.

She blinked up at me, her cheeks turning a soft pink. Ducking her head, she tucked a piece of hair behind her ear. "So are you."

I couldn't stop my smile. "I promise I'll take care of you. Always. You don't have to be scared."

I wasn't sure if I imagined it or not, but her breaths sounded shaky. Like she was fighting against some intense emotion and struggling to regain control. Then she looked me in the eye, and the sweetness turned hard. "I'm not scared."

It was my turn to blink. This little wolf had bark. I liked it, but I didn't know what to do with it. My mother had always been so soft-spoken. How was I going to tame her?

"We'll have a good life together, Sunshine. I swear it. I'll do everything I can to make you happy."

I glanced down at my pack, all of them now in their

wolf forms as they watched and waited for me to shift and make my claim known. All she had to do was accept me.

They howled in unison as I undressed, closing my eyes and turning my face to the moon. "Accept me, Sunday. Be mine?" My voice was a harsh whisper, but I knew in my heart she was meant to be mine. We were fated. There was no way she'd say anything other than yes.

Then my entire world shattered as a single soul-crushing word left her lips.

"No."

DON'T MISS A SECOND THIS SUPER SPICY PARANORMAL REVERSE HAREM PRE-ORDER YOUR COPY OF REJECTION NOW!

ALSO BY MEG ANNE

BROTHERHOOD OF THE GUARDIANS/NOVASGARD VIKINGS

UNDERCOVER MAGIC *(NORD & LINA)*

A SEXY & SUSPENSEFUL FATED MATES PNR

HINT OF DANGER

FACE OF DANGER

WORLD OF DANGER

PROMISE OF DANGER

CALL OF DANGER

BOUND BY DANGER (QUINN & FINLEY)

THE MATE GAMES

A SPICY PARANORMAL REVERSE HAREM

CO-WRITTEN WITH K. LORAINE

OBSESSION

REJECTION

POSSESSION

TEMPTATION

The Chosen Universe

The Chosen Series: The Complete Series

A Fated Mates High Fantasy Romance

Mother Of Shadows

Reign Of Ash

Crown Of Embers

Queen Of Light

The Chosen Boxset #1

The Chosen Boxset #2

The Keepers: The Complete Series

A Guardian/Ward High Fantasy Romance

The Dreamer (A Keeper's Prequel)

The Keepers Legacy

The Keepers Retribution

The Keepers Vow

The Keepers Boxset

∼

Gypsy's Curse: The Complete Trilogy

A Psychic/Detective Star-Crossed Lovers UF Romance

Visions Of Death

Visions Of Vengeance

Visions Of Triumph

The Gypsy's Curse: The Complete Collection

∼

THE GRIMM BROTHERHOOD: THE COMPLETE TRILOGY

A SEXY & HUMOROUS URBAN FANTASY ROMANCE

CO-WRITTEN WITH KEL CARPENTER

REAPERS BLOOD

REAPING HAVOC

REAPER REBORN

THE GRIMM BROTHERHOOD: THE COMPLETE COLLECTION

ALSO BY K. LORAINE

REVERSE HAREM STANDALONES

Their Vampire Princess (A Reverse Harem Romance)

All the Queen's Men (A Fae Reverse Harem Romance)

THE MATE GAMES

(co-written with Meg Anne)

Obsession

Rejection

Possession

Temptation

ABOUT MEG ANNE

USA Today and international bestselling paranormal and fantasy romance author Meg Anne has always had stories running on a loop in her head. They started off as daydreams about how the evil queen (aka Mom) had her slaving away doing chores, and more recently shifted into creating backgrounds about the people stuck beside her during rush hour. The stories have always been there; they were just waiting for her to tell them.

Like any true SoCal native, Meg enjoys staying inside curled up with a good book and her cat, Henry . . . or maybe that's just her. You can convince Meg to buy just about anything if it's covered in glitter or rhinestones, or make her laugh by sharing your favorite bad joke. She also accepts bribes in the form of baked goods and Mexican food.

Meg is best known for her leading men #MenbyMeg, her inevitable cliffhangers, and making her readers laugh out loud, all of which started with the bestselling Chosen series.

About K. Loraine

Kim writes steamy contemporary and sexy paranormal romance. **You'll find her paranormal romances written under the name K. Loraine and her contemporaries as Kim Loraine.** Don't worry, you'll get the same level of swoon-worthy heroes, sassy heroines, and an eventual HEA.

When not writing, she's busy herding cats (raising kids), trying to keep her house sort of clean, and dreaming up ways for fictional couples to meet.

Printed in Great Britain
by Amazon

23384311R00247